THE EDGE OF DARKNESS TRILOGY

INSATIABLE

BOOK 1

LEIGH RIVERS

Art designed by Zoe Maxwell (@kowai_girl_tattoo on IG)
Cover Design By: Ashlee O'Brien at Ashes and Vellichor Designs
Formatting by Charly Jade *of* Designs By Charlyy

Edited by Laura at Ten Thousand Editing
Proofread by Lauren at PSR Editing

Distributed by Zando

First Edition: August 2026

978-1-63893-546-9 (trade paperback)
978-1-63893-606-0 (BAM signed edition)

10 9 8 7 6 5 4 3 2 1
Manufactured in the United States of America
LAK

PLAYLIST

Digital Bath – Deftones
Spiracle – Flower Face
Party Monster – The Weeknd
Skin – Rihanna
The Hills – The Weeknd
broken – lovelytheband
Waste Love (Madison Love) – Machine Gun Kelly
THE DEATH OF PEACE OF MIND – Bad Omens
Take Me Back To Eden – Sleep Token
From Now On – The Greatest Showman
Do I Wanna Know? – Arctic Monkeys
4runner – Brenn!

The Edge of Darkness Trilogy playlist can be found on Spotify.

CONTENT WARNING

This trilogy may be considered darker than the pits of hell.

Insatiable has numerous kinks such as exhibitionism, possessive and toxic behaviour, praise and degradation, breath play, gun play, probably too many hand necklaces, and sex next to a dead body. As well as having graphic sexual and violent content with mentions of rape, pregnancy loss and attempted suicide, it also has more potentially triggering material.

A detailed list can be found here -
https://www.authorleighrivers.com/

Your mental health is extremely important to me. I highly recommend readers not to continue with this story if any of the listed warnings are triggering.

DEDICATION

For the good girls who like to dance in the dark while being watched by the devil.

PROLOGUE

KADE

SIX YEARS AGO

I fucking hate people.

Especially parties.

It might be my fifteenth, but that doesn't mean I'm going to participate in the celebration like my twin sister keeps insisting. I don't like the attention or being around groups in general.

Mum told me we could have a joint party; we've been doing it this way for years. But fuck that – I hate it. And if I hear the song "Single Ladies" one more time, I will lose my shit. Most of the people here are fourteen still and have a crush on anime characters, for fuck's sake.

I had to escape to my room like I always do.

Locking my room door is mandatory, because sack having any

of them tell my mum I'm smoking out on my balcony. Ewan, my stepfather, caught me last week while having a draw in the pool house and said if I did it again, he'd tell her.

No one wants that woman yelling at them, scary bastard that she is.

I like my privacy, my own space where I'm unbothered. I have my key jammed in the hole, the latch on and a chair against the door. No chances of anyone ruining my peace.

I'd rather fill my lungs with smoke.

It makes me feel weird, to be honest. People might think it's great to be the centre of attention when they walk into a room, but I can't stand it. I'd rather be invisible. I'd rather no one knew who I was, or my family history, or do everything they can to talk to me.

They don't want to know who I am, not really.

You'd think living in one of the largest manors in the west of Scotland, they'd struggle to find my room, my wing, but unfortunately, they have, and if one more person knocks my door, I'll put a cig out in their eye.

I should go to the party before Mum or Ewan can bang on the door and give me shit, but I can't seem to move from the balcony.

Because I'm preoccupied.

She has no idea I'm watching her.

Away from the rest, away from the party, a girl with long dark hair, wearing a little black dress, sits on the edge of the pool with her feet in the water.

Something about her intrigues me, so I keep my eyes on her.

I like to watch people from afar. I'll study the way they act, their facial expressions and body language in certain situations, the tones of their voices. I intentionally make people uncomfortable just to see their reactions. My teachers are forever complaining to my parents.

Mum tells me to stop it, but it's a great way to pass time and try to understand things that don't come naturally to me.

I tilt my head to the side and stare at the girl with intense fascination.

Why is she not at the party? And who the fuck is she? I've never seen her before.

I can't stop looking at her – I don't want to stop – unable to tear my gaze away as she stares at the starry sky. She must be cold, surely. September is nothing short of fucking Baltic.

Maybe I should take her down my hoodie and…

What? Shut the fuck up, Kade.

I stub out my smoke then toss it into the ashtray hidden under my balcony ledge, keeping my eyes on the mystery girl while I shove on my trainers.

Mum will come for me at any moment for the birthday cake. I waft the smell of cigarettes from my room and cover it up with air freshener.

My phone dings in my pocket, and I quickly pull it out while I brush my teeth. The group chat I have with my two best friends pops up. Dez is pissed he isn't here. And Base asks if I want to go to a real party followed by Russian words I don't understand.

Before I can reply with a *yes,* I hear footsteps.

My shoulders slump. *Here we go.*

"Kade!" Mum bellows from the other side of my door.

I roll my eyes, place my toothbrush back in the holder and switch my phone screen off.

"Are you in there?"

I kick aside the chair and pull the latch. "Yep."

When I swing it open, I'm met with her scowling at me, arms crossed, tapping her foot on the ground. She's smaller than me, with blonde hair that's nothing like my dark. Similar eyes, blue and sleepy, but hers are glaring at me while I look at her, giving her a bored expression.

"Were you smoking again? I can smell it from the stairs."

"No," I lie, dodging her and making my way down the spiral staircase my stepdad Ewan designed for me.

"Your sister was looking for you. You missed the cake."

I pull up my hood and tighten the strings, burying my hands into the front pocket as I grunt. Luciella has always been the golden child, the favourite, the one who doesn't give my mum and Ewan any problems. They both worship the ground she walks on. I get it. I'm not like them. I'm not like my twin sister.

Luciella would never be caught smoking or drinking at the age of thirteen, and definitely wouldn't be brought home by the police after punching an officer.

He deserved it.

I'm sure everyone sees me as the bad kid. The one the family dreads when they get together. I used to give a fuck and attempt to fit in, but now I prefer my own company – the loner. They keep their distance, and so do I.

Mum does try though, probably too much.

She thinks I didn't hear her crying to my dad over the phone about my "mood swings", begging him to help her deal with their "unfeeling" teenage son. But I'm not a completely emotionless robot. I care about Dez and Base, and, when she isn't a pain in my ass, Luciella. I just don't see the point in following stupid rules or talking about feelings I don't really get.

There's nothing wrong with who I am. Even Dad tells me I'm special and never to take offence at how others view me.

He's probably the only person on earth who truly understands me, yet he lives thousands of miles away in a mental institution – he's committed numerous crimes and is deemed too dangerous to live amongst the public.

It's pretty fucking promising for me that he remembers feeling the same way I do.

The famous Tobias Mitchell, American psychopath. The insane killer who took over every news channel in the world. He's labelled as ruthless and unpredictable. Dangerous. A threat to life. Yet, when we visit the institution, he's a caring dad who wants to know everything that's going on in our lives. He tries to be involved as much as he can and looks at my mum like she's the only woman in the world, full of complete adoration.

Even though he tried to kill her.

Yep. He can keep his crazy; I have my own.

My stepdad has been in my life since birth and does what he can. He takes me for boxing lessons in an attempt at some father–son bonding, like he did with my stepbrother Jason. But he's grown up now and has his own life, so it seems Ewan has moved on to me.

I finish pouring a drink of juice and walk around the table.

Some of my sister's friends are giggling, whispering between them while openly watching me, and it makes me uncomfortable. The mystery girl by the pool isn't here though.

Not that I'm looking.

I make a quick escape by pushing through the crowd and going out onto the grounds. The glow from the spotlights leads the way to the pool house.

When I reach the end of the path, I glance over my shoulder to make sure no one has followed me before continuing. The ripples from the water reflect on the glass door of the pool house, and I lean against it, pulling out a cigarette.

I look out to the loch, the moon resting just above the Munros in the distance. The manor is surrounded by water and green forests, and it's kind of relaxing.

I close my eyes as the nicotine burns my lungs, releasing it in a cloud of smoke.

The sound of splashing has me frowning, nearly dropping the cigarette from my mouth when I see the mystery girl is still here. She's perched on her elbows, casually chilling at the edge of the pool, still admiring the stars in the sky.

I shouldn't feel a rush of excitement, but I do.

What do I do? Talk to her? Walk away? Hide?

"Who are you?" I ask, taking another drag as I walk towards her.

She doesn't acknowledge my existence, and I really want her to look at me. I try again. "Hello? Who are you?"

I don't like being ignored, especially by a random person who resembles a ghost with freckles all over her body. I wouldn't usually try to socialise but colour me fucking intrigued.

From her side profile, I can openly admit she's pretty. The thought smacks me upside the head because I've never thought of someone as pretty before.

I assumed I was defective in that department, but since I like the way she looks, perhaps I'm not. It's hard to study her the way I do others, but I'm more than happy to just… look at her.

Getting annoyed with the silence, I huff. "You should go back inside. It's too cold out here, Freckles."

Grimacing, I mentally punch myself in the dick. *Freckles? Really, Kade?*

Still silent.

If she ignores me one more time, I'm shoving her in the fucking water.

I shake my head.

Sitting on the bench next to the diving board, I inhale, unsure why I keep talking. I never talk. "You don't go to my school."

I freeze when she looks up at me, and fucking hell, her eyes are insane. Coughing out the rest of my smoke, I lean my elbows on my knees as she stands, shaking off the water from her legs and slipping on her shoes.

I don't get it. Or her. Or why she's walking around the pool towards me.

Wait.

She's walking towards me.

Oh shit. What the fuck is she doing? *Go away.*

My breath is slowly being ripped from my lungs as she draws closer. In fact, I don't think I'm breathing at all.

Her hair flows down her back in curls, freckles dusting over her skin, and those eyes are fucking killing me. They aren't blue, maybe a light green mixed with silver, like a forest in winter.

What the fuck is wrong with me?

She sits beside me and takes the cigarette from my lips, then places it between her own. The touch of her fingers against my lips doesn't make me uncomfortable.

I try not to show how much she's affecting me by looking away, but my insides are somersaulting.

I clear my throat while she smokes my cigarette like it's hers. There's a breeze and fuck do I inhale the sweet vanilla – she smells good.

I turn my head and watch as she rests back, the end of the cigarette bright orange. Then she blows a cloud above us, eyes closed as the smoke dissipates in the air.

Her eyes open, and now she's looking at me. I'm stuck gazing right back at her beauty.

Fuck.

Once she's done, she places what's left of the cigarette back in my mouth. Her fingertips graze my lips and send a spark to my chest, and I'm not sure what that means. I toss the finished bud aside.

"My name is Stacey." Her voice is soft, quiet and calming. Colour me even more fucking intrigued. "I joined Luciella's dance class a few months ago."

I wouldn't mind watching her body move, to see her in her element. I bet she moves beautifully too.

Stop.

I light another smoke since she finished mine, eyeing her every few seconds as we sit in silence.

Stacey.

A name for the mystery girl.

"What age are you?" I ask.

She smiles at me, and shit, I've never liked someone's smile before. I find myself faintly smiling back at her.

"I just turned fifteen. Same as you."

Same as you.

The three words have me wanting to know more about her.

Her grin grows when I hum, a dimple denting deep in her cheek, and she looks away and tucks a strand of hair behind her ear.

Butterflies, I think.

I wonder if she feels them too?

I must be ill. I'll need to ask Mum what the fuck is wrong with me.

"You sound American *and* Scottish," she says. "So does Luciella."

We spend a lot of time in America visiting our father. It was only natural we picked up the accent over the years. Mine is a lot stronger and deeper.

Hearing people yelling for Stacey, I sigh, knowing our meeting is about to be cut short.

As much as I'd love to sit here and stare at her like a creep, I need to leave before she thinks I'm a weirdo trying to chase some girl I don't even know.

"Giving you a heads-up," I begin, flicking the cigarette into the grass as soon as I see my sister's blonde head. I narrow my eyes. Even though I don't want to say the next words that leave my mouth, my impulsiveness wins. "Just because you're my sister's friend doesn't mean you can speak to me. Stay the fuck out of my way."

As I turn to leave, she lets out a mocking laugh.

"Funny," she snaps back, and I halt in my tracks, brows knitting together as I glance over my shoulder at her.

She pops out her hip and crosses her arms. "And cute. I was just about to say the same thing to you. So why don't you stay the fuck out of my way, *Kade*?"

I like the way my name sounds on her tongue.

I smirk, loving this side of her. "Or else what?"

Ah, fuck. Freckles is even prettier when she's mad.

The butterflies are going fucking wild, and I have no idea how to repress the feeling.

She barges into me with her shoulder, and I can't stop the grin pulling at my lips as she marches away with my sister.

Her scent lingers, her dark hair bouncing down her back, but she keeps facing forward, refusing to give me that one last look at her I'm desperate for – until she's about to vanish down the pathway among the trees, when she turns and gives me the middle finger.

Fucking hell. Why am I smiling?

1

STACEY

SIX YEARS LATER

I pull the duvet away, slowly and quietly, and slide my legs out of the bed first. He stirs and reaches across the mattress, but I'm out and on my feet before he can touch me.

My dress and underwear are scattered across the floor, my heels probably on his stairs or in the living room. A Tinder date that began in the pub, something to keep me busy. After a few drinks and endless flirting, he invited me back here.

Is it bad that I can't quite remember his name? He's either Bryan or Byron. They do sound the same. I'll need to check his profile before I delete the app.

I notice a few missed calls on my phone from my best friend Lu, one from my other best friend Tylar and several messages from my stepbrother, demanding to know my whereabouts.

I groan, rubbing my temples to try to ease my headache, then open Luciella's contact and type out a message.

Me: *Can you pick me up? I'm at Branchton. There's a row of houses across from a church. Do you know the place?*

I tiptoe down the steps with my heels and jacket to hand until I reach the bottom, sitting on the bottom step.

My phone vibrates.

Lu: *On my way. Be there in five.*

Thank God.

I know my friends are going to want the details. I can already hear the high-pitched squeals they'll make when they hear I finally had sex after months of not being the slightest bit interested.

The last person I slept with told me that as much as I'm a lovely girl, he couldn't meet up again. Weirdly enough, he went missing a few days later, and still is.

Being called a *lovely girl* at the age of twenty-one annoyed the hell out of me.

There's a car horn sounding outside, and I sigh in relief.

Luciella's stepfather bought her the car for getting into university. Ty is planning on taking over her family's dance studio.

I'm still trying to find myself, and I'm okay with that. I'm in no rush to sort my shit out. I'm a dancer and an aerialist, an instructor three nights a week for kids' and adults' classes, and we train for shows and competitions.

My mum died when I was thirteen, and when my dad fell in love with Nora Fields, he moved us to this town to live with her and her two boys, Kyle and Chris.

My dad died two years ago, but Nora and her sons insist on me staying there until I save up enough money to move out; she kept all the inheritance that was supposed to be for me.

I don't need to pay dig money, which is good, despite the utter nightmare of living in that house. It means I can focus on my goals.

It's nearly the break of dawn as I step outside. The black Audi R8 waiting has me freezing. The tinted windows hide the driver, but I know exactly who it is, and the fine hairs on the back of my neck rise, my heartbeat accelerating.

The alloys are shiny, as if they've been freshly polished, and the headlights nearly blind me. I grimace, wondering if I can turn around and walk away.

Lu is going to catch a slap when I see her later.

The horn sounds again, making my shoulders tense.

"Unbelievable," I mutter under my breath, seeing no other way to get home since an Uber will take forever to get to this side of town.

With my heels dangling from my fingers, messy hair, and make-up far from fresh, I feel nervous. Out of everyone who could pick me up after a one-night stand, he's the last person I want.

Unhurriedly, I make my way to the car, opening the passenger door and throwing myself into the seat. I don't look at him – I keep my eyes forward, tossing my heels on the floor in front of me as I attempt to put my belt on. It retracts twice, and I blow out a breath when I finally manage to click it in.

I try to ignore the addictive scent of mint, cigarettes and Tom Ford's Noir. The same aftershave he's used for years. I try to ignore *him*, but his presence is everywhere, even after two years of silence between us.

I cross my arms in front of me, glancing at him sideways. "Lu said she was picking me up."

He doesn't respond, looking bored as he types on his phone, his elbow perched on the leather divider between us. He has a fresh tattoo on his hand, which somehow makes it look even more veiny.

I gulp, quickly looking away before he notices me letting my gaze travel up the new tattoos littering his body.

His knees parted, gym shorts showing off his legs, he leans back against the driver's seat, still texting. My scowl deepens as I watch him reply to messages instead of driving me home.

He must have been working out in the home gym at the manor. His top is tight against his chest, the taut muscles still swollen from his session. There's a cigarette tucked behind his ear, and wavy black hair nearly as dark as his soul falls over his forehead.

He has a sun-kissed tan that makes me look like a ghost.

As much as I'd like to say I've forgotten everything about Kade Mitchell, I'm a terrible liar.

I roll the window down, ignoring the chill taking over me while I try to stop his scent from clouding my judgement. Yes, Kade might be handsome, a person that ticked every box for me at one point, but he's my best friend's twin brother and completely off limits.

I know that now.

The last conversation we had was two years ago, and he hasn't as much as looked me in the eye since. I know Lu must have given him shit to get him to come pick me up.

He'd never do this off his own back.

Fucking Luciella. She's aware of how much we can't stand each other. She knows I try to dodge him every chance I get. I mean, she doesn't know *exactly* why, but still.

After nearly three minutes of rock music playing low and him typing away on his phone, the sun starts to rise. My jaw rolls in annoyance, my gaze flitting between the steering wheel and the front gate of the house I left.

"Are you going to drive or just sit here?"

As usual, I'm met with silence. He clicks away on his screen, the corner of his mouth curling up into a smile.

I try not to stare at how handsome he is, despite being a reincarnation of the devil; how soft his skin appears under the harsh black ink. He doesn't smile often, so who is he talking to? Annoyingly, my traitorous heart beats faster. Who's making him grin like that?

No. Stop, Stacey. Who cares who makes him smile?

I can't stay in this car. I need to get the hell out of here.

"I'm getting an Uber," I say, unbuckling my belt, but Kade catches it before it can retract, yanking it to click back in without a word, eyes still on the screen. He types with one hand, the other holding my seat belt in place until he eventually shuts his screen off and turns the car back on.

The engine rumbles beneath us, and I'm rocketed back into the chair as he accelerates at a ridiculous speed.

He turns the music up, and I stare at him, at his beautifully harsh features, while his silvery-blue eyes blaze into the road. I eventually put the window up to stop my hair from blowing wild.

I open my messages and see one I must've missed.

***Lu**: Kade's coming instead.*

***Me**: I hate you.*

She replies instantly.

Lu: Sorry! He was driving his friend home. Please don't kill each other.

***Me**: I really hate you.*

I click my screen off and stay silent, staring out the window at the trees whizzing by. My phone vibrates uncontrollably in my hand – a chain of messages from my stepbrother.

***DoNotAnswer**: Where the fuck are you?*

***DoNotAnswer**: I'm on my way home and you better be there.*

***DoNotAnswer**: I mean it, Stacey.*

I roll my eyes and sigh as I ignore him. It'll come back to bite me, but I can't deal with him right now. Not while I'm in a car with Kade fucking Mitchell, trying not to breathe the same goddamn air as him.

"You should've told Luciella no," I eventually say, loud enough so he can hear me over the music.

Kade's jaw tenses as he speeds up.

I huff, resting my elbow on the window, palm to the side of my head. "I would've waited for an Uber or walked."

He doesn't answer me, just like I knew he wouldn't.

Kade takes the cigarette from behind his ear, sparks it, then tosses his lighter into the divider between us.

He licks his lips, his sleepy eyes on the road, and I watch his mouth as he takes another draw.

You're nothing. You're fucking dead to me.

His voice echoes in my mind, a memory of the last time we spoke. Words he threw in my face; words I'd rather forget. I look away from him, keeping my burning eyes on the outside world as he drives into my housing estate.

The security is tight – all the houses need codes to enter the grounds. Nora asked me when I was growing up if I wanted to have sleepovers for my birthday, celebratory parties or anything that got my friends here, but I always said no.

I didn't want any of them near the monster that lives inside those walls.

Kade stops at the biggest house – three floors of white brick and unused horse stables at the back. An empty pool and overgrown weeds make it look eerie.

He turns his engine off and flicks the cigarette out the window without turning to look at me. He taps his finger on his lap, the muscle in his jaw straining.

Say something, I want to shout. *Yell at me. Anything!*

I drag my gaze away from him, letting out a sigh as I grab my heels. I don't say anything as I unclip my belt, and I stay quiet as I open the door and leave the car.

I reach the gate, ready to push in my code, when I hear the engine start again. I peer over my shoulder, and our eyes meet like a clash of thunder. Goosebumps erupt over my skin, a thrill of electricity rushing in my veins. His eyes are as electric as I remember, but there's something else behind them.

Something dark that wasn't there before.

"Thank you," I whisper. "For driving me home."

For a split second, I think he might actually say something back. But instead, he looks me up and down slowly, taking in my after-sex appearance, and draws his gaze away from me with a shake of his head.

He's disappointed.

Kade lights another cigarette and turns his rock music up loud enough to wake my stepfamily before speeding off without giving me another glance.

Yep. He still despises me.

And after what I did to him, he has every reason to.

I quickly make my way to my bedroom on the top floor of the manor, letting out a breath of relief when I shut the door behind me. My back presses to the wood, and I close my eyes.

My eyes burn, fighting tears I refuse to let fall.

The first time I ever felt this way, this overwhelming feeling, was when we met. He'd interrupted me by the pool at his manor.

I remember the way he looked at me, and how it made a warmth build in my chest. His eyes were so full of life. We'd smoked a cigarette together in blissful, comfortable silence, before he turned into an asshole.

I'd tried to ignore him for years. But being around my best friend's twin brother was too much – there was too strong a pull between us.

Until *that* night, when everything changed.

Kade Mitchell has been the broken shadow in my life ever since, and it's all my fault.

My heels drop to the floor, and I lick my lips, remembering a time when I'd do it and be able to taste mint and faint tobacco.

I shake my head, pushing away the lone tears sliding down my cheek.

Without turning the light on, I pull my dress off and unclip my bra, ready to remove my underwear. But before I can do anything else, a firm grip wraps around my throat, causing a strangled gasp to catch in my chest as the person backs me away from the door and slams me into the mattress.

Air rushes out of my lungs from the impact in a choked-out

cough. Pressure builds behind my eyes as they fly open in fear to see Chris – my evil and deluded stepbrother – above me.

I try to slap his arms as hard as I can, so he'll release his painful hold, but it only causes him to tighten it and lower himself onto me, crushing my nearly naked body between him and the bed.

"Who the fuck was that?"

2

STACEY

I love dancing in the dark.

When I'm surrounded by carnage, which is often, it's peaceful – an escape. I enjoy mentally vanishing from existence, even if it's only for a moment.

Sometimes, I close my eyes and block out everything as my body moves around the hoop, or as the silks wrap around my limbs while I hang mid-air. Usually, halfway through my routine, I'll free flow, head lolling to the beat, imagining a silent audience that can't take their eyes off me.

Music will play, the genre completely dependent on my mood. I'll tell myself that anxiety and unnecessary voices don't exist. That they're nothing but void thoughts desperate to destroy my calm. As each chord strikes, the black tendrils around my heart will shrivel away.

There was a time when one person was able to make me ignore that side of myself. I helped him with his own darkness, and he made me feel alive, sustaining me with tender touches and words, stolen kisses and nights in his bed when no one knew. I was happy.

I thought I was safe. I thought I was free.

Until I wasn't.

But the past is the past. It's nothing a bit of music can't temporarily fix.

"Spiracle" by Flower Face echoes around the studio I've been dancing in since I was a teen. Whenever this song plays, I think of him.

I remember the way I felt sitting on the sofa across from Lu. Nervous. On fire. Wishing I was brave enough to touch him. His hand was so close to my own, and I dared myself to take it, to feel his palm in mine, to know how soft it was, but I was terrified of his refusal.

He hated being touched – it would make him flinch and look as if he was in pain. Then his pinkie grazed mine under the blanket that we shared, eyes on the TV, and I fought a smile.

It was from then that it really started. It wasn't a dare – it was real.

The studio is empty, like it always is after classes end. The colourful LED lights are dimmed, but sometimes, I turn them off completely. It's relaxing, just closing my mind off from this world and being in my own – my axis shifts, and everything stops while I dance.

But in a few hours, Chris will pick me up, and it will all come crashing down – and I'll remember my true reality.

The music cuts out, and I stop, gripping the hoop while I stay suspended upside down, one leg hooked over to keep me stable. I narrow my eyes at the screen of my phone – the text that's popped up has interrupted my song and disconnected the Bluetooth.

I flip down onto the crash mat, tightening the bobble in my hair as I walk to the other side of the room, my bare feet slapping over the flooring. Leaning against the fully mirrored wall, I open the messages in our group chat.

***Lu**: My mum and Ewan just left. I think Kade and his friends are going out, so we'll have the entire manor to ourselves for the party.*

***Ty**: I'm still at my aunt's house. But I'll see you soon!*

Her mum and stepdad Ewan are going to America for a few weeks, something about a meeting with her biological father's therapist to possibly get him accepted time in public. But so far all his appeals have been declined.

I mean, I can't see him ever being allowed time away from the institution. He's terrifying. I spoke to him on the phone once while Lu hurried out of the bathroom, and his voice alone sent shivers through my body. He knew my name and warned me not to hurt his son like *I* was the monster.

His voice was so deep and dangerous, I think I'd honestly pass out if I ever met him. As much as his son resembles him, I'd run in the opposite direction of Tobias Mitchell.

He's a diagnosed psychopath. A killer.

After replying to say I can't wait, I quickly send Chris a text telling him not to bother picking me up. I have the dress with me I'm wearing tonight, and I can grab a shower at Lu's too.

My stepbrother will definitely be pissed, but he's always mad at me.

A few days ago, after Kade dropped me off, I begged him to release me and lied that it was Luciella who drove me home.

I have concealer hiding the faint bruises he left on me.

I connect my Bluetooth back up to the speakers that surround the hall, restart the song and take in my sweaty appearance in the mirror.

When my gaze drops to my chest, I stare the small scar on my sternum, purple and deep. As much as my breasts hide it, it's there. That was why Chris ripped a key against my skin – to deter others from touching what he thinks is his.

He made me lie to Nora and say I did it to myself, and she believed me. She'd wanted me to seek help from a therapist, thinking I was harming myself.

No. Your son is just a fucking monster, Nora.

I run my fingers up the titanium poles. There are seven of them spaced out throughout the hall, a hoop in the middle hanging from the ceiling and deep-pink silks at the back. In the next room, there's a huge dance area where the kids go.

Tylar's family owns the building, and she's had plans to expand into somewhere bigger for the last year but has been caught up in her studies while her parents work on a project in Rome.

I wrap the silk around my wrist, getting a good grip of the material, then do the same with my foot and pull myself onto it. Flipping myself upside down, the material twists around my thighs, holding my weight safely as I quickly fix my hair.

Then I let the music take me on a lyrical adventure, using my flexibility and rhythm to map out the perfect choreography I could use at the Festival of Fright Night at Halloween.

By the time the song finishes, sweat is layering my skin, and my limbs ache from the constant pulling and tugging on the silks. I flip myself upside down once again, settling in a full straddle, and pull off my top to reveal my sports bra.

But when the material at the hook tangles and I start to spin slowly, my entire body freezes – there's someone watching me.

"Chris!" I snap. "You aren't allowed in here!"

My stepbrother shrugs as I untangle myself and drop to the floor.

I narrow my eyes at him. "What the hell are you doing?"

He smirks, making me step backwards as he takes one step forward, eyes dropping to my chest. "You know I like to watch you."

Uncomfortable shivers rush through me, bile rising in my throat. "I told you I'm going to my friend's house."

"I'll drive you. I'm not taking no for an answer."

"I don't need you to drive me."

Chris lifts his hand to me, and I instinctively flinch away before he can touch the strands of hair that have fallen into my face.

"You'll do as I say, little sister," he says. "Unless you want me to lock you in my room again. Maybe I'll chain you to my bed this time?"

I blanch. "No."

He smiles. "I'm driving you."

I gulp and nod, knowing I won't win with Chris.

I turn my back on him and head for the small changing room, throwing on my top as I go. I still feel far too exposed to be around him. After putting on my socks and shoes and wiping my face with a towel, I yank on a hoodie then pull my coat up my arms.

He's going to try to make me cancel tonight, but he can shove it.

Not only would giving in to him make him feel powerful, but Lu would also hunt me down. This has been planned for ages, a secondary celebration of her twenty-first.

A knock at the door makes me jump out of my skin. "Hurry the fuck up before I get you ready myself."

I scoff silently, shaking my head as I slide the strap of my bag on my shoulder, ignoring him when I swing the door open and try to walk by.

He catches my wrist and hauls me back, pinning me against his chest and lowering his mouth to my ear. "Drop the attitude." Chris turns my rigid body to face him, caressing my arms. "I've been good, Stacey. Stop attempting to piss me off by acting like a child."

"I haven't—"

His rough, unwanted hands silence me as they travel up to my shoulders in a firm stroke. His thumbs run across the faint bruising there before cupping each side of my neck. "What have I told you about talking back to me? Do you want to make me angry?"

He sucks his bottom lip, chewing on it as his eyes search my face, waiting for a snarky retort so he has a reason to throw me onto the floor or bite my cheek.

My back hits the wall, causing the mirrors along it to ripple. His body crushes mine, and I grit my teeth to fight the revulsion, fists clenching by my sides.

"So pretty and defiant," he mutters, nudging his knee between my legs to force them open. His palm travels up my side. "Do you remember what happens to bad little girls like you?"

"Get the fuck off me, Chris," I warn him, shoving his chest but failing to move him away from me.

He grins. The bastard loves when I get mad. I feel his excitement against me, and I swallow the strangling lump that's building in my throat.

Chris has been like this with me since I joined the family years ago. I tried to tell my dad when he'd barged into my shower the day we moved in and forced his mouth on mine. My dad refused to listen when I told him that the boy four years older than me had watched me undress on numerous occasions when I was only fourteen.

Nope. I was apparently a teenage troublemaker, rebelling from the death of my mother.

Chris has kissed me on numerous occasions, mid-argument. But every time, my lips have clamped shut – hard enough to cause me pain – to deny the tongue trying to pry its way into my mouth as I fought back.

As far as I'm aware, we've never fucked. But he's drugged me. Hit me. Made my life hell. I tried to run once, but it only made things worse. He became more violent.

It feels like there's no escaping someone as monstrous as Chris Fields, but one day, when I figure out a good-enough plan, I will.

His lips part; he's probably about to describe how loud I'll scream for him, but a noise behind us stops his words.

Thankfully, the studio door opens, causing him to jerk away, and I can finally breathe.

Tylar stands in the entryway, mouth open, brows knitting together, confused as she looks between the two of us. "Um… Who are you?" she asks Chris, and I close my eyes, hoping he doesn't introduce himself correctly.

"Members only." She points to the sign on the wall then stands aside, opening the door wider, silently telling him to fuck off.

I want to hug her.

"Of course," Chris replies, glancing at me, spinning his car keys on his finger and licking his lips.

He leans in and whispers against my ear, "Just wait until you get home, little sister."

I stare at him, waiting for him to leave.

Before Chris turns away from me, his smile drops. "Behave."

Tylar raises a brow at me as soon as he's gone. "Who the hell was that?"

My own worst nightmare. The stepbrother you don't know about.

For my own sake, and my friends', I've kept his identity a mystery and do my best to make sure it stays that way.

My older stepbrother Kyle is an angel. He loves me like a brother should. But then there's Christopher…

"Just some guy," I lie through my teeth, turning the speakers off and switching the main lights on to kill the colour-changing glow. "I thought you were at your aunt's place?"

"My mum wants me to deposit money into the bank," she tells me, pulling open a small cupboard in the corner of the hall and unlocking the safe. She counts notes, about eight hundred pounds' worth, then shoves the pile into her purse.

"He wasn't that Bryan guy, was he? I remember you describing him differently. That one was hot. I'm digging the smile and the shaggy blonde hair. Plus, he's tall."

I huff, scrunching my nose at her calling Chris hot. He's nothing but vulgar in my eyes. "No. That wasn't him."

"Well, whoever he was, please keep it in the bedroom," she says, tilting her head towards the door. "Come on. I can give you a lift to Lu's."

The drive is filled with Tylar reeling off the rules of the studio, and I stare out of the window as I offer sounds of acknowledgment. But when she tells me that a house is currently on fire in Branchton, I look at her with pinched brows. No casualties, but apparently the homeowner was beaten to a pulp.

The name hasn't been released.

My phone vibrates, and when I look down, I roll my eyes. The usual threat. One that used to make my skin crawl and dread returning home. But now it's just routine from him.

***DoNotAnswer**: Be a good girl tonight.*

I snarl at the screen, my fingers moving before I can stop them.

***Me**: Leave me alone.*

The drive to Luciella's takes us through to the loch, and the trees surround the road. We stop at the electric gates of the extravagant manor I still find breathtaking. Tylar tells me she'll catch up in a few hours before driving off.

Once she's gone, I ring the bell; the two dogs start barking like crazy, which has me smiling.

As soon as the door swings open, my smile drops, and I'm trapped under Kade's dark scowl. It's full of so much hatred and betrayal. If I'm not mistaken, he'd rather see me beneath the wheel of his motorbike than standing on his doorstep.

His two Dobermanns, Milo and Hopper, who are usually away with him at university, sniff at my legs and hands, both growing excited when they recognise my scent.

Instead of cowering with my tail between my legs or backing down from their owner, I lower myself to fuss over the dogs while I level him with a look just as grim.

He breaks eye contact first, turning his large muscular back to me as he whistles for the dogs to follow. He's wearing a hoodie, a backwards cap to hide his messy hair and has a beer bottle in his hand. I'm guessing he's not going out tonight.

I roll my eyes and mumble, "Great," under my breath as I close the door behind me.

This will be fun.

3

STACEY

"If I wear the red dress then I can't wear a red top tomorrow," Lu says, alternating pressing each hanger to her chest. "But the blue is a little short."

"Then wear another – you have plenty of dresses," I tell her as I paint my nails, a towel wrapped around me and wet hair down my back. I'm lying on my front, on her bed, while she loses her shit every five minutes about what to wear.

"But I want to wear the red dress."

"Then wear it," I say, twisting the lid onto the polish and blowing on my nails.

"You aren't even helping me, Stacey!" she replies with a huff and tosses both hangers onto the floor. "I can't wear red. I'm wearing a red top tomorrow."

My best friend is insufferable at times.

"Oh yeah, I meant to tell you that Kade and the others aren't going out tonight. They cancelled their plans when Dez told them I was having a party."

"I gathered," I reply, not looking up from my screen, staring at the annoying messages from Chris I've left unanswered.

I'll eventually have to respond, because if I don't, he'll track me here, and that's the last thing I need.

When I go home, I'll dodge him. There are five rooms he can't unlock from the outside; I'm well versed in the manor's hiding spots.

One day, I'll be free. But I guess that's the same day I slash his throat, because other than death, I'm not sure anything will stop him until I'm fully his.

The thought of giving in to Chris makes me feel sick.

Lu chucks a pair of rolled-up socks at my face. "Did you hear me?"

"What did you say?"

She sighs. "I know you're not a fan of Kade and his friends. I'm hoping they stay away so you don't leave."

I snort. She knows me too well, but I wouldn't be leaving because I can't stand them – I just can't stand the looks *he* gives me. "Did you tell him to stay on his side of the manor?"

"God, yes. I don't think I can handle Base and his constant need to talk about sex. If they decide to have a full-on orgy again, I'll kill them all."

"You weren't even there," I say. "It's not like you witnessed it happening."

"I sat on the sofa Base was humping on two days later," she mumbles.

I giggle, trying to rid myself of the memory as if I hadn't been there without my best friend knowing. Tylar wanted to spy on Dez at the pool house, because she was still head over heels for him. She asked me to go with her, and obviously, so I could catch a glimpse of Kade, I agreed.

I wish I hadn't.

We walked into the building and froze on the spot while a full sex-fest went on in front of us, music blaring.

Base, the Russian heir to an entire empire who never takes his eyes off Luciella, was snorting lines of coke from a set of tits while getting his dick sucked.

Dez had someone bouncing over him and froze when he saw Tylar.

Kade kept his scowl on me as he took his place behind a blonde bending over a pool table, naked, unbuckling his belt with a slowness that made me grit my teeth.

He didn't take his eyes off me as he pushed into her.

I hadn't felt pure rage until he smirked.

Bastard.

"I think Base just tries to get your attention," I say. "To make you jealous or something. He's been trying with you for years."

A darkness unravels over Lu's face. "Well, he can stop. Just like Dez and Tylar stopped. It never ends well."

Ty and Dez had a thing; Lu found out and went crazy, declaring that none of her friends should go anywhere near Kade's little trio. As much as I tried to tell her to calm down, that they were harmless, Ty called things off with him.

And I know it hurt her and Dez when she did.

Tylar and the rest arrive an hour later, and the night begins as we stand in a circle, taking shots that burn my chest.

Luckily, this house is big enough that Kade's little get-together is non-existent compared to the party Lu is throwing. And since alcohol is slowly slithering through my veins, a part of me is wondering if they'll invite loads of girls over.

The music's loud enough that my ears are ringing. Someone brought strobe lights. The flashing has bodies glitching while they dance.

My phone vibrates, and I tut.

> ***DoNotAnswer**: If you don't reply, I'm coming to get you from whoever it is that you're fucking.*

I roll my eyes, muttering, "Asshole."

"Who the hell is that?" Tylar asks with furrowed brows, looking over my shoulder.

I put my phone in my bra, shrugging as I take her glass and down the vile, strong drink it contains.

"Hey, you bitch!" But she smiles as someone pulls her away from me, onto the makeshift dance floor.

I make my way to the bathroom on the first floor. My vision is a bit messy from the strobes as I relieve myself then lean against the sink.

I glare at my phone, which is sitting beside the sink. Maybe I'll accidentally drop it in the water? Break it? Step on the screen so the messages are illegible?

DoNotAnswer: *I'll rip his jaw off. You're mine.*

I scoff at the text. Daily, hourly, I wish I could strangle my stepbrother in his sleep without him thinking I'm trying to make it sexual.

Me: *Can you stop? I'm at my friend's party. And I'm not yours. I'm your fucking stepsister, you sick freak.*

DoNotAnswer: *I'm coming to get you.*

Anger builds as I quickly turn off my phone.

Surely it's wrong for him to want me so badly?

I hurry upstairs to Lu's room and toss the phone on her bed. I know I should be doing as he says to stop the abuse, but I'm at my limit. I want to fight back.

By the time I get back downstairs, most of my friends have moved into the main kitchen. Some are sitting on the counters, some at the breakfast bar, while hyping two people sitting on the floor for everyone to see. She's straddling him and grinding against his...

Oh.

My eyes widen when I notice him taking her nipple into his mouth, grabbing her breast while he licks and sucks, as if he's starving. Her dress rides up over her behind, where his other hand is gripping and moving her against him.

A girl from Lu's college class stops in the doorway, her jaw nearly hitting the ground. "You do know we can see you, right?" she asks the pair, but they wave them off as they continue kissing and grinding.

"They're just going to..."

"Fuck, yes!" someone confirms for her when she struggles for words.

Luciella walks in. "Absolutely not! This is my mother's kitchen, goddammit!"

I continue to sip my drink, shoulder to shoulder with Ty while we watch them stand and disappear out of the kitchen, the girl giggling as he smacks her ass and asks where the spare rooms are.

Lu pops a hip out with folded arms, tapping her foot. "There are over thirty. Take your pick."

Someone tells her there's a smashed lamp in the lobby, and she sighs before vanishing.

"Such a spoilsport," a voice says behind us.

Ty groans when she realises it's Dez.

"You wanted to watch, didn't you?"

"Get fucked," she retorts without turning around. "Go back to the other side of the house where you belong before Lu sees you talking to me."

"But we're here for the free booze and the eye candy. Is Satan's twin going to ruin that as well?"

Tylar's eyes flutter as Dez lowers his voice to a whisper. She ignores whatever he says, but I see her flush, and one of his hands takes her hip, pulling her back to him. "If I put my hand up your dress, would your cunt be soaked, remembering how it felt to have me fuck you in every way possible?"

I clear my throat and suck on my straw, averting my eyes.

"Stop," she says, but her voice is breathy.

He grunts. "You weren't telling me to stop the other night."

He obviously can't see how devastated Ty looks. She shrugs him off and storms away. Dez just laughs and takes a swig of his beer, eyes finding mine.

I glare at him. "Why do you need to do that?"

He hasn't taken her ending things with him very well and is forever teasing her, knowing it drives her crazy. He's always texting and calling, and Tylar being Tylar, she answers.

"She loves it," he replies, taking another drink of his beer.

I raise a brow and glare as I nod towards my retreating friend. "Oh, evidently."

Dez winks at me with a smirk, pulling himself onto the counter. Before I can search for Tylar to console her, Dez glances over my shoulder. "You want another beer, Kade?"

I freeze.

He must nod, because his friend reaches out a bottle towards my shoulder. A warmth radiates against my back as Kade takes the drink, knuckles all bloodied and cut open. I hold my breath, trying to ignore my treacherous hormones as heat coils at my spine.

I can smell him, the spice of his aftershave and the shampoo he uses on his hair. It's intoxicating, memories flooding me of my fingers wrapped in his waves, the scent of his pillow, the sound of his laugh when I sing terribly.

Still standing closely behind me, he only hums, and the deep rumble goes straight from my chest to between my legs, tingling all the way down like fireworks.

My cheeks are most likely red. I haven't been this close to him in such a long time. The alcohol is numbing my common sense, because my body should not be reacting this way.

Does he feel the same way I do right now? Is he itching to grab me and drag me into an unoccupied room? Probably not, since he hates my guts.

Dez glances at a tall, leggy redhead walking in and tilts his head at her. "Did you not fuck her last night?"

I walk away before I can hear Kade's response.

"I could look at you all day, do you know that?"

"Stop being romantic, Kade – I might get the wrong idea."

A low laugh, and... "Just another thing you taught me, Freckles. Don't go home tonight. Stay with me."

I nod, and he presses me to the mattress, nudging my legs apart...

No.

I refuse to go back to that memory, the moment I knew what

he meant to me.

At that point, he was everything.

And I lost him.

4

STACEY

When I eventually stop dancing and sit down next to my friends, I can breathe. They gossip, play Never Have I Ever, where I completely dodge most questions when they discuss our firsts, then take the remaining shots set out on the table.

I'm not sure why Kade has suddenly started making an appearance. For the past two years, I've only seen him a handful of times.

And I'm either met with silence, glares, derisive snorts or passing comments muttered under his breath that he doesn't think I can hear.

He's changed so much from the timid boy who couldn't understand basic emotions, who needed to be shown that it's okay to feel, who got nervous when he had no idea what he was doing in the bedroom to *this* version.

By the time the crowd starts to disperse, it's four in the morning. Lu's in bed, leaving Ty, myself and a few others to play more drinking games.

We're all pretty drunk, happy, laughing while taking shots to prolong our buzz – until Kade, Dez and Base walk into the sitting area, two girls under Base's arms.

Tylar, sitting beside me cross-legged, won't even glance at them as she pours another drink and asks who's next.

"We're playing drinking games," someone says. "Wanna join?"

Tylar blurts, "No," at the same time Dez says, "Sure."

We all shift on the sofas to make room, and the large coffee table between us fills with everyone's drinks.

"I think we should spice up these little games though," Base adds, sitting down and dragging both girls onto his lap. "Depending on how adventurous you all are."

Kade drops onto the couch opposite me, and to my absolute horror, one of the girls on Base's lap moves over to him. He pauses for a second, giving her a confused look, before a tattooed hand grasps at her hip. I gulp deeply, trying to ignore my jealousy.

I have no right to feel this way.

"You're talking about How Much Can You Handle, aren't you?" Tylar asks, frowning when they all nod. "You're aware that Stacey and I are here? Lu will freak."

"Just no one touch Kade, and she won't kill us." Dez nudges his friend, but I don't look at him to see his reaction as I study my nails. "Base can pair up with Stacey. You said you wanted to fuck her, didn't you?" he asks his friend.

Oh man.

Base shakes his head. "You're a dick."

Kade shifts on the couch, lighting a cigarette and tossing the clipper onto the coffee table between us.

"If Tylar accepts, then she can have me," Dez says, winking. "You game?"

She nods slowly, her cheeks blushing with the alcohol. "I'm game."

"If you can handle me." He smirks, slapping his friend on the chest. "And Kade already has Abbie, so there won't be a riot from the twin dragged from the pits of hell."

"Stop saying that shit," Base says. "She's not that bad."

"But she's Satan's twin? We all agreed."

"If you want me, then stop talking about my best friend like that," Tylar says, crossing her leg over her knee and quirking a brow.

I can see from the edge of my sight that Abbie's hand is high on Kade's lap. He's paying zero attention as he takes a draw of his smoke and blows it between us, a cloud coming straight for my face.

She's pretty. Her body is perfect – wavy brown hair, a nice rack, with long, smooth legs that dangle over his lap. Her dress is tight, accentuating every curve.

But I know he hates it when someone plays with his hair or presses a palm to his chest the way she is. It took ages for him to be comfortable with my touch. He's either fighting the urge to not cringe away, or he truly has changed.

Have they had sex before? Or is it more? Does he talk to her about… everything?

Tylar tilts her head at me. "I don't think Base could keep up with this one." Her elbow digs into me. "She's had a lot of practice lately."

I slap her knee. "Hey!"

She winces and apologises with a kiss on my cheek.

Base – a taller, more muscular version of Dez – responds with chocolate brown eyes and a grin. "I'm up for the challenge if you are, Rhodes."

Oh God. Shitting shit.

He would tear me in half.

And I'm not about to fuck one of Kade's friends, no matter how much we hate each other.

Kade glares at me when I look at him – if it were possible, I'd be on fire from how angry he appears. Which is stupid, considering Abbie is whispering something in his ear and stroking her hand up his bicep, and he's allowing her.

I shrug as our eyes clash a little longer, unbothered as Base nods in agreement.

I'll play along with this for a minute, just to see Kade's reaction, then I'll go to bed before anything happens.

Would he even care? Doubtful, since he has Abbie trying to draw his mouth to hers. He isn't kissing her. He isn't even looking in her direction.

He's looking at me.

"How do we play?" one of the guys asks, completely interested.

Dez's eyes are on Tylar as he explains the rules. "Choose a partner – or partners – and fuck until you can't."

Abbie, perched on Kade's lap, lets out another flirtatious giggle, leaning back to whisper something into his ear again. His eyes move to her, and his brows furrow.

"Stacey, there's someone at the gate asking for you," a voice says from the doorway of the sitting area. One of the guys who was waiting on an Uber. "He's pretty fucked up."

Shit.

"Is it the guy from earlier?" Ty asks me, a smile on her lips, and everyone around us is listening. "The one you were seconds from screwing in the studio? You could invite him in. Sorry, Base, but he was hot."

I grimace, and so does Dez. "We weren't going to—" I stop, sighing as I place my drink on the coffee table in front of us. "Start without me."

"He's pretty mad," he tells me. "He's shouting for you to get out there."

Kade's cigarette freezes halfway to his mouth.

Ty abruptly stands, but I tell her it's fine and ask her to stay where she is, telling Base and Dez the same when they, too, get to their feet.

"You sure?" Dez asks, concerned as he fists his hands. "I'm happy to tell him to get to fuck."

Base nods in agreement.

"Yeah, I'm sure. It'll be fine."

Standing and smoothing over my dress, I ignore Kade's eyes following me as I walk out of the room.

When I reach the gates, hugging myself with how cold it is, I huff out a foggy breath. "Really, Chris? Why are you here?"

My stepbrother's eyes are bloodshot, as if he's had far too many drinks before coming here. "You weren't answering me."

His words are slurred, and saliva slips from the corner of his mouth.

"Are you high?"

"Will it make you come home with me if I say yes?" he asks, fingers curling on the rods of the metal gate I refuse to unlock with the code.

I shake my head, gritting my teeth in annoyance when he staggers to the left. "You look cold, little sister. You know I can heat you up."

My stomach twists. "Go home."

"You're my home," he replies with a hiccup. "Don't make me mad. I don't like being mad with you. Come with me. We'll go back to the house and I'll... I'll make love to you."

He loses his balance, tumbling to his side. I groan, taking a few steps and reaching my hand out to try to help him to his feet. Every single time he gets this messed up, I need to help him, even though I don't want to. It'll be worse for me if I leave him like this, and I'd rather not meet those consequences.

But this time, when I try to help him, he grabs my wrists and yanks me to him, slamming my body into the metal separating us.

A flash of pain momentarily seizes me as my face hits the hard surface between us.

"Let go of me," I snap, tasting blood from a cut on the inside of my lip.

"Who are you fucking in there?" His thumb runs along my lips as he stares at them, his eyes wholly black from all the drugs he's consumed. "Whose cock has been in this mouth?"

He lowers his hand to grab between my legs, and I flinch from his unwanted touch before he can make contact.

He smirks, catlike and evil. "This is all mine. Every inch of your body belongs to me."

I manage to shove myself away from his grasp as he tries to kiss me, falling back a few steps and catching my breath. I'm thankful the cobble path to the gate is far from the manor as I begin to raise my voice. "You need to stop! You're sick. You can't do this with me!"

"You want me!" he rushes out.

I stare at him, shaking my head.

"You want me, and you deny it. You love—"

"I don't."

He glares at me, eyes watering, until they aren't on me any longer.

"Who the fuck are you?" Chris snaps, his rage building. His eyes flicker between me and the person now standing behind me. "Who is he, Stacey?"

I know who it is without the need to turn. I can sense him; I can always feel when he's nearby. The faint smell of spice, smoke and mint from the hoodie I've slept in only confirms it.

Kade snakes his arm around my waist, already making me feel safer. His other hand is wrapped around the neck of a beer bottle, a joint between his fingers.

He blows a cloud of toxic smoke towards Chris.

His arm tightens around me, his hand fisting the material of my dress at my hip. In a deep, threatening tone, Kade says, very slowly, "Walk away before I make you one sorry motherfucker."

"Who are you?" Chris asks again, one of his hands slipping from the poles of the gate.

"Just go," I beg him as Kade lowers his chin to my shoulder, inhaling deeply.

Chris will most likely come for me when I get home. He's big and bad around me, but I watch the sliver of fear in his eyes as they shift to Kade again.

"She's not yours."

Kade chuckles. "She's not yours either. Clearly." He points behind Chris. "Leave."

Chris pushes himself from the gate and spits on the ground before getting back into the car he certainly shouldn't be driving.

I breathe, closing my eyes as the lights start to vanish in the foggy driveway. Kade hasn't released me, but I haven't moved away either. My core twists with a deep sensation I haven't felt for a while as he brings his mouth to my ear, whispering, "Who was your friend, Freckles?"

"No one," I manage to answer, holding in a gasp as the tip of his nose traces the shell of my ear.

As I tilt my head to give him better access, my chest heaves as the delicate yet powerful touch travels to the sensitive area of my neck that has my inner walls pulsing. He knows what he's doing, tempting me, teasing me. "No… No one."

He takes another draw of his joint, then has a swig of his beer, still holding me to him. "You sure? Wasn't that who you were apparently close to fucking earlier?"

"No."

Kade hums, the rumbling sound vibrating against my back. "He doesn't seem your type. Far too young." He lowers his voice. "You prefer your quick fucks older, don't you?"

I don't reply, concentrating on my unsteady breaths and the heat coiling around my spine.

When Kade's fingers tug at my chin, forcing me to look at him over my shoulder, I lick away the metallic taste on my lips, trying to hide any evidence of Chris hitting my face against the gate.

So close. His mouth is so close to mine. If I tilt my head, our lips will collide.

When he turns my body to face him, his eyes are burning into my soul. He backs me up against the gate with a palm on my chest then moves it to my throat, holding me in place. My pulse is hammering against his hand, and as he squeezes slightly, a whimper slips from my mouth.

My entire body is on fire with his touch. The total opposite of when Chris tries to manhandle me.

His pupils dilate under the moonlight.

He releases my throat and grasps a handful of hair, roughly tugging it to tip my head back. "Is that what you want? A quick fuck?"

Kade waits for me to respond, tightening his hold when I let out a whimper from how close he is, then releasing me and stepping back.

"If that's what you want," he says, and I frown at him. Kade tips the bottle in the direction Chris went, fighting a snarl on his face. "By all means, go. Or you can have Base as planned. We both know how desperate you can be."

Before I can come up with a snarky response, or at least tell him to go fuck himself, he scoffs, shaking his head and turning away from me. He tosses back the rest of his beer then chucks the bottle, my shoulders tensing as it smashes on the cobbles.

You prefer your quick fucks older, don't you?

Fine. I might have deserved that.

5

STACEY

Something is licking my face.

Two somethings.

I crack my eyes open to see Milo and Hopper on each side of me. I pat their heads while looking over at the door I'm certain I shut. "How did you two get in here?"

They stare at me, then Milo tilts his head, and I lie back down as they roll onto their backs to get tummy rubs. Hopper nudges my face with his wet nose, and I wrap my arms around him with a huge grin.

"Did you both miss me?"

Both heads tilt this time, and I laugh and scratch their ears.

Kade must've kept them away from the party last night. He's always extremely protective of them. I'm surprised he hasn't booted the door down and demanded they leave me alone.

The sun beams in my face as I peel the duvet off me, screwing my eyes shut as I search for my phone. When I find it, it's dead, and with how much I drank last night after going back to the party, I think I'm dead too.

No sexual games were played thankfully.

I slip my shoes on and leave the spare room, Milo and Hopper sprinting away down the lobby. I walk three doors down and knock lightly. "Ty?"

The latch on the door unlocks, and my friend sneaks out, leaving Dez asleep in bed. Her hair is a mess, and there's a bite mark on her throat. She blows out a breath as she looks at me. "I'll call an Uber. I'm too hungover to drive."

We step over a sleeping Base at the entranceway and slip out the front door.

The manor is strangely silent. "You wouldn't think it was noon. Luciella must've given the staff more than one day off."

"Three days, I think. She hates having them around."

The outside air hits us, and we both shiver.

"I'm going to come stay at your place for a few days," I tell Tylar, shivering even more at the thought of going home to Chris. "When do you leave for Rome?"

"Sunday," she says as we sit on the steps, waiting for our ride. "I know you want to ask. So ask."

I shrug. "What you and Dez do is none of my business."

"It was that stupid game," she says, sighing. "I thought I was going to sleep with him, then Kade made them all leave."

When I'd gone back into the manor last night, Kade had grabbed Base by the collar before he could take a line of coke from the coffee table and dragged him out of the room. Then when Dez decided to come up for air after devouring Tylar's mouth, Kade had said that the party was over.

I had a few more shots, and then me and Tylar went to one of the spare rooms. She snuck out once she thought I was asleep, and I heard her giggling outside the door.

The gate opens, and I watch as a black motorbike drives in and stops next to us. The rider stands tall, tugs off his gloves and then the helmet to reveal dark messy hair and sleepy blue eyes.

Kade drops the helmet on the ground; he looks like he hasn't slept in days. He rolls his shoulders as he gets off the bike, and as he lifts his gaze to me, I notice a bruise under his cheek. I gulp and look away.

"I think Base might be dead," Tylar says, yawning. "He's lying in the lobby in just a pair of boxers."

Kade nods, and I want to look at him again so badly, but I don't.

He walks up the stairs on my right, and my skin prickles at his nearness before he vanishes into the manor. My shoulders jump as he slams the door.

"So moody," Tylar says. "I wonder where he went? Dez said he ran out the manor at seven this morning."

I don't reply as I stare at my shoes, kicking imaginary stones.

When the Uber arrives, we run down to the gates and jump in. Tylar lives an hour from here, and her place is smaller, filled with loads of art, statues and plants. Her cats press up against my legs as I try to walk to her room, nearly tripping me on the stairs.

Instead of showering and getting dressed, or doing anything productive, Tylar and I put on fresh pyjamas and climb into bed. We stay there for the rest of the day, and when I finally charge my phone, Luciella video-calls us for an hour to make plans for our upcoming trip to America. She's flying out to meet up with her mother and Ewan, and see her dad, and has invited me along for a holiday.

I fall back to sleep after we eat pizza.

We do this for three days, and over those three days, I ignore every single message from Chris. They only grow angrier, more threatening, and even after I block him, he uses a new number to ask me to come home.

Or begs me more like.

Tylar finally drives me home after we collect her car from Lu's, reminds me that I'm covering her class tonight then air-kisses me as I leave the vehicle. I rush to my bedroom, sighing in relief when I reach it and close the door, putting the chair beneath the handle to stop Chris from getting in.

I shower and lean against the tiles, remembering how close Kade was to me by the gate. His arm was around me, and then his hand was on my throat. I slide my hand up to my neck and bite my lip, closing my eyes and imagining it's him.

The moment breaks when someone bangs on my bedroom door, loud enough that I can hear it in my bathroom.

Chris stares at me like an angry owl from across the dining table while Nora discusses with Kyle the importance of being more involved with the family instead of partying all the time.

I can barely swallow my food without feeling his vomit-inducing gaze on me. It's murderous – like, serial killer murderous. If there wasn't anyone else around, I fear what he'd do.

If Chris grips his fork any tighter, it'll snap.

Psycho.

"When are you going to America?"

Nora's question is enough to pull his concentration to his mother. He had no idea I was going away. Great, more punishment.

When I tell her that I'm leaving tomorrow, she asks, "And will adults be going?"

"Can we not do this? I'm twenty-one."

"Regardless of your age, the last time you went over there, you came back with multiple bruises and a broken arm. How are you going to prevent that from happening again?"

I shrug. *Your son has a screw loose.* "Maybe not drink and fall in front of oncoming traffic?" That was the lie he'd made me come up with.

"There's no need for that tone, dear. I'm just worried about you. Whenever you go away with your friends, you come back injured."

"Why are you going there?" Chris asks, and I know he's going to strangle me against my door when we're alone, to try to squeeze every little last detail from me.

I can't say, *Oh to see Tobias fucking Mitchell with his children,* can I? First off, they'd freak because he's famous around here. And then they'd lock me in my room, so I'd never see that family again.

When I don't respond, he kicks the table. "Who are you going with?"

"Friends."

"Who?"

"Fucking hell." Kyle tosses down his fork, Nora scowling at him for his bad language. "Does it matter? Let her breathe, man. You're unbearable at times. And so are you," he says to his mother. "She's old enough to do what she wants."

"Fine. But you will call me every day," Nora says, before continuing to eat her dinner.

I mouth a *thank you* to Kyle and finish eating, ignoring Chris's death stare while I gulp down my glass of wine.

Kyle isn't aware of just how insufferable his brother is. He thinks Chris is possessive over me because he'd always wanted a little sister growing up, but if he really knew what he was like, I'm not sure who would murder who.

There have been so many occasions where I considered telling him. So many times, while he rushed me to Accident and Emergency, I debated telling him the truth, because I think he'd believe me. But then again, my dad didn't, so it isn't worth the risk.

Plus, I don't want Kyle getting hurt.

If I told Lu or Tylar, they'd demand I leave – pack my bags and run away. But not only do they not know Chris exists, they also wouldn't understand just how psychotic he is, the lengths he'd go to in order to control me. I think I'm the only one who knows what he's truly capable of.

He makes Tobias Mitchell look like a saint.

It's like being in an abusive relationship without the sex and emotional connection. I'm not *not* leaving because I'm his partner and I love him and part of me hopes he'll change. I'm not deluded into thinking he has any capacity to be sane. No, not even close. I'm still here because I'm far too scared to run away and I'm broke.

And even if I did manage to escape, he'd hunt every inch of this earth to find me.

I want a voice, but I have no idea how to use it or how I'd stop his wrath if I did.

We continue eating, but Chris just stares at his plate. There's nothing in his eyes, nothing in his tone. Nothing but pure rage. And all his anger is towards me. Like he's calculating how hard to throw the knife to make sure it goes right through my skull.

I clear my throat, turning to Nora. "May I be excused?"

The corners of her eyes crinkle as she smiles at me. "Of course. Take the rest of the wine with you."

"Thank you." I turn to Kyle and Chris and say with a nod, "Goodnight."

Chris scowls at me as I grab the bottle and leave the table.

The walk to my room is nerve-wracking – my feet can't possibly go any faster. I get to my door before I'm thrown against the wall.

I was so goddamn close.

"The fuck was that all about?"

Before, when he started being more aggressive with me, I'd cry and plead with him to leave me alone, but now I simply roll my eyes and look anywhere but at him. "What did I do this time?"

"You know what I'm talking about. Saturday night. And you've been ignoring me since."

When I raise a shoulder, he snatches the wine bottle from my hand and takes my jaw in a painful grip. "Who was he?"

Chris was so gone from reality that he hadn't noticed who was holding me; he hadn't noticed it was Kade Mitchell with his arms around my waist. He definitely knows who he is – the entire town does – but I guess he can't remember his face because he was on so many narcotics.

The grip on my jaw tightens, and Chris crushes my body with his.

"You're not going to tell me, are you? Did you forget what happened the last time?"

Even as my heart shatters, I grit my teeth despite how close they feel to cracking.

Chris yanks me from the wall and shoves me into my bedroom, slamming the door behind us. He still has the wine bottle to hand, and I already know what he's going to do.

"Lie down."

I fold my arms. "Absolutely not."

"Tell me who he was," he continues, walking me around the

room as I try to get away from him. "Who the fuck had his hands on you?"

"I'm your sister."

He snatches my jaw again, angles my head right back, and before I can yell at him to fuck off, or even take a breath, he pries my lips apart and pours the wine into my mouth.

"*Step*sister. So I can do whatever the fuck I want to you. You're mine, remember? Now, since you like to drink so much, fucking drink."

I choke, slapping at his chest, face and arms, but he doesn't budge as the alcohol glugs down my throat. I cough as it flows into my eyes, up my nose, down my top and soaks my clothes, and I try to close my mouth, to clench my teeth or cough the liquid away, so I can fill my lungs with air, but his hold on me only tightens. Pain erupts all over my face from his grip, and tears mix with the red wine on my cheeks.

My chest is burning, sick rising up my throat with the wine he's drowning me with.

The tears falling down his cheeks make him look like he's hurting, but he's the one abusing me. He always cries.

He stops and steps back, wiping his face with his sleeve. I drag in breaths and try to blink away the burning in my eyes, nearly vomiting my dinner back up as I drop to my knees and gag.

"Are you going to answer me now?"

Barely able to fill my lungs with air, it takes me a full minute to make sure I don't pass out. The room is blurry and spinning, and so much pressure is building behind my eyes and my head.

"Fucking answer me!"

When I ignore him again, his foot drops down on the back of my head, my mouth colliding with the ground, and I instantly regret coming home.

6

STACEY

"Right, I have a proposition for you," Lu says excitedly.

I stare at myself in the bathroom mirror, wiping away the condensation from my shower. There are black circles beneath my eyes, probably from my lack of sleep over the last few days. I have a gash on my cheek from where my face smacked into the floor, and I'm certain my pinkie is broken from Chris stomping on it.

This needs to stop.

I just have no idea how to end it. Even if Nora or Kyle would believe me when I told them, I don't think they'd be able to stop Chris from burying me in the garden. I even contemplated telling Kade a few years ago, because I knew he'd do something about it. But every time he asked me where I got my bruises, I'd lie and say they were from dancing.

I always lie. And I hate it.

"What's the proposition? And no, I'm not taking your classes when you get back from America. I'm far too busy."

"You did before!" she exclaims, and I can tell she's probably throwing her arm around and pacing her bedroom. "Please. I really can't be bothered teaching a bunch of kids."

"No."

She sighs. "Fine. But wait, you said when *you* get back, not we. Are you not coming?"

"I am. I'm just tired is all. Who's going again?" I ask, rubbing my towel into my hair to dry it a little then putting her on loudspeaker to brush my teeth.

"Just us I think. Mum and Ewan are there already obviously, and Jason didn't get time off work. My grandmother is apparently meeting us at the hotel near my dad's institution, but we'll see. She never shows up."

I shouldn't be disappointed, but I get why Kade isn't going.

"Your dad's mum?"

Lu huffs. "Unfortunately. I can't stand her, and I'm certain my mum wants to punch her in the face every time she talks."

Her phone beeps, and she's silent for a beat.

"Oh shit, yeah, my brother just reminded me that him and Dez are fixing the ceiling at the studio tonight. Aren't you taking the dance class?"

Oh fuck off.

"Awesome." I sigh. "Yeah, I am. I'm taking over for Tylar's classes until she gets back from Rome. It's the advanced class."

By the time she hangs up, my hair is nearly dry, and my nerves are ready to explode at the thought of Kade being at the studio. I rub moisturiser over all the dark tattoos on my body – most are on my arms, but there are a few on my legs and torso.

Some of them Kade designed for me. They were supposed to be matching. I refuse to cover them up like he did.

I leave the bathroom, quickly making sure the door is locked before getting dressed and sorting my dance bag. I pack my Pleasers and fishnet tights to wear with my bodysuit.

The last time Kade saw me dressed like this, dancing with fire for a competition I never got to participate in, I ended up bouncing over his cock on the studio floor until three in the morning.

Once I make sure the coast is clear, I run down the stairs as quickly and as quietly as possible, managing to escape the mansion before Chris can tackle me into a room.

I've never come across someone so messed up, not even when I spoke to Tobias Mitchell on the phone.

My son deserves better, he'd told me. *You ruined him.*

I mean, he was half right – Kade did deserve better, but I definitely didn't ruin him. He seems to be happier than ever with his alcohol, drugs and fucking everything around him. He never partied like this before, but now it seems to be all he does.

He seems happy.

So no, I didn't ruin him. But I did earn a spot on his block list.

I thank the Uber driver that drops me off at the dance studio and climb out of the car. The coldness of the night bites into my skin as I hurry down the steps into the building – then nearly scream out profanities when I slam into something.

Or someone.

His dark brows knit together as he glares down at me, his blue eyes so intense I struggle to look at them.

"Um, sorry," I mutter as Kade leans down to grab my dance bag, tucking it back onto my shoulder. The hallway is narrow, cool, but having him so close is making the place feel like an inferno. "Is Dez here too?"

He nods once, pulling the cigarette from behind his ear, then eases past me, heading for the exit.

Back to the silent treatment, I guess.

"Where are you going?"

He raises the lighter and cigarette above his head as he makes his way to the stairs.

I glance at my phone screen to check the time and quickly say,

"Um, my class doesn't start for an hour. Do you want me to go to another hall? I need to warm up and run through my routine."

Kade turns to face me, still walking backwards. He honestly couldn't look more unbothered as he shrugs. "I've seen you dance plenty of times."

My cheeks heat at the fact he's speaking to me, even though it means nothing. He spoke to me that night at the manor. I mean, it wasn't exactly a *positive* conversation, but it was the first time he'd broken a breath towards me in two years, even if it was only to insult me.

"My music will be loud," I add. "Very loud."

Another shrug. I might slap him if he shrugs again.

"I like loud music."

I stare at his powerful, well-built back as he takes two stairs at a time before I head in. I give Dez a half-smile when he ducks down from the ceiling.

"Alrighty, Rhodes."

"Hi, Desmond."

He chuckles. "Don't start that shit." He waves a screwdriver at me. "I told that prick my real name in confidence and she told everyone."

"Tylar would take offence at being called a prick."

He leans his elbows on the top of the stepladder. "Then she's the biggest prick of all pricks. And you make sure to tell her that."

He looks at the entrance and lowers his voice. "She's not in tonight, is she?"

They obviously aren't in contact right now.

"No, she's still in Rome."

Dez nods, and I can tell he wants to talk about her more, but he taps the metal of the ladders and gets back to work, burying his head in the ceiling.

I quickly pull off my tracksuit and yank my tights on, button my bodysuit at the crotch, then tie my knee-high Pleaser boots. They're new, and the leather squeaks a little when I move my ankles.

Kade comes in as I connect my phone to the speakers, and I can feel his eyes on my back. It's distracting me from searching through the notes for my routine. As I glance up at the floor-to-ceiling mirrors that span one side of the hall, I can see him staring at me. More specifically, he's looking at my legs, dragging his gaze upwards.

He might as well have dragged his tongue over my skin with how hot it makes me.

"Pass the flathead screwdriver," Dez says, causing Kade to break away from eye-fucking me. "This won't tighten, piece of shit wiring."

"Let me try," he replies in a deep voice, and I try to focus on finding the notes I've saved on my phone outlining each move.

The hall is big enough that they shouldn't cause a distraction, even with the corner of the ceiling hanging down.

I sit down in front of the mirrors, playing "Party Monster" by The Weeknd, and quickly swipe through my notes, then I sink into the splits, each leg straight out with blocks beneath my ankles. Usually, I'd do this without heels, but Kade being here has completely thrown me off what I usually do to prepare for classes.

Flexibility has always been a positive for me. I bend in all ways, which makes it easier to dance, work out and...

Yeah.

I roll my hips forward to deepen the split, leaning down so my elbows rest on the grey wooden flooring.

"Ah, shit," Dez blurts out, the metal creaking as he jumps down from the ladders. "I need to head, man. Are you good to finish this up?"

Kade must nod or something, because I don't hear a reply.

I smile at Dez as he gathers his things then says goodbye to us both. Annoyingly, I can hear the joke in his tone as he says, "You two have fun."

We most definitely will not.

My bodysuit is like a thong and does nothing to hide my ass in this position. My netted tights make me appear more sexual, and my boots are nine inches of red leather that go to just above my knees. Of all the times to be left alone with Kade! I mentally pat myself.

"How long are you going to be?" I ask, keeping my gaze fixed on my phone screen. "Will you still be here when my class begins? I'll need to turn the lights out and the LEDs on."

When he doesn't respond right away, I glance up. He's walking to the mirrors in front of me to go through his tool bag. He flips a hammer in his palm then checks his phone, staring at the screen before tossing it down.

"I'll leave before your class starts. You can put the LEDs on now though. I'll use a head torch."

Seeing Kade working does things to me. Ewan has been trying to get him to work with his company for years, but he only does the odd job here and there.

University was his plan.

That's where he'd vanished to, only coming back every now and again and ignoring me in the process. I've no idea why he's home now.

Maybe he quit?

Once the lights are out, and a soft red glow takes over the room, I scroll through Spotify, finding "Skin" by Rihanna. Before pressing play, I finish my stretches and turn to Kade, who's at the top of the ladder with his head in the ceiling.

"Are you sure you want to stay? This is like... a *really* slow dance routine."

I feel my nerve endings catching fire as he lowers his head from the ceiling, his eyes lingering on me for a split second before he goes back to work.

The lyrics are about rough fucking, for crying out loud.

With my ex right here.

I could scream.

I mentally say a prayer for myself as I get into position. It's not that I'm embarrassed; my classes aren't for someone else's pleasure. They're for body positivity and feeling good about yourself, taking an hour away from real life and escaping reality.

But dancing the way I'm about to in front of him, especially with the way I get into the zone of things, I must say I'm a little nervous.

He's seen me dancing, but not for a long time.

Hopefully he keeps his head in the ceiling.

The vocals start, and I lie back, raising one knee so my heel drags on the laminate, then the other, alternating for the introduction as my back arches off the floor. I flip onto my front, flicking my hair and leisurely, sultrily sliding up to sit on my haunches while my hands roam my body, my hips moving all the while.

Kade stays in the ceiling while I keep going, working up a sweat by the time I get to my feet. I slowly walk around the pole, then pivot around it twice, one hand exploring myself as the other grips the cold metal. My eyes lift to the mirrors, and I nearly stop moving.

He's no longer in the ceiling – Kade's leaning his elbows on top of the ladder, watching me as I slide my back down the pole to squat, twirling my hips as I descend.

I wrap my long ponytail around my fist. "Stop looking at me."

He shakes his head.

I roll my eyes and keep going, trying to focus on my routine. But I can't. He's staring at the way my body moves to the beat, the rhythm of how I sway into each word she sings.

I abruptly stop and put my hands on my hips, facing him with a scowl. "You're distracting me."

Both his brows raise as he points at his chest. "Me? You're the fucking distraction here."

"I told you it was a slow song. If you don't like it, then leave or pay attention to your work."

I ignore whatever he mutters under his breath, stopping the song and putting it back to the beginning before I get back into my starting position on the floor. I'm far too hot, and I'm desperate to remove my tights.

The music takes hold of me, and this time he keeps himself busy while I do the entire routine, then a second time. On the third, I hear him huff and fold away his ladder. I don't stop as he tidies up the corner, and I don't look at him while I'm air walking on the pole as he walks right past to pack up his things in front of the mirror.

Rihanna stops, The Hills starts automatically, and I'm a panting mess on the floor, star-fishing while I attempt to cool down. Kade, in his navy-blue top and shorts, stops at my feet. His dark hair is messy, hanging over his forehead; a tattoo curls up from his collarbone, and his arms look stronger than before.

Kade's blue eyes are burning into me.

"What?" I snap, still panting as The Hills get into the chorus.

"Base is going to message you."

I sit up, perching on my elbows and crossing my legs at the knee. "And?"

Kade's gaze drags up and down my body before his Adam's apple works in his throat.

Hm, I've licked that throat.

"He wants to fuck you. Don't bother."

God, I should not be smirking right now. I also shouldn't feel a tightness in my chest. Not because Base wants me, but because it seems to annoy Kade. A guy who apparently hates my guts and thinks I'm dead to him.

I tilt my head. "I wasn't going to – not that it's any of your business."

He scoffs. "Not old enough for you?"

I sigh and get to my feet, still nowhere near his height even with my heeled boots on. "If you have something to say, then get it over with."

Kade steps forward, his expression serious. The defined lines of his face are highlighted by the red LEDs, his eyelashes long and dark, the vein in his neck more noticeable the closer he gets.

"You want me to get it over with?"

I nod.

"Fine."

He slowly eats up the distance between us, and my heart beats harder in my chest. My breathing becomes laboured, deeper, especially when he takes my hip and my throat, backing me up against the mirrored wall.

"I have plenty to say to you, but all I can think of is how sick you make me."

I give him a teasing smile that touches my eyes. "That's all?"

"I hate you."

"Yeah?" I manage to respond, even as he closes the infinitesimal distance between us. We're almost chest to chest. "Not as much as I hate you."

His thumb strokes the side of my neck, and he might as well have shoved his face between my legs and sucked on my clit with how wet it makes me.

His jaw ticks. "Stay away from Base." His grip tightens on my throat, and my eyes flutter with the sensation. "I don't need you poisoning his mind as well."

My knees shake, but as he goes to release me, I stop him, pressing his hand to my throat. It's not the same as when Chris does it, and it feels good – a replacement for usually being terrified.

"You like that?" He stresses his words by cutting off my oxygen momentarily.

All I manage is a nod, and his eyes flash with something dark and sinister.

As he applies pressure to my throat, his thumb to my pulse, I remember what he said and decide to fuck with him. "I must admit, I'm tempted." My voice is strained. "Base looks the wild type in bed."

Lie. He knows I'm lying too. One, Base wants my best friend, and two, he's Kade's best friend. And three, I have no interest in the Russian Scot.

The hand that was on my hip is travelling up my side, burning a trail in its wake. Every touch from him is scorching; every touch goes straight to the coiling sensation that begins at the base of my spine. Our chests rise and fall in rhythm as we wait for the other person to speak, to fill the silence. Our bodies are so aware of each other, remembering all the times we'd been joined as one.

Seventeen minutes until class starts.

I must be insane, because although I want to slap Kade and call him every name I can think of, I also want him to lift me into his arms and fuck me senseless. I want all his anger pushing inside me. His rage. His harsh words against my ear as he makes me scream his name.

"If you're going to do something, then hurry up."

"I don't want to go near you," he replies, lowering his forehead to mine, his dilating eyes showing his lie. "I can't stand you."

His fingers tighten around my throat, and my pussy clenches.

My hand drops between us, feeling the hard ridges of his cock through his shorts. He's so big and thick, just like I remember. My heated body also remembers, and it tenses along with Kade's, a hiss dropping from his mouth as I squeeze the length of him.

I tilt my head, whispering in his ear, my lips grazing the shell, "If I disgust you so much, then why are you hard?"

He uses his grip on my neck to push me harder against the glass. "It means nothing." Kade's face comes closer to mine, his breath hitting my lips as his thumb presses just underneath my breast. "It's a lie."

He doesn't stop me from rubbing my palm up and down the length of his cock through the material of his shorts. He twitches against my hand, and his breaths hit my cheek as they become heavier the harder he gets.

Kade's grip grows tighter on my throat; his other hand stops at the strap of my bodysuit, and he curls his fingers under it and drags the strap down my shoulder with haunting slowness. My breast bounces free as the material slips beneath it.

Reaching under his waistband, I take his hard cock in my hand. He's warm, smooth and the veins are as thick as ever. The same veins I've traced with my tongue once upon a time. "Does this make you sick, Kade? To have me touching you this way? Is this a lie too?"

He swallows, but the way he moves into my hand tells me he's lying when he replies with gritted teeth, "Yes."

I continue stroking him, swiping away the bead of wetness from the tip and lifting my thumb between us, so he can see me lick the precum.

His lips part gradually, his eyes heavy as he watches my tongue run up my thumb. I close my eyes to revel in the taste and lower my hand between us again, wrapping it around his thickness.

A moan slips from my lips as he pinches my nipple, my underwear drenched from the sting. Kade thrusts into my hand, breathing the same air as we both gasp.

My other hand fists the front of his top. "Will I stop?"

Right now, as he nudges my nose with his, pushing himself into my fist with a deep groan, I think he might kiss me. His lips are close to mine. But even though I'm touching him, I will never let him kiss me again. I slant my head to put distance between our mouths.

He grabs my jaw and shoves his thumb into my mouth, pressing on my tongue, before lowering his head and taking my nipple between his teeth. He sucks so hard, I think I might explode.

Kade sucks my breast into his mouth, his tongue circling my nipple as he fucks my hand. It's enough to make me see stars in the room full of red.

His thumb slides from my mouth. I breathe, "You—"

Before I can finish what I'm about to say, the main entrance of the studio opens, and the sound of my girls chatting echoes down the hallway.

Kade stiffens and swears to himself, yanking away from me. He steps back to put distance between us as he stuffs his hard cock back into his shorts and grabs his phone from the floor.

When he sees how tented he is, he tucks himself up into his waistband, shakes his head at me and huffs as he drags a tattooed hand through his messed-up hair and down his face.

He looks mad – fuming. His jaw clenches, dark brows lowering to a scowl. His eyes follow my fingers as I pull the strap of my bodysuit back onto my shoulder, concealing my breast.

Everything within me is on fire, tingles reaching my toes.

"Relax," I say through deep breaths, like it hadn't made me feel alive – as if I hadn't been asleep for two years and only just awoken from our temporary connection. "It means nothing, remember? It's a lie."

Kade shakes his head, glaring at me before walking out.

A text from Base pops up on my screen, asking if I could talk Luciella into a threesome, because it seems to be his last resort to getting what he wants. I kindly decline. Then I open Kade's contact and try not to look at all our previous messages.

Me: *You left your screwdriver here.*

I lift the tool and flip it in my hand as my students walk in. One giggles that Kade Mitchell looked at her, and her friend mentions how angry he was, which only made him appear hotter. Another girl fans her face like she's close to passing out.

My phone dings, informing me the message has bounced back, and I roll my eyes with a tut.

Still blocked, it seems.

7

KADE

My hands are fucking shaking.

As soon as I get into my car, I slam the door with more force than necessary and grip my steering wheel until my knuckles turn white. Then my fist slams into it. Once. Twice. Three times. None of my anger fades; none of the thoughts slow down, not the way they used to when I lashed out.

Not when it comes to her.

I can't see past my fingers clutching the leather of the wheel, can't fill my lungs, can't see past the blinding rage that surges through my veins from the sight of her. The sound of her voice, the feel of her soft skin. Every single thing about her pisses me off.

The erratic beats in my chest don't calm down, even though she's nowhere near me. She's in that stupid building, dancing around unaffected like the venomous snake that she is.

Fuck.

What is she playing at?

The fuck am I playing at?

I've dodged her for the past two years. I kept my distance when I visited at the weekends. Yet here I am, sitting with a solid, raging hard-on, imagining fucking my sister's best friend in every position possible.

All I wanted to do, when her hand was wrapped around me, was rip her clothes off and remind my dick what it feels like inside her. I wanted to have my fingers between her legs, to hear her moans in my ear as I sank into her. I wanted to bend her over and twist that idiotic ponytail around my fist while she screamed for me.

Jesus fucking Christ. If I wasn't in a car park, I'd finish myself off.

As soon as her students leave, I'm going back in. This is just an itch to scratch. That's all. I'll fuck her against the wall and tell her to stay out of my way until I have to leave town again.

The fuck? No.

Then I'd just be playing into her little game of emotional fucking turmoil, and I refuse to go down that road again. Not this time. But I'd be lying if I said that seeing her tonight hadn't woken a side of me that needed to touch every inch of her body.

Stupid urges.

Repress that shit.

That's all they are. Urges. Because am I fuck ever going back to that.

Not that I could, even if I wanted to.

Stacey Rhodes is the devil in disguise. She's hot as hell on the outside, has a personality that makes you fall for her, but is utterly ugly and fake on the inside. My traitorous cock clearly doesn't know the difference between a snake and an angel and needs to stand the fuck down.

The hard-on is painful, even as I adjust myself and lean back.

I shouldn't have watched her dance. I shouldn't have volunteered to fix the stupid ceiling. I should've known after seeing her at the party that I should be keeping my distance. Now my dick is twitching in my shorts and begging me not to drive away.

Did she reply to Base? He's been saying for weeks that he wants her after seeing a video of her dancing with my sister. He'd messaged our group chat, asking if we thought he should send her a text. I ignored him obviously, but Dez told him to enjoy the full-on rejection she'd toss at him.

Which seemed to have egged him on more.

I nearly cracked his head open when they planned to partner up at the weekend. The girl on my lap was about to be thrown off me and a blade thrust through his skull.

She'd warp his mind like she did to me, and no one wants a broken Base.

But if he were to go there, I'd kill him. I'd regret it as soon as I did, but I would slaughter him in a heartbeat.

Impulsive. I'm far too impulsive.

Thank fuck I made my friends leave the party. I watched her through CCTV going to sleep in the guest room and felt like I could relax.

But then Tylar left her on her own.

My obsessive tendencies – a trait pointed out by my old therapist – meant I kept checking on her. I couldn't sit at peace without the need to make sure Base, or some other drunken wanker, hadn't snuck into the bed against her will. I was fully prepared to sleep against the door with my gun, just to make sure that didn't happen.

I'd quietly opened the door and ushered my dogs in with her, because I knew no one would try to slide into the room if they were there.

Plus, irritatingly, Milo and Hopper missed her.

I watched her sleep through the cameras and drank until I could barely see while she cuddled into our— my dogs.

But then *she* called, and I had to leave.

I got dressed, made sure my gun was fully loaded, and filled my holsters with blades and other weapons before leaving.

My phone dings – a reminder to download my boarding pass.

When Luciella said that Dad had booked two extra tickets so I could also visit, I'd thought about asking Dez to come with me instead. Not out of favouritism, but I didn't want to spend the entire time listening to Base talking about how he should approach my bitch of an ex. He doesn't know about our past – she begged me to keep it between us until she was ready to tell Luciella, so my best friend now wanting to screw her is just fucking great.

Maybe I'll burn his passport before he can board?

No. Impulsive, controlling prick. They can do what they want. He'll be the one to look like an idiot when she fucks him over. Because that's what she does. She draws you in, feeds you lies and feelings and fake bullshit, only to drop it all on your head.

To say that I'm a bitter cunt about it is an understatement.

I hate her with a fucking unrelenting passion.

I grab my packet of smokes and light one up, rereading the message I received in the studio. Safe to say my cock has gone soft.

***Bernadette**: You were warned not to make a mess. You had a contract to eliminate the owner, so why were eight bodies found at the casino?*

***Me**: They shot at me first. What the fuck am I supposed to do?*

***Bernadette**: Watch your tone. Do something for me.*

An annoyed huff lets out, and I inhale as much smoke as possible to burn my lungs.

***Me**: What?*

***Bernadette**: Come see me tonight.*

I sigh, quickly firing back a response and hoping she leaves me alone.

***Me**: Can't. Busy.*

***Bernadette**: I wasn't asking, Kade.*

"Fuck's sake," I mutter, flicking my cigarette out the window.

> ***Me:** I fly to America in the morning. Have your husband fuck you instead.*

As usual, her response is immediate.

> ***Bernadette:** You have an hour to get here, or there will be no visitation rights for your father for the next year.*

I roll my eyes at her go-to threat, toss my phone on the passenger seat and head to her address while I play music. It's loud enough to drown everything out.

Bernadette is nearly forty, married with a kid nearly the same age as me. She can literally do whatever and whoever she wants, and her repulsive husband allows it. She approached me when I was nineteen, told me a bunch of lies about being able to help with my dad's case and I've been trapped with her ever since.

I wanted to get the fuck away from her the first night I woke up after being drugged, but after everything she's made me do – all the people I've killed for money – it's not something I can walk away from, especially with clean hands.

When I buzz her gate, I try to form excuses that might keep her away from me, but I know there's not a chance of that happening.

I open my glovebox for my safety net, tucking a gun she doesn't know about into the back of my shorts, then pulling on my hat and flipping it backwards.

I quickly shoot a text to my assistant Barry, telling him that plans are still going ahead in America, to set up a meeting point and that I'll be out of reach for the rest of the night.

I hide the messenger app I created for me and my team in a secured file, so Bernie won't find it if she decides to go through my phone.

It started when I tried to kill Barry in England, only to find out he was innocent. He was my age and had a ten-grand bounty on his head. I helped him fake his death, and he became loyal, offered to work with me to help others like him. Over time, we created our own group to try rescue people trapped in the firm grip of the underworld.

All of them are free to leave my company, but none of them will. Not only do I pay them well, but they also get to travel, experience the adrenaline rush of fighting and saving, and they're part of the family I somehow created. A group of ghosts – dead to the underworld but very much alive.

And I'm their leader.

A huff, a shake of my head and I head in.

Standing in the foyer, I watch Bernadette strut towards me with a glass of wine, her dyed-red hair bouncing, fake tits nearly falling out of her tight black dress. Her heels click on the white marble, and the sound vibrates through my body, nearly enough to make me visibly shiver. It aggravates so much that I can't look her in the eye.

The woman is a blackmailing monster. Probably the worst kind I've had the displeasure of meeting. Bernadette's nails drag along my chest as she passes by me, and I follow her into the office.

She pulls out a folder and slams it down on her desk between us. "Bryan Tiernan," she says, flipping it open to an image of his broken face, "filed two charges against you this morning. Assault and arson. I had to pay him off and tell him not to speak a word of it again. Care to explain why you're attacking random people in their homes then setting it alight?"

I stay silent. Tap my fingers on the armrests. I should've killed him like I killed the last guy she slept with.

No one fucks Stacey and gets away with it. I can't have her, but nobody else will.

"I can't keep covering for you when you go off course. I tell you who your targets are. I don't need to make sure things like this aren't happening." She points at the paperwork, teeth bared. "You weren't trained like this. You had no reason to break into his house and hold him at gunpoint, and you certainly had no reason to beat him until he was nearly unrecognisable. This could have easily been an attempted murder case. What if one of my colleagues got the report instead of me?"

I shrug.

That pisses her off enough to grit out, "Why. Did. You. Do. It?"

I lean back in the chair, resting my ankle on my knee. "I had my reasons."

She raises a perfectly plucked brow. "Care to explain them?"

"Nope." I'm unhinged – that's the only explanation. "It's none of your business."

She snarls, leaning forward. "Careful, Kade. I can easily hand over your file and have you locked up for the rest of your life. They'll stick you in a facility like your father."

When I stare at her, attempting to tamp down my anger, she smirks and closes the file. Not the first time she's said something along those lines, and she has enough power to do just that. She does run an entire empire in the underworld and holds a senior rank in Police Scotland.

I have nowhere to run.

"However, you are going away for a while, and as much as you'll be doing work for me in America, I'll miss you dearly." She walks around the desk; pulls herself onto it in front of me. "Archie will be home in an hour. Will we wait for him to join us, or will I show you our new pet now?"

My eye twitches. "New pet?" I don't like the sound of that. "Meaning?"

Bernadette grins, kicking off her heels and settling her feet right between my legs. Her dress rides up her thighs, showing me that she's bare beneath. No underwear. No boundaries. No fucking shame.

I fight a grimace and look away.

"You'll like her." She hops off the desk. "Follow me."

On the third floor, she chuckles and turns to me. "Remember when we had Rachel join us? Well, she's even prettier. And more adventurous."

I might just shoot myself in the head right now. The gun is

burning into my back, begging to be used.

But if I kill her or myself, my entire family will be obliterated – Bernadette's annoying tripwire if I ever turn on them.

If I refuse to do certain work, Luciella gets threatened. If I refuse to fuck someone, then Dad doesn't see my mother for weeks.

No one in my family knows the reasons behind their bad luck. I'm apparently a university student, living his life in Stirling.

But that's far from the truth.

One day, I'll get away from her; I'll escape this life.

When she opens the door to reveal a blonde fingering herself on a four-poster bed, moaning and writhing on the velvet sheets, Bernadette tells me to unzip her dress, and I pray this will be a quick night.

But then she pushes the needle into my neck and any chance of that goes out the fucking window.

8

KADE

FLASHBACK 1
THREE YEARS AGO

Three tents are pitched. One for me and my friends. One for Luciella and hers. And far away from the group of eighteen-year-olds – bar Base and Dez being twenty – are Mum and Ewan.

She *is here.*

Not that I'd ever have the balls to talk to her nicely.

Ever since we were fifteen, I've gone out of my way to piss her off.

Points for maturity.

Me and Base sit on the log in front of the fire, him passing me the joint when Mum and Luciella aren't looking, while the girls attempt to make their own fire.

I train my eyes on a certain dark-haired specimen while my friend talks about his weekend in Moscow. Stacey laughs at something Tylar said.

She's not even funny.

"Fuck being in a relationship," Base says as he looks at people kissing. "It's hard to find loyalty."

I snort, looking away when her eyes find mine. "You have the biggest choice out of us all since you fuck both men and women."

He passes me the joint, blowing out smoke. "There's a difference. I'm sexually attracted to both, but emotionally and romantically, I could only ever date a woman. Does that make sense?"

"It does." Base took ages to come out and say he was bisexual, worried we'd view him differently, but we all got drunk and celebrated instead.

"It doesn't mean I have a bigger choice. Like, no offence, mate, but I wouldn't go near you. You're too tall and I reckon you'd be dominant. I'd fuck Dez though, but don't tell him I said that."

I chuckle. "I won't."

For the next five minutes, Base texts on his phone while I people-watch. The guys have coolers filled with beer outside the twelve-man tent, and some of them are chatting with the girls.

"What about you?" Base eventually asks.

I frown, opening another beer. "Me?"

He nods. "I've never seen you with anyone. Me and Dez spoke about it a few times. We reckon you're a virgin." He winces. "That sounded bad. I don't mean it that way. You just don't spare anyone a glance."

I go silent, wondering if I should stand up and walk away before I punch him or admit that I've never been attracted to anyone, or had the urge to kiss or fuck or anything like they do. I've never had a one-night stand like they all have.

I used to be embarrassed about it, but I guess I don't really give a fuck anymore.

It's not like I'm completely devoid of sexual arousal – my hand does a good-enough job without emotions or the feeling of someone else doing it.

No – one person is on my mind. She's my sister's best friend and she hates me.

My eyes search the campsite until they land on her, sipping her drink and staring at the barely lit fire. I've figured out a lot about her by watching what she does. She's not very sociable, doesn't talk that much. She's a fantastic dancer. I may have walked in on her stretching at the studio once, and the image of her bending over has imprinted on my mind.

She has a few tattoos. Nothing drastic. She suits them.

She smiles at something Dez says, and my hand grips my beer. As much as she looks innocent and sweet, she's annoying; steals cigarettes out my mouth and walks away, rolls her eyes when I correct her, even if I'm right. She's called me every name under the sun, and it makes my day ten times better.

I shouldn't look at my sister's best friend the way I do, but when Stacey Rhodes walks into the room, you can't not *look.*

She glances at me again, but this time, I stare back, feeling the cool air against my neck.

Base nudges my shoulder, and I break her gaze. "So, are you?"

I look at him as he sparks another cigarette. "Am I what?"

"A virgin?" he asks. "You can tell me. I'll help you get laid."

I grind my teeth. "Fuck off."

Base laughs through the smoke. "Relax. I'm not trying to make fun of you."

I hum and stand up. "Don't ask me that again."

He raises his hands. "Fine. Anyway, we should tell the girls to sit with us," Base says as he follows me to the tent to grab another beer. "Their fire is pathetic and I'm liking your sister's ass. That's allowed, right? Or do you have rules?"

I scoff. "You can do what you want with Luciella, but don't give me any details. I mean it. And hurt her, I'll strangle you."

He laughs then tips his beer towards the girls. "And Stacey. She seems to get hotter every time we see her. How is that even legal?"

Tossing my friend into a fire could be passed off as an accident, right?

I huff when the girls join us, sitting in a circle around our fire. Music plays, people talking among themselves, and I focus on the flames.

Through the fire, I see her again. This time, she's already looking at me. There's a jolt in my stomach, then a flutter.

I don't know how to stop feeling this way.

When they all decide to play a game of dares, I huff and contemplate going to the tent to sleep. I lean my elbows on my knees. "I'm not playing dares when my fucking sister is here."

Dez speaks next. "Right. Why don't we have a rule that you need to go into one of the tents to complete the dare in two minutes? That way it's more private."

"Sorry to break it to you, but I last a lot longer than two minutes," Base says, smirking as he drinks his beer. "But I can make an exception if it's a certain blonde."

"Shut up, Sebastian," Luciella retorts.

They argue back and forth until she gives up, and Tylar makes the first dare for someone to down their beer. The next is for someone to take their top off, and the third is for Dez to run around the campsite naked.

"I dare Luciella to kiss me," Base says, and I drop my head at his desperation. "Let's go, princess. I hope you're ready for two minutes in heaven."

"What happens if I say no?" she asks, crossing her arms. "I can't kiss him!" My sister looks at me. "Tell them I can't!"

I shrug. "Do what you want."

She levels me with a deadly look of betrayal before her nostrils flare. She gets to her feet and follows Base into the tent. He zips it up, and someone starts the timer.

To pass time, I sit on my phone, scrolling through social media. I click on a certain profile. I want to follow her, but she'd probably block me.

I click on her tagged photos, angling my screen so no one can see. Hanging upside down on an aerial hoop, Stacey wears a red bodysuit, showing off her incredible flexibility.

I screenshot it.

The tent unzips, and I click off my screen. Base gives us the thumbs up, and Luciella looks like she wants to kill someone.

Dez and Tylar are dared next, then three others. The dares get a little more intimate, and the timer gets longer to a point that I kind of panic.

Stacey hasn't been dared to do anything with anyone, and neither have I.

"Kade," Tylar says, grinning.

My soul leaves my body with the look she gives me.

"I dare you to make out with Stacey."

I nearly drop my phone.

"What?" Luciella sounds disgusted. "Are you joking right now?"

"You just kissed Base," Tylar says with a wave of her hand. She tilts her head at Stacey. "Go on then."

"I'm going to bed," my sister says with a grimace.

"You want me to keep you warm?" Base asks.

She fakes a smile. "I'd rather burn in hell, but thanks."

Everyone laughs, but I stay silent, watching the flames and wondering if it's possible to disappear. Breathing heavily through my nose, I glance at Stacey getting to her feet.

Oh shit. This is happening.

Nope. I can't fucking kiss her.

I know I'm turning the brightest shade of red, hands shaking.

I watch the girl I've obsessed over since I was fifteen strut towards the tent with no care in the world, her hips swaying, hair falling down her back – frozen until Base taps me.

It's only a kiss. I'm fucking old enough to handle a kiss.

I'll know what to do. I'm not going to make a cunt of myself by messing up. She's probably kissed loads of people, and this is nothing.

I think I'm going to pass out.

I follow, thankful for the music playing – it drowns out the thoughts going wild in my head. Stacey goes in first, and I zip the tent up again once I'm inside.

Without hesitation, Stacey sits, facing me. "We can pretend if you want. I know you'd rather be doing this with anyone else. I won't be offended. Really."

Well I'm fucking offended.

The view I have is delightful as her dress rides up her thighs, but before I can pitch in my shorts, I drop down to my haunches, mirroring her. "If you're scared, you can admit it." I don't know how I manage to say that without throwing up. "Do you want to pretend?"

She clears her throat, fidgeting her fingers. "We have two minutes. I think thirty seconds have already gone by."

I nod. "Okay."

"Okay," she counters. "Is it a full kiss?"

"Tylar said 'make out with Stacey'."

I want to move the strand of hair from her face, but I fist my hands instead.

"Don't laugh," she says, chewing on her lip, "but I haven't done this

before."

I inwardly sigh in relief, inching my body forward until our knees touch. "Neither have I." Stacey's gaze widens, but I continue before she can talk. "Just close your eyes."

"Don't lie to make me feel better. We all know about your reputation."

I narrow my eyes. "Meaning?"

She raises a shoulder. "You know what I mean." Then she shakes her head. "It doesn't matter."

"Any reputation I have like that is a lie," I say, turning the setting of the torch to a soft glow. "A lot of people talk shit about me to get themselves seen or to get a story. I'm in the same boat as you here. Okay?"

She swallows, and I watch her throat move. "Okay," she quietly responds.

"Close your eyes and stop being nervous," I say as my entire body fights a tremble.

Her eyelids close, dark lashes, thick and long, settling under her eyes on the soft skin. "Don't laugh if I do it wrong."

For a second, I look at her, as if I haven't a million times already, allowing myself to study each freckle close up, her perfect cheekbones, the way her dark hair curls around her face and cascades around her. She licks her lips, and my eyes are drawn to the act. They're naturally plump, a deep shade of pink, and she always bites the bottom one.

My breaths are heavy through my nostrils as I lean forward, closing my own eyes. Heart racing to a dangerous rate, my nose glides against the side of hers until our lips are aligned, and I hesitate.

I'm going to fuck this up. Heat is radiating around us, and I can't fucking breathe. There's a pain building in my chest.

Panic slams into me, and I ease back an inch, about to tell her we'll just pretend to everyone. But Stacey pushes forward and presses her lips to mine, and the world stands still, time halting. "Broken" by Lovelytheband fades, and so do the giggles and chatter of the group nearby, until it's just me and Stacey.

Her palms slide up my chest to rest on my shoulders, and I bristle from the touch, unsure how I feel about it. She notices the way I freeze mid-kiss and removes her hands. "Sorry if I..."

I grab her before she can shy away, pull her back to me and reciprocate the kiss. It's firm yet gentle, and as I go in for a second, more relaxed kiss, her tight grip returns on my shoulders.

I've wanted to do this since I was fifteen but never had the balls to approach her. As hot as she is, she's terrifying when it comes to cursing me out. In all honesty, I think she'd run in the opposite direction if this wasn't a dare.

The thought annoys me.

We tilt our heads in sync, and the kiss deepens to a point that I suddenly need to part my lips and taste her tongue, to touch her with my hands, to discover how delicate her face feels under my palms, but I don't want to scare her off. Instead, I kiss her bottom lip, then the top, sucking lightly each time. She bunches the material of my top into her fists.

I don't like touch. It makes me feel uneasy, but my hand has a mind of its own as I feel the sharpness of her jawline, gliding my fingers up until they're brushing into her thick hair.

Stacey shivers in my hold, and I want her to do it again, to show that she can react to me. It's addictive.

She drags my bottom lip between her teeth, sending blood to my cock.

My thumb strokes the soft skin under her eye, and just as both of our lips part, and I feel the heat from our mouths and tongues, Base – the dick – calls out, "Time's up!"

Neither of us stop. Stacey moves her hands to both sides of my face and kisses me harder, coming closer until my fingers curl at her nape. A tingling sensation shoots to my chest and triggers something animalistic in me. She whimpers as I possessively snake my arm around the small of her back and pull her to me.

"Keep going," she orders, panting against my mouth, and I nod, breathing heavily.

She's so warm and comfortable. No bad thoughts are running rampant in my mind, telling me to get away from her.

Everything is calm. Everything is quiet. Everything is okay.

The tip of my tongue darts against hers, and I groan accidentally, yanking her even closer as her legs part around my knees so she's nearly in my lap. She tastes just as I expected. Sweet and fruity, with a hint of mint to cover the smoke she has now and again. Stacey Rhodes tastes fucking divine. Addictive.

I eliminate any space between us until she's sitting on me, causing heat to build at the base of my spine. Harder than a rock, I try to keep her at a safe distance, so I don't freak her out.

Her fingers bury into my hair, tugging it as her tongue moves against mine. She's devouring me, and I'm letting her. Hungrily, we swallow each sigh we drop, and I'm getting fucking harder. Especially when she brackets her hips at my waist.

I can feel her smile against my mouth.

And then... butterflies. I have fucking butterflies while kissing someone. What the fuck is wrong with me?

"Hey," Base says, hitting the fabric of the tent. "Will we keep playing without you?"

Stacey pulls away first, falling from my lap, and I'm certain I hear her squeak. "Oh shit," she mutters. "We're coming!"

"Too much info, Rhodes."

From what I can see, her pupils are dilated, her cheeks flushed, and her chest is rising and falling uncontrollably.

I want to kiss her again, but as she gets to her feet and hurries out without giving me any words, the bubble bursts, and the moment is gone.

9

KADE

My phone rings, pulling me out of the dream I wish I could erase from my memory. As much as reliving that night makes me want to smash everything in the room, it keeps me grounded when I'm in positions like I am now.

My mind always goes back to her when I lose control, blacking out, and when my body betrays me. Memories play out like fucking nightmares, mocking me for what we had and what she destroyed.

My phone rings again, my sister's name flashing up on the screen.

Shit.

I untangle myself from two sets of arms and legs, naked and slick with sweat and God knows what else. Bernadette groans, but instead of waking and yelling at me to go back to sleep, she reaches for… whatever her name is and cuddles into her tits like they're cushions.

Messages fill my screen, from Luciella and my mum. I have fifteen missed calls.

> ***Luciella****: Where the fuck are you? We leave for the airport in an hour!*

> ***Luciella****: Base is here, and he said he hasn't heard from you. If you don't get home soon, I will leave without you!*

> ***Luciella****: Answer the phone, you dickhead!*

> ***Mum****: Your dad is happy you're joining us; he hasn't stopped smiling. This means a lot to him, sweetheart. I'm glad you're putting aside everything that's happened and coming to visit. I'll see you soon.*

Not going to lie, the last one hurt. Our last encounter ended with me flipping a table and storming out of the meeting area after him bringing up Stacey and our split.

Another text appears as I type a reply to Luciella, telling her to calm her shit. I read it twice and my right eye twitches.

> ***Base****: Get out of whoever's bed you're in and move your fucking ass before I track you down. I need to go pick up Stacey (high-five me if I get a kiss) but am I fuck going to America without you.*

I scowl at the message. I read it again and again and again. Why the hell is he picking her up? His bracketed text fucks me off more than I'd like to admit. Stacey won't kiss him for picking her up. Perhaps he noticed how I go silent and stare at her whenever she's around, and he's trying to piss me off?

I dodge a hand trying to wrap around my waist and sit on the edge of the bed. I read the text again and my thumbs start to type before my brain can catch up to what I'm saying.

> ***Me:** I'm heading home now. I'll get Stacey on the way.*

I fume at myself but don't take the words back. She lives on the opposite side of town from Bernadette. But as I said, I'm an impulsive, controlling prick and I refuse to let him go anywhere near her if I can help it.

It's a lie, I'd said while her hand was wrapped around my cock, and that alone was the biggest fucking lie.

I wish I could erase her from my life.

Even when I'm working in different countries, I'm checking her social media like a stalker, logging into the CCTV to watch her walk into the studio or around the manor, or asking Luciella about their weekend plans just to know what they're getting up to. I even hacked my sister's phone to read their messages once, and it was the biggest regret of my life.

Two years of obsessing over a girl who drove me to insanity.

I type back another response to Luciella, telling her that I'm en route before I tug my clothes back on and tuck my gun – which I slid under the bed without Bernadette seeing – into the back of my shorts.

Where the fuck is my hat?

Once I take a piss, noticing the scratches on my cheek and the multiple bite marks on my neck and chest, I soak my face in cold water and debate shooting Bernadette while she's asleep.

Maybe I'll suffocate her with a pillow and make it look like the other girl did it.

Too risky. As much as I'd love to end her, I can't. I have too much emotional baggage to risk it. Maybe I should take a leaf out of my dad's book and not give a fuck about anyone. Everyone seems to think I'm just like him – might as well prove them right by killing the head of the Scottish underworld.

Archie greets me halfway down the steps. "Morning," he says, holding a coffee in one hand, a bowl filled with boiled eggs in the other. "She didn't keep you up all night, did she?"

I scoff out a laugh and ignore him.

This man is deranged. A political leader who works with numerous charities for animals, schools and victims of all kinds of abuse, yet the sick fuck was perfectly fine with having a forced threesome with teenage me then abusing me after I passed out. He was fine with feeding me drugs and booze while I begged to leave the house.

He was fine with watching me kill. Watching me torture people who'd wronged them.

He was fine with weaponising me, a rage-filled kid desperate to keep his family safe, blackmailing me so I can't ever stop. I did move to Stirling and buy an apartment with the money I earned from the contracts, in the hope they'd lay off me, but they still have their claws in me. Hotels rooms and yachts. Cars and clubs. Anywhere they can have me, they do.

I want to kill him the most. His time will come.

Here he stands with a smile, in a silk robe, asking me if his wife kept me up all night. I want to kick him back down the stairs and make him choke on his fucking boiled eggs.

My shoulder hits his arm as I storm past him, down the steps two at a time until I reach my car, where it takes me ten minutes to control my breathing.

I pull my phone out, open my secret folder and send Barry a message that I'm contactable for the next few days. He lets me know that two cars have been sitting outside, waiting for me.

Always waiting.

I might not fear much, but that doesn't mean I don't need my own security team. They're always there. Out of sight but ready for anything thrown my way.

Bernadette doesn't know about them obviously, because they're there to protect me from her twisted games. She likes to play them when I piss her off – randomly sending someone to try to beat the shit out of me or shoot me somewhere non-fatal.

Everyone she's sent so far has turned up dead, without the need to use my guards. If she didn't want her men killed, then she shouldn't have sent me away to different countries for intense training in weapons and martial arts.

My team doesn't know how extreme it gets with Bernadette and her husband, and if I can help it, I'll keep it that way. They're my soldiers – one word that I'm abused, and they'll open fire and lose their lives.

I have hundreds beneath me, but Bernadette has tens of thousands. I know the probability of surviving that kind of war.

I turn on my engine, still controlling my breathing and the need to go in there and put a bullet between everyone's eyes. I'm pissed off more than usual, probably because of Base's message.

After a night of hell and threats and unwanted sex, all I'm thinking about is what Stacey replied to Base. If he's said he's picking her up then, surely, she must've accepted his offer?

Fuck, I hope not. I'm in no mood for drama. Thankfully, Jason isn't going to America, eliminating that issue. I'd rather drown myself than spend any time with him.

The sun is starting to rise as Stacey's estate comes into view, and when I stop outside her house, I hide the gun back in my glovebox.

I look up at her window; the curtains are closed but for the small gap she usually leaves in the middle, so the sun can wake her. Despite what happened, I'm drawn to her so much that I've climbed up to her window four times over the last two years and watched her sleep. Even contemplated sneaking in once.

I could do it now, right?

Fuck, no. I need to repress all these impulsive thoughts.

I turn down my music, pull out my phone and stare at her contact details.

Freckles.

She's been blocked for nearly two years. I doubt she even attempted to message me within that time period. She probably deleted my number and moved on to the next sad bastard to poison.

I stare at the last messages between us.

***Freckles**: She's asleep now. Meet you at the pool house?*

***Me**: I'll race you.*

Freckles: I always win, remember?

Only hours later, the messages went from cute and playful to desperate and pleading.

Freckles: Please answer the phone, Kade. Let me explain.

Freckles: I want to fix this. Please.

Loads of missed calls, and, a week later, she says:

Freckles: Luciella said you moved out. Where did you go? Please talk to me. I love you.

That last part made me go feral. I'd taken my first line of coke that night and gone on a four-day bender with Base in America.

I love you. Nope, she didn't love me. She had no idea what love was. I blocked her right after I typed several responses without sending any.

It was only days later that Bernadette approached me outside of the dance studio as I contemplated going in, and I wish so fucking much I'd walked away from her false offer.

Gritting my teeth, raging at myself for reading the messages again – something I've done a billion times while off my head on drugs or drowning myself in booze – I do the unthinkable.

I unblock her number.

My blood is roaring in my ears, fingers trembling as I change her contact name and type a message to her.

Me: I'm outside.

There. Simple and straight to the point. No need to overcomplicate it. After two years of keeping my distance, I broke my rules by following her to the front gate, by watching her dance, by approaching her and letting her touch me, by letting myself remember every sound she'd ever made for me.

When her hand wrapped around my cock – the lie that wasn't a lie – I forgot what she'd done. But I remember now. And I refuse to let her fuck with my head again.

My heart races as soon as my phone vibrates in my hand, nerves shattering into fragments at her three-word response. I'm a pathetic piece of shit.

***Stacey**: Well hello, stranger.*

I stop my lips from tugging up into a smirk, my chest tightening as I swallow. "Waste Love" begins playing, and I turn it up slightly, but not loud enough to wake her family. I remember her saying her stepmother hated visitors, hated anyone in the house, which is why I was always climbing through her window.

***Me**: Move or I'll drive away.*

She types, deletes, types, deletes. I nearly send another message when she responds.

***Stacey**: I'm rolling my eyes at you. Be 5 mins.*

Her bedroom light turns on, the curtains opening to reveal her glancing down at me in only her bra. My skin prickles with goosebumps at the fresh memory of my mouth on her tit, heat rushing up my spine and making my dick twitch.

After a longer second of our eyes clashing without looking away, she gives me the middle finger and vanishes from my view.

Little shit.

I don't block her again, but I do swipe up on the chat box and instantly despise myself as I read all our older messages. Mostly flirty and teasing, telling the other that they're fuckably hot while in the same room as my family. Pictures from trips that we'd secretly taken. I want to scrap them all, but when my finger hovers over the delete-all button, I decide not to.

After I was dared to kiss her years ago, I lasted all but a few days before cornering her in my kitchen and daring her to kiss me again while no one was around. I pulled her onto the countertop and let my hands roam her body, close to having a panic attack from thinking I would do something wrong.

That version of myself doesn't exist now. I don't get anxiety around her because she's pretty and I have no idea what to do with her. No, I reckon if I fucked her now, I wouldn't be able to stop myself from strangling her to death.

The anchor who broke me.

Fucking ridiculous.

She appears nearly fifteen minutes later, rushing out with a suitcase rolling behind her and a bag over her shoulder. I should get out and help her, but I pop the boot and relax into my seat instead.

I shouldn't be nervous. I shouldn't be wondering what to say to her. I definitely shouldn't be thinking about her words to me last night.

Relax. It means nothing.

I guess it never had. Not to her.

I gulp down air as she drops into the passenger seat in a band top and jeans. Her perfume and shampoo take over all my senses, and I have to roll down my window more and light up a cigarette to block them out.

Stacey leans forward, looking up at her window. When I follow her eyes, I see a shadow standing there, but whoever it is quickly shuts her curtains.

Must be her stepbrother Kyle. I never met him because he was always away studying, but she spoke highly about him often.

She doesn't say anything as she clips in her belt, or when she pulls out her phone and starts scrolling social media, ignoring whatever messages keep popping up on her screen.

Not a *hello*. Not a *hey, what happened last night was a mistake,* not a fucking word about it. Fine. I won't bring it up either.

It shouldn't annoy me this much.

As I drive out of her estate, I turn up the music. But when I go to press the accelerator, I chance a look at her as if I'm looking for traffic, and my eyes drop to her neck.

My brows furrow, and I almost stop the car to inspect the bruises she's tried to hide with make-up.

My first instinct is to hunt down whoever hurt her and kill them, but then I remember the way I grabbed her at the studio, and I grip the steering wheel tighter.

Surely I didn't cause those bruises? I didn't... Fuck. No, I wouldn't hurt her. She wanted me to hold her firmly.

I should pull over and apologise right now. I should tell her that I never meant to mark her. I'm not a psychopath that hurts the people I care about. Yeah, I've shot people in the head or disfigured them, and I've tortured people for information to help Bernadette, but never have I lifted a hand to Stacey.

Fuck. Maybe I did do that. Maybe the hold I had on her throat last night was tighter than I thought. Maybe everyone's right, and I am like my dad and out of touch with reality.

A lump sticks in my throat, and I run through every possible way to say sorry.

But then my sister calls her, and she turns off my music to speak. She tells her we're on our way, groans and asks her to stop shouting, then huffs and hangs up.

"They're leaving now. They don't want to be late. They'll get us at the airport."

She trains her gaze on the scratch on my cheek; the obvious bite marks on the side of my neck. I probably smell like sex too. If any of it bothers her, she doesn't show it as she goes back to typing on her phone.

Why would she care? She's heartless.

She tucks a strand of hair behind her ear then leans down to grab something from her handbag at her feet. My eyes fall on our initials woven together on the exposed part of her back. I shake my head and look away.

I light another cigarette and turn up the rock music.

When we get to the manor, she walks my dogs while I shower and dress. She chats with the staff; I glare at them. We don't talk on the way to the airport, or while we're stuck in a traffic jam that doesn't seem to be moving.

I keep looking at her throat, noticing that she's touched up her make-up and the bruises are barely visible now. Maybe it wasn't from the studio, and like me, she was fucking someone else last night.

The thought irks me enough to clench my jaw. I'm a walking, talking contradiction.

You don't hate her, son. You're just mad at her, my dad had said when I last visited.

But he's a liar. I do hate her. I'm not trembling with anxiety because I'm mad at her – I'm fucking losing it because all I can think about is her with *him*.

"Shit," she blurts out. "The motorway got closed off from a bad crash. That's why we're stuck here."

I frown. "Does it say how long until it's cleared?"

"Could be hours," she replies, slouching. "We'll definitely miss our flight. I'll tell Lu."

And to make things even better, we do miss our flight, and the next one from Glasgow isn't for two days. Instead, we have to drive to Edinburgh, book the only hotel near the airport with any availability and wait until tomorrow to fly out.

Base wishes me good luck, and I swipe away from Bernadette's message regarding a contract. She tracks my every move – the ones I allow her to track anyway – so she knows where I'm heading.

I spy one of my cars nearby – Barry is sitting in the passenger seat with a laptop. I nod at him on the way in, and four guards dressed casually walk behind us, staying far enough back that Stacey doesn't catch on.

When we reach the hotel reception, I'm certain someone is playing a joke on me. I'm fully expecting someone to jump out of a plant pot with a camera.

Stacey turning a shade of white just adds to my annoyance.

There's only one fucking room available.

10

STACEY

Kyle: *Was that Kade Mitchell?*

Kyle: *Wait... Am I losing my mind right now? Are you hanging out with* the *Tobias Mitchell's kids? Is Lucy Luciella? The twin?*

Kyle: *I know I'm being the overbearing big brother here, but do you know who he is? Have the twins given you fake names? Shit. Do you remember our emergency code if you need me to come and get you?*

I lie in the small double bed, reading each text. Attached in his next message, he sends news articles dated from when Tobias Mitchell was arrested. *Psychotic killer ordered to live out his life sentence in an institution.* One of them has a picture of Kade and Lu as kids, smiling with their dad in an artificial park within his institution in America.

Legendary Tobias Mitchell finally granted visitation with his children.

There are related articles at the bottom of the page, and I click on the one about Aria. *Doctor Miller finally finds true love with a former flame. But what does Tobias think?* Somehow, they got a hold of their wedding photo, where the twins are around seven years old. Lu has a huge grin, Kade is scowling and their big brother Jason, who is eleven years older, has his hands on their shoulders.

I remember I used to think he was a son of Tobias too, but he looks like Ewan. Aria isn't his mum, but she treats him the same as she does Kade and Lu, especially since his biological mother overdosed a few years ago.

He's been a ghost to the family for a while now.

The last article I read is from two months ago – Kade with a cigarette hanging from his mouth, leaving a nightclub in London with a girl on his arm. They call the brunette brave then go into detail about the pair sharing a hotel room, which she left a few hours later with *messy hair.*

I close the browser.

Kyle sends another message, asking if this is a code red.

I've only been able to read his texts. When we were in the car, my phone wouldn't stop buzzing, and the last thing I wanted to do was discuss Kade with my stepbrother while sitting in the passenger seat.

It was awkward when he first picked me up because I had no idea what to say, especially after what happened in the studio, but I grew less anxious when no rude comments came from him. It was a comfortable silence I've had many times with that side of him.

Well, the version I had to myself for nearly a year. The version that held my hand under the covers and smiled at me when no one was looking. Kissed me in the pool house. In the car. In random hotel rooms all over the world while we watched *The Greatest*

Showman for the billionth time.

The version I've missed every day since he walked out of my life – and I let him.

That side of him quickly shrank back into its shell when he tossed his bag into our room and stormed off, muttering a *fuck's sake* under his breath hours ago. I'd sat on the small bed, kicked off my shoes and pulled the duvet over me, and I've been here ever since.

He's back to his usual dickish self. I won't be surprised if he's drunk in the bar downstairs or in a taxi on his way to a random girl's house.

Should I text him and ask if he wants to grab food, or will he tell me to go fuck myself?

On cue, my phone dings, and my heart stops, thinking it's him. But it's Kyle sending a question mark.

I forgot to reply. No doubt he's sweating and pacing the floor, worrying about my safety. He really is the total opposite of his younger brother.

***Me**: Sorry. My phone was on silent! I'm okay. Promise me you won't tell Nora or Chris who they are. I don't want them freaking out. But yes, they are his kids.*

A few minutes pass, then my screen lights up once more.

***Kyle**: Fucking hell. Yeah, sound – I won't say anything. What are they like? Cool? Dickheads? Do they boast about who their dad is? I read something about Kade being exactly like that psycho. Did you see the article on him when he was 12? It says he has death in his eyes. The fuck does that even mean? Oh shit, I don't think I want to know, but you aren't dating him, are you?*

I sigh, shaking my head. Some of these articles are ridiculous. If these reporters knew the side of Kade I did, they'd never say those things about him. Regardless of how he acts now.

Tobias struggled with *every* emotion and had no idea how to control them. Whereas his son can feel them to some extent, can certainly show them when he's comfortable enough and doesn't go on a killing spree when things don't go his way.

I reread the last part of Kyle's text, narrowing my eyes. I'm not about to tell him that Kade is my ex or that we have a heavy history that could write an entire book.

I'm not going to tell him that one time, while he was knocking on my room door to see if I needed anything from the shop, Kade had me pinned to the floor with his hand wrapped around my throat, tight enough to nearly cut off my oxygen supply while roughly fucking me.

No. I definitely won't tell him that.

Another message, and I huff.

***Kyle**: I'm uncomfortable with the delayed response. I wish to retract my question.*

***Me**: Shut up. I'm not dating him. And they're normal people.*

***Kyle**: Okay. Cool. I thought your flight was hours ago? How do you have a signal?*

***Me**: I missed it. I need to stay in a hotel until tomorrow.*

***Kyle**: With the psychopath's son? Damn.*

***Kyle**: Remember... orange emoji with your location and I'll be there.*

I send him an *okay*, and he goes offline. I've blocked Chris thankfully. When the first string of abusive messages came in as soon as I sat in the car, I made sure he couldn't contact me for the remainder of the trip. My body still aches from his violent "lesson" last night. I don't think the bruises and cuts are too noticeable, but I used a thick concealer to cover them up, just in case.

Is it bad that I welcome his fists? If he didn't hurt me that way, he might resort to sexual attacks, and I'll die before I allow that.

It's the middle of the afternoon, but I didn't sleep much last night. I yawn, stretch under the covers and quickly text Kade to tell him I'm going for a nap. He reads it, and when ten minutes pass without a response, I sigh and put my phone on charge. As soon as my head hits the pillow, I'm out.

It's been hours since I woke up and there's still no sign of Kade. TV is boring, social media is dead, and I keep rereading the same line of a rom-com book and failing to register the words. It's late, the light from a lamppost shines through the window, rain pelting the glass, and I'm in dire need of a cold can of juice.

I'm starving too. I think the entire hotel can hear every time my stomach growls at me to feed it. But my laziness has so far won, and I've settled on the bottle of water from the mini fridge.

Did I go through his things hunting for a snack and settle on stealing his crisps? Yes. Yes, I did.

Luciella called. They landed an hour ago. She said she was close to punching Base in the face and sending him home. She didn't appreciate him suggesting a quickie to get them both in the mile-high club. She hung up on me when I started laughing.

A beep sounds from the door, and it swings open, banging off the wall. I shouldn't flinch – I don't mean to – but my heart races momentarily and I pull the duvet to my chest as if Chris is about to fly in and smash his fist into my face.

Kade pauses in the threshold as if he's forgotten I'm here, his brow raised at my scared expression, before he slowly closes the door.

I let my grip on the covers go and pretend to read my book,

refusing to acknowledge his presence. But the energy changes when he's near – if I couldn't read before, I definitely can't now.

I keep the book open anyway and watch him over the top of it.

He tosses his car keys on the hotel dresser, shrugs out of his jacket and drops it on the little chair on the way to the bathroom.

Hello to you too, asshole.

His phone dings on the dresser once, twice, a thousand bloody times. I ignore it as the news reporter on the TV announces a horrific death in the centre of Edinburgh. I glance up at the screen as she stands with a microphone in the rain, explaining that the body of a man was found decapitated in the middle of Holyrood Park a few hours ago. A harrowing murder in broad daylight.

"Woah," I blurt. I turn the volume up, my book forgotten as it slides off my lap, and shift to the foot of the bed, watching the footage of police officers cordoning off the area. Another view comes from a helicopter hovering over the park.

"Did you see this?" I call out to Kade, but of course, he doesn't answer me. "This is so close to us."

They're still looking for the attacker – someone tall, strong and wearing a black balaclava. No evidence has yet been found except for a snippet of CCTV but they have no way of identifying the perpetrator. The officers are on foot and in vehicles, hunting for the person who did it.

I could never take another person's life, despite what I've sometimes thought about doing to Chris. The idea alone makes me tremble and pull myself back into bed. I mute the reporter, trying to refocus on my book. Maria – the main character – is going on a blind date and hoping to end her three-year dry spell.

My one-night stand with Bryan-or-Byron was the last time I had sex, and quite frankly, I can't say it was memorable. To be fair, I haven't heard a peep from him either, so I guess we're mutual on it being a one-time thing.

I can't risk touching myself at home with Chris under the same roof. Maybe my need for pleasure explains why things went as far as they did at the studio. It explains where I got the balls to even make the first move, considering my nerves were all over the place just from having Kade's hands on me.

Is it normal to hate him *and* want to feel him inside me?

Is it normal to wake up sweating and seconds from orgasming from memories alone?

Probably not.

If the girls hadn't shown up early for class last night, I strongly believe Kade and I would've ended up on the studio floor again. It's still there – the tension that cripples me, the pull towards him that has me internally screaming. All the feelings I've locked away. Each time my eyes land on his, I want him. But I also want to slap him hard enough to hurt him.

The bathroom door opens and closes, and I glance up. "Did you eat?" I ask, my voice cracking at the end when I see he's only in a pair of boxers.

Holy mother of God.

I grab my book and hold it tight in my grip as I let my gaze fall down his body.

He was lean before, but now? He's *huge.* I let my eyes take in his powerful back, muscles upon muscles bunching as he pulls things out of his bag. His arms look different without a top on, like he could crush my skull with his bare hands. My lungs give up when he straightens and turns to me, flashing his abs, chest, that perfect V of muscle and happy trail.

Dark tattoos litter his tanned skin – ones he didn't have before that cover older ones that had meaning for me. There are snakes. A lot of snakes. An hourglass with clock hands behind it covering what used to be a blooming rose he'd had done for me over his heart.

Despite that, he's a work of art – he always has been, but the Kade I once rolled around in bed with and laughed with while watching our usual movie is even hotter than before.

"Yeah."

And his legs? They could suffocate someone with their size. He has designs wrapping around one and distorted animals on the other. The ink vanishes up into his boxers, and I wonder if he has his—

"You done?"

My eyes quickly fall to my book, a blush creeping up my neck to my cheeks. "I was daydreaming. Don't get any ideas that I'd waste my eyesight on you. And you can sleep on the floor."

I can feel his anger. If he can talk to me like shit on the bottom of his shoe, I can do the same to him.

"Why would I?"

"Because I hate you," I reply, deadpan. "I'm not sharing a bed with you."

He knows I don't mean it.

He chuckles, pulling on grey cotton shorts and grabbing his toothbrush and toothpaste. "For the record," he starts, pausing as he starts brushing his teeth, "I'd rather set my balls on fire than share a bed with you."

"Charming. Is that how you usually get the ladies into bed?"

"Nope. It comes naturally," he says around the toothbrush. "You of all people should know the tricks of getting into people's beds. What was it Tylar said? You've had plenty of *practice* lately."

"Plenty." I flip a page and fail to hold in my anger when I look up at him. "I'm seconds from smacking you, Kade. Either get into bed or fuck off."

"This angry side of you doesn't work. You're as scary as a puppy."

I scoff.

He washes his face, turns off the bathroom light then crosses his arms at the foot of the bed. After a few seconds, I feel his gaze on me, my skin heating as I attempt to not look back. "Problem?" I ask, keeping my eyes fixed on my book.

I flip three pages instead of one – completely unfocused.

"If I get in, do you promise not to grab my cock again?"

My gaze flies to him in horror as he walks to the other side and lowers himself onto the bed beside me.

"I need to answer work emails, and the last thing I need is an unwanted hard-on like last night."

An aggravated groan is pulled from my throat as my eyes return to the book. He can claim it was unwanted all he wants, but I felt how hard he was and had his heavy breaths on my neck. He was all over my boob, for crying out loud. Nope, fuck him. He can have my silence, if only to keep him from issuing any more insults.

I swallow when he gets comfortable beside me. My silk shirt

is buttoned to my neck, but the matching shorts mean my legs are bare, and my nerves catch fire as he leans forward.

"What are you reading?"

I shut the book. "Go away and stop distracting me."

Kade smirks. "Do I distract you a lot, Freckles?"

"Stop calling me that."

"Too innocent for you now?"

"Okay." I throw the duvet off. "I'm sleeping in the car."

He captures my arm, and the electricity running through my body has me inwardly gasping.

I grit my teeth. "Stop being a dick. Really, Kade. You know this is awkward, and you being an idiot is making it worse."

"I'll stop," he says, his gaze a little droopy now he's closer to me. "It was a joke."

I can tell he's tipsy by how hooded his eyes are. He's always had beautiful sleepy eyes. When he's been drinking, they fall nearly closed. Even then, the silvery blue is still noticeable. Still breath-taking.

It's annoying when I'm supposed to be mad at him.

I put a pillow between us. "Don't come on my side or I'll poke you in the eye."

There's a shadow of a smirk on his face.

Silence falls. The lamp on his bedside table is still on. This is bad. My heart shouldn't be racing and threatening to blow through my chest. I shouldn't be nervous. We're two people sharing a bed because there's no other option.

Except, I fear that my body will gravitate towards him in my sleep. And this new version of Kade who hates my guts will push me away and probably knock me off the bed.

He sits up, and my eyes linger on him as he types at rapid speed on his phone. Call me nosey, but I can't help it. He's replying to emails. At least, I think they're emails – I don't recognise the app he's using. I chew on the inside of my cheek, pull my own phone out and start scrolling, bored.

Ten minutes pass. "Why are you replying to work emails so late?"

Kade doesn't stop typing. "Because some people need to actually work, regardless of the time."

"Where do you even work? Last I knew, you were helping Ewan and studying."

He opens a new email and types to someone with a name starting with B, then angles his phone so I can't see what the message says. "None of your business. A lot has changed in two years."

So he isn't going to tell me where he works? Weird, but okay. Noted.

"Did you see the news? Someone was killed not far from here. Decapitated. The person who did it is still out there."

Kade doesn't look up from his phone, and with the most monotonous, bored tone, he replies, "Shame."

11

STACEY

I wake to Kade standing by the window, looking out with a hand in his pocket, drinking a glass of what I assume is whisky that he must've picked up from the bar downstairs.

Ice cubes clink against the glass as he takes a drink – and the gulp is so audible that I can picture the way his throat shifts as he swallows.

I perch on my elbow and rub my knuckles into my eyes to rub away the tiredness. "Do you ever sleep?" I ask groggily as.I yawn.

"No," he replies sternly, taking another sip. "Go back to sleep."

"That's all I've done since we got here." I sit up fully and stretch my arms, rocking my head from side to side to fix the cramp in my neck. "How long until we fly out?"

He walks slowly to the bedside unit and checks his phone for the time even though he's wearing a watch. "A few hours."

"You should lie down."

"No."

"You look tired."

"I'm not."

"Kade..."

He rolls his eyes. "Will you shut up if I do?"

I fall back on the bed. "You're insufferable – do you know that? There's no need for you to speak to me the way you do. What's done is done. Stop being a dickhead."

He laughs dryly, not even slightly amused. "What's done is done." Kade licks the whisky from his lips as he stares at me. "Move over."

I begrudgingly move over to the edge of the bed.

Kade settles on top of the covers, sighing and rubbing his eyes with his thumb and forefinger. He looks exhausted, and his knuckles are freshly cut again.

I turn onto my side. "Were you fighting?"

He glances at his hand and puts it down at his side, staying quiet as his gaze flickers around the ceiling, as if he's thinking. His eyelashes are so long and dark, and I impulsively want to tug at them.

The bed is small, and our elbows brush for a millisecond as he gets under the duvet. The touch is more of a graze, but it's enough to make heat rush to my cheeks.

I lie on my back and fold the duvet around me, my arms straight against my sides.

Kade reaches over to turn the lamp off, bathing us in darkness, but the moonlight gives us a good-enough view of each other's faces.

The aftershave he used to use when he was younger has been replaced by something more expensive, and it fills my nostrils. I fidget my fingers and try not to breathe too heavily.

He pinches the bridge of his nose, huffing to himself – either because of our situation or the fact that Aria convinced him to come on the trip, and it's already going sideways.

My chest rises and falls in the quiet as I try my best to remain calm. Sharing a bed with him is fine. We can be mature about this and not make it a thing.

We can pretend my hand wasn't around his cock last night while he sucked on my nipple. We can pretend that we weren't in love at one point. We can also pretend we aren't sharing a hotel bed while hating each other's guts.

We've shared loads of beds; albeit his dick was always inside me, but still. Does he feel it too? The gravitational tug between us? It's bringing a thin layer of sweat to my skin, and I want to slide my hand to the right and touch his pinkie with mine.

Like we did when we were teenagers, with the blanket over us so no one would see.

"Can I ask you something?" His deep voice and tone rumble through me. "And I want you to be honest with me."

Oh God. This could go in so many directions. "What?"

He takes a deep breath and sits up, perching on his elbow so he's facing me. "Did you blame me for what happened? Is that why you did it?"

My heart twists in my chest. I've tried not to think of that heartbreak. I shake my head. "How could I blame you for something like that?"

"When you—" He stops, licks his lips then runs his thumb along them. "I've convinced myself it was some sort of twisted revenge."

I wish I could tell him the truth, but I fear the damage is already done. He deserves the real story – I know that. But it would start a war, and I have no idea how that might end. Chris is diabolical, in every sense, so the thought of him and Kade clashing terrifies me.

Even if I did tell him, nothing can change. What's lost is lost, and I'm stuck trying to find my strength and voice.

How do I tell someone what happened that night without them looking at me like I'm filth? I can only shake my head and hope he drops it. "No. It wasn't like that."

He stares at me for a long second, studying my face, the way I'm holding back the audible gulp and the tears threatening to fall. "Forget I asked."

We had everything, and now we have nothing but lies and grudges. I can't be mad at him – not really. But he walked away so easily, and I couldn't fight for him.

I sink my teeth into my bottom lip and, without waiting for him to say anything else, I turn my back to him and hike my knees up to get comfortable.

The ghost of a touch on my spine sends shocks in every direction. My momentary lapse in judgement means my top has ridden up, and every bruise and scar Chris has left on my back is now in full view.

"The fuck?" His voice is a growl – deadly. "What happened to you?"

My blood turns to ice as he touches my scars, tracing them. I gulp. "Dancing."

"Don't lie to me. Do I need to kill someone?"

I scoff. "No. I'm not lying. They're from dancing."

"Really?" he asks. "Why didn't you have these before?"

I close my eyes as I feel him pull my top up more, exposing every scar and bruise.

"Fuck no, Stacey. Turn around."

"No," I say quietly.

"Turn. Around."

I sigh and glance at him over my shoulder. He looks furious, brows furrowing, his eyes full of rage.

"I do silk routines now, remember? They rip at my skin."

My phone starts buzzing, a random number popping up on my screen. I silence it as Kade grips my shoulder, pulling me back so I lie flat on the mattress. He's so close again as he hovers above me, inspecting me. One hand is buried in the pillow beside my head; the other pulls my top up to just under my breasts, revealing a messy scar under my belly button from being dragged across the ground and cutting it on glass.

"Stop it, Kade."

His finger glides over the dented skin. "You didn't have any of these before."

I yank my top down before he can see between my breasts. There's no way I could lie about that and blame dancing.

"Leave it."

"What about the bruises on your neck and the marks on your face? Dancing?"

He'll know I'm lying, so I bite my tongue before responding quietly, "No."

His eyes flicker over my face. "Me?"

My phone begins buzzing again. "No," I reply.

"They must be from me," he replies, frowning deeper as he traces a bruise on my shoulder, and then one on my throat.

I shouldn't shiver, but I do, and he notices.

The touch shouldn't be sending me into a spiral or causing heat to gather between my legs. Yet here I am, getting wet and needy from Kade simply being near me.

My eyes widen slightly as he mimics the hold he had on my throat in the studio. "I held you like this. It was me." He looks horrified, his eyes darkening a fraction as he takes in my appearance. "I hurt you."

"It wasn't you," I whisper.

"So you fucked someone last night?" His eyes flash with something threatening. "Since when are you into getting beaten up during sex? Who was he?"

My pulse flutters beneath his thumb, and I know he can feel it. His jaw clenches as he stares down at my neck, and the need to wrap my legs around his waist is too much.

"I'm not answering those kinds of questions from you." I can't. All I can see is the real reason I'm battered and bruised. "Drop it."

Kade sucks on his bottom lip, breathing through his nose. He's still above me, and the heat radiating from him has me nearly squirming.

"I want to know who." His voice is frightening, the mania sobering him. "If you don't tell me, I'll find out. Don't go near him again if he's going to do this to your body."

A wave of anger hits me. "I can sleep with whoever I want. Just like you screw whoever *you* want."

I gasp, my body coming alive as Kade lowers himself on top of me, settling between my legs and gripping my throat – but more gently than he did in the studio.

"That's right. We can fuck whoever we want, when we want, in any position we want. And I will. Because I want nothing more than to rid the image of you grabbing my cock last night."

Said cock is rigid between my legs, and I fight the urge to raise my hips. "Yeah?"

He nods, minty breath hitting my face. "You irritate me. You're a poisonous snake that won't fuck off from my mind. You're everywhere yet nowhere. A fucking disease."

I frown at him. "A disease? I will hit you."

A gasp rips between us as he grinds into my pussy over our clothes. "You could try."

I want to clench my legs around him so badly, which is strange, since he just called me a goddamn snake and a disease. My breath hitches as he rocks his hips into me once more, fighting his own urges.

"Fuck. I hate you. I fucking *hate* you."

I raise my hips. "You feel like you hate me."

He shakes his head, fisting my hair until I feel pressure on my scalp. "Who did you fuck?"

I stay silent, although my breathing has become a little heavy from how hot I'm getting, how soaked I am beneath my shorts, and the random jabs of his cock against me. "Questioning me while you're doing that isn't going to get you an answer."

I gasp as he grinds harder, the head of his cock pressing right against my entrance, and I wish my underwear would rip.

The fourth time the phone buzzes, Kade swears under his breath and shifts to lie by my side, breaking contact.

I'm going to hex whoever this is. I sit up, take a shaky breath and hide my flushed cheeks as I grab my phone. "Hello?"

"Wow," Chris drawls and my heart sinks. "She actually answers."

I rush to climb on top of Kade, straddling him and pressing my hand to his mouth in case he tries to speak.

"What do you want?" I attempt to discreetly turn the volume down on my phone.

But Kade notices, his brows knitting together as he studies my horrified expression.

"Where the fuck are you?"

I flinch at how pissed Chris sounds. Kade glares. Both of his hands are resting beside my knees in tight fists.

"Why aren't you in America?"

"Complications," is all I say, silently begging Kade to stay quiet. I press my palm to his mouth harder when he tries to break away. "I missed my flight."

I'm not sure how I'm sounding, because all my concentration goes when I try to pin Kade more firmly, nearly flinching as I feel him rock solid right *there.* His hands fly to each side of my waist, gripping me when I try to get off.

He digs his fingers into my flesh, pulling me tighter into him, so the hard ridge of his cock presses into the material between my legs.

I want to rock my hips again. The need is almost robbing me of every responsible thought as Chris continues to yell.

Thank God I turned the volume down – even I can barely hear him.

The clench in Kade's jaw tells me he feels it too. The struggle to not grind into each other. To not move and feel the pleasure we know awaits us. If I move my hips, rock them, the underside of his cock will rub against my clit again and definitely drag a moan from my throat.

My hand slips from his mouth, and I press my finger to his lips to warn him to be quiet. He doesn't like being told what to do, but I think the fear in my eyes makes him compliant, because he's not making himself known to the person on the phone.

His hands are so large they nearly circle my waist. His fingers move from gripping my hips to my ass, tugging me even closer.

"Rock your hips into my cock, Freckles," he whispers quietly, and I nearly whimper. "I fucking dare you."

Even as Chris continues ranting down the phone, we keep our eyes on each other. His darken as a string of my sanity snaps and I shift against him once.

My body sings at the sensation.

He tightens his hold to control me and moves his own hips in a way that has my lips parting. From base to tip, the length of him smooths over every sensitive area of my pussy.

My underwear is drenched already, soaking through to my PJ shorts.

I rest my hand on his chest and roll my hips once more. His heart is thudding against my palm, his chest rising and falling with each deep inhale and exhale. I've no idea what Chris is saying, neither of us paying any attention to the phone as we dry-fuck each other.

Kade keeps his voice low and quiet, the blue of his eyes taken over by his dilating pupils. "Does he make you scream the way I used to?"

Oh, he thinks I'm sleeping with my caller. But it's either that or he questions me more about my bruises and cuts, and to be honest, I'd rather keep dry-fucking him while my abusive stepbrother is threatening me, none the wiser to my actions. A huge fuck you, Chris.

With the phone still to my ear, I move my hand from his chest and slide it up to his neck as I roll my hips, grinding against the underside of his thick length. He meets each movement, and if I don't hang up soon, Chris is going to hear me whimper.

Kade pulses against my pussy as I tighten my grip on his throat. He stops me from moving with his hold on my ass, watching as his cock drags up my core with each rise of his hips. My spine tingles, heat gathering up my legs all the way from my toes.

"Answer me or I'll stop," he warns.

Between each breathed-out word, the tip of his cock presses against my entrance before sliding up to my clit, making me tense everywhere. I bite my lip with each stroke, my thighs wet.

"Does he make you scream the way I used to?"

"No," I whimper.

"No what?" Chris asks in confusion, pausing his rant.

Kade loses his patience and takes the phone from me, ending the call and returning his hands to my waist. "Do you remember how to scream my name?"

I gasp with each solid stroke as his hand reaches for my shoulder, pulling me down on him. Before I can say anything, before I can even think of forming any sort of response, I grasp a handful of his hair just as a coiling sensation wraps around each vertebra, burying deep within and leaving me close to detonating.

Kade yanks down my shorts and sinks his fingers inside me. My every nerve ending is on fire.

I let out a moan and slam my palm against the headboard. He

thrusts hard and fast, and my legs shake with how roughly he's fucking me with them.

He stops, and I gasp for breath, whimpering as he smacks my ass with his free hand. "Ride my fingers, you little slut. Just like you used to."

My head drops back, my long dark hair a mess as I do what he says until my legs are trembling relentlessly.

Kade takes over again, fucking me even harder, curling his fingers so they hit that sweet spot that has my vision blurring.

"*Kade.* We shouldn't be doing this."

"I know. Keep fucking doing it." He grips my ass cheek with his other hand. "If Base tries to fuck you, you'll remember this. Me – having you moan *my* name."

He goes deeper, and I tense all over.

"You're making a mess, Freckles. Fucking dripping all over my hand."

With my eyes screwed shut, I moan, whimpering as his fingers hammer into me with delicious force. His breathing is laboured, and he drops his own groans as I lower myself enough to rub his cock with my soaked thigh.

On my knees above him, my gaze clashes with his. Both of us are completely taken over by lust and the liquid heat in our veins. But something flashes in Kade's eyes.

"You won't let anyone harm you – do you understand me?" He presses his thumb to my clit, and my lips part in a hum of pleasure, the orgasm that's been building and building close to combusting.

"When I find out who hurt you, I'm going to fucking destroy them. I'll make sure to bleed them dry then fuck you next to their corpse. You got that?"

Driven by the sensual strokes of his fingers, his thumb against my swollen clit, I nod.

"Words, Stacey." He slaps my clit and I cry. "Give me fucking words."

"Yes! Okay, yes. I won't... *fuck...* Kade, this is so wrong."

His eyes blaze into me. "Are you tapping out?"

My head shakes, hips rolling against his hand. "No."

"I want to hear what it sounds like, just like old times. I need to hear you screaming my name."

He pulls his fingers out, and I debate punching him.

"I want you to sit on my face." He yanks me up to his mouth, and I catch myself on the bedframe. "Suffocate me with this pussy."

Kade yanks me down by the hips and buries his face between my legs, and I moan so loud, I think the room next door hears.

His tongue is wet on my clit, and he groans as he sucks loudly on it – then he takes it between his teeth and sinks two fingers inside me, causing me to scream.

He strokes himself with his free hand, groaning against my needy cunt and alternating between fingering and tonguing my entrance, taking each piece of flesh between his teeth, dragging his lips all over my pussy then diving between my legs and tasting me after attacking my inner thighs.

Like an electric shock, everything inside me lights up when my orgasm hits – a strike of a match that spreads like wildfire all over my body. My walls clench and throb around his fingers, my vision blurring to darkness.

Both my hands are in his hair, tugging as I ride his face, grinding against his fingers and mouth as I explode – and keep exploding.

Kade's tongue lashes against me, my body spasming as liquid lust wraps around my spinal cord like one of his tattooed snakes.

"Oh fuck."

He bites at my clit, and I yelp through my orgasm.

"Louder. Grip my fingers with your soaking cunt and scream my fucking name like the dirty little whore you are."

Such derogatory terms should have me slapping him, not clutching his fingers inside my pussy, needing him to keep the dirty words coming. My head falls back, and I see stars.

Air rips from my lungs. The intensity of my high reaches breaking point, and his name slips from my lips with a string of curses. But it's a whisper – a gasp.

"Louder."

He sucks on my clit so hard, I nearly pass out as I remind him exactly what it sounds like when I scream his name.

12

KADE

I had five rules I stuck to for two years.

Rule one*: Stay away from your toxic ex-girlfriend.*

Rule two*: Don't unblock her number.*

Rule three*: If you're both in the same room, don't fucking look at her – it's a trap.*

Rule four*: Under no circumstances will you have any sexual interactions with her.*

Rule five*: Never forgive Stacey Rhodes.*

Yet here I am with two fingers buried inside said ex, her cunt dripping down my chin, moaning my name so loud her voice breaks.

I fucked rule one the day I came back home for a break Bernadette gave me after a heavy job in Africa. I picked Stacey up from a one-night stand like a fucking idiot.

My drug-fuelled fury drew me back to that house to knock the shit out of him, set his house alight. He was supposed to die. It's the same with every guy she comes across. How did I miss one?

Rule three went out the window when I found out Luciella was having a house party and Stacey would be there. After having her in my car again, after being tortured by her fucking vanilla scent, being in the shadows was no longer enough. I told Dez and Base that we'd be crashing the party.

I followed her to the front gate. Went against my own mind to have a shred of alone time with her and see who she's been fucking.

I've stalked her long enough to know who she speaks to, who she meets and who the fuck touches her, and I wasn't aware of whoever that was at the gate.

I still have no idea. Barry is working on it.

Rule four went tits up the second I let her grab my cock in the studio. The instant I felt her palm on me, the rage I'd been feeling simmered a touch. Not fully – just enough to curb the craving to rip someone's head off.

My anger knows no bounds these days, especially when it comes to a pretty little dark-haired dancer named Stacey fucking Rhodes.

Then it came to me unblocking her, another rule broken.

But rule five will remain solid. The idea of forgiving her makes me sick. I'll never fall under her spell again.

Don't get me wrong, the sight of her above me is wonderful. She's always been hot – a wet dream; she's always made liquid heat rush through my veins. Her tits are bouncing as she moves against my mouth, thighs tightly bracketing my head as she rides my face, and her taste on my tongue has me eating her out like a starved man.

I don't deserve nice things. I don't deserve to have her look at me like I'm her fucking God, but she also doesn't deserve me. I meant it when I called her a snake, yet my cock is pulsing as I fuck my own hand, tasting her orgasm on my tongue.

I can't say I'm amused with myself, to be brutally honest. I have those five rules for a reason. This girl broke my teenage heart, yet here I am pleasuring her.

Stacey moans loudly as I suck and lick through her orgasm, and my dick thickens in my grip.

I'm harder than a rock. The urge to flip us over and fuck her brains out is strong.

Her hands grasp at my hair as she grinds against my mouth. "*Kade*," she whimpers over and over again, head dropping, and the shake in her voice and tremble of her thighs has my dick dripping with precum and sensitive as hell.

"I can't," she breathes. "It's too much."

She's swollen and pink and tastes like a dirty sin I'd feast on every day.

I haven't enjoyed pleasuring someone in years, and my dick certainly hasn't been like fucking steel while going down on someone. I haven't willingly participated in anything sexual for so long – or been turned on by the taste and sound.

Everyone after her was either a distraction to make her jealous or an unwanted assignment.

I've never claimed to be a saint when it came to sex. I'm not a gentleman who can offer sentiments and roses. Not anymore. I'm a creation of being used and abused, and there's nothing I can do to stop it. It's my life now; I just need to live it.

So fucking sue me if I'm going to stay beneath her for a little while longer and drag out her orgasm. It feels right. And it fucking annoys me that it does. I'll suffer the consequences of this later, when Stacey inevitably tells me this was a mistake.

I suck harder on her clit, and a hum of deep, mind-boggling pleasure falls from her lips, driving her towards another orgasm that leaks down my chin. My balls tighten. I might actually cum from eating her out.

She's soaking for me as her cunt clenches around my fingers, quivering and throbbing as I curl them again, pumping and sucking.

Her high hits a breaking point as her body shakes, and my grip tightens around my cock as her mouth opens with a silent "fuck", pupils blown and wild.

I don't give her a second to realign with reality as we swap positions, my cock pressing into her inner thigh as she pants in my face beneath me.

"Another," I order, hand coming between us to rub circles on her clit. "One more, Freckles, then I'll fuck you."

I'll pound her so hard and fast, she'll never forget me again. When she goes back to whoever screws her on the regular – that's if I don't find him and kill him – she won't be able to have an orgasm without seeing my face.

The thought pisses me off more.

"Don't stop," she breathes.

As I bring her to orgasm again, her fingers twist in the bedding. Her thighs try to crash together, but I spread them with a knee as her walls crush my fingers through each spasm.

She captures my wrist, her pleading gaze begging me to stop because it's too much. I remove my fingers from her pussy and lick them clean while she watches; I fight the deep groan threatening to leave my lungs from her addictive taste.

My mouth lowers to hers, and before I can capture her lips, she tilts her head to the side. "No. Don't kiss me."

She kissed him.

My nostrils flare with rage, and I flip her. "On your hands and knees. I don't want to look at you." The words feel like poison on my tongue.

She complies, slowly, then glances at me over her shoulder with a raised brow.

"So I can picture you as someone else."

She rolls her eyes, pulling a pillow under her body. "You're such a dick."

Of course that doesn't bother her. She's here to be fucked and that's it.

Her ass hikes, and I spit on her back hole. She flinches and glares at me while I swirl the tip of my thumb around it.

"What?"

She grits her teeth and swipes at my hand. "If you even *dare* put anything in there, I'll rip your balls off."

I fight a laugh, giving her ass cheek a slap, my cock twitching as she whimpers from the sting. I can see everything – her glistening pussy and the forbidden hole I want to stick my tongue in. I revel in the fact I was the first to break in every area.

I slide the head of my cock up her thigh, capturing wetness, then rub it over her pussy and ass. She winces, and I ease back before I ignore her threat and try to shove into the back hole.

She's dripping, and I rub my thumbs into her inner thighs, spreading her cum. Then I bunch her top in my hand, push it up to her head and shove her face into the pillow.

Her back has some tattoos to go with those on her arms and legs. She's like a fucking work of art of all my designs. I love ink; I love drawing tattoos, especially for her.

I spot my favourite, which I drew when we were in a hotel in London, the same night we lost our virginities to one another. I have the same tattoo – *K* and *S*, integrated in a twisted design of meaningful scripture, roses and vines that makes our initials hard to notice.

She didn't want Luciella or Tylar to notice. Because I was her dirty little secret, and she wanted to keep it that way.

A tightness tugs in my chest, but I bat it down and shove two fingers inside her again. She's ready.

There's a veil of darkness lowering in my mind that I'm always fighting against, and now of all times is not the fucking moment for it to descend. My eyes involuntarily flutter into a rapid blink I'm unable to control, and the room blurs.

Bernadette's voice is in my head, as if she's whispering over my left shoulder about what a good boy I am and how well I'm doing – how much the girl below me is enjoying herself as I screw her brains out.

Nails clawing at my back and tearing the skin.

The woman's whimpers to go harder.

A gunshot and blood.

She's dead, and Bernadette wants me to keep going, but I can't.

Stacey's voice pulls me from my spiral. "What are you waiting for?"

My fingers aren't moving inside her.

Fuck, did I space out?

I swallow. "Seems I need to gain some courage to be inside you again."

She tenses all over as I begin thrusting my fingers in and out once more, hammering into her as I grip her shoulder and shove her face back into the pillow.

"How many guys have been in here anyway?"

I don't need her reply; I already know the answer.

My heart is fucking racing though, and I feel dizzy. My cock is throbbing in my hand as the girl I've never forgotten about bends over for me.

I'm seconds from fucking my ex, and I'm freaking out.

Embarrassment.

I don't know how to have casual sex nowadays. The last time I did, I had some girl bent over like this in the pool house and held Stacey's burning gaze as I drove into her.

She was mad. I didn't give a fuck. That was a fraction of the shit she put me through.

"If we do this, it doesn't mean a thing. A transaction of sex and nothing more."

She's scowling at me over her shoulder again, dark hair falling down her back. "If that's the case, I'll make sure to imagine your best friend and moan his name instead."

I clench my jaw until it hurts and lean down, capturing her throat from the front. "Shut the fuck up." I'll murder Base before he gets the chance. "You'll stay away from him."

She swallows, her throat working against my hand. "Make me."

God fucking dammit.

I let go of her throat, grabbing her hips and dragging her ass to me.

I ignore her infectious giggle that nearly pulls a smile onto my lips and line up to her cunt, before gliding through her soaked slit. Her hands fist the pillow as I ease my swollen crown through her welcoming entrance, her warmth encasing the head of my cock like I'm home.

Fuck me, she's tighter than I expected.

Was she this tight for him?

"Are you going to move?" Stacey, although being extremely patient with my drugged-up ass, is seconds from strangling me. "Or are you admiring the view?"

Shit, I zoned out again. I shouldn't have taken those lines earlier. I can't function with or without them nowadays. If Stacey knew I was on something, she would kick me out of the hotel room and tell me to go fuck myself.

I don't even have a condom on, and I don't care. I'll fill her with every drop of my cum and watch it leak from her cunt.

If I get her pregnant, then she's shackled to me forever.

The fuck am I doing?

I drag myself away from her, shoving my cock into my shorts as I back away from the bed. She turns, sitting up and pulling her top down to hide her tits then holds it to cover her pussy. She looks at me questioningly, confusion all over her face.

"You never change, do you?" My words come out before I can think.

Annoyingly, Stacey is truly beautiful and sexy, and everything mixed together.

But she's the devil. A twisted snake.

Stacey isn't an assignment. She's not paying me to sleep with her, and I'm not being held at gunpoint until I cum.

But she's not innocent either.

Her brows knit together, and instead of snapping at me for my attitude, she asks, "What's wrong?"

A part of me wants to confide in her. A part of me still sees my Stacey and how we used to be. But then I remember who she is and the video of her flashes in my mind.

"You're pale."

I storm into the bathroom with my phone and lock the door. My back hits the wood. I slide down it and attempt to control my breaths. My head throbs in pain, like there's acid behind my eyes, my dick instantly limp.

In and out. Just breathe in and out.

Stacey knocks on the door, but I can't make out her soft voice or what she's saying.

My hands are shaking, my knees bouncing as I fist at my hair and feel the layer of sweat on my face. My vision blurs, and I feel myself losing consciousness.

Fuck. It's happening again.

Fuck.

13

KADE

FLASHBACK 2

"Slow the fuck down!" my stepbrother Jason bellows, reaching his hands out to slam his palms on the dashboard. "Why am I teaching you to drive if you're not going to listen to a word I say? We've been at this for six months!"

I tut and shake my head. "I'm doing thirty, you dramatic bastard."

"On a roundabout," he replies, huffing and sitting back in his chair. He puts down his window, airing himself. "Fuck. I might message Giana and tell her I might not make dinner tonight."

"And then she'll come for me. Keep your dog on her leash."

He smacks my arm, and I burst out laughing. "You're not ten years old anymore. I can beat your ass with my eyes closed."

"I'd love to see you try."

"I'll just tell Aria you're smoking joints in her pool house."

I roll my eyes. "Could you be any more like your dad?"

He scoffs. "I think you're too like your *dad."*

I narrow my eyes at my big brother. Step, but still my brother. We always take the piss out of each other, so we're used to the dad slander and the occasional brawl.

Ewan is sound. He's basically another dad for me and Luciella.

"I'm going to intentionally crash," I tell him, and his eyes go wide. I cut him off before he can speak. "And I'm going to unclip your seat belt right before we hit a tree." I press down on the accelerator. "Unless you say you're sorry."

He pales when I speed up, not looking at the empty street, keeping my eyes on him.

Adrenaline courses through me as I go over the speed limit, and I know there's a bend coming up on the road.

"Shit. Okay. Okay!" Jason blows out a breath and mutters, "I'm sorry."

I smile and slow down, turning up the music. "Pussy."

He wipes the sweat from his face. "Shut up, you impulsive psycho. Do another parallel park."

He's been teaching me to drive for months. Ever since I got my provisional and passed my theory, we've been going out when he finishes work if his girlfriend doesn't have plans with him.

"I think I'm going to ask Giana to move in with me," my brother says as I reverse into his chosen spot, do a three-point turn, then head towards Loch Lomond. "We've been together for years. Surely we're ready for that step, right?"

I raise a shoulder. "You're asking a guy who doesn't understand that shit."

"Oh yeah, the frigid virgin. Got it."

I exhale. "Anyway," I begin, wetting my lips and wondering if I should mention her name. Would he give a shit if I kissed my sister's best friend? Is that even a bad thing? "See how you weren't able to come camping..." I stop, knowing he's going to laugh at me when I say it was my first kiss. He knows I'm a virgin, that's about it. "We all played dares."

Jason grimaces. "Glad I didn't go. Was Luciella there?"

"She left five minutes in."

He nods. "Good."

I might not give a shit what she does, but he's the protective big brother that I should be. Though sometimes he's a controlling prick and wants to wrap her up in cotton wool and keep her away from all men in the world.

"I was dared to... to k-kiss someone." I swallow, annoyed with myself for stuttering. "I did kiss someone."

"Right," Jason replies, confused. "Is that a big thing?"

"It was the first time I'd ever done it."

With a disbelieving sound, he tilts his head. "You're eighteen, dude. The fuck have you been doing?"

I shrug. "I've not been interested."

He crosses his arms. "Do you fancy her?"

Don't laugh, but I haven't done this before. The best eight words I've ever heard in my eighteen years of walking this earth.

"Yep."

He slaps my shoulder and I tense, only relaxing when he pulls it away. "Well, at least the little bro is off the mark. Did you bone her?"

I laugh. "No one says bone, Jason. Old bastard."

"I'm twenty-nine, you dick."

I sigh. "Well Stacey—"

"Woah. Wait. You kissed Stacey? Does she not hate your guts?"

I huff, pulling up at the manor gates and waiting for security to open them. "Yes."

Jason blows out a breath. "Good luck with that."

I know. I'm going to need it. Because when I get into this house, I'm going to have to hide in my room. Luciella is having an indoor pool party with her friends. As much as I've witnessed Stacey in a swimsuit countless of times, I don't think I'd handle seeing her now, knowing what it feels like to kiss her.

And I'm going to do it again.

Luciella is going to fucking hate me.

Keep going, *Stacey had said to me in the tent, while in my lap with her tongue down my throat, and I fully intend to keep fucking doing so.*

"We're out of ice!" Tylar exclaims. "Stacey, it's your run."

When she nods and gets out of the pool, I avert my eyes. Seeing her wet body will only make my fascination worse. I already screenshotted and cropped a picture Tylar posted on social media an hour ago before my friends forced me to come down here.

All those years of teasing her have finally come back to bite my ass. It's typical that the first girl I'm interested in turns out to be the one I've bullied since I was fifteen. My friends helped by targeting Tylar and Luciella, but my sole purpose was to make Stacey's life hell.

For absolutely no reason.

I've lost count of how many times she's given me the middle finger, shoved me and called me a fucking asshole.

All deserved of course.

Her breathy voice is in my head, and I tighten my grip on my bottle of beer. It's like a fucking mantra, constantly drawing me in, begging me to act on my impulses. I'm back in that damn tent again, with her in my lap.

Keep going. Keep going. Keep going. Keep going. Keep going. Keep going. Keep going. Keep going. Keep going. Keep going.

I want to keep going.

Fuck it.

No one asks me where I'm going as I leave the pool room, water dripping onto the carpets as I make my way to the kitchen. The staff glare at me, but I ignore them. I don't bother putting on a top.

I just need to get this off my chest.

Kiss her. At least finish the kiss. Then I can forget this thirst for more.

I'm telling myself I'm going for a snack, and it's sort of true – the snack being a five-foot-four tattooed aerialist with delicious curves, toned from exercising, who's badly singing along to "Wrecking Ball" as it echoes throughout the manor.

She has no idea I'm leaning against the doorframe as she belts out each word.

She's a terrible singer.

Well, not everyone can be perfect. But Jesus, she could wake up a dead person with that horrendous voice.

Her bikini – a tiny black thing – hugs her body. It's fucking imprinting on my mind as she moves around, slamming cupboards, still singing along as the song hits the chorus. She searches the freezer, then the chest freezer in the corner, none the wiser that I'm here.

She won't find ice in here, but I'll let her continue.

It's a delightful view.

My hooded gaze shamefully drops to her ass as she stretches up to reach the top cupboard, groaning when she fails.

"The ice is in the walk-in freezer down in the basement," I tell her, smirking when she jumps in surprise and spins around.

"Fucking hell, Kade!" She presses her palm to her extremely naked and wet chest. "I think my heart just exploded."

I chuckle then stop myself. I don't laugh in front of people I don't feel comfortable with. And she's the last person in the world who could make me feel comfortable. She makes me dizzy and crazy and fucking nervous.

Instead, I blink and push off the doorframe, walking until I'm in the centre of the kitchen. "That would be a heart rupture, and it's more common a few days to weeks after a heart attack."

"It was a figure of speech, asshole," she retorts, and I can't stop myself laughing.

She slams the freezer shut, placing her hands on her hips. Hips that I've held in my palms. Hips that I want to hold again.

She wets her lips, and my gaze falls to her mouth.

Fuck.

All I've been picturing is Stacey since that night, and it's starting to piss me off.

She did this to me, so she can fucking fix it.

"What do you want?" she asks, crossing her arms. "If you're here to tease me about kissing you and how bad I was at it, don't bother. I'm in no mood for your bullshit tonight, Kade."

The way she throws out my name has anxiety prickling at my skin. I want to just come straight out and say I have to kiss her again, but instead, I stupidly reply, "Ice."

Her brows furrow. "Ice? You're drinking bottles of beer. Why would you need ice?"

Fuck. Okay, think, Kade, you stupid bastard.

"You were taking too long," I say, leaning my elbow on the island counter. "And you were looking in the wrong place."

"Whatever."

Before she can head to the stairs that lead to the basement, I side-step to block her. "Wait."

She tries to hide it, but I definitely just saw her looking at my body. It's still wet from the water, as is hers.

She gulps and takes a step back. "What?"

"The kiss..." I have no idea what the fuck I'm doing or saying or thinking. I'm certain my hands are shaking. "What did you think of it?"

I'm a tit – an embarrassing fucking tit. Why don't I tell her that I chugged one off while thinking about her not even twelve hours ago while I'm at it?

She shrugs, not giving a fuck. At least she isn't laughing at me. "I had high expectations given how full of shit you are, but I've had better."

The fuck she has.

"Liar. I was your first kiss," I reply, imagining myself grabbing her face and pressing my mouth to hers. Imagining *being the key word. Because I'm too much of a fucking pussy to actually do it. "And you were mine."*

"See, that I struggle to believe. If you need an excuse for how crap it was, don't beat yourself up too much. I know you were disgusted by the dare as much as I was."

I shouldn't be hurt by her comment, but I am. "I wasn't disgusted."

She quirks a brow.

I lose patience and slowly advance towards her. Even though she seems to be acting cocky and unaffected by all this, I know her pulse is hammering in her neck. I'm close enough to see the skin fluttering at the side of her throat.

I want to pull that area between my teeth.

"Do you want me to prove I'm not disgusted by it?"

No idea where that came from, but the words have already left my lips. I actually said that. Me. Kade Mitchell. Just asked Stacey Rhodes if she wants me to prove I'm not disgusted by the kiss. By... implying I kiss her again? I don't know.

"Freckles?" I push, seeing her bad-girl image falter as she starts to chew on her lip nervously.

I move closer, feeling warm from my inner panic, and she blurts out, "I'm wet."

I tilt my head. "That's very forward of you. Not sure if you know this, but so am I."

My hair is wet, just like hers. Little drops keep trailing down her body, and they're fucking with my head.

She stays quiet, but I can see the rage in her eyes. It makes her even hotter.

"You told me to keep going," I point out, my own pulse racing as I take another step, eliminating even more distance between us. "Or are you going to lie about that as well? We both know neither of us were disgusted."

Her eyes sparkle, her throat working as I rest my trembling hands on the counter on each side of her.

Stacey lifts her chin. "It was a dare."

The corner of my mouth curls. "Then I dare you to kiss me again."

"Your sister might walk in," she says shakily, and her gaze flicks to the door then to the back entrance. No staff. No people. Just us.

My sister won't walk in. She's a lazy bitch, and the kitchen is too far away for her. Anyway, Base will be distracting her with his flirting. He's probably shoved her in the pool by now.

Drops of water roll down her chest, and I try not to watch as they soak into the swell of her breasts. "Then she better walk back out."

"She'd kill me."

We're both teetering on the edge of this pull, the rope tightening only to loosen again, neither of us making the move, and fuck do I want her to, because I have no idea what I'll do if she denies me. I'll go to kiss her and knock teeth or hurt her.

Come on, Kade, *I say to myself.* She wants to. Just fucking kiss her and ignore how much you're freaking the fuck out.

"I highly doubt she'd kill you."

She scoffs. "Um, are you joking? Didn't you see how mad she got because we were dared?"

"I honestly don't give a shit," I say, my lungs burning with pressure. "I'm going to kiss you, and then we're going to go back to the party, alright?"

Her gaze drops to my mouth then moves back up to meet mine. "Why do you want to kiss me?"

"Because I liked it," I admit easily, and her eyes widen. "So I need another taste, Freckles," I say in a low tone, my hands itching to touch her, to run through her hair and tug it until her head falls back, giving

me enough access to devour her throat. "Then I'll leave you alone."

All she says is, "Fine."

My chest rises and falls, matching hers. "Fine," I repeat, fingers flexing on the counter beside her.

I swallow and count to three, but I don't bend down to capture her lips. This girl has been my obsession for too long, and ever since that night in the tent, I haven't been able to think about anything else. It's wrong, and as much as I don't want to be like my dad, I think I might be.

Who gets this way after one kiss?

Was he this way with my mum?

Am I going to be doomed to pine after this girl forever?

I knock aside all those thoughts as she says, "But..." I watch as she glances at the door again. "Lu..."

She's worried we'll get caught. That's a good thing, right? She wants me to kiss her. I think. I honestly don't give a shit if my sister walks in. She can fuck off and stay out of this. Whatever this is.

Keep going.

I grab her jaw between my thumb and fingers, and lower my head, my nose nudging hers. "You told me to keep going."

"I... I did," she breathes.

My thumb strokes across her chin and the swell of her soft bottom lip. "Will I?"

A few moments pass, and something claws inside my chest, until she finally whispers, "Yes."

Instead of going for her lips, I press my mouth to her jaw, and revel in the taste of her skin as I trail kisses along her jawline. Feeling her breath hitch, I nip at her, dragging my lips to the erratic pulse on her neck I haven't been able to stop looking at.

I flinch a little when her palm slides up my naked chest, the muscles pulling taut under her gentle touch. She tries to draw back like she did that night in the tent, and my free hand captures her wrist to hold her there.

Touch is repulsive and unnecessary. I barely hug my own mother. A person openly wanting to touch and cuddle and feel makes my skin crawl. I've always been this way, but when Stacey touches me, even if it's just a hand on my chest or shoulder, it feels different.

Not repulsive at all. But it's still foreign to me. Unknown. Yet I want to explore it more. I press her palm to my chest, and I don't let it go.

She must think I'm a weirdo, but I like her touch.

I like how she tastes.

I like the way her breathing stutters as I kiss her neck.

I suck the skin of her throat, bringing it between my teeth. The sound she makes causes me to falter. I've never done this before. Never kissed a girl's neck while releasing her jaw to grab her hair and tilting her head to the side, giving me more access. I don't know how I even know how to do this. I just... do it.

My eyes screw shut as she brushes her fingers through my hair, the feeling far too intimate and invasive. She catches on and rests her palms on my shoulders as I keep devouring her throat.

A slow rock song is playing now, but all I can hear is her. She whimpers, arching her back as I suck on her skin, and I'm certain I hear my name whispered like a fucking prayer.

I straighten, cup her face between my hands and press my lips to hers properly.

Breathless, we both fall into the kiss, her fingers digging into my shoulders while I lower my hands to her hips, gripping them as she parts her lips, allowing me to run my tongue against hers.

This is the same, yet different.

Before, we had to do it. This time, we're doing it off our own backs. I'm deepening the kiss and pressing her into the counter harder because I want to. She's sucking my bottom lip into her mouth and biting it because she wants to.

She doesn't taste like alcohol. A fruity drink, but definitely no alcohol. I accidentally groan as she sucks on my tongue, and without thinking, I grab the back of her thighs and lift her onto the counter.

We're kissing again, deeper, her legs parting so I can stand between them until she locks her ankles behind my back, wrapping her arms around my neck.

"We need to be careful," she says against my mouth, still running her tongue against mine. "Anyone." Another brush of her tongue. "Can walk in."

Her bare skin beneath my hands is heated and soft and addictive, and if it was acceptable, I'd kiss her thighs and suck on the flesh until I left permanent marks. I'd lick all the way up to her...

No. *That's too far. If I don't stop, I might scare her off.*

I pull away first, shoving my hand down my swim shorts to cover how hard I am. "You forgot the ice, Freckles."

She slips off the counter. To my own pleasure, she smiles as she bites her lip, the same one I had between my teeth. "Show me where it is."

I grin as I follow her out of the kitchen, watching her ass from behind.

I lied when I said I'd leave her alone. She's feeding into my obsession, and it's only going to get worse. This is only the beginning.

14

KADE

I blink away the blurriness in my eyes, sitting up against the door of the bathroom. The light blinds me, the headache edging close to being unbearable.

A knock sounds at the door. “Kade?”

I close my eyes and ignore her, the ache in my temples growing. I lean forward and take a deep breath before grabbing my phone and bringing up my messages.

Trembling fingers fly over my screen as I send a text to my mum.

***Me**: Are you still with Dad?*

She sees it right away, but my vision blurs so badly that I rub my palm into both eyes. I only took two lines earlier, not the full bag, but I feel like I’m seconds from passing out from another overdose.

If I black out and think of Stacey again, I’m going to be more than pissed.

> ***Mum****: Yes, sweetheart. Do you want to talk to him? Is everything okay?*

> ***Me****: Yeah. I'll call in ten.*

I wash my face with more force than necessary, ignoring another knock on the door. My lungs are struggling for air, a painful ringing in my ears so intense I'm surprised there's no blood spilling from them.

I grip the edge of the sink and drop my head, knees trembling.

Something is sitting on my chest – crushing it.

My car keys are sitting next to my washbag, so I take them – and immediately drop them on the marble floor. "Fuck," I mutter.

Stacey's soft voice annoyingly soothes me. "Kade? Are you okay? You can talk to me." She's right there, on the other side of the door. "I'm sorry."

I groan into my palms. She better fuck off.

I put my head under the running tap to soak my hair in ice-cold water then dry it with a towel, but I feel no better for it.

Whatever is rushing through my body is crippling me – my hands are cramping, there are tingles all over my face and the last thing I'm going to do is ask *her* for help.

"We won't make this awkward. I know it meant nothing, okay? We can forget it happened if it makes you feel better. Come out and we can watch a movie or something."

Jesus, why can't I just fucking *breathe*?

I bring up my messages again, staring at the most recent ones from Bernadette.

> ***Bernadette****: I sent you a contact to deal with while you wait for your flight.*
> *No mess – do you understand?*

> ***Bernadette****: Are you at the hotel alone?*

***Me**: Yeah.*

***Bernadette**: Two hours, Kade. This has a big payment for the both of us – don't fuck it up.*

My response to her, not even an hour later, was confirmation that the job had been completed and a picture of the guy's head. Although I'd intentionally made quite the mess for her to clean. The target was an abusive wanker. He deserved it.

Bile rises in my throat to go with the anxiety riddling me right now.

Stacey's sitting on the bed, legs crossed and looking worried when I exit the bathroom. I grab my bag and throw it over my shoulder.

"Kade."

She's up and coming towards me now. I dodge her hand.

"Don't fucking touch me." The words are strangled and forced.

"Where are you going?" She stops in the middle of the room. "Talk to me. Don't make this awkward."

I don't respond as I slam the door shut and make sure it's locked. I quickly message Barry and tell him to put a guard outside the room. He confirms instantly.

I nod to one of my team as I leave the hotel reception; outside, a black SUV holds more of my guys waiting for instructions. Wherever I go, they're always nearby.

Always watching my back. Always on alert. Always waiting.

When I drop into the driver's seat of my R8, I shake my head at the scent of her everywhere.

Can I not escape her? One – she's my *ex*. Two – she's my sister's best friend and always there. Three – she's coming to America. Four – I'm stuck in a damn hotel room with her.

And five – the biggest mindfuck of the year – I want to go back and screw her brains out, to hear her moan my name again, to feel her skin beneath my hands and the taste of her on my tongue.

I press my forehead to the steering wheel to rid all the thoughts and call to mind the video – the one that started all of this – thankfully losing the semi that was growing.

Mum answers on the second ring. "Hello, sweetheart. We have ten minutes before the visitation ends."

We do the whole back and forth on how the day has been while I try focus. It's sunny over there, raining here. Luciella has argued with Base all morning, and she can't wait to see us.

She whispers something to my dad: "I'll go to the bathroom and give you two some peace."

My lungs are still on fucking fire. "Thanks, Mum."

There're a few seconds of silence.

"Kade?" the deep, threatening voice rumbles through the phone.

As much as the world is terrified of Tobias Mitchell, he's my dad. He has his issues, and a terrible past, but I'm not much better. I've taken over one hundred lives in only two years, whereas he's killed four people.

He has the excuse of not understanding right from wrong, but I know fine well what I'm doing when I track a person down and make them bleed and beg for mercy.

"Dad…" I stop, a lump strangling me. Everything is hitting me at once.

"Son?"

My eyes close. "Can… Can anyone hear me?"

"Just me."

I grit my teeth, unsure how much I can say. He doesn't know that I'm tied to Bernadette and her fucked-up world, and I don't think even the institution could keep him on a leash if he found out.

He would start with Archie, and decapitate him while Bernie watched in horror. I want to be the one to end her though.

The crushing pressure against my chest amplifies, and I'm certain my team sitting in the SUV across the car park can see me hunching over my steering wheel.

I take as much of a deep breath as I can. "We missed our flight. The next one is tomorrow." I pause, gulping, sweat breaking out all over me. "We need to share a hotel room with only one fucking bed."

"Language." He sighs. "What did you do?"

"Too much." I manage another gulp as sweat drips down the side of my face. "Dad… I can't breathe properly and my… my chest is killing me. My lips are tingling and so are my hands. The way it used to happen when I was a kid."

We haven't talked in a long time. Nearly two years. But I know he can talk me out of this. He always did before.

Dad hums, and a few seconds go by. I can hear the thundering of my erratic heartbeat in my ears. "Can you see?"

My jaw clenches and unclenches repeatedly, fingers obsessively tapping on my steering wheel. The coke should be slowly leaving my system now. "Yeah. I can see."

"Five objects you can see. Tell me."

I exhale, my eyes scanning the area. "Other cars. A lamppost. The hotel car park sign."

"Good. Keep going."

Dad stays silent while I try to concentrate. Slowly, the pain in my chest eases a touch, but not fully. "A fox just ran across the small hill in front of me."

"Do you remember Luciella wanted a fox as a pet when she was ten?"

A smile tugs at my lips. "Yeah."

"One more, son."

My mind isn't against me. All this panicking is just in my head. "I can smell her in the car. She's still wearing the same perfume."

I know he's nodding. "The one you bought her?"

"Yeah."

I stare at the passenger seat and imagine her soft legs, toned from years of dancing, and her hair flying around her face as I drive faster. She's giggling, then crawling into my lap.

"Same one. Flowerbomb."

"You've had to spend time with her."

I look away from the hallucination of her beside me. "Yeah."

"And how does that make you feel?"

"That I was okay with breaking the first four rules. But now I regret it, because at the end of the day, she doesn't deserve for me to break the fifth."

Dad helped me form the five rules. I was spiralling right after we broke up, and he knew I was seconds from losing it. He thought it would help me get off the booze, completely unaware of all the drugs I was consuming.

I needed something to fill the void, and partying myself into a comatose state was the best way when I had Bernadette over my shoulder, leading me into the underworld like an animal into a slaughterhouse.

"I watch her," I admit. "When she's in the manor, at the studio, or walking around the mall. If I don't see her at least once every day, I lose my mind. I've climbed to her window to see her sleep, and I've been trying to hack her phone for the last year. I hacked Luciella's."

And I hunt down the people she sleeps with and make them disappear, but I keep that part to myself.

"That's extreme," Dad replies. "But I understand."

Of course he does. "I can't stop hating her though."

"It would help if you let her explain."

My hand nearly crushes the phone to my ear. "No. We've already talked about this. Neither of them deserves to be fucking heard."

"Stop swearing." Dad is silent for a beat. "What else has happened? Your mother is worried about you."

I divert his attention from me. "Stacey has a lot of bruises," I say. "They look fresh. When I saw them, she said most were from the studio." It's quiet for a long second, and I add, "It's making me think."

I pull a cigarette out and spark it, glad my lungs are functioning enough for me to get the dose of nicotine I need. The ember casts a soft glow around the car as I suck and inhale deeply.

"What are you thinking?"

I blow a cloud of smoke out the window. "She's a good liar, but Luciella does the same training as her and she isn't black and blue. Someone hurt her."

Stacey is probably the best, most manipulative kind of liar. I know. I've been on the receiving end of her lies.

"You didn't notice anything while stalking her like a crazy ex-boyfriend?"

My eye twitches at his tone. "No."

"Where is Stacey now?"

"Hotel room. The door's locked, so she won't be able to get to her." I inwardly groan as soon as the words fall from my lips.

"Who?" His tone is dangerous.

"No one."

"Kade. So *who* can't find her?"

"It doesn't matter."

His hand slams down on something. "Don't keep something like this from me. Who are you in trouble with?"

I take another draw, enjoying the burn of each inhalation. "If I tell you, you'll try to escape. You're better off not knowing. I'll deal with it."

He laughs, and it sends a chill up my spine. "You think I'm stuck here? That's insulting, son. It would take me less than a day to be out of here and halfway to Scotland."

My brow raises. "You could escape?"

"In a heartbeat. Now tell me what's going on?"

I ignore the second part. "Why haven't you escaped then?"

"My family is happy – why would I ruin that? I hurt your mother by trying to love her the way she needed. As much as she will always be everything to me, I could never give her what she wanted."

I hang on to this subject, knowing he's so deluded when it comes to my mother that he'll stay on it. "I think she still loves you. I see it in the way she changes when you're there."

It's true though. Mum's face lights up as soon as she sees or speaks to my dad. She loves my stepdad Ewan, that much I know for a fact, but she's totally different and more *alive* when she's around my dad.

If he wasn't a psychopath who put her through hell when they were in their twenties, then maybe they'd have a shot. But, in all honesty, from reports I've read about them, they were toxic.

Besides, I like Ewan.

Silence. And then. "I wish that were true, son. Ewan is the love of your mother's life, and she is the love of mine. There's no changing that."

"Sounds miserable," I say, flicking my finished smoke out the window then rolling it back up with the press of a button. "You've been locked up for over twenty years and you still love her?"

"Not a day goes by have I ever felt less."

Yeah, as I said… miserable and deluded.

"I can tell you're feeling better. Good. We're allowed to have bad days too. It's late for you. Why don't you try to get some sleep before your flight?"

My eyes close as my head drops back against the headrest. "She's there, remember?"

A pause, and he scoffs. "Then have some self-control around her."

I hear Mum asking if everything is okay, to which he says *yes* and that he'll be right there.

"I'm going to spend time with your mother before she leaves. Go to the room and sleep. And for fuck's sake, son, keep your dick in your pants and stay out of trouble."

Mum scolds my dad for his language.

I chuckle. "Right."

He hesitates. "And Kade? I apologise for what happened the last time you were here. I had no idea she meant so much to you."

The call ends.

I stare at the screen with a bitter taste in my mouth. Dad knows more than anyone what it's like to want someone you can't have. His block is himself, whereas mine is that I don't trust a hair on Stacey's head.

We have six hours before our flight. There isn't a chance in hell I'll survive that. I'm honest enough with myself to say that I'm terrified to be back in that room with her.

My phone vibrates in my hand as I walk over to Barry's car.

Speak of the devil.

> ***Stacey**: You're not seriously going to sleep in the car? There's a killer on the loose! I'll sleep on the floor or the bathtub. Some dude is at the door too – he told me to wait for your return when I tried to come out for you. What's that about?*

Little does she know that I'm the monster that goes bump in the night.

I chew on my lip as she types again, still tasting her even after vigorously washing my face.

Barry is silent as I get into the passenger seat of the SUV.

***Stacey**: I get it, you hate me. What happened tonight was a lapse in judgement from both of us, but we need to be mature adults about it. We'll make a deal not to go near each other, even if we're tempted, okay?*

***Me**: Stop texting me.*

An impulsive reply I regret as soon as she reads it. I try not to smile when she sends an emoji of the middle finger. Her war cry.

I glance at Barry, who's watching with a raised brow and waiting for me to speak, his fingers hovering over his laptop. "Are you *smiling*?" he asks me. "Don't do that, it's weird."

"Fuck off. Can you trace who called her about an hour ago?"

"I can try. Her phone is still jammed – I can't break into the damn thing."

"She's bruised too." I rub my face. "I think whoever the bastard is is beating her. Can you look into it? My hands are tied while I'm with her."

Barry nods. "I'll see what I can do. You should sleep."

"Yeah," I say with a yawn.

I'm tempted to go back to the room, just to see her, but that would just be feeding the possessive side of me that watches her every fucking step on a daily basis.

I'm my own worst enemy.

I hate her, but I can't live without knowing what she's doing.

After ten minutes and another smoke, I pull up my secret app, transfer funds to it and make different travel arrangements.

I have more than enough from contracts, clients and business shares, so money isn't an issue when it comes to travelling. With the number of assignments I've done over the last two years, my bank account could rival my mother's and Ewan's combined.

Tonight's contract earned me three hundred grand. It took me less than an hour to get the job done. I used to hate it, but not as much now. It's fuelled a deep hunger in me for blood and havoc.

I get an adrenaline rush when I hurt people.

I know it's wrong, but it's built into me now. I can still see the blood of the guy I beheaded tonight and hear his screams for help as I chased him with a machete in my balaclava.

Once I arrange a time and place for my jet to land and refuel, I message Stacey.

***Me**: Get ready. The jet leaves in a few hours.*

***Me**: And deal. Try to keep your hands to yourself.*

15

STACEY

My body is on fire.

Kade's lingering touches are like ghosts on my skin.

I have no idea what happened. One minute, I was on all fours and ready – waiting for Kade to fuck me from behind. My heart was beating so fast, a spark in my chest that we were so close again. And next he's white as a ghost and rushing into the bathroom with his usual crappy comments.

You never change, do you?

Apparently not. Not when it comes to him. How can we be apart for two years and fall back into this? Before, we were learning about each other's bodies and ways to make the other feel good.

We would explore and live and love, and then we'd lie in each other's arms after. There was no rudeness or him degrading me in hurtful ways.

Embarrassment burns through me. From him noticing the bruises and scars Chris has littered me with to letting him – someone who claims to despise me – make me orgasm… *multiple* times.

He hates me. That much I'm aware of. But he's also confusing me. We went from close to fucking to him telling me we're travelling on a private jet.

And why was there a security guard outside my room? Kade excused him when he came to the room and grabbed my bags, not answering any of my questions about how it's possible we're getting on a private jet.

I'd shoved on my closest outfit – a black summer dress that sits mid-thigh. He'd raised his brow when he saw what I was wearing – it'll be perfect for America, but it's the middle of the Scottish winter here.

Now we're driving in silence, and I keep fisting my dress from the thick tension still between us.

I continue glancing at Kade while he drives us to a twenty-four-hour McDonald's before the flight, waiting to see if he'll break the silence. But he's on his third smoke and blasting music, so I highly doubt he will.

"The Death of Peace of Mind" by Bad Omens is playing loud enough to hurt my ears, and when I try to turn it down, he grabs my wrist without looking at me. "Don't touch my fucking radio."

I yank my arm away from his electrifying touch, huffing and slouching in the seat. "I prefer the old Kade. This new one is a buzzkill and a moody prick. You don't need to keep treating me like shit."

No reply. Not even an insult.

When we reach McDonald's, he doesn't ask what I want – he orders us both Big Macs and a side of mozzarella dippers.

"What if I wanted something else?"

Kade pulls out of the drive-through lane and parks up. "You don't like anything else."

I blink. "For someone who can't stand me, you seem to remember a lot about me."

A smirk. Curbing it, he unclips his seat belt and readjusts

himself with parted legs. "Unfortunately."

We eat in silence. The radio still plays, though he's at least turned it down now, and his phone keeps buzzing with messages. He denies a call then tosses the phone into the divider.

"That might've been important."

"Just eat your food, Freckles."

"Don't call me that."

He glares at me until I look away with heated cheeks.

After another few minutes of quiet, he takes all the rubbish and puts it in the bin he parked beside. The radio switches to the news; the gruesome murder is the lead story, and the reporter explains that someone's been detained but another suspect is still at large.

"Head of Police Scotland Bernadette Sawyer is here with us. She's been personally working on this case for the past few hours. Is there anything you'd like to say to the public, ma'am?"

Kade holds his breath and slows down.

"Certainly. I'd like to reassure the public that we have the best of the best on the search and strongly urge anyone who has any information to come forward. We believe there were two attackers, and we have detained one. Holyrood Park will stay closed until further notice."

"Is there anything you can say about the innocent life that was taken?"

"Is it not weird to ask that on—"

"Shh."

I roll my eyes and cross my arms as Kade turns the volume up.

"The body has been identified as Matthew Barnwell, a thirty-year-old man who was on his way home from work. The family has been informed, and love has poured in from social media for this respected member of the community, with hundreds of people expressing their condolences."

Kade tuts. "Respected." He shakes his head. "Fucking ridiculous."

"Did you know him?" I ask, puzzled. "The man that was killed?"

"Of course not."

I narrow my eyes, brows furrowed with confusion. "Then what's ridiculous?"

"She doesn't know him. How can she say he was respected?

She's full of shit."

"Well, at least she sounds hot," I say. "A singsong voice."

Nothing. Not a word. His eye twitches as he slams his foot down on the accelerator. He pulls onto a long stretch of road towards the airport, with no streetlights in a tunnel of trees.

Another Bad Omens song plays, and I tap my foot to the song.

I ask what time we take off – no response.

I ask why he's being an idiot – no response.

I ask if he wants to talk about what happened earlier, and, of course, there's no response. Slapping him would be acceptable, right?

"Come on, Kade. Are you going to give me the silent treatment the *entire* trip?"

"I don't plan on *seeing* you this entire trip," he replies, monotone. "As soon as we land, this nightmare is over."

I grit my teeth, annoyance and fury in my veins.

Kade has every right to be mad at me, but he still walked away. He still claims to despise me.

Yet right now I'm wearing his jacket because I was cold. If Kade truly, truly loathes the ground I walk on, why is he even taking me on this jet with him? Why did he back me against the wall in the studio? Follow me out of the manor to see who I was out talking to at the gate? Why pleasure me?

Why did he try to kiss me?

I gather enough courage to speak and turn to him. "I didn't know what I was doing," I say, filling the silence and attempting to calm my nerves.

I twist my fingers together. I've imagined this conversation a million ways, and it's always easier to speak out in my head. Why is it so hard to admit what happened?

Kade driving faster and ignoring me isn't helping.

"That night, I was—" *Raped.*

I stop, a lump sticking in my throat. I fail to say it aloud.

"It wasn't…" *What you think.* "I didn't…" *Want to do it.* But all I can finish with is, "I'm… I'm sorry."

I look out the window to hide the tears building behind my eyes as I try and fail to use my voice. If I tell him what happened and how many times, he'll think I'm dirtier than he already does. Used. Worthless. Or he'll say I'm a liar. He might not believe me, and then I'd be called an attention-seeker, a manipulator – toxic.

I want so badly to tell him the truth, but it won't come out.

Still no reply.

"Sorry," I say again.

Kade scoffs. "Don't waste your breath. I really don't give a shit."

I shake my head. "You obviously do, or you'd stop having such a terrible attitude with me."

I turn to face him again and let a tear slip down my cheek, my lip trembling. "I *loved* you. I wanted everything with you. Why would I ruin that? I would never intentionally—"

My body jerks forward as Kade slams on the brakes, the tyres screeching on the road until the car comes to a stop. Hair over my face, hands on the dashboard, I watch him with wide eyes as he heaves in breaths and grabs his lighter.

He shoves the door open and climbs out.

"Where are you—"

My voice is cut off by him slamming the door shut. I turn to look behind the car and see him running both hands through his hair.

I open the car door. "Do you know what? Fuck you, Kade!"

I walk towards him, his sleepy, fuming eyes on me as he puffs on a joint, and stop in front of him. "You left me. I needed you, and you left without even trying to fight for me!"

"Why would I fight for you?" he sneers. "I saw what happened in that video, and that was enough to show me your true colours. *What's done is done,* right? Get back in the fucking car and get out of my sight."

I snatch his joint and throw it away. "I didn't know what I was doing! I wanted you—"

"Stacey, I swear to fucking God. Shut the fuck up."

He moves closer. "You don't deserve time to explain why you did what you did, and I really don't care. I dodged a bullet getting away from you."

My teeth clench, fresh tears spilling. "I wanted to go home to you. I cried for *you.*"

"You cried for me? When? While you were on top of him?"

Kade takes a step towards me. There're inches between us, and I don't flinch as he takes hold of my jaw. It's not firm or painful but enough to show he could dominate me in a second. Despite his words, I can see the hurt in his eyes.

"I saw the proof of you with him." He releases my jaw and shoulders past me. "They're waiting for us at the jet. Move or I'll leave you here."

Defeated, I stand there and consider my options. I can either grab my bags and call an Uber to take me to the main terminal for our original flight, or I can go with Kade to this ridiculous and expensive jet and stay silent the entire trip.

Because fuck him. Losing your voice to everyone is one thing, but losing your voice to someone you loved – trusted – is ten million times worse.

I've never been heard. My dad didn't even listen when I told him about Chris abusing me.

Staying silent is like being in a mental prison.

A chill blows up my dress, and I decide to walk back to the passenger seat and slide the door closed.

"I hate you," I immaturely say. "You'll never touch me again."

"Noted." He speeds down the road, his elbow resting on the side of the car door.

He scans a badge at a fence, which then slides. He drives straight into the hangar to a small silver jet with a sharp nose.

I've never seen one before. Sure, Nora is rich, but we always fly commercial whenever we leave the country.

A man in a suit stands at the bottom of the pulled-down steps.

Kade nods to him when we walk towards the jet. "Barry."

"Sir," he replies. "We'll get your bags." His eyes land on me. "Miss Rhodes."

I tilt my head. "Hello."

"He's my assistant," Kade informs me as he leads me to the steps.

"How can you afford this?" I ask in awe, my eyes like saucers.

Kade's only response – to my surprise – is to wrap his fingers around my wrist as I stumble at the top of the steps after seeing the cream leather and oak interior.

"No, really, how can you afford this?"

I'm staring at the minibar full of wine and champagne and other expensive things. It's like a mini home in a plane with the sofa and the eight chairs with tables between them. I know his family has a lot of money, but not this much.

So what the hell does he do to be able to afford this?

I'm so damn confused.

Kade nudges me forward when my feet refuse to move.

The door closes and the young man with the English accent – Barry, Kade's *assistant* – talks him through the flight plan and a meeting he has scheduled while he's in America. He confirms that Kade's dogs are currently out in the manor grounds with the staff, and that they'll attend their advanced training lesson later in the day.

I raise a brow when Kade pulls his laptop out.

I take the seat across from him, still unable to find any words beyond *fuck* and *Jesus*. I've forgotten I was just yelling at him as I admire our surroundings.

"Don't tell Luciella about this," Kade says.

Barry pours us each a drink and informs us we'll take off in five minutes.

"She'll tell my mum and I can't be fucked with her interrogating me with annoying questions."

I tilt my head. "Are you going to answer any of mine?"

He takes a gulp then sets his glass back down on the small table between us, his eyes going back to his laptop screen. "No."

"You're not some crazy paid hitman, are you?" I ask with a smile, trying to lighten the mood. "Oh wait, you're paid for sex." Then I pause, thinking. "Drug dealer?"

He glares at me. "Your voice is giving me a headache."

I roll my eyes and look out the window as the jet pulls out of the hangar. An uneasy feeling reaches deep inside my chest when I think of all the ways Chris will make me pay for hanging up on him, or for going on this trip in the first place.

I allowed Kade to hang up on my psychotic stepbrother so I could dry-hump him. Which resulted in me sitting on his face. Then being bent over and so close to being fucked.

And now he's sitting across from me in a fancy jet, has an assistant, is strangely rich, and all I can think of is finishing off what we started back in the hotel. I hate him. Loathe. I think I could slap him and not feel bad about it for ten full minutes.

I can still be attracted to him though. Especially when he runs the tip of his thumb across his mouth as he looks at something unsettling on his laptop. He shifts, his legs wide open, and accidentally bumps his knee into mine.

He glances up at me, catching me staring, and I avert my gaze to my hands, which are fidgeting in my lap.

This is going to be a long flight.

16

STACEY

The novelty of being on a private jet is gone six hours in. I've slept. I've drank. I've slept the drunkenness off. I've begged this idiot to play a game of I Spy with me, which he obviously declined.

What is he typing? His brows are knitted together as he concentrates on the screen, and I watch him. He yawns, and it annoys me that he even manages to make that look hot.

I lean my elbows on the table between us. "Do you not sleep? You look terrible."

His eyes are sunken in, bags under them, and his hair has seen better days. This guy hasn't slept in over twenty-four hours, and the finger he taps on the table when he's not typing and the way he bounces one knee has me studying him.

He's... different.

I'd almost say he was coming down from a high, from what I remember of Chris taking drugs and waking up on my bedroom floor. Or the way I'd feel the morning after he'd forced pills down my throat.

Kade taking uppers seems out of character though, considering he's a fitness freak.

I nibble my lip. I know he smokes pot, but Kade wouldn't take anything harder. I remember how much he hated drugs when we were younger. He took medication to help regulate everything going on in his mind; I know this because I always sat on the sink and handed him a glass of water to swallow them with.

He hated tablets; hated pills that controlled him.

Has that changed?

"There's a sofa at the back of the plane – why don't you go lie down?"

His blue eyes stay on the screen. "I'm not tired."

I sigh. "Rich, rude and apparently an immortal who doesn't need sleep. You truly are a catch."

A faint smile touches his mouth, but he wipes his hand down his face to cover it up and continues typing. "Go back to sleep. Your company was better then. I'm too busy."

"Doing what?"

"Working," he replies bluntly, ending our conversation.

I yawn and smile at Kade's assistant. "What else is there to do in here?"

He points to the TV, but I shake my head.

"We have board games, if you're interested in any of them?" he offers.

"Will you play with me?" I ask Kade, but he grunts and shakes his head, without looking away from his laptop. I grin at Barry. "You?"

His glances at my best friend's brother, his expression worried. "Sir?"

"Do whatever she wants," he says, waving a hand towards me dismissively. "She'll probably suck your cock if you ask."

"Kade!" I exclaim in horror, turning to apologise to the guy, who nods to me and returns to his usual seat in the corner. I slam this tit's laptop shut. "Was that really necessary?"

Slowly, his nearly silver eyes slide up to meet my green ones, his dimples denting as he attempts to scare me off with a raging look. I raise a brow, not caring he's about to blow.

He grits out, "I was in the middle of something."

I rest my elbow on his laptop, lean my chin on my hand and beam. "And now you aren't."

"Fuck." He shakes his head with an unbelievable look as his back hits the chair. "You are *insufferable*. What do you want from me?"

The laptop is tossed to the table beside us, and he pushes the one between us up until it clicks into the holder. Elbows on his knees, he leans forward. Large, tattooed hands rub at his face as he sighs, and I remember a few hours ago where those hands were, and my body screams for me to climb into his lap and fuck him into submission.

His wet tongue was inside me not long ago.

I remember the way the release felt above him, how powerful it felt to grab his hair and ride his mouth.

The way his name on my lips was so natural.

How his hard cock had pressed into me from behind, and how much I'd wanted to push back so he filled me.

I think he might be thinking this too, because he sits back and readjusts himself in the seat. "Stop looking at me like that."

"Like what?"

His eyes darken. "You know what. I don't like you, and you don't like me, so why do you keep staring at my cock like it's inviting you to suck it?"

I tut, even though my cheeks heat. His assistant definitely heard him. "Can't we just put aside everything and be friends?"

The look he gives me makes me squeeze my legs together, and I have the sudden urge to accept the invitation to suck his cock. He pleasured me, so it's only fair I do the same.

Apparently, I'm easily turned on by an angry Kade.

"We didn't choose to be stuck travelling together, so get it out of your head that we're even *close* to being on a friendly level. Stop trying to talk to— What the fuck are you doing?"

I slide off my seat and onto my knees, grabbing his thighs and digging my nails into them. "Tell your assistant to leave."

Kade swallows. "Fuck off, Barry."

He smirks but hides it as quickly as it shows. "Yes, sir. Let me know if you need anything." He nods to me. "Miss Rhodes."

On my knees, I smile at him.

Kade grabs my jaw. "Stop looking at him like that," he warns.

I look away from Barry gathering his laptop into a case. "Or what?"

"Provoking me isn't a good idea, Stacey." He shifts on the seat. "Don't look at my staff. Ever. Got it?"

I roll my eyes.

A soft click follows, and Kade is still glaring at me as I settle into a comfortable position between his legs and rub my hand up his bulge. Already solid. He says nothing as I tug at his shorts slowly, lifting his hips so I can pull them down to reveal his Calvins. His length strains against the white material.

He hisses as I rub him, and I look up at him with a hooded gaze. "You hate that you want me, don't you? It's written all over your face."

He closes his eyes, dropping his head back as I run my palm up and down the underside of his cock. It makes him even harder, the swollen head edging out of the top of his boxers with a glistening bead of precum.

"Will I keep going?" I ask in a sultry voice as I slowly pull down his boxers. "Or do you want me to stop?"

His hips rise, jaw clenched as he opens his eyes and watches me slide down his boxers. "I'll throw you out of this jet if you stop."

The empty threat shouldn't turn me on, but there's an ache between my legs. The fact "Take Me Back To Eden" by Sleep Token has started playing only intensifies the neediness.

I grin, sucking my lip to hide my smile as I free him completely. Thick, long and cradled by veins, his cock barely fits in my hand as I wrap my fingers around it, stroking gently and twisting when I reach the tip.

I move my hand up and down, enjoying the way his muscles pull taut, his eyes on mine. "Use your mouth."

"Say please."

He raises a brow, tensing as I spread the arousal of his precum with my thumb, bringing it to my mouth so I can taste him.

He stares at my lips, his chest rising and falling. "I do not beg."

I shrug and go to stand, but he grabs my shoulder and shoves me back down. He breathes through his nostrils and fists my hair. "Are you going to suck my cock, Freckles? If so, stop playing with it and put it in your fucking mouth."

My pussy flutters at his dark tone. "Make me."

I sink my nails into one of his thighs as he grabs my jaw, pries my mouth open and slaps my lips with the leaking tip of his cock. He smears his precum across my bottom lip, then releases my hair to shove two fingers into my mouth and presses down on my tongue.

I gag around his fingers, my eyes watering.

"I'm going to fuck your throat, and you're going to be a good girl and swallow every drop of my cum."

He doesn't wait for a response; he removes his fingers and shoves his cock into my mouth, then grabs my nape and forces my head down to take him deeper. I choke around his thickness, needing air yet wanting to suck and feel him sliding in and out of my throat.

I look up at him to see he's biting his lip, desire all over his face as he fists my hair and controls the bob of my head. His cock pulls out ever so slightly, then gags me again as he goes deep.

Saliva trickles from the corners of my mouth as he moves his hips, fucking my mouth.

My thighs beg to open wide. To reach between my legs to give myself some relief, or at least crush together to cause some friction. There's something about watching a man screw his eyes shut and curse while being pleasured that makes me wetter.

"*Fuck*," he blurts as I push against his abs to halt his movements and roll my tongue around the sensitive head, sucking lightly, tasting his arousal. I pop it out of my mouth and go back to stroking him, which earns me an angry stare.

I'm not giving him the reins on this. I'm the one with the power. I'm in control. Beneath him and on my knees, yet above him.

I go to take him into my throat of my own accord, but he grabs my face, forcing me to look at him.

"Eyes on me," he orders. "Keep them on me."

I feel comfortable as I wrap my lips around his cock again and tease him a little more by pulling my mouth away. I feel comfortable as I run my tongue up the underside and cup his balls. And I definitely feel comfortable keeping my eyes on his, watching him on the edge of snapping as I stop sucking once more.

Our deal to resist temptation has gone south.

My lips press to the tip and I whisper, "Beg me to keep going."

Kade grabs a handful of my hair. "*Please* put my cock back in your fucking mouth."

He doesn't give me a chance to do anything before he pushes the tip through my parting lips and fucks my throat again with rapid rises of his hips. I gag around him, but it only seems to drive him deeper into my throat, robbing me of air as my eyes water.

He pulls my hair, his cock leaving my mouth to let me breathe. Strained, he asks, "Why?"

I gasp to fill my lungs, tears running down my cheeks. "Why what?"

He glances at his cock.

I shrug with a soft smile. "I owe you one."

He doesn't like that response. His eyes darken, and he grabs his dick and slaps it against my bottom lip, sliding it against my cheek to wipe away my tears.

"This doesn't change things." He slides a hand in my hair and pulls until I feel a smidge of pain, and my inner walls quiver with desire. "You fucked me over and I can't forgive you. Expect nothing from me. If you want to suck my cock, do it, but with zero expectations—"

"Then stop stopping me, you idiot."

I take him deep into my throat again, swallowing around him, and his fingers tighten in my hair, eyes rolling to the back of his skull.

He groans. "Fuck, Stacey."

I hold him there for a few seconds, sucking and licking, his cock swelling with each throb. A deep, vibrating moan comes from his chest as I take him to the hilt. My eyes water more, but I keep watching him as I stay there for a few seconds before coming back up for a lungful of air. My nipples tighten under my dress, and I fight the urge to rip the fabric off and caress my aching breasts.

Against his swollen, leaking tip, I whisper, "Still hate me?"

He groans and fights a snarl. "Stop talking."

Kade silences me further by shoving both hands into my hair and yanking my head back down. And then he fucks my mouth, making saliva gather – faster and harder, until I gargle for air, and I'm certain his assistant can hear me choking on his cock.

His grunts and moans and breathy curses fill the air, almost drowning out the music playing from the speakers at each corner of the aircraft.

Kade sucks on his bottom lip, and I can tell he's close as his cock twitches through each pull and lap, and the caresses of my hand. His hands are still twisted in my hair, holding me in place as he raises his hips with brute force. I gag and choke and moan around his thickness, falling into a hum as his thrusting slows down.

"You like this, don't you?" he rushes out. "I can tell how turned on you are. Such a whore, my Freckles."

My mouth is stretched over his base, and he buries himself deep, watching my eyes water. He moves strands of dark hair from my face and wipes the tears away with his thumb. "I want these tears. None of these other dramatics. Tears from sucking my cock. You're dying to touch yourself, aren't you?"

I manage a nod with a mouthful of dick. If I don't get some sort of release, I'll scream. I'm aching between my legs, my breasts feel heavy, and I'm absently grinding my thighs together.

Kade blows out a breath, chest heaving, as he slowly pumps his hips into my mouth. "Show me how wet you are."

With no hesitation, I reach under my dress to feel how soaked I am. Moving aside my underwear, I groan around his head as I circle my clit with the tip of my middle finger, finally getting the pressure I need. I dip in and lift my dripping fingers up to show him.

He continues thrusting. "Keep touching yourself. I want your fingers deep in your cunt while I cum in your mouth."

I whimper around him as I sink two fingers inside my pussy and rub my clit with the other hand.

Kade throws his head back. "Fucking hell. I've missed your mouth."

I push a third finger in, and I'm close to exploding. I struggle not to sob from the surreal feeling of my walls clenching around my fingers with building heat.

"You can take me deeper. Suck me into your throat." He thrusts into my mouth, and his swollen crown hits the back of my throat then slides down.

"Just like that. All of it. Take every fucking inch. Now swallow around my cock. *Fuck*!"

I can already feel the snake of pleasure wrapping around my spine and coiling deep within my core. Both of Kade's hands fist in my hair again to still my head bobbing on his cock as he groans deeply and empties right down my throat.

The length of him pulses and thickens through each twitch, and he swears, gripping my hair painfully as I suck hard and my own orgasm hits, wet, blinding-hot heat coursing through my body.

He watches me scream around his cock as I rub my clit until I can't any longer. My heart rate has sped up to a dangerous pace, my thighs soaked, hair a mess.

I remove my fingers, and he captures my wrist so he can suck them. The warmth of his tongue working against them and the way his gaze stays fixed on mine has my heart beating even faster.

Wetness drips from my mouth as I slowly drag in air to my starved lungs, a string of drool stretching from his crown to my lips. He runs his thumb across my mouth. "Good girl. If there's anything I miss about us, it's how well you suck my cock." He's still hard as he snatches my throat. "Now climb up here and fucking ride me."

His reload time has always been impressive.

There is no hesitation – I move right onto his lap and hike my dress to my hips. Kade wraps his arm around the small of my back as he fists his cock between my legs.

Just as I go to lower myself onto him, I yelp in surprise as Barry walks through the door, informing us we need to take our seats for landing.

Like a bucket of ice-cold water has been thrown over me, I twist my hands into the material of Kade's top and bury my face in embarrassment.

Pulling my dress down at the back to hide my ass, he glares at Barry over my shoulder as he walks past us on the aisle to grab something from a bag.

I close my eyes. Neither of us move from our current position.

I can feel the head of his rigid cock nudging at my entrance, and he rubs it against my slick pussy. I shake and lower myself a little. His tip pokes through my slit, and he twitches. One movement, and he'll be properly inside me.

"I might kill Barry," I whisper against Kade's ear, feeling him shiver.

Kade sighs and drops his head to my shoulder, gripping my hips before lifting me up enough to break the intimate connection. "I'll do it for you. I have a gun in my bag."

I laugh, but the way he's scowling at Barry while he helps me to my feet and fixes my dress, before pulling his boxers up, I have a feeling he isn't joking.

17

STACEY

Poor Barry has to endure death stares from Kade the entire landing.

He offers us water. Kade ignores the kind gesture but keeps his eyes on him. I accept a glass and thank him, just to make the guy feel better. I can tell he's been working for Kade for a while and is used to his mood swings. He doesn't flinch at his abrupt tone, and when Kade tells him to sit down and leave us alone, he gives him a look, glances at me then fights a smirk as he goes to sit down and put his belt on.

While I wipe the mascara from under my eyes and fix my hair, I fight a scoff.

Kade might come across as intimidating and unapproachable, but he isn't *that* scary.

He sits with his elbow on the armrest, fingertip to his temple, legs wide open. The white top he's wearing stretches tight across his firm chest, the fabric ruffled at his shoulders from where my hands were fisting, and I try not to gawk at his build. His ink. His muscular, veiny arms.

I cross my legs and gulp, still studying him.

A dark brow raises, and I'm caught staring. Again.

Instead of blushing and averting my eyes, I narrow them, wondering if we should ignore the fact Barry is here or that we're descending. We could get this off our chests, this tension and sexual frustration, with one quick fuck. Maybe then we can move past this atmosphere and be civil.

I hold his gaze until he eventually looks away. The pressure of descending has my ears popping and my stomach flipping. Kade swipes at his phone screen, unbothered, while I try not to imagine the plane crashing.

The jet jolts as it touches the tarmac, tyres screeching until it slows to a steady pace. I breathe a sigh of relief. I hate flying, but the worst part is the landing. There wasn't any turbulence the entire journey, but I did spot a bolt of lightning from afar earlier, which made the little hairs on the back of my neck stand up.

Kade only grimaced at me when I asked what would happen if it hit us.

I look outside the small window; take in the pouring rain and the way the wind beats against trees. I flatten my lips and look down at my summer dress.

Finally, Kade breaks the silence as the aircraft carries us to the middle of a private hangar. "We're not supposed to land until tonight. It's five in the morning here."

"An extra day in the States then."

His phone rings. "You don't understand," he says, turning his phone over so he can't see the caller ID. "My family will check when our flight lands. They don't know I have this kind of money. We'll need to stay somewhere until we apparently land on the commercial flight."

"You're quite the sneak, aren't you? Tell them we got an earlier flight from somewhere else." A shrug. "No biggie."

"Stop being difficult and listen to me."

I mouth a *fine* and shrink into my seat, and he continues. "I need to do something. I'll drop you at a hotel."

My eyes widen as I unclip the belt from around my waist. "You visit your dad as soon as we're supposed to be landing. You're not a robot, Kade. You have to sleep."

He dismissively waves me off.

I get to my feet when Barry says we're good to go. He opens the door and lowers the steps, smiling at me, but drops his gaze as soon as Kade looks at him.

"I'll send you all the details," he tells Barry. "Stay close." Then he glances at me. "And stop smiling at her."

"Sorry, sir," he replies, his cheeks going red.

I glower at him. "Stop acting like that."

Kade raises a brow and turns me towards the steps, then follows me down. "Like what? Barry has been my right-hand man long enough to know not to piss me off."

My heart jolts in my chest, because does he mean Barry looking at me pissed him off?

"How does he know who I am?"

Kade lights a cigarette, apparently deaf, then hands our suitcases to a man in a suit and thanks him.

It's dark and a little chilly in the rain, but nothing like Scotland.

Kade offers me his jacket again, which I gladly accept, trying not to inhale too deeply as he shrugs it onto my shoulders.

For someone who claims to despise me, his actions are the complete opposite.

A man nods to Kade and hands him a set of keys.

My eyes widen. "No way," I blurt. "A Bentley..." I study the mirror-like alloys, gun-metal grey paint and the black-and-white interior. "A sporty Bentley?"

"It's a Bentley Continental GT," he says, bored.

"Were there no normal cars left to rent?"

"It's not a rental."

My eyes widen even more. "What exactly do you do for money?"

This aggravates him. "Shut up and get in."

The first two hours of driving with Kade's playlist are relaxing, to say the least. The seats are comfortable and heated. The car drives smoothly as "Digital Bath" by Deftones plays. I absently watch him, the way he turns the wheel with his palm heel, grips it as he speeds, his elbow resting between us while he smokes.

He stops to get us food, a bottle of water for me and an energy drink for himself. I fall asleep near the end and only wake when he pulls into the car park of an old warehouse.

"Where are we?" I ask, rubbing my dazed eyes with my knuckles. My mascara must be a riot. "Is this the hotel?"

"No. I need to do something then I'll take you. This was on the way. Just stay here," he tells me. "Keep the doors locked, and don't you fucking dare follow me."

My chest tightens with instant anxiety. "Where are we?"

"I have business to deal with. Just lie in the back seat. No one will see you."

There's a knock on my window. I flinch and look to see a man with a brow piercing and a tattoo of a gun down the side of his face. He's missing nearly all his front teeth to devastating and disgusting decay. He wears a denim coat with badges all over it.

Stay quiet, Kade mouths to me as he rolls down his window.

The man stands tall and walks to Kade's side, where he's joined by a second guy. "Mr Mitchell. Welcome back." He taps the other man's shoulder. "They call him Nāve in other countries, because he is a man of no heart. Deadly, merciless and always finishes the job."

Kade rubs a hand down his face in annoyance. "Sure."

Huh?

"We weren't expecting you until tomorrow."

I haven't the slightest clue what the hell is happening.

He waves to someone behind him, and the warehouse doors open to reveal more people. They look like a biker gang.

"I see you brought a different whore this time. Where is the blonde you brought before?"

Um, excuse me? Whore?

Kade doesn't bother with a response. "Let's get this over with," he says, then turns to me. "Stay here."

"And risk all the scavengers getting her?" The man bellows a laugh, his hand slapping the top of the car. "Don't be ridiculous. The more the merrier." Toothless turns his back to us and waves to his friends. "Nāve is here. Let Crawley know."

Four others appear by the car, and Kade groans. "Fuck's sake. Stay behind me," he warns. "Don't speak to any of them. Don't look them in the eye. Keep your head down. Got it?"

I gulp. "You're scaring me."

"Good," he retorts. "You don't fuck with these guys. I should've dropped you off at a hotel."

"You still can." The panic in my voice is obvious, my heart racing. I don't want to go inside, not with all these people who look like they'd put a blade in my back without hesitation. "Please take me to a hotel, Kade. *Please.*"

He turns the car off, his window sliding up. "They'll follow me there and have someone watch you. Just stay behind me and don't speak a word. I don't have time to have my team come for you."

Kade gets out first and comes to my side, opening the door then leaning in to open the glovebox.

I gasp, covering my mouth. "Why do you have a gun? I thought you were joking when you said you had one!"

His tanned skin and abs show as he pulls up the hem of his top and tucks the deadly weapon into his waistband.

"Do you even know how to use that?" I ask quietly.

He gives me a look as he unclips my belt, and I feel cold metal on my leg as he slides a blade up my outer thigh and tucks the handle into the side of my underwear. His voice is low, and even though I'm scared, my pulse is racing from the touch of his hand on me. "A precaution."

"Kade. Really. I'm scared," I admit slowly as his palm slips from my thigh, and he wipes a tear from my cheek. "Do you know these people?"

He offers me his hand and helps me out of the car. "Yes. Stop asking questions."

I instantly regret wearing a short dress, but at least it's long enough to conceal the small blade trapped under the waistband of my panties.

He drapes his jacket around me once more, and I clutch his arm as we walk towards the warehouse. More men appear as we go in, and I wish I waited for the commercial flight.

I'm uncomfortable as dozens of eyes watch me walk down metal steps barely lit by flickering lights.

Cameras follow our actions, and the frigid air creeps over my skin.

"I don't like this," I whisper to Kade. "Can I please go sit in the car?"

We get in an elevator, and someone stands behind me, far too close for comfort.

Kade glares at the man and yanks me in front of him, my back to his chest, and snakes an arm around my waist. "Stay calm." A murmur against my ear that doesn't settle the rapid palpitations of my heart. "If they see you're afraid, they'll feed on it."

I manage a nod. Having his arm around me doesn't shoot zaps of pleasure to my core as it should, but it feels good. Safe. I want to stay here forever – his breath hitting my neck, lacing our fingers, his body cocooning around me as the elevator descends – even though I know he's just pretending I'm his whore and safeguarding me.

"Breathe, Freckles," he whispers. "You're safe with me."

The gun tucked into his waistband is digging into my back, the blunt side of the blade is pressing into my thigh, and I'm terrified as I shake in his hold.

I've been in places like this before with Chris, but there were never weapons or a threat to life. Booze, drugs and sex. Pain, forced kisses and paid pleasure.

I thought those parties were the den of Satan; I didn't know there was a place deeper than the pits of hell.

There's a foul stench when we reach the bottom. More gang members are standing around a table when we enter a room full of boxes and overhead lamps. Illegal plants. White powder. Pills. A glass screen that looks onto a lone chair in the middle of an interrogation room.

Fear claws at my bones, seeping into my blood and threatening to stop my organs.

"*Nāve,*" one of the gang members says. He has a long white beard and gold teeth. His hands rest on the table between us, where a brown envelope with Kade's nickname on it sits. "We didn't expect to see you until tomorrow."

"I'm aware, Crawley."

I'm standing behind him again, my arms crossed as I stare at the ground.

"I'm here for the contract and fifty."

"Only fifty? The last time you wanted three hundred."

"Fifty," Kade says again. "Put it into a suitcase."

My skin crawls as two guys smelling like beer come up beside me.

"Is your whore here as entertainment?" one says as the other hums and adds, "I'd have a piece of this."

I yelp as he slaps my ass.

"I—"

His words are cut off as Kade's arm snaps out, his elbow slamming into the nose of the guy closest to me, breaking it in a bloody crack. His gun is pointed at the other one, and he seems unbothered by the multiple weapons now aimed at him.

"Touch her again and I'll blow your fucking head off."

Oh God. We're going to die.

Kade doesn't blink, doesn't lower his gun.

I rest my hand on his back. "Please..."

Please stop. Why are we here? Why do you have a gun? Where is the Kade I grew up with?

"We've heard the stories about you. I'm not afraid of you. I'll take your whore off your dirty hands, and you'll never see her again."

Kade sighs, as if this isn't traumatic or terrifying in the slightest. "Last chance." His voice is clipped. "Back off."

He laughs before baring his teeth. "Or what? I'm one of five leaders here, and I—"

Kade pulls the trigger.

I jump with a strangled gasp as the blast rings in my ears. The man's body falls to the ground, lifeless – dead – while red trickles from the hole between his eyes.

My palm crushes to my mouth to muffle my scream, bile rising in my throat.

Unfazed, Kade tucks his gun into his waistband. "None of you will lay a finger on her – are we clear?"

Dark and intimidating, his tone feels like an arrow glazed in ice shooting through my chest, poisoning me with liquid fear.

"You want my business, none of you will touch her, look at her or even acknowledge her presence."

To my surprise, they all agree and lower their weapons with hands raised in surrender, and I stay in shock as they continue their business. The man's blood puddles on the floor at my feet, and I try not to vomit.

If I run, I have nowhere to go.

I grip Kade's left arm tighter as they discuss drugs, weights of bags they pack into a suitcase, and a contract that should apparently be *easy* for Kade, considering his experience.

My eyes burn, but I struggle not to look at the dead man next to me.

18

KADE

FLASHBACK 3

I haven't seen Stacey in three days, and I'm debating asking my sister for her number.

It would be way easier if I had it. Or… she'd ignore me and say it was a mistake and that I forced her to kiss me.

Wait. Did I force her? Technically, I barricaded her against the kitchen counter and dared her to kiss me again. Oh shit. That's not good. Maybe I should apologise? Would she even hear me out?

Dad told me a few nights ago to chill out, because I kept thinking I imagined the kiss. He told me to take a deep breath and name three things I could see, two things I could touch and one thing I could smell. It worked. My lungs filled again, and my blurry vision lessened.

Then he told me to get out of my head and speak to her.

Safe to say I'm still in my head.

Nicotine infiltrates my lungs as I watch the water of the loch rippling, the small boat rocking side to side against the wooden pier, the soft glow from the lights illuminating the outdoor pool.

I still find it ridiculous that we live in Scotland – where it rains almost every day and we get a week of summer a year, if we're lucky – and have an outdoor pool. I've been in it four times, and each one resulted in shrivelled balls and left me close to catching fucking pneumonia.

Luciella and her friends are in it a lot. Not that I intentionally stand exactly where I am now and stare at a certain black-haired beauty for hours on end. Base sat with me once, and I was in my head again, thinking he was looking at her too.

Regardless, he can't have Stacey. I've claimed her and no one else can have her but me.

Kind of. I think. Probably not, but I'd like to.

Wait. How does one claim a person?

If I spoke these thoughts aloud, she'd flee the country and I'd be locked up with Dad. And I can't have that, because I need to kiss her again. Or speak to her. Or have her attention for longer than one minute while my virgin hands shake.

The hard-on I keep getting every time I think back to that moment in the kitchen is becoming a biological hazard.

I pull out my phone and see Luciella has posted a picture of our main sitting area with the TV, captioned movie night *with Stacey, my mum and Ewan.*

The cigarette nearly drops from between my fingers.

She's down there.

Knowing she's down there has me quickly showering, brushing my teeth and shoving on a pair of boxers and sweats. I don't bother putting on a top – the manor is roasting.

Before I can leave my room, I halt in my steps, blow out a breath and run my hands through my hair before pulling my phone out.

I open my messages with Jason.

Me: She's here. What should I do?

Jason: Giana said to be cool and pretend nothing happened.

I frown. That sounds like the worst advice ever.

Me: Why?

Jason: Who the fuck knows. She winked when I asked. Just chill and don't stab her like your dad did to Aria.

Rolling my eyes, I chew my lip to suppress a laugh while firing back a response.

Me: He didn't stab her; his friend did, dick. One day, when my dad comes for you and your dad, I'll stand back and watch.

Jason: Haha! Now fuck off and don't embarrass yourself. Good luck. You need it with those looks.

Asshole.

I stuff the phone into my pocket, spray on some aftershave and head downstairs. I try not to look at Stacey; she's sitting on the sofa in a little red dress and fluffy bed socks.

"You're coming this time, right?" Luciella asks her.

"Can't."

"Why?"

She shrugs. "I just can't."

I sit on the one-seater between the two main sofas, one of which is taken up by my sister and Stacey, the other by Ewan and my mum.

Pausing the TV, Mum asks, "What are we watching?"

"Is The Greatest Showman *there?" I ask.*

Luciella groans. "We've watched that, like, a thousand times!"

I huff. "It's a good movie."

"What's it about?" Stacey asks, and every drop of blood in my body turns to ice when she looks directly at me.

"Some money-hungry dude and a musical," my sister thankfully answers. "He cheats on his wife and still gets a happy ending. Bullshit."

Mum's mouth drops open. "Language!"

I snort and shake my head. "It's a good movie."

My sister lifts the remote. "I'm in the mood for a horror."

The lights dim, and the movie starts, but all I keep thinking is that I should've beaten my sister to answer Stacey.

I would have given a better fucking description. Nevertheless, I'm intrigued enough to stay down here instead of escaping to my room.

The movie has been on for at least an hour, and I haven't paid any attention to it.

Luciella keeps screaming and jumping out of her skin; Ewan looks like he's ready to fall asleep.

A chill wracks my body, but I can't be fucked going to get a top. I grab a blanket from the basket near the sofa instead.

"Kade, sweetheart, can you share that with Stacey?" my mum asks. "She looks cold."

There's a space beside her, Luciella on her other side, but I'd rather stick pins in my eyes than take it.

Kissing her is fine. Sharing a blanket sounds like a fucking nightmare. I'm nervous about being in her vicinity as it is. I'll have an arterial rupture if I get any closer.

I get up from my comfortable seat and sit beside her, offering her half of the blanket.

It only takes my family ten minutes to decide they need to leave the room. Ewan and Mum for food, and Luciella to talk to our dad on the phone.

Leaving me with Stacey. Alone. Sharing a damn blanket.

Shoot me.

"This movie is terrible," Stacey says, crossing her arms. "I don't know how people enjoy being terrified every two seconds."

I gulp. "Yeah."

"I'd rather watch the film you mentioned – The Great Man?*"*

*Smirking, I rest my elbow on the arm of the couch. "*The Greatest Showman,*" I correct. "You were close."*

She chews her lip, and my eyes drop to her mouth. "Do you think they'll notice if we change it to that?"

"Luciella would notice if we fast-forwarded it by five seconds."

"Hmm. True."

Our eyes clash, and the insatiable desire to wrap my hand around her ponytail and yank her to me increases with each passing moment. I could look at her forever – the different shades of light green looking back at me; the way her pupils dilate as I absently reach my hand forward, twirling a dark strand around my finger.

"Why did you let me kiss you?" I ask, remembering her mouth on mine in the kitchen a few days ago. "I teased you for years. You should have slapped me."

Stacey blushes. "I, um, I wanted to."

The hair springs free from around my finger. "Slap me?"

Fidgeting with the edge of the blanket, Stacey sighs. Her tone is like a caress on my cheek. "Are you playing a game here? Make the girl want you only to toss her to the ground so you can get praised?"

"How can I get praised if no one knows I kissed you again?"

"You know what I mean."

I hum. "Can't say I do."

The door handle jiggles. I twist my body to look behind the couch to the door as Mum pops in to say she's making pizza. I nod, running my hand through my hair as the door closes again. The movement causes the blanket to shift.

No, it's not the movement. It's Stacey knocking it away to climb on top of me, settling on my lap with her thighs bracketing my hips. "If you meant it, then..." She grabs my face to look at her, at the neediness in her forest-green eyes. "Kiss me again."

Frozen. Completely and utterly frozen, all I can do is gulp down the building lump in my throat that's threatening to suffocate me.

I want to kiss her. Fuck, do I want to. But being caught off guard makes me uneasy. I have no time to think it through or plan how to touch her or what to say. I always want to be in control, so having her like this has knocked me off my axis.

Having her touching me without preparing myself has my blood roaring in my ears.

My heart races to an unbearable pace, my hands fisting at my sides. I want to snatch her hips and pull her closer. I want to taste her mouth and hear her whimper. I want to feel her body all over me.

But something is stopping me from moving.

Sensing my anxiety from the sudden change in the atmosphere, Stacey's brows furrow before realisation hits, and she rises to her knees above me.

I'm staring at her like she has two heads while mine takes far too long to process our position. A beautiful girl is straddling me and all I can do is sit here like a wide-eyed statue.

Why the fuck do I need to be so weird? Why can't I be normal and not panic and freeze and fuck this all up?

She lets go of my face, and some of the bad friction alleviates from my chest.

"I... Oh God. I'm such an idiot."

Her face is red as a strawberry as she tries to get off me. Embarrassed. My hands move without me thinking, and I grab her hips and bring her back to sit in my lap.

"Don't." One word, my voice thick and pleading. "Don't."

"What do you want me to do?"

"Be patient with me," is all I say before I capture her lips with mine.

Our mouths melt together, and most of my worries fade away as she drapes her arms around my shoulders and kisses me back. It's a little overwhelming, but I can handle it.

I slip my tongue past her lips, and she opens for me just as a groan leaves my throat. Taking from me what she wants, Stacey slants her head to deepen the kiss, until my fingers are digging into the material at her waist. The visceral need to touch her naked skin is unbearable. I want to tear her fucking dress off and lick and bite every inch of her.

It's a ridiculous urge, considering my experience is sitting at a solid zero and I'd probably get stage fright.

She takes my bottom lip between her teeth, and I hiss. She sucks on it, licks, and then forces my head to the side to trail her wet mouth down my throat.

My cock hardens until it's painful, and my sweats do nothing to conceal it.

Nearly settled between her legs, my dick begs to be released from its restraints, but that'll only scare her off. Like me, she hadn't kissed anyone before, so I imagine her virginity status is the same as mine.

My teeth clench as she devours my neck, her hands travelling down my naked chest and back up to curl around my shoulders. I can tell she's tracing the ink down my left arm, and it causes shivers to course through me. Testing where she can touch without me tensing, she explores me while her mouth moves over mine.

She takes my hands, pulling them off her waist. I frown, and slowly, she places my palms just above her naked knees. "Is this okay?" she asks me, dragging them up and up, slipping under the material of her dress. "Or is it too much?"

I almost smile. She gets me, understands why I need to go slow. "Yeah."

"Tell me if it gets too much, okay?"

A deep sound vibrates in my chest, and I nudge her nose with mine and peck her lips.

And then she's kissing me again while I massage my way up to her hips then trace the fabric of her underwear. Lace. Probably white and innocent.

My breath hitches as she lets out a whimper from my touch, and she delves her tongue into my mouth while fisting both hands in my hair. She tugs, and I tighten my hold on her hips, dying to drag her forward to grind against me.

Too soon. Far too soon.

"I took your number from Lu's phone," she says into my mouth, drawing my tongue between her lips and sucking hard. "If I message you, will you respond?"

I grin, my hands moving of their own accord to grab her ass. Which is belting, by the way. All those dances and aerial sports she does definitely pay off.

If I bring her forward a little more, she'll feel my dick and how solid it is for her, and I'm not sure either of us is ready for that.

"I guess you'll need to find out for yourself." She whimpers as I nibble her jaw. "Sneaky little Freckles, stealing my number from her best friend's phone."

She giggles, and I feel every muscle in my body go warm and taut with how fucking much I want to hear her giggle again.

I flip us, and I settle on top, one hand next to her head, holding myself up. My mouth is on hers once more, our tongues sliding together as my hand goes from her hip to her hair then back to her hip, tasting and licking and biting until we're breathless.

She parts her legs, and my annoying nerves start to kick in again.

I'm solid. My dick hurts. My balls are tight, and our kisses are growing more demanding, more intimate as her ankles hook behind my legs, digging her nails into my back to bring me closer.

Anyone could walk in right now and see me on top of Stacey.

Regardless of this, of the heaviness on my chest that only worsens by the second, I bunch her dress at her hip and dip my hand under her arched back to get a good grip on her ass.

Absentmindedly, as my tongue tastes hers, my hips rock, and the length of my cock grinds between her legs at the same time as I drag her against me. As much as I have to fight the urge to grit my teeth with the tingling sensation at the head of my dick and in my balls, my mind catches up with me, and I freeze.

My mouth pulls away first, then my hands leave her body, shock rushing through me.

With widening eyes, I stare at her. At the blush on her face. "Sorry," I force out, my heart fucking pounding in my chest, before I move away from her.

"Sorry," I say again, swallowing deeply and moving back into my original position while she slowly sits and wipes her mouth. "That's not what I was trying to—" I stop as the door opens, the blanket already thrown over us.

Ewan walks in first with pizza, and thank God I pulled away in time, or he would've got a full view of me pinning Luciella's best friend to the sofa and dry-humping her. Mum comes in next with two bowls of food, Luciella trailing behind with a tray of drinks.

I glance at Stacey. She's chewing her thumbnail, her eyes trained on the paused screen, a blush still creeping up from her neck to her cheeks.

We both control our breathing as Luciella tells me Dad is calling me tomorrow, and that she's forgotten what was even happening in the movie. It restarts to reveal the girl is screaming for her life.

I can taste Stacey on my lips, raw from her biting and sucking them. The heat that radiates between us is still there, and it only amplifies when my fingers touch hers, and she takes my hand under the blanket.

In any other circumstance, I'd pull away from that sort of physical touch and picture the person in a million pieces. I'd get pains in my hands. But with Stacey, I return the sentiment by lacing our fingers.

Me. Kade Mitchell, at the age of eighteen, *holds hands with a girl for the first time.*

And I like it.

When the movie ends, and we need to let go, I head to my bed, finding a message from an unknown number.

Unknown: I know you weren't trying to… you know. We both got carried away. It's okay. Don't overthink it.

Unknown: And I want to watch the *Great Man* movie with you.

I chuckle, save her number and type a reply.

Me: Not if you keep getting the title wrong. There's only so much disrespect I'll put up with for that masterpiece.

Freckles: *The Greatest Showman*! But yeah, I want to watch it with you. You can say no. I don't want you to feel like you HAVE to.

Me: Do I really have a choice?

Freckles: Of course not. I'm staying here on Wednesday after practice. Will you be home?

No girl has ever been in my room, unless I count my mum when she shouts at me. Dez, Base, Jason and Ewan, but no one else. I like having my own space, but something about having Stacey here feels… I don't know.

Me: Come to my room when Luciella falls asleep. If you get the title wrong once more, I'll kick you out and tell my sister her friend is a shit kisser.

Freckles: YOU WILL NOT!

Me: See you on Wednesday, Freckles.

19

STACEY

My feet carry me unconsciously out the warehouse, too in shock to stop.

Kade says my name, but I can't stop or speak or even breathe. I wrench the knife from my underwear and toss it on the ground. All I can see is the red footprints from my shoes on the warehouse floor.

"Stacey."

I bypass the car, aiming for the front gates and repeatedly telling myself that it'll be okay. The only thing I need to do is get a ride to the hotel and find Lu's room, where I'll be safe. I just need to get away from all his chaos and danger.

I need to get away from the man I once knew as a nervous teenager – the man who just shot someone in the head like it was nothing.

"Stacey."

The gate slides open as I approach it, but Kade wraps his hand around my arm and spins me to face him before I reach it. "Keep your mouth shut about this."

I clench my teeth hard enough to hurt. "Fuck you."

I yank free of his hold, but he steps in front of me.

"Be mad at me all you want – I don't care. But you can't speak a word of this to my sister."

"I want to get away from you. I won't say anything, but this is fucked up." I cover my mouth to stop the sob. "You murdered him!"

Kade blinks once, unfazed as he flips the blade in his hand without breaking eye contact. "Shit happens."

I have no way to respond to that. My body is still shivering, my heart is still rattling in my chest and I have a headache. Blood is splattered on my dress and stains my skin. If I don't wash it off soon, I might bring up everything I've eaten in the last twenty-four hours.

"I'll take you to a hotel. We can go meet everyone later."

"I'll get an Uber," I answer. "I'm not going anywhere with you."

He sighs. "Come on, Freckles."

"No! You don't get to call me that!" The tension in my head gets worse. "You killed someone!" I cry. "What happened to you?"

"Let me take you to a hotel – you're covered in blood."

"*What happened to you?*" I hold my ground, my vision blurring. "I have no idea who you are. You aren't the Kade I fell in love with."

He nods and lowers his head. "I suppose I'm not."

I'm certain I'm pale.

Kade looks up, takes a careful step towards me and tries to move strands of hair – now sticky with blood – from my face, but I flinch from his touch.

His hand freezes, then he drops it to his side. "You're afraid of me."

I avert my eyes.

"You are aware that you're the only person in the world I'd never hurt, right?"

"If that was the case, then you wouldn't have walked out of my life when I needed you the most." I shake my head. "You already did hurt me."

"We aren't doing this," he says, exhaling and putting his hands in his pockets. "I shouldn't even be speaking to you."

I laugh sarcastically. "Oh yeah, that was definitely the case a few hours ago, wasn't it?"

"You know what I mean."

"No. I don't know what you mean. What happened to the guy who despised when his friends took drugs? Now you're buying fifty grand's worth, you apparently have whores and you *kill people*?"

His jaw clenches. "This has nothing to do with you. Stay in your goddamn lane and drop it, alright?"

"I can't..." I turn my back to him. "I can't drop it. They knew who you were and asked why you didn't have your other whore with you. You... You didn't need to shoot him."

Kade sniffs, the sound of his lighter flicking before I smell the exhaled cloud from his joint. "I can assure you he won't be the last person I shoot."

Understanding his words is difficult. I once fell in love with him. He was the pain-in-the-ass brother of my best friend who liked to tease me, but it was harmless and fun, and I would do anything to go back to that.

Oh how differently I would do things if I could go back. No lies. No secrets. No holding back on telling everyone we were together.

I try to walk away again, but Kade grabs my wrist. "You're being dramatic. Not here. Get in the fucking car."

I tug out of his grip and turn, but I only get two steps before he swears under his breath, snatches me off my feet and throws me over his shoulder.

The world turns upside down, and I gasp as I beat my fists into his back and kick my legs. "Put me down, you asshole!"

My thrashing around does nothing given the muscles he has.

"I don't have time for your bullshit, Stacey."

"That's a lovely name," a voice says, and Kade stops walking.

I try to see who Kade is looking at, but I'm stuck staring at his ass.

"I'll have to ask your boss how much she costs. When is your time up with her?"

"Step out of the way, Crawley."

I grip the material of Kade's top at his back, frozen in fear as two more guys appear at our side.

"*Dvigatsya,*" Kade says, and I frown at the language I had no idea he spoke. His tone lowers. "*Ona ne prodayetsya.*"

The man chuckles deeply. "*Ona seichas.*"

"Stacey," another one says, chuckling as he leans down to my eye level and grins at me. "I'd pay a pretty penny for you."

One of Kade's arms vanishes from around my legs, though he still keeps me secure over his shoulder, and I hear a gun cocking. "Don't make me tell you again. Step out of the way."

The man looking at me stands up, then he's out of sight.

"Relax," Crawley says, back to English. "We come in peace. We're just curious about your little raven here."

Kade tightens his grip around my legs. "Get out of my way or I'll put a bullet between your eyes."

I groan and cover my ears, waiting for the bang. My dress is somehow still hiding my ass – maybe thanks to the way Kade has positioned his arm.

I hear footsteps on the gravel, and Crawley, the old leader, is watching me as Kade makes his way to the car with the gun at his side, finger still on the trigger.

I'm tossed off his shoulder, my back pressing to the cold metal of the car as he opens the passenger-side door.

"Stop looking at them," he hisses. "Hey…" He tips my chin. "Eyes on me. Calm down. You're breathing too fast, and I can't be fucked with you passing out."

I had no idea I was panicking until now, until the words hit my ears, and I realise my heart is racing to an unsettling pace, my eyes burning.

I don't remember getting into the car or clipping my seat belt on. I think he did it.

Another door slams, and the engine turns on, rumbling beneath me. He reverses out of the area like he's being chased, and I need to grab hold of the dashboard, only narrowly avoiding whiplash, as he swerves the car to the left and accelerates down the road.

"Tell me three of your favourite things."

I glance at Kade. "W-What?"

"Three favourite things. Go."

I focus on my breaths. "Dancing."

"Keep going," he pushes as he veers around a corner, not looking at me.

"*The Greatest Showman.*"

He pauses. "Another."

"The..." I breathe out a breath. "The dogs. Milo and Hopper. I miss them."

Kade accelerates again, pushing my back to the seat, and I realise his questions have distracted me – I'm now breathing properly again.

A few minutes pass, the car still speeding along, and I eventually sit back on the seat and cross my arms.

He slows down, then stops at a set of traffic lights. "You should've got into the car when I told you to the first time. Now they know your name."

I don't reply – I just stare out the window.

The lights from shops and lampposts merge into one blazing colour. My eyes sting, but I keep staring out the window, unable to take in anything he's saying.

He's not happy. He's complaining, but I ignore him, which pisses him off even more.

I'm not sure what he was expecting, taking me into a building full of people like that.

The sun is rising in the distance, but as beautiful as the orange and yellow hues are, I can't focus. I try to close my eyes and sleep.

My hands are still trembling, and I keep seeing the man's body dropping to the ground every time I close my eyes. I hear the sound the gun made when he pulled the trigger and feel the way my heart stopped when I witnessed someone being murdered. I remember the way Crawley and his men looked at me – Kade's whore.

I've witnessed Chris beating the shit out of people, watched illegal cage fights and people being bottled and stabbed to injure. But not death. Not murder.

Kade could get arrested and jailed for a long, long time.

"Get out of your head."

Screw you.

We arrive at the hotel. He takes our bags to reception and asks for a room.

"Two rooms."

His striking silvery-blue eyes are on me, but I block him out. I need space, and the last thing I need is to be around Kade when part of me fears him.

"Two?" the lady repeats, watching Kade. Thankfully she hasn't noticed the blood on my face.

A nod, and he sighs. "Yeah."

He pays for both rooms then thanks the woman. The elevator takes a few moments to arrive, and he scans a card to take us to the eleventh floor.

My room is across from his. He unlocks my door, and I push it open and head inside. He follows me, setting my bag and suitcase next to the bed.

"I have work to do," he says. "Will you be okay?"

No. "Yes," I reply, keeping my eyes on the red carpet. It's almost the same colour as the blood that puddled at my feet. "Please leave. I'll get an Uber to Luciella later."

"Look at me."

I shake my head.

Kade stands in the doorway, tapping the top of the frame. I flinch as he goes to step forward, and he freezes.

"Don't be afraid of me, Freckles. Sometimes people need to change to survive."

I stare at my fingers, twisting them together. "What language was that you spoke?"

He runs his thumb across the seam of his lips, a freshly rolled joint at the back of his ear. "Russian."

I nod, unable to ask anything else.

He waits a long minute before he leaves, the door closing with a delicate click. I don't hear him opening his own room door, but I do hear his footfalls growing quieter as I head to the bathroom and fill the sink.

Washing the blood off my face takes a few minutes. Then I tug my dress from my shaken body and stare at my exhausted, distraught reflection.

There's no light in my eyes, only tears for the boy I once knew.

I wash in the sink again, but it's not enough. I feel dirty.

Showering does nothing to warm the chill in my spine. Neither does wrapping myself in a blanket and watching the sun move across the sky.

A few hours later, I hear sirens. Are the police on their way to arrest Kade?

My lip trembles again, and I get annoyed with myself for being so weak. I handed that boy my heart when I was a teen, and even now, years later, he still holds it. But this time, he's crushing it with vengeance, for things out of my control.

I wasn't lying when I said that what happened wasn't my fault. I had no idea what I was doing or what goddamn reality I was in. All I knew was that I'd never felt that level of panic before. I'd just wanted my boyfriend and only found out the following morning that I wasn't in my boyfriend's bed.

I've no idea what happened to him since we split up, but I'm not sure the Kade I fell for still exists.

I curl into the bed and attempt to relax my thoughts. It takes me nearly four hours to feel less on the verge of a breakdown. When I do, I pull my phone out of my leather backpack and turn it on.

My notifications go wild. Most are from an unknown number – Chris on a burner.

In one text he describes in alarming detail what he's going to do to me when I get home, but instead of feeling fear, I swipe and delete the chain then block the number.

Kyle tells me to have a safe flight.

Lu informs me she is never surviving this trip with Base. They went out last night for drinks with her mum and Ewan. Base had a threesome in the room beside hers then asked if she wanted to join in.

I'm tagged in a few videos and pictures from the studio. My girls are practising for the competition coming up soon. A few others are pole and hoop stunts, stretches and dance moves.

Once I respond to some of my students, my phone beeps with illegible messages from Kade.

***Kade**: Stcy Awke?*

***Kade**: Goooodnghjt freecks.*

20

KADE

"How many do you think are inside?"

Barry sits beside me in the car, which is parked across from the building Stacey and I left two hours ago. Three SUVs are parked up too, keeping an eye on the surroundings as I strap the ammo belt around my waist and fill each compartment with magazines and daggers.

I look over and tilt my head from side to side as I contemplate my answer. "Maybe fifty."

"Easy then," he says in his Geordie accent.

I huff a laugh at his sarcasm. "They're all armed, so probably not."

"Are you sure they know her name?"

"Do you not listen?" I snap, scowling at him. "I've gone over the exact conversation five times."

"I just find it a little dramatic to be doing this over a name."

"You've been working for me for over a year and you think *this* is dramatic?"

He grimaces. "There was that time you tried to burn someone's house down. For the same girl, may I add. Is this not a step too far?"

I stop loading my belt and pinch the bridge of my nose. "If they tell Bernadette her name, she'll track Stacey and then probably manage to dig up our past. I don't want to imagine the shit she'd do to her to make me more compliant."

Barry knows everything. I had to tell him, or he would've thought I was just stalking some innocent girl. He sends reports to me when I haven't the time to watch her. He thinks, as a twenty-one-year-old, I should find another obsession that doesn't drive me to murder.

Am I extreme? Yes. But for my own fucking sanity, I need to know what she's doing. Is that weird? To hate her yet need to know what she's doing? Even though she's a snake?

A snake who still belongs to me.

"You plan on killing an entire gang for a girl who apparently cheated on you?"

I grit my teeth and try not to smash his face in. "Yes," I reply as I throw open the door. "Did you manage to find out who called her back at the hotel?"

"No. The phone has a fucking steel barrier around it."

"Keep digging."

Barry doesn't respond as he, too, gets out of the car and checks his ammo belt, hidden under his suit. I made him wear the same one as me, since the material takes most of the power from gunshots.

Fifteen guys follow us, but I have three more on standby and a sniper on the roof of the building across from the warehouse. Heavy-metal music plays from inside as we hack the gate.

Our steps are silent in the warehouse, our guns aimed as we take the stairs. I send some guys left, another group right, and Barry and three others follow me.

"Clear," someone says through my earpiece as another says, "One down."

I keep my gun raised, aiming forward as I side-step from a

corner, the silencer muffling the shot I take. The bullet sinks into the man's skull, killing him instantly. Four more go down, and we stick explosives to the walls.

Bernadette sent me to Russia for intense training with their armed forces, a group of soldiers working under her pay who didn't hold back on torturing me while I learned how to fight, shoot, stab and resist interrogation tactics.

Barry stands beside me as I put away my gun and grab two blades, fisting the handles and signalling for my team to follow me.

I shove a knife under someone's chin, ripping his jaw clean off, then stab him in the eye while covering his mangled mouth with my palm.

"Go to sleep," I whisper in his ear as I yank the blade from his eye and slice it across his throat.

His body drops at my feet, and I step over it as I wipe my knife on his denim vest.

"The leaders will be in the basement," I say to Barry. "Leave Crawley for me."

As the elevator lowers, the rest of my team take the stairs down. I check my pistol is loaded then flip a blade in my hand while I wait. It was only hours ago I was in this shaft with Stacey, holding her in my arms to try to calm her down.

Now I'm covered in blood, adrenaline in my veins like a kid at Christmas Eve.

As soon as the elevator reaches the bottom, the sliding metal doors creak open, and gunshots are fired from both sides. The impact of a bullet hitting my armoured vest throws me into a wall, the searing pain stealing my breath away.

Before the dickhead can finish me off, I launch a blade at his face, and Barry breaks his neck.

We set a few more explosives as we run through the basement, shooting anyone and everyone. I dodge an axe coming straight for my chest.

Through my earpiece, one of my guys says, "Fuller is injured."

I swear to myself and head towards them to find Fuller with a bullet wound in his chest.

"Keep pressure on it." I point to one of my newest members.

"Take him to our medic. Do *not* go to the hospital."

He agrees and heads off as Barry and three others stay on my left. We dodge and shoot, killing at least twenty gang members before we plant the last explosive.

The heavy-metal music is still playing, and as I load my gun, I absently nod along and whistle to the tune.

I grin at Barry like a crazy person. "Ready?"

"You're insane – do you know that?"

"Yep."

Blood stains my face, and Barry is almost unrecognisable under the crimson splatters on his. I signal for everyone to follow us out, and once the elevator has taken us back up – the metal doors barely stopping the bullets from penetrating them – I cut the power.

A fist flies at me from behind, the burn on my cheek welcoming through all the adrenaline pumping in my veins.

Crawley limps to the side and grabs hold of the wall, evidently trying to flee the place and leave his men behind. I order my team to lower their aim.

"Sir?"

I look at Barry. "Leave. All of you."

My assistant lingers for a second too long before he tells everyone to get back to their vehicles.

I sigh and pull the joint from behind my ear, amazed that it managed to survive the gunfight. "Thinking you could hit me and get away with it was an error, but your worst mistake was looking in her direction."

Crawley scoffs as he clutches at his thigh, blood seeping between his fingers. "Your whore?"

My jaw strains as I stare at him, my patience worn to the point of snapping. "She is not my whore." I light my smoke and inhale, hoping it'll calm my temper, because I'm not in the mood to torture this guy. "Have you been in contact with my boss since I left?"

"Why would I have contacted Mrs Sawyer?" he asks, confused as he grips his wounded leg tighter and stumbles into the wall, sliding down it until he's on his ass. "Was the girl her daughter?"

I grimace and exhale. "No. Cassie is even more insufferable."

"Is that why you are here? Because of your whore?" He laughs.

"Sharing is caring, Nāve."

I roll my eyes. "Stop calling me that. My name..." I grab his jaw in a painful grip that has him thrashing. I press the bright, hot end of my smoke to his cheek as I say, "My name is not fucking Nāve."

He yells as his skin burns beneath the ember, tears filling his eyes.

I let go, reach behind me to grab one of the blades in my ammo belt and bring it between us. "My name is Kade. Kade Mitchell. Son of Tobias. Maybe I should carve it into your skin? Will you still call me *Nāve* then?"

"F-Fuck you."

I knock his hand away as he tries to punch me, weak and slowly dying from blood loss. He must've been shot.

Instead of giving him a quick end by putting a bullet between his eyes, I carve each letter of my first name into his sweaty forehead in block capitals until he has spittle dripping down his chin, unmovable, nearly unconscious.

"There," I say, admiring the four crimson letters with a smile. "Now you'll never forget who I am."

"You *are* Death," he says in a low, slurred mumble. "Your time will come. You and your whore."

I throw my hands out to the side, exasperated. "She's not my fucking whore." I lean my elbows on my knees. "In fact, she isn't a whore at all. She's the girl I watch, the girl I obsess over until I feel like I'm going fucking insane. I gave her my heart when I was a teenager, and do you know what she did? She *shattered* it. She's a venomous snake. Wait. Do you understand a word I'm saying, Crawley?"

He's fading, not listening anymore.

The light leaves his eyes, and I roll mine and drag the sharp side of my blade across his throat to make sure he's actually dead. Blood pours from his neck and drenches my hand. I massage the warm liquid between my thumb and fingers before I stand.

Stacey would look wonderful covered in blood. As long as it's not hers.

I shake off the thought. "Blow it," I order.

"You're still in range, sir," Barry says through my earpiece. "You need to leave the area."

I smirk and wipe the blood of Crawley's men from my face – it's already starting to dry – then glance at the elevator shaft. "I'll be fine. Just blow it."

There are a handful of men still down there, trapped and wounded, trying to get out. The stairway is blocked, electricity cutting off the elevator.

They'll be entombed in the warehouse basement.

All of them stared at Stacey. All of them wanted her. But no one ever gets to have her – not even me.

I pull off my suit jacket and throw it to the side, then roll my sleeves up to my elbows with my blade still in hand. I unbutton my stained shirt as I walk through the car park and yank out the bullet lodged in my armoured vest.

That'll leave a bruise. I already feel the sensitive skin and the ache on my side where it impacted.

I reach the car to find Barry sitting in the passenger seat. "I said to blow it."

"As immortal as you seem to think you are, I'm not going to put your life in danger, sir."

"I gave you an order."

He sighs. "For your safety, I chose not to follow it."

"You *and* Stacey are starting to annoy me with this talking-back shit."

He chuckles and then taps on his phone screen, bringing up the app that connects all the explosives and triggers them. The flash comes first, and then the thunderous sound of the world blowing up nearly ruptures my eardrums. The ball of flame erupts like a volcano into the skies, and I smile at the artwork we created. I would have been in pieces if he had blown it when I said.

I announce to everyone, "Nice going, team. Pack up and get some rest."

I turn to my assistant. "I need to complete a contract. You good to clean this up, head to your hotel and wait for word?"

Barry nods and climbs out, patting the front of the car.

I look at what was once a warehouse filled with a gang, now obliterated and filled with dead, incinerated bodies.

If Bernadette finds out I eradicated an entire MC, she'll flip. I can't be fucked with that. I'll need to lie and tell her we had an altercation and they threatened to out us, so I simply had to blow them up.

It was unavoidable. A travesty. A huge shame.

Maybe people will learn not to mess with my things.

21

KADE

As the sirens buzz in the distance – Barry's clean-up team, not the emergency services – I make sure everyone has left, and then I input the location of my target, groaning when I realise it's a security-infested manor. I follow the map, stopping at a wooded area to burn my clothes and pull on a fresh suit I had stowed in a suitcase along with the drugs I'll use to gain entry.

Before closing the suitcase full of gear, I take two lines of coke, hating myself a little more than I did a moment ago. But I need to ease the vibrating in my bones, something that happens when I go too long without an upper. The drugs aren't being forced into me now though; I think that stopped when I started craving the highs they offered.

I pull the suitcase from the car, slide the handle up and drag it behind me as I walk onto the driveway that leads up to electric gates. I press the buzzer and introduce myself as a distributor for Mr Lennox, and whoever it is on the other end lets me in.

I roll my eyes at the security team. How easy was it for me to walk right in here fully armed?

I'm directed to the main room, where an overweight, greasy-looking man is planted behind a desk, smoking a cigar. Gold rings flash on every finger. "What do you have for me?" he asks, coughing through his smoke.

He sits back as I throw the suitcase onto his desk and open it, showing him all the white powder inside. A grin, and he disgustingly gargles in his throat.

But Mr Lennox doesn't have a chance to lift even one bag to inspect it before I yank my gun out from my waistband and shoot him right in the chest four times, the silencer quieting the *pops*.

His body slumps instantly, and I snap a picture and send it to Bernadette, demanding the rest of my pay.

I leave the suitcase behind, but I only manage to reach the main stairs before shots are fired at me.

I throw myself behind an overturned table, laughing at my luck as I pull my other gun out, so I have two firing as I run to the pillar, dodging the bullets that whizz past my head.

The coke isn't helping my accuracy, so I drop one of my guns and pull out a blade, then grab a guy from behind and shove it into his neck, using his body as a shield as I make my way to the back entrance.

I'm not sure how the fuck I reach my car, or how long they chase me until I overturn my Bentley in a ditch. I somehow escape unscathed, but I'm pissed I wrecked my new car and have to run on foot until I lose their tail.

There's blood in my eyes, turning my vision red as I type a message to my assistant on my cracked phone screen.

Barry picks me up at a nearby gas station, and he huffs all the way to the hotel, telling me I need to be more careful. He offers me a handkerchief for my face, but I shrug him off, thank him and jump out of the car.

The receptionist doesn't ask me if I'm okay as I storm past the desk and head for the elevator. A couple get in on the second floor, but they keep to the corner of the small metal box, far away from me – a man covered in blood with an ammunition belt on full display.

I think my lip is cut; it stings a little.

My steps are clumsy and unbalanced as I get off the elevator, the bright lights making me squint and shield my eyes with a flat hand.

When I reach our rooms, I send Stacey a text that I think might be illegible, and when no response comes, I ignore my own room and sit outside hers, entertaining myself on my phone.

The first clip I have saved is from our last holiday to Greece. I watch the video from the karaoke bar, us on the balcony, another of Stacey sunbathing and me zooming in on her face – to her tanned, freckled skin. One she recorded of us holding hands and walking along the sandy beach. I pause the clip when she kisses my cheek, studying the smile on her face, which matches mine.

Videos upon videos, images upon images haunt me, yet I can never delete them.

I fucking hate myself for opening the file. I usually have it locked and securely hidden from prying eyes. It's torturous, the way it makes me feel. I've struggled with emotions since I was a kid. I felt alive for the first time when I had Stacey, and now everything within me is black.

I'm dead inside.

The thumb I'm using to swipe through the pictures is crusted with blood. Every single image stabs a hole in my already hollow chest; I want so desperately to jump back into that reality, to hide from the person I've become. But it doesn't exist. She's not the same Stacey from then, and I'm definitely not the same Kade either.

I scroll through our messages, all the way up to some of the first ones we exchanged.

Our first picture together: me asleep with my arms wrapped around her, from when she accidentally stayed the night. She's smiling at the camera, the usual middle finger up. The caption makes the corner of my mouth lift, even though it shouldn't.

You snore so loud, asshole.

We were kids blinded by emotions.

We had everything. And she fucked it all up.

Killing high-profile people, dealing with drug lords, drinking a ridiculous amount of alcohol, beheading and disembowelling, and even walking into a gang's territory to unleash hell I can deal with – but not a cheat. Not a fucking liar who made me think they were someone to me when they weren't.

How anyone could look someone in the eye and tell them they loved them, only to go fuck someone else hours later is beyond me.

I've been sitting outside Stacey's hotel room for two hours now, a lot more spaced out than planned. Maybe it's the joint I smoked ten minutes ago that was packed with green, or maybe I'm just tired – that seems like a strong possibility.

Or maybe the coke from that MC gang was dodgy, and I'm sparkled from tampered drugs.

I don't want to go into my room. If someone survived and followed me back, I need to be on alert. They might go into Stacey's room.

Another death on my hands won't be an issue.

I like killing people who deserve death. It gives me great pleasure to watch the light go out in their eyes as they take their last breath.

It's only two in the afternoon, and I've already killed at least sixty people and earned one hundred and fifty grand. Stacey would be disgusted with me if she knew.

She hasn't responded so I can only assume she's asleep.

Good. I might say something I'll regret while I'm fucked like this. You'd think taking uppers, I'd be in a great mood, but I feel like I could noose myself. I wouldn't though – that would leave a mess behind, and no one needs to deal with that shit.

Would she care if I died?

I'm not afraid – if it happens, it happens, but a part of me would want to know how she'd feel. Regretful? Sad? Relieved? Would I see tears on her cheeks like I did on the jet?

A flash of her on her knees before me has my head dropping back to the door, my traitorous dick annoyingly twitching. I want to slap it.

I can still feel her lips tight around my cock, see her tears sliding down her face from choking, and the way she swallowed every drop of my cum. It's driving me fucking insane. I was seconds from being inside her, and I would've been if not for fucking Barry. I've never wanted to kill my assistant before. He does my head in most the time, but never have I pictured him dead.

I even wanted to hit Base when he said she was hot.

She makes me more dangerous than I already am.

If she pointed at a random person and told me to shoot, I'd pull the trigger with no questions asked. Yet I can't stand to breathe the same air as her. I've even pictured myself killing her once or twice and regretted the mental images instantly.

The sooner she meets up with Luciella, the better.

Fuck. My head is banging. The lobby is bright, and I can barely strain my eyes enough to see. The walls are morphing together; the floor is lava yet soft under my palms.

Definitely dodgy drugs.

The door I'm leaning against opens, and I fall back into Stacey's hotel room.

Dark hair comes into view, green eyes staring down at me, confused and terrified.

"What the hell?" she hisses before frowning at the crimson stains all over my clothes and body. "What in the world happened to you?"

I mumble and rub my eyes with my finger and thumb. As much as words are running wild in my head, I'm too fucked up to speak properly. What I want to say is that I finished work and want to know if she's still scared of me, but I slur each word in messy syllables.

I try to get up, but my body refuses. I look like an overturned turtle on coke.

"Why are you covered in blood?" she asks, glancing up and down the hallway before opening her door wider.

It's not my blood. I'm perfectly fucking fine.

"Get in."

Demanding Stacey is hot.

I can't move though.

"Oh for God's sake."

Somehow, she manages to drag me into her room, picking up the blade I'd kept by my side and shutting the door.

"What did you do?" She's pretty when she's mad. "Are you drunk?"

I haven't touched a drink, but I won't tell her that.

Not that I could, because the room is fucking spinning and I feel like I'm floating. I rub my eyes with my knuckles. Nope, I'm losing my sight.

That's new.

The room goes dark – or are my eyes closed? I don't know.

I feel something wet and gentle against my face. Stacey kneels to wash the blood off me with a hand towel she's dipped in warm water. I wince as she drags her fingers through my hair, catching and tugging.

She doesn't stop me from holding her hips to stay upright.

"How did you get blood in your hair?"

Freckles, darling, I'm a fucking animal. You should've seen me Jackie Chan my shit today.

"Are you going to answer me?"

"Don't..." I pause, trying to slow my thoughts as cocaine rushes through my veins. I open my eyes, and they burn with lack of sleep. "Don't... be afraid of me."

My vision blurs again as Stacey wipes the cloth across my forehead.

"I can deal with you hating me, Kade." She scrunches the cloth to soak my hair, and my head drops to her shoulder as she rubs the fabric on the nape of my neck. Water trickles down my back. "I can't deal with you throwing your life away on whatever trouble you've got yourself into."

I weakly snort.

If you didn't cheat on me, I wouldn't have been outside the studio that night, contemplating going in to see you, and Bernadette wouldn't have found me.

My inner voice is selfish.

I can't blame her for the monster I've become. Nope, that's on me.

Her face is the last thing I see before my vision blurs, and I lose consciousness.

22

KADE

FLASHBACK 4

After I passed my driving test two days ago, Jason took me out, and I drunkenly asked Stacey if she was still coming to my room to watch a movie. She said yes.

I'm a wreck, a bag of fucking nerves as I tidy my room for the hundredth time. Mum had brought up a pile of clean clothes earlier and asked why I was hoovering my curtains at eleven at night.

Fair to say she took the vacuum from me and told me to go to sleep.

I'm overthinking tonight. I've even wiped down my TV screen.

We've been texting all day, and I've realised a few things. When she's home, she either has no signal or doesn't bother checking her phone. The only reason I've had so much of her attention today is because she's out with her dad at some event.

I'd like to think she isn't messaging me because she's bored. The idea that she's willingly not talking to me all the other times makes me feel itchy and uncomfortable.

Maybe I should shower again?

I reread our recent messages to pass time.

Freckles: *Are you sure you want to see me?*

Freckles: *It's okay if you don't want to.*

Me: *Shut up.*

Freckles: *Your communication skills are shit. What does shut up mean in this context?*

Me: *If you don't come to my room later, I'll kidnap you from your bed and drag you here.*

Freckles: *Oh, okay. That's slightly threatening but a little sweet.*

I'm not sweet. I don't know how to be. When I read that message earlier, I'd stared at it for a whole five minutes before going for another smoke.

With a gnawing in my gut, I wait. Smoke another cigarette, brush my teeth again and check my room once more for any mess I missed.

My phone dings, and it takes me everything not to pounce on it. Desperation isn't attractive, and apparently – according to Jason's girlfriend – I should wait at least ten minutes before responding.

I last barely thirty seconds before I read and reply.

Freckles: *She's asleep.*

Me: *Come up.*

By the time a knock sounds at my door, I've already paced the room so much I'm surprised there isn't smoke coming from my carpet.

I swing open the door and anxiously stand aside to let Stacey in.

She's wearing jeans and a knitted sweater, her hair tied back. "Hi."

"Hi," I reply shyly, closing the door and locking it.

I don't know what else to say, and she obviously feels the same. She looks around my room, and I follow her as she explores. It's big, bigger than most bedrooms, and the double doors leading to my balcony intrigue her.

"I see you standing up here a lot." She goes out into the cold, looking down at the manor grounds. "Always smoking."

"I can't smoke in my room," I tell her, leaning on the stone wall beside her. "My mum would kill me."

She smiles, her perfect teeth white and straight.

When we go back inside, I notice her shiver. I close the balcony doors and offer her more comfortable clothes to watch the movie in. Her jeans look good on her, but something about her wearing my clothes seems way better. I don't expect her to accept my offer, or for her to take my top and shorts and go into the bathroom to change.

I lie on my bed and set up the movie, trying not to think about how my heart is racing or the thin layer of sweat forming between my brows.

"This is huge on me," Stacey says as she opens the bathroom door. My top is nearly to her knees. "I don't think I need the shorts."

Oh, fuck me.

She places them on my dresser, and I gulp as she walks towards my bed.

"My dad is picking me up in the morning. I'll go back to Luciella's room after the movie." She places her knee on the edge of my bed. "She really can't find out I'm here. Did you tell anyone?"

"Nope," I lie. Jason and my dad are fully aware. "What's the big deal if she finds out anyway?"

"Are you kidding?" she replies, and my eyes follow her as she crawls up beside me to settle against the headboard. "I'd need to escape the country if she knew I was here."

"Seems dramatic."

"Is this movie actually good?" she asks, changing the subject. She crosses her arms at her chest, and I must admit, seeing her body clad in my black top makes me want to never start this fucking film.

"The best. If you don't like it, then I'm afraid this little thing between us isn't going to work."

She snorts. "No pressure, asshole."

I just said we were a thing, and she hasn't corrected me. That's a positive, right?

Her bare legs are right next to mine, and the way she's sitting, my top is riding up her thighs. Against my better judgement, which tells me I should look away and start the movie, I say, "If you plan on mauling me again, I recommend not doing it while we watch this."

Stacey slaps my leg. "Shut up or I'll leave."

Nope. She isn't leaving. Not until we reach the credits, and I've kissed her at least ten times. I should get the first one in while anxiety isn't clawing at my chest and overthinking.

My nerves don't get the better of me as I lean forward, my knuckles to her chin to tip her head back, and capture her lips with mine. A caress of our mouths – so soft and so fucking addictive when she hums. Stacey's palm instantly presses to my cheek as she kisses me back.

I could kiss her forever.

I don't know why it's taken me so long. I should have done this years ago. Maybe if I did, I would have had her for longer. She'd be my girlfriend by now, and everyone would know she was mine and I was hers.

We part our lips, tilting our heads to deepen the kiss. I tangle my fingers in her hair and pull her to me. Close enough. My free hand embarrassingly clutches at my bed frame.

I want to keep kissing her. I want to keep tracing her tongue with my own, to hear her heavy breaths and the feel of her teeth taking my bottom lip between them. I want to touch her skin and climb on top of her. I want to do everything I've imagined.

But I don't.

I pull back, sinking my teeth into my bottom lip and tasting her fruity lip balm. Her chest is rising and falling; so is mine. My forehead is against hers, and instead of fully moving away from her, I kiss her again.

It's deep and feral. Stacey matches each stroke of my tongue as she positions my hand on her waist, snatching my shoulders and dragging me on top of her. I like that she's taking control, because I really don't have a clue what I'm doing.

She tastes like sweet intoxication as she tugs at my hair. I'm not sure how long we stay like this, but my lips are raw, my dick is harder than a rock and my top has ridden so far up Stacey's body, I can see her underwear and the underside of her bra.

The image will haunt me forever. In a good way. I think.

I break the kiss, rising on my knees and dragging my hooded gaze down her body. Each curve. Each inked design. I want to touch her everywhere.

"You aren't real, Freckles." I splay my hand on her stomach and slide it up. "So fucking beautiful. You were made for me."

"As much as I don't want to stroke your ego, you're not too bad yourself," she replies with a giggle, and the way she says stroke has my dick jerking.

There's no hiding how aroused I am. I'm not small, and my shorts do nothing to conceal the tenting of the fabric. She keeps glancing down at it.

"We're going slow," she says. "Right?"

We.

I nod and remove my hand. "Right. But if you want something," I say, eyes trailing back down the length of her body, "tell me."

She puts my hand on her ribs. "I want you to kiss me again."

Oh thank fucking God. If she'd asked me to eat her out or to fuck her, I would've disintegrated into a pile of dust.

I lower onto her and crush my mouth to hers, devouring her lips. She sucks on my tongue, and I groan into her mouth as her ankle hooks behind my leg.

"I trust you," she whispers to me, snatching my jaw, so my gaze is pulled back to meet hers. Her hair surrounds the pillow; green eyes, full lips. "I want you to trust me too."

She takes the hand on her ribs and slowly slides it under her bra – thin black lace with stitched detail in rose that matches her panties. I grit my teeth and control each breath through my nostrils at the softness of her skin there.

"I trust you," she says again.

My hand freezes, my lungs seizing. The fuck am I doing? I can't sit here and fondle her. I can't do any of this without messing up. I'll do it wrong.

She notices my hesitation. "You won't hurt me."

"I could."

She holds my cheek delicately, her voice low. "No you couldn't, and you won't."

"You want me to do this?" I ask as I cup her breast, needing confirmation. She was the one who put my hands on her, but right now I need to hear her say that three-lettered word.

"Yes," she breathes. "I want you to. But I don't want you to do anything you aren't comfortable with. We can stop – or slow down. Just tell me."

Without having to think again, I slip my other hand under her bra and palm her other breast. My mind hasn't caught up with my body yet, so as I shove her bra to her chin to get a full view, I caress her. Her tits are handfuls, full and perky, and I want to know what they'd feel like in my mouth. How much pleasure would she get from me kissing them?

Her nipples tighten to peaks as I swipe one with my thumb, and she lets out a quiet moan.

"Fuck," I blurt.

Stacey sucks her bottom lip into her mouth and bites it, her breathing heavier. "They aren't big or anything special."

"Be quiet."

She grins, but it falls, her mouth open as I roll her nipple between my thumb and forefinger. I lean down to kiss her again, swallowing her little whimpers as I pinch and roll, caressing her breasts while I devour her.

Finally, I release her nipples, shift onto my back and pull her on top of me.

I tug at my top. "Take this off," I order, nearly exploding in my boxers as she whips it from her body and tosses it behind her. "Fucking perfect."

She breathes deeply as I reach up and palm her tits again. My dick is straining in my shorts, and the fact she's sitting an inch from it isn't helpful. I've never looked at someone and wanted to fuck them. Yeah, I've imagined myself putting Stacey in every position possible, but I've never wanted to act on those scenarios.

Not that she isn't fuckable; I'm just not that type of guy.

But with Stacey in only her underwear, straddling me in my bed, her pupils dilated and a flush to her skin, I want to sink my cock into her deep enough that I'll never get it back out.

We're kissing again, and I gain some confidence in letting my hands explore her nearly naked body. From her bare ass to gripping her back, to rolling her nipples and pinching as she whimpers my name.

She moans into my mouth when I pinch harder, my lips travelling down her throat so I can suck on her pulse, which hammers against my tongue. I want to keep going, to take her nipple between my teeth, but I go back to her mouth instead.

She whimpers as I pull her hair, flipping us again so I'm between her legs.

"We're never going to watch this fucking movie."

"What was it called again?" she jokes, smiling as I nip at her jaw and move hair from her face.

I drop to her side, lacing one hand with hers while the other twirls a strand of black hair around my finger. "You said you'd be a good girl."

When I texted her drunk the other night, she said I had to take her for a McDonald's every week now that I had a licence, and I said only if she was a good girl.

Her response?

I'm always a good girl, Kade.

I nearly died.

She fake gasps. "Am I being a bad girl?"

Inwardly, I groan as I look down at her body, clad now only in her panties. "Very."

"Then you better put the movie on." Stacey bites my knuckles playfully before – sadly – putting my top back on. "Or I'll go watch it with Luciella instead."

"Lie. She'd never willingly watch it."

Stacey cuddles into my side, and I wrap my arm around her shoulders. The movie starts, and we both focus our attention on it, quiet unless she's asking me questions about it. She smiles a lot. Her eyes go wide a lot. She tightens her fingers around mine a lot.

It feels nice.

I feel her sink into my embrace as the opera singer starts. I don't watch the TV screen; I'm staring at her. Her eyes are fixed on the movie; she's hanging on to each word, each lyric that belts from the redhead's lips.

"Why is this sad?" she asks with a trembling chin. "His wife can see the way he's reacting. I want to hug her."

"I know."

"But the song is so heartbreakingly beautiful."

"I know."

We watch the rest of the movie, and by the time the credits come up, we're both yawning, legs tangled together, her wild hair in my face.

"I loved that," she says with another yawn. "We need to watch it again."

"Whenever you want."

I'm seconds from falling asleep. I've never shared a bed with anyone. Even when I was a kid and Luciella got scared of the dark, I slept on her floor until she calmed.

The thought of sleeping next to someone has never occurred to me. I never wanted to. Never even imagined it. Yet, with Stacey buried into my side, her knee hiked over me, I would happily close my eyes and fall asleep. I hold her thigh, my nose in her hair, and I don't bother asking if she's staying.

Jason is right – I do like her. Is that weird, .considering I've only kissed her a handful of times? Is there a timeline for feelings and all that emotional bullshit?

She doesn't know it yet, but she's kind of stuck with me. I can't say that aloud without her running for the hills, but the fact that I've never once looked at another girl with interest or thought of them as beautiful until I saw her speaks volumes.

But I have no idea what to do with her.

Stacey moves beside me, resting her head on my chest; she can probably hear how fast and hard my heart is pounding. She's patient with me. She'll give me time to adjust to all of this. Even the way she places her palm on my chest next to her head is gentle.

The scent of her shampoo and the sound of her deep breaths are the last things I remember before I drift off. I fall into the first peaceful sleep I've had in years as we both cuddle into each other.

When I wake in the morning, the top I gave her is neatly folded on my dresser – and she's gone.

I reach for my phone and notice I have a text from her. A picture she sent an hour ago. I'm passed out, spooning her with my face buried in her hair. She's sleepily grinning and giving the middle finger, with a message beneath the image that says, You snore so loud, asshole.

23

KADE

My eyes strain against the light as Stacey follows me out the hotel.

She hasn't spoken a fucking word to me. I woke up in her bed, her on the floor with a blanket – shivering. I draped the duvet over her and snuck to my own room before she'd woken up.

She washed all the blood from my hands, arms and face, even my hair, and then slept on the hard floor.

I texted her an apology, and all she said was that we had fifteen minutes before we needed to leave.

The silence is starting to piss me right off.

When I ask if she wants to grab food, she hums. *Hums.* What the fuck is that? A yes or a fucking no?

"Where's your car?" she asks, looking around the car park.

For a second, I have no clue as I look around too, then it dawns on me, and I blow out a breath, even more annoyed I wrecked it. "We need to get an Uber."

"What happened to your car?"

I shrug and pull out a smoke. It's probably still buried in a ditch, unless Barry cleaned that up too, but I haven't heard from him yet.

She types on her phone as she leans against a wall, crossing her arms with a scowl on her face, then checks the time on her watch while tapping her foot. Amused, I lean against the railing and fill my lungs with something not nearly as poisonous as her.

My side is badly bruised, but I welcome the ache. It stops me from staring at Stacey and wanting to spark a conversation with her, to see her smile or have her on her knees again.

I think she was touching the bruise when I was asleep, unless I was hallucinating. I remember opening my eyes to her face screwed up in confusion as her fingertips traced the purpling skin, her lip quivering before everything went black again.

Just as I go to ask, she storms towards our ride. I have to hurry to catch up with her.

I should thank her for at least looking after me when I obviously couldn't even speak.

"About earlier—"

"Don't," she warns. "Just get in the car, Kade."

I frown at the way she says my name. "Fine. Luciella thinks we just got off the flight," I say as we both get into the Uber. "We'll stop somewhere for food and head to meet them. My gran won't be there. She sadly has the flu." The last part is sarcasm.

Nothing. No response.

If she wasn't Stacey, my violent side would want to smash her head into the glass for ignoring me. Make her bleed. Scream for forgiveness.

The silent treatment I give her is for her own good.

Her ignoring me now is just childish behaviour.

I shouldn't care that she won't look at me, but I find myself growing agitated and a tad nervous that she's blanking my existence. She's the only person in the world to ever make me feel like this, and that makes me fist my hands in rage.

I'm Kade Mitchell. I don't do emotions. I don't care about

people, especially not people who fuck me over. So why can't I stop looking at her?

My phone dings with my next contract. Half a million. A club owner from where we'll be staying. Known groomer.

The last part confirms I'll enjoy it.

I read the file while Stacey stares out the window.

He got off with rape, stealing thousands from an old lady and drugging an underage girl before getting a blowjob off her.

When I get a hold of this prick, I'll make it hurt. The family of the young girl is paying Bernadette – and me – more than enough to drag out the pain. They reached out to Bernie a few weeks ago, after hearing about her from relatives back in Scotland, and specifically asked for her best.

And I don't ever disappoint.

The hotel we're staying at has a pool round back, surrounded by loungers. Base has been sending me pictures of him on one with a beer. Mum and Ewan have made the most of the bar, and Luciella has impatiently waited on her best friend, who's currently typing on her phone with a frown and chewing her thumbnail.

The silence is making me uneasy. Fuck it. "Sorry," I say, folding my arms. "For waking you up. I was just..." High as fuck. "Drunk."

She doesn't take her eyes off her phone. "It's fine."

It's not fucking fine. Look at me. Yell at me. Do fucking something.

We've spent the last twenty-four hours bickering and getting each other off, and now she can't spare me a glance because I shot someone who was trying to sexualise her? Of course, she has no idea what happened the rest of the day, but I've just been doing my job.

A job I don't fucking want.

But if I tell Bernadette that I'm out, both me and my dad will likely see a death sentence. The rest of my family will get worse.

I refused a contract not long ago, and she threatened my dogs. My fucking *dogs.*

Shaking my head, I lean my elbows on my knees. "Fine." *I'm useless.* "Forget the last twenty-four hours."

"Already forgotten."

My hands fist with unnecessary rage, and I roll my jaw. "Good."

When we reach the hotel, Stacey blanks me and leaves the car.

I need to tamp down my irritation and tell myself not to drag her into a room and bend her over my knee. This attitude of hers is absurd.

I hug my mum and nod at Base to follow me to our room as Luciella lets out an excited scream and grabs her friend for a cuddle.

"Mate, I have so many fucking stories for you," Base says as he unlocks the hotel-room door. "We're going out later, right? I had a threesome last night and kept their numbers!"

Luciella screws her face up as she and Stacey stop a few doors down from ours. Perfect. Just what I fucking need.

"Please, Sebastian, stop being so vulgar."

Despite my infuriation right now, I fight a smirk as Base glares at her. "Don't call me that."

"It's your name, is it not?" She opens her door; Stacey slips in without a word. My sister's eyes burn into me. "Be ready in an hour. And don't you dare ruin this for Dad."

I narrow my brows. "Who the fuck do you think you're talking to?"

She shakes her head. "Someone who used to be my brother, but now he's possessed by a fucking battered demon. Get a grip of yourself, Kade. When did you last sleep?"

I stare at her.

Base folds his arms in a huff. "Don't call me Sebastian."

"Okay, Sebastian," Luciella shouts as she slams the door.

"I might kill your sister," he says, shaking his head and picking up one of my bags. "She's been doing my head in ever since we left the manor. I asked if she wanted to join—" He stops. "Never mind."

Lovely.

The room is large, with two single beds, an en suite with a shower and bath, and a balcony that looks over the pool.

"Think they'll come out tonight as well?" he asks as he drops onto his bed. "Luciella won't give me the time of day, so maybe I'll approach her best friend."

"Sounds toxic."

"Because I, Sebastian Ivanovich Prince, *am* toxic." He winks at me, then says in Russian, "I'll make your sister realise I'm her one true love by fucking her best friend."

Eye twitching, I head for the bathroom to shower – again.

"Wait. Did you understand what I said?" Base sits up, confusion on his face. He has no idea I'm multilingual. "Hey, what's up with you? You said you were cool with me liking Luciella?"

"I am." I stop before I can close the door. "I'm just tired."

He grunts. "Fine. I'll make plans. Give me your phone. Mine is dead."

I toss him it. I have all my work shit under passwords – the last thing I need is him knowing the secret life I live; that I'm not the engineering student he believes I am.

But he tilts his head as soon as he unlocks it. "Eh, Kade?" He rises from the bed, turning the screen to me, and my heart sinks. "Why do you have a picture of an ultrasound on your phone? You knock someone up?"

Before he can inspect the picture and see the woman's name, I swipe it out of his hand. "Charge and use your own fucking phone, and no, I didn't knock anyone up."

"That was a baby scan."

I shake my head. "I mean it, Base. Drop it."

"I'm your best friend. You can tell me this shit. Who did you get pregnant? When are you going to be a dad? I need to know this shit! I'll be Uncle Base!"

If only he knew how old this scan is.

I glare at him as I grip my phone in my palm. "Stop."

Raising both hands, he stands back. He doesn't believe me, but I don't push the subject before getting back into the bathroom and trying not to fucking pass out from how fast my heart is racing.

Once the door is locked, I turn on the shower, waiting for the place to steam up with my head in my hands. I have the worst migraine building, I feel like I have blood and guts all over me, and I'm uncomfortable as fuck.

The scalding water burns my skin for ten minutes before I shut it off, get dressed and head down to reception to meet my mum, Ewan and my sister.

Base and Stacey aren't coming to see my dad. Mum suggests they go for a drink and wait on us, which grinds my gears because

I know for a fact Base will flirt with her until his tongue falls off.

The Uber to my dad's facility takes half an hour, and Ewan talks to me about his new project and ways I can help. He's been trying to get me back into construction with him; he'd probably noticed I'm a bit off the rails. I always enjoyed helping – it kept my head straight – but right now I have neither the time nor the mental capacity to focus on something like that.

Ewan tells us he'll catch up in an hour, that he's going to speak to someone in the building about a contractor. He always wants to give my parents time together. It helps Dad to have time with my mum. It's quite the bond they have, considering their horrific history.

It's a twisted love, and it's warped Dad's mind so much that he can't focus on anyone else without comparing them to her or instantly becoming obsessive again.

He's a diagnosed psychopath who loves Mum in his own way – learned, studied, even if it's not the same way a neurotypical person would love. It's limited, the way he feels, but it's enough to never break the bond they have.

Kind of sad if you think about it. Being in love with the same woman for over twenty years and knowing they'll never have a happy ending must be hard. Sometimes I compare their story to mine and Stacey's, and wonder if I'll still be watching her in twenty years.

Probably.

Shit. I am like my dad.

As soon as we get into the main area of the facility, an indoor park with a man-made pond, we spot Dad at the picnic bench – the one he always sits and waits at for visits.

He glances over his shoulder, and his eyes light up. "Hi, sweetheart," he says as he gets to his feet and hugs Mum. They hold each other, as if they hadn't just spent hours together yesterday. "Did you get a good sleep?"

"I did," Mum replies, cupping his face and smoothing her thumbs over his skin. "You shaved. Did Luciella's comment about getting grey hairs in your beard go to your head?"

He smirks. Mum grins and blushes.

Me and Luciella stand behind them in silence.

Dark and threatening eyes land on me, and for the first time in God knows how long, I think he might hit me. Anxiety scratches at me as he moves, studying my face, my eyes, all the tattoos I've acquired in the last two years. "Hello, son."

Lips flattening, I nod. "Dad."

Usually, when I visit, he'll pull me in for a hug or offer me some words of encouragement about how good I look, how much my workouts have been doing me justice. But this time, he just stares, trying to read me.

With minimal sleep, a sore side from being shot, a bruised face from Crawley's punch, a comedown and barely looking after my health the past three days, I'd be surprised if I looked normal right now. I'm probably drawn and looking exhausted. And I definitely forgot to sort my hair. It's an abomination of curls and waves in all directions, hanging over my forehead.

Luciella breaks the awkward moment by cuddling him, and only then does he perk up and lead us to the pond area.

He holds my mum's hand, Luciella hooks her arm around his and I walk behind them – silent, unable to even think of a conversation starter while they discuss what they're planning to do over the next few days.

I shouldn't be here. There's no reason for me to be here.

He lost another appeal, but I already knew he'd lose it. He wanted to visit Scotland for a weekend, but because I failed to do as I was told, Bernadette made sure the appeal fell through, and now he's permanently blocked from ever entering the United Kingdom.

I highly doubt any country would let him in anyway. He's known worldwide as a psychotic madman.

Luciella slows to walk with me. "What's wrong with you? Talk to him."

I shrug. "I don't know what to say."

I haven't visited my dad in nearly two years. The last time we had a huge argument and I overturned one of the picnic tables. He has more grey hairs now, but he's kept at the gym they have here and eats healthily.

You'd think a man in his forties would at least look forty, but he's just a slightly older version of me, with the same level of fitness. He'd probably be able to beat the shit out of me without trying.

"Maybe apologise first," she says, watching him and my mother laugh about something as she rests her head on his shoulder. "You did call him a lunatic, a waste of oxygen and told him he was better off dead for what he did to Mum, before walking out on him."

As soon as those words fell from my lips, I regretted them. But I was too fucking furious with him to turn around and say sorry, to take them all back. He was hurt by what I said – it was the first time I'd ever seen him cry.

He'd tried to agree with me, that Mum deserved everything that didn't involve him, but I didn't wait to hear him explain. I stormed out, blocked the institution's number and went on with my life.

All because he tried to talk to me about Stacey. *You don't hate her, son. You're just mad at her.* He knew everything about us. *There must be a reason she's acting this way.* Every trip. *No one can change overnight.* Every time I felt happy. He even knew when I asked her to be my girlfriend. *You need to hear her out, Kade. If you love her, let her explain.*

Tobias Mitchell wasn't the person to give relationship advice. I mean, come on. He went off his meds and kidnapped my mother to blackmail her into being in a relationship with him.

He's a million shades of psychotic obsession, but somehow, he was the one who made me see that I was falling in love with Stacey when I was a teenager.

"We should come back in a bit," my sister whispers to me as our parents talk about their night. "Maybe get a coffee?"

Dad glowers at me, and I feel all the blood drain from my face. "Yeah. Good shout."

We leave them in peace and head to the cafeteria. I take a seat at one of the tables while Luciella goes to order, returning with a large tea for her and a latte for me.

"I'm sorry about what I said earlier. About the not being my brother thing."

I snort. "It's fine. I haven't exactly been around."

"Are you… Are you really okay? You know you can talk to me."

We were as close as siblings could be once, but when her best friend ruined me, I couldn't bear to look at either of them. I almost told her about us so many times while drunk-calling home, almost told her that me and Stacey were sneaking around and that I was sorry.

But the apology would have been a lie.

"I have a question," I say. I formulate a lie so I can give Barry more information. "When we were on the plane, Stacey was trying to take her hoodie off. She had a few bruises." I sip my hot drink, ignoring the burn on my tongue. "She said they were from the studio."

I need to know who did them. If my sister tells me she's seeing someone, I'll make sure the last week of his life is lived in terror. I'll blind him, take his fingertips, shove a screwdriver in his ears and make him choke on his own cock.

Luciella frowns. "One thing we're all jealous of is how much it takes Stacey to bruise. Are you sure they were bruises?"

"I'm certain. She has scars as well."

My sister studies her paper cup. "I noticed the scars. She said most of them are from falling or some silly accident. I've not noticed bruising. We're going out with you and Base tonight, so maybe I'll ask her to wear a skimpy dress and see what she says."

I stop drinking and set down my cup. "You and Stacey are coming out with us? Since when?"

"Base asked me earlier," she replies, shrugging a shoulder. "And I said yes."

I don't want to go out with fucking Stacey tonight. I already have plans, and I need to complete the contract by three in the morning.

"I could straight-up ask her how she got bruised," she says, biting into her pastry.

"Don't put her on the spot like that."

She arches a brow and looks at me until I feel itchy. "Why are you so concerned anyway? I thought you two couldn't stand each other."

"I don't care. It was just an observation. No one likes to see another person looking beat-up."

She hums in agreement and finishes her drink. "I'll keep an eye on her," she says, then her eyes widen. "Oh, the cashier said there are loads of paps outside apparently. They must've found out we were visiting Dad."

"Awesome," I say sarcastically. "Where are we going later?" I ask. I know Base has already planned it.

I'll just make sure I leave, complete my job and get back without them noticing.

"The place across from the casino near the promenade. Begins with an M?"

I inwardly scream. This day cannot get any worse.

Of all the clubs we could go to, they pick the one whose owner I need to fucking kill?

"Your dad wants to speak to you." Mum has appeared at the entrance of the cafeteria. She tips her head to the corridor. "Alone."

I sigh and follow the signs back to visitation while taking deep breaths.

As soon as I walk in, Dad pins his raging gaze on me. "Sit the fuck down."

Without flinching, I do as I'm told.

"From the beginning." I try not to look away from the intensiveness of his gaze. "Tell me what the fuck is happening... From the very beginning, Kade."

I shrug. "I don't know what you're talking about."

"Don't play dumb."

"Nothing is happening." I shake my head, looking at him with a serious expression. "Don't bother yourself with my life."

Darkening eyes stare at me like I'm the villain. "Are you on drugs?"

I'm certain the whites of my eyes still have a tint of red, and I absently sniff and look at my bouncing knees beneath the table. "No."

The way I reply means there can be no doubt it's the biggest lie I've ever told him. I don't have time for any of this.

"I'm going to ask you again. Are you on—"

I abruptly stand from the table. "I'm not fucking doing this," I snap as I walk towards the exit.

Dad yells something at me, but I block him out and gesture to the doorman to let me out.

He knows I'm on something, which means my mum will soon know. And then my plan of staying under their radar is fucked.

24

STACEY

I love Luciella, but with the number of dress shops she dragged me into before we headed back to the hotel, I contemplated pushing her in front of a speeding car.

Apparently, the club we're going to is fancy and expensive, so she wants us to mix in with the glamourous girls by wearing the skimpiest goddamn dresses I've ever seen.

You'd think she was trying to get me naked with the scraps of material she's picked out. She's never been one for flaunting her body, so why tonight?

I said no to every dress she threw at me, settling on the one with the most material.

I'm not in the mood tonight. Spending hours with Base while he listed all the reasons Luciella and him should get married has given me a headache.

And I don't want to spend any time with Kade. Even seeing his face annoys me.

He had another argument with his dad earlier, and Lu told me he stormed out. It was the first time they'd seen each other in two years. They've talked on the phone briefly, but Tobias apparently wasn't happy when he saw his son.

I lie on the bed reading while Luciella takes hours in the bathroom. I message back and forth with Tylar, tell Kyle that I'm having fun and might need picked up at Glasgow when I land, and delete the usual texts from Chris and his half a dozen numbers.

I received two an hour ago, and I refuse to respond.

Kade*: You out your mood yet?*

Kade*: I take that as a fucking no.*

The guy can get fucked. He literally told me to forget what happened between us, and now he's annoyed I'm ignoring him?

The door clicks open, and I quickly come off the messages as my best friend walks out with a grin. She's wearing a navy dress that contours every curve on her body, accentuating her chest, her blonde hair curled and pinned back. She looks beautiful. Even though she and Kade are twins, they aren't identical – she's taken after her mother, and Kade – obviously – took his looks and personality from Tobias.

Luciella's smile falls to a frown, her hands now on her hips. "Why aren't you ready?"

"I need to shower."

She groans dramatically. "You could have showered in my mum's or Kade's room."

I'll pass on the latter.

By the time I'm washed and ready, Lu stares at me like she hasn't seen me dressed up millions of times. "Damn, you look sexy. We need to wingwoman each other tonight."

"That would've been possible if you didn't agree to us going out with your twin and Base."

She harrumphs. "It was in the moment."

The black silk of my dress glides against my smooth legs as I walk to the mirror. There's a slit right up the leg to the hip, and the dress dips into a deep V at the front so my cleavage is on display. The mesh detail and my breasts pressing together thankfully hide the scar there.

The dragon wrapping around my leg is like word art. From my knee to the apex of my thigh, the tattoo is made up of quotes from my favourite books, movies, lyrics, and stupid phrases Kade and I used to pass back and forth. They're small enough that you'd think they were just lines and shading – unless you looked closely – so it took five sittings to finish.

Kade designed it for me.

The "From Now On" lyrics from *The Greatest Showman* are my most cherished. We watched the movie together the first time I came to his room, and it quickly became our favourite – more like a paired obsession.

Kade might have covered up the ones he got for me, but I'll always keep mine.

She stares at my throat when I ask her to fasten my chain. "What's with the bruises? They're everywhere."

All the blood drains from my face. They aren't deep purple and blue anymore but faded yellow. I thought they'd be less noticeable by now. "Oh, I…" *Think. Think, Stacey.* "I fell down the stairs."

"Hmm. Must've been quite the fall," she says as she types on her phone with rapid thumbs. "The ones at your house?"

I chew the inside of my lip. "Yep."

She gives me a look. "You can trust me. You know that, right?"

"I fell, Lu."

"If someone is hurting you—"

"Lu, really, stop. I'm fine. I fell down my stairs when I was late for class the other day, okay?"

A few seconds, and she turns to the mirror to do her lipstick. "As long as you know you can talk to me."

And thankfully, she drops it.

I think.

Luciella closes the door just as Aria walks down the hallway, linking her arm through Ewan's. "Oh, you girls look lovely," she says, giving us a warm smile. "Remember what I said, sweetie. Call me if you're lost or if you drink too much."

She sighs. "I'm twenty-one, Mum, not twelve."

"Then stop being a brat." Kade's deep voice comes from behind us, and although my blood hums at his nearness, I paint on a blank expression as I turn to find him leaning against his doorframe with his ankles crossed.

I avert my gaze when he glances at me. I plan to give him the cold shoulder like he's done to me for ages – but I reckon I'll struggle tonight.

My eyes trail back to him, and his gaze flicks to his mother.

I've always found Kade hot, from the moment I met him down at the pool house and he was rude to me. Fifteen-year-old Stacey felt flutters in her chest every time she saw him.

But this... this is my favourite version of him. He's wearing black suit trousers, without the jacket or tie, and a crisp white shirt rolled to the elbows to show off his expensive watch. His dark hair is as messy as ever, just the way he likes it.

I know if I lift his shirt, I'll see a huge bruise on his side, and I want to feel him shiver beneath my touch again.

It was inappropriate of me to touch him, but the deep purpling of his skin had me far too curious.

Kade's eyes are fixed on his twin. "We're late for the reserved booth."

"I know that," Lu snaps, turning to her mum. "I left my purse in your suitcase."

Ewan unhooks his arm from Aria's. "Come on," he says, ushering Luciella along the hallway. "I need to go grab my wallet anyway."

When they vanish, I'm left with Kade and his mum, feeling very, very exposed in what I'm wearing. She smiles in the silence, then says to Kade, "You look smart. I hope you're feeling better."

Aria tuts at his silence, and I look at her as she checks her watch. "I'm going to see what's taking them," she says. "Maybe you'll have better luck pulling words from him."

I lower my head.

Silence fills the corridor.

"Any reason why you're ignoring me?" Kade asks.

Impulsiveness and idiocy have me turning on my ridiculously high heels to face him. "I'm going to ask Lu to go somewhere else, away from you and Base."

"I'm sure Base will be heartbroken." He shoves both hands into his pockets, licking his lips as he watches me. "He was going to make his move on you since my sister isn't giving him any attention. Not really your scene though, is it? You prefer older men and spare rooms."

"Fuck you," I seethe, the broken memory from *that* night caving my chest. "When I eventually let Base have me, I'll make sure you're around to witness it like I had to watch you in the pool house."

"Immature." Kade laughs deeply. "I expect nothing less."

"Expect nothing less of what?" Lu asks, appearing behind me, her head tilted to the side in confusion. "Never mind. We need to leave!" She turns to her brother. "Where's Base?"

"Here, princess," he greets as he leaves the hotel room next to us, and I pale at the thought he might have heard us. "Sorry. Had to shave my balls."

"Lovely," she responds with a contorted expression. "Let's go!"

She walks ahead, Base following her until they're out of sight around the corner.

Kade pushes away from the wall, leaning down to whisper, "If you weren't such a twisted snake, I'd tell you how hot you looked tonight."

I roll my eyes even though I feel like my nerves are on fire as we walk towards the elevators. "Your insults are getting weak."

"A little like yourself."

I suck my teeth. "Call me weak again – I fucking dare you."

"We don't exactly have the best track record with dares. Do we, Freckles?"

I snap my head to him, halting my steps, and he nearly knocks into me. "Don't call me that. What happened to forgetting?"

"Forgetting what?" he teases, a glint in his eyes. He seems awfully cheery compared to how he was earlier.

He doesn't reek of alcohol, but his pupils are a little bigger than usual.

I turn away from him. "Stop talking to me. You're annoying."

Kade snorts, and we keep making our way down the hallway. "I'm making conversation, not trying to fuck you."

"Thank God. I've faked enough orgasms with you to last a lifetime."

I gasp as Kade snatches me by the throat and pins me to the wall in a flash, his chest and grip holding me in place as his heavy breaths hit my ear. "I'll tell Base to take my sister without us and prove just how full of shit that fucking statement is."

Shivers work their way down my spine, my pulse thrumming against his palm. "I'd rather you didn't." I pat his shoulder, hoping to deflate his ego in some way and hide how much he affects me. "But thanks for the offer."

His jaw clenches, eyes blackening as he steps back and releases my throat. His hands fist at his sides, but the feel of his skin is still on me, shadows wreaking havoc on my hormones.

"I wish you never met Luciella." And the bucket of ice that hits me then washes away that feeling. "I wish I didn't kiss you that night."

Punching him would be bad, but I fucking want to right now. "I wish I never sucked your dick." I turn my back to him. "But *shit happens.*" I throw his own words back at him – the same ones he used outside that warehouse of horrors.

"I wish you never rode my face," he mutters low enough that only I can hear – Base and Lu are waiting for us by the elevator. "But sacrifices need to be made when one is bored."

"It was the worst face ride of my life."

"With how loud you screamed my name, I very much doubt it."

My nails sink into my palms as we reach the bickering pair.

I intentionally step on his foot when we enter the elevator, and I swear I see him trying to hold back a smirk. The dimples I've traced with my fingers countless times dent deep, and I need to look away before Lu notices me eye-fucking her brother.

He stands beside me as the doors close. Mirrors line every wall, and I look up to see him staring at me through our reflection.

While Lu checks her phone, and Base watches her, I give him the middle finger like a grown-up should.

He stifles a smile and shakes his head.

Base looks me up and down, then looks at Lu. "Fuck me," he groans. "Kade, would you kill me if I had a threesome with your sister and her best friend?"

I laugh.

Kade's scowl turns deadly.

Luciella slaps his head with her purse and tells him to shut up.

25

STACEY

The busy club is large enough that we've barely seen each other. Kade and Base stay at the bar while the latter flirts with everyone. Me and Lu sit at a booth, and I think I've drunk all of her shots.

Luciella yells over the music that Tylar is flying over, that she finished work early and has a week off. She thinks she's lying, because Dez is also flying over to meet his friends.

She doesn't like this very much.

"Why is it such an issue if they're together?"

She looks mortified. "Imagine I went there with Base! He's my brother's best friend."

"Right, I get that. But Dez isn't your brother."

She chews on her cheek. "I just don't want things getting complicated. What if they broke up, and it was messy? It would be awkward. If he cheated on her, I'd kill him. I'd tell him to stay away from my house, and then it would cause a war between me and my brother." She shrugs. "I don't want any of that."

I understand, kind of. If she feels that way about Tylar and Dez, she'd hit the roof about me and Kade – past and present.

Base falls into the booth beside Lu and throws his arm around her. "You up for that threesome yet, ladies?"

She shakes her head, trying to hide the smile on her face without moving his arm. "In your dreams."

He winks at her. "Dreams can come true, princess."

And I take that as my cue to leave. "I'm going for a stronger drink."

I know Base isn't serious. He wants Luciella – not me.

I order a vodka as a young man in a fitted black suit, his golden hair styled to perfection, appears beside me; he smiles as he gives me a second glance, leaning against the bar and looking me up and down.

I thank the bartender and sip my drink through a straw, ignoring him.

"Gerald," the guy says in his strong American accent. "This lady's drinks are on the house."

I nearly choke. "What? No."

"I'm the owner. Someone as beautiful as you shouldn't be paying for drinks."

My brows rise. "And why would you do that?"

Shrugging, he drags his gaze up and down the length of my body again. "I'm a nice, *generous* person." He winks and takes his drink before he vanishes onto the dance floor.

A firm hand lands on my hip, sending instant flutters down low as a familiar voice whispers in my ear, "You need to stop flirting with my half-a-million-dollar target."

I don't turn around, but I do tilt my head a little, my eyes on the owner of the club, who's now laughing with a group of girls. "He's worth half a million?"

My breathing stops as he pulls my back to his chest, the slit of my dress giving him access to skin-on-skin contact as he moves his hand lower. "The more dangerous, the more I get paid."

I stare at the guy bobbing around the dance floor with a goofy grin. "He doesn't look dangerous."

His chin rests on my shoulder, and my gaze shoots to the booth Lu was at, but she and Base aren't there.

"Looks can be deceiving," Kade says, his knuckles running up and down my ribs, the other hand dangerously close to an area that's currently puddling with liquid heat as he drags his fingers along the slit of my dress, sending electric shocks to my core. "Stay away from him. I need to do my job and I don't need you getting in the way."

I gulp. His touch is soft and caressing as the laser show from the DJ booth amps up through the intense song playing.

Breathless, I manage to turn my body to break the contact, looking up at him as I reply sternly, "Don't tell me what to do."

Kade laughs, pushing his tongue against his cheek. The smile on his face has my skin buzzing. "But you take orders so well," he says, rubbing a tendril of my dark hair between his fingers. "Don't you, Freckles?"

"Don't call me that." I furrow my brows at him, ignoring the growing pulse between my legs. "And you tell me: do I follow orders well, *Kade*?"

Flirting with him like this – well, our version of flirting – is ridiculous and stupid. Luciella could appear at any moment and see our closeness, the way Kade releases my hair and cups my cheek with his hand, leaning into my opposite ear.

"It was one of my favourite things about fucking you."

The hum in my blood, the nerves catching fire like an inferno, has me fighting the slam of my thighs. Against the neediness between my legs, remembering all the shitty comments he's thrown at me, I move his hand from my face. "If I remember right, you were the one who had to be given directions on how to get a girl off. Stop belittling what I was in our relationship to make yourself look better."

He chuckles, taking a sip of his drink. "These tantrums you keep having are cute."

"Cute? No, you're a walking, talking version of whiplash. One minute you act like you hate me, then you're trying to have sex with me or messaging me. You can go hump your hand for all I care."

Then a smile plays on my lips, because I want to piss him off, to push him as much as he's pushed me over the last two years. "I'm going to go over there and dance with your target, then I'm going to tell him to take me home and fuck the image of you out of my mind forever. Does that live up to your expectations of me?"

Drink halfway to his lips, he freezes. "If this is you trying to make me jealous, it won't work. I've had two years to get over you."

I snatch my glass up from the bar. "You won't mind if I excuse myself then."

"Where are you going?" he asks as I slip off the bar stool.

"To find out if your target knows how to properly make a woman scream his name."

"I wouldn't do that if I were you."

"Good thing you aren't me," I retort.

His eyes don't leave mine as I back away, deadly calm, and I'm certain he isn't breathing. I can feel his stare on my skin as I make my way through the dancing crowd.

I felt blistering rage when I saw him with that girl in the pool house. Yeah, I saw him in the magazines and newspaper columns that loved to cover his wild weekends with multiple women, but being there – seeing it in person – was way worse.

He saw a short clip of me being violated, and from the way it was edited, it looked like I was willingly fucking someone else.

It looked like I was enjoying it, cutting out the moments I tried to leave or begged for my boyfriend, but he took it as me cheating. I understand why he took off and refused to hear me out. I saw the video, and it looked terrible on my end.

It didn't show any of the other people who attacked me while my brother watched. I didn't consent to a single thing that happened to me that night.

Slut.

You prefer them older, don't you?

You're dead to me.

I was dead to myself too.

Kade's target lights up when I approach, dancing and wrapping my arms around his neck, and his greedy hands immediately find my hips. I let the beat flow through my veins, ignoring his whispers in my ear about how smoking hot I am and the way he bites me; how he drags his palms all over my body. No fire is sparking in my core, no butterflies or the desire to rip his clothes off.

The more dangerous, the more I get paid. Ridiculous. This guy is harmless and cheery and even looks like he'd be sweet.

He twirls me around and around, pulls me back into him, and I want to glance over my shoulder to make sure Kade is watching us. To see if he's angry.

Because I know he will be.

He wants to wring my neck just as much as he wants to fuck my brains out.

The feeling is definitely – annoyingly – mutual.

We turn, No Name's back to the bar, my hands on his chest, and I can see Kade over his shoulder given how short his target is. He's sipping on his drink with a blank expression, but his eyes don't leave mine.

He tips his glass in my direction with a slight nod.

Anger spikes, and when No Name plants a kiss on my lips, I don't push him away.

Fuck Kade. He's treated me like shit and spoken down to me. I might have been on my knees and riding his face not long ago, but I'm doing exactly what he wants.

I'm forgetting what happened.

I feel absolutely nothing as No Name presses his lips to mine – sloppier now – and cups my ass firmly.

I need to get this guy out of here before he ends up dead. Not for No Name's benefit, but so Kade doesn't have yet another death under his belt.

When the unfamiliar tongue tries to nudge through my lips, I don't allow him entrance; I pull away and continue dancing with him.

I hope Kade is fuming.

My immaturity levels have risen to the high heavens by now.

Kade's drink is gone – now he's leaning against the bar with his hands and glaring at me. Just to be extra mature, I give him the middle finger, whispering to No Name to take me out back.

I know Kade can read the words on my lips.

No Name's hand clutches mine, and he drags me off the dance floor, through the narrow corridor where the bathrooms are and out the back entrance into a dark, wet alleyway. There's barely any light, and we're closed in by high walls. I instantly feel uncomfortable and cold.

I don't go home with random men. It took me everything to join Tinder after what happened to me. This is purely to save his life.

"You need to leave," I say as he clicks the door closed.

He doesn't listen, pulling me into him and caressing my face with both hands. "But the fun only just started, beautiful."

I keep myself calm as I push against his chest, but he doesn't move an inch from the hold he has on me. "Let go of me."

He crushes his mouth to mine painfully, and panic sets in. I bite on his lip, hard, until I taste copper then stomp on his shoe with my heel.

No Name wipes blood from his lip, eyes wide, before lunging. "You fucking teasing—"

A fist flying into his face cuts him off, launching him into the wall with such force, I'm surprised his skull isn't cracked open.

Kade takes my chin as he searches me for any injuries. His thumb swipes the blood from my lip. "Did he hit you?"

I pull my jaw free. "No. It's his blood."

"What the fuck are you playing at? What part of *he's dangerous* do you not understand?"

He smashes his elbow into No Name's face when he throws himself towards Kade in a weak attack. No Name drops to the ground again, groaning and holding his excessively bleeding mouth.

My ex points at him. "Stay the fuck down. I'll deal with you in a minute."

I cross my arms. "I told you what I was doing," I state. A huge part of me wants to run back into the club to get away from No Name, away from his horrid advances, but I also don't want Kade to kill someone else. "Just let him go."

This version of him isn't real. It can't be.

"It's my fucking job," he snaps.

When No Name gets to his feet again, Kade grits his teeth and grabs him by the throat, slamming him into the wall. "Did you enjoy that? Did you enjoy having her fucking attention?"

"Dude, come on." He laughs, teeth stained red as he spits to the side. "I have a lot more than her if you're looking for quality."

I frown at the comment.

Kade headbutts him – his nose bursts with crimson, his skull cracking against the wall. He frees his shirt from his waistband and pulls out the gun he had earlier, pressing it under his target's chin.

I rush forward. "Kade, stop! You don't really want to do this."

"Stop?" he retorts, fisting the guy's hair. "Do you know why I was assigned to kill him?"

No Name's eyes go wide, begging and pleading silently, but Kade's attention is on me. "A father contacted my boss and wanted him taken down for drugging his underage daughter and raping her."

I stop breathing, my stomach roiling.

"He's a filthy bastard. Aren't you, you little prick? How many girls were victims of yours?"

No Name smiles. I need to bleach my mouth. "Then you know I have enough ass to make you a good bargain."

He drugged and raped someone.

I no longer see the young American but Chris and numerous other men standing in Kade's grip, uncaring as they talk about all the ways they wanted to fuck me that night. The way Chris egged them on. Charged per fuck. Videoed it.

I see my brother hovering over me while I hallucinated, begged him to take me home and cried that I wanted my boyfriend. The way his lips felt on my forehead while he let someone else violate me with their mouth. Teeth sinking into my breast, leaving a wound that took weeks to heal.

No Name isn't No Name. He's another Chris, who drugs and destroys, breaks and manipulates. He's a monster.

I fist my hands at my sides, not caring how psychotic I sound. "Hit him again."

26

STACEY

Kade punches him in the stomach, knocking the air from his lungs. "Again?"

Tears burn my eyes. "Yes. Make it hurt."

The butt of the gun meets his head three times, and No Name slides down the wall with blood trickling from his hairline.

"He was supposed to serve ten years," Kade says, kicking No Name's legs as he tries to get up. "I read your report. Disgusting pig."

You want to fuck her? Give me three hundred and she's yours.

Do I need to pay for my services too?

What about a big-brother discount?

Kade turns to me. "What do you want me to do now?"

Adrenaline courses through my veins, and I need to release it. Deep breaths fall from my lips as I study Kade. As my eyes hold his, my chest caves with how much I wish we were back in the hotel room, on the jet, on holiday or lying on a beach somewhere.

It's so foreign, this intense feeling. Like seeing Kade this way has something switching on inside me. This once. I can have him this once and get him out of my system.

I tilt my head to No Name. "Knock him out."

Kade's knee belts into his face without hesitation, and he slouches on the ground.

He turns to me, gun still in hand, waiting. "What now?"

My skin burns with deep need, my nipples tightening, rubbing against my dress, which is begging to be ripped off. I shouldn't be turned on by his violence.

He's a machine, and I want him.

"Finish what you started."

He takes a careful step towards me, and my heart stutters.

"What did I start?"

I raise a brow.

"You want an audience?"

He slowly closes the distance when I don't reply, because my body is too alive and charged with energy to do anything but wait for his touch. "I asked you a question."

I raise my chin, my heart racing, my pussy clenching as Kade's eyes travel up and down the length of my body. "Do you hate me?"

He frowns. "What?"

"I said, do you hate me?"

"Yes."

"Do you want to hurt me?"

"Sometimes. But not the way you think."

My gaze drops to the weapon, and I wrap my fingers around his wrist and bring it to my face. I manipulate his hold to press the barrel to my forehead, and like I thought, my clit throbs from the danger. "Does this make you feel better? You hate me, so you could end it now."

The faint click tells me he turns the safety on, but he doesn't pull the gun away.

"You could kill me right now."

He gulps and grips the handle.

Everything deep within me is vibrating, all the way down to my toes as Kade pushes the barrel of the silencer harder against my forehead, making me back into the wall.

"You would love to shoot me, wouldn't you?"

Kade licks his lips, finally speaking. "It would be more hassle than it's worth."

"Because you'd have the mess to clean up?"

He shakes his head. "Because I'd go insane without being able to watch you. I do hate you. I hate who you are, but I can't stop thinking about your cunt strangling my cock while I throttle you. I picture you covered in blood that isn't yours. My name on your lips. Screaming for more while you apologise over and over and fucking *over* again." He presses the barrel harder to my forehead. "Hate is not the word I would use when it comes to you."

I smirk. "Always the romantic, Kade."

He hums, the barrel of the gun slipping down the side of my face gently. He drags the metal across my lips, pulling the bottom one down before he trails the metal between my breasts.

The coldness against my heated skin has me panting.

"The year we spent together was the worst year of my life," he says. "If I could take every moment back, every *lie*, I would."

There's no venom in his words, because his eyes are hooded, his cock is hard and pressing against my thigh, his breathing unsteady.

"Sounds like you definitely got over me in those two years."

Kade glares at me, eyes filled with a growing void – his soul rippling into a vortex I want to dive into.

My lungs seize as he drags the gun down, down, down, until he reaches the slit of my dress. "I got over you, just like you easily got over me."

The tip of the silencer inches between my legs as Kade grabs my hair, elongating my throat. I gasp as the weapon presses to my cunt at the same time his tongue swipes up my throat, teeth nibbling my jaw.

"I want you to cum on my gun." He moves it against my pussy, my underwear in the way, and I let out a moan.

Stopping his movements, he sucks on my jaw. "Keep going. Rub yourself on it."

I grind my hips against the gun, needing more pressure. My spine tingles, a coiling heat pooling in my core from how intense it feels, having Kade's mouth on my body and his gun against the material of my underwear.

"You like that?" His voice is low, and his tongue tickles my earlobe as he speaks, his breath hitching in my ear as I palm his cock. He groans. "Fuck."

Moaning, I grind harder, chasing that electricity. The tug of my hair, the bite on my shoulder blade, the way his energy merges with mine causes me to shiver as I head to euphoria already.

Whimpers are ripped from my lungs as heat builds in my core, my legs shaking as the silencer runs from my clit to my entrance, sliding and grinding, making my toes curl and my hands grip his shoulders.

I yelp as he rips my underwear off and slides his gun between my legs again, pressing it to my cunt but not entering. "*Kade,*" I breathe as the pleasure intensifies.

He hisses as I scrape his skin when my orgasm hits like a tidal wave, holding the metal to me as I pulse against it.

It intensifies as he sucks on my pulse and hisses, "That's right. Fucking cum all over my gun."

I moan loud enough that the sound echoes around us, throwing my head back as my legs shake, and Kade has to hold me up.

My high goes on for what feels like forever, and I welcome it as he holds me. When I gasp, my heart racing as the pinnacle hits, he spins me around, presses his chest to my back and sinks his fingers inside me. His hard cock is against my ass as he pulls up my dress.

I bite my lip as he curls his fingers inside and fucks me with them – hard and fast.

Ready – I'm desperate for him to replace them with his cock.

I flinch as he pulls them out.

"I need inside this cunt," he growls as he shoves me forward, bending me over, the leaking tip rubbing against my clit and entrance. He points the gun at No Name, who's barely conscious.

With one punishing, harsh thrust, he drives home, fully sheathed inside me. I can't contain the scream I let out or the slap of my hand over my mouth. My pussy welcomes his cock, clenching around him. He's large, thick, and my tight walls are clutching as he slowly pulls out – then pushes back in until each inch fills me once more.

Full. I'm so full.

He yanks my hair to lift my head to the side, forcing me to face No Name.

"She's beautiful, right? You agree, or you wouldn't have fucking kissed her."

I gasp as he thrusts harshly, pushing deeper, my eyes fixed on the gun he's pointing over my shoulder.

"Watch what I do to her. Watch how well she takes my cock while you lie there and wait for death. Let her screams for more be the last thing you fucking hear."

No Name is barely able to open his eyes, his head lolling but I don't care. The sensation of being so complete, so tight around Kade, has me pressing back, meeting his movements.

For some diabolical reason, having my best friend's brother screw me while a version of Chris lies in front of us makes me even more turned on. He's at gunpoint. About to die, and the last thing he'll see is me being fucked by Kade Mitchell.

My pussy grips his pummelling cock, the faint music of the club hardly drowning out the sound of how wet I am.

When he slows, I beg, "No. Don't be gentle."

He wraps my hair around his fist, tugging my head back. "You don't deserve it gentle, Freckles."

And with that, he roughly fucks me like I'm his enemy, each snap of his hips nearly pushing me out of my heels. I cry as he hammers into me, my dress bunched at my waist, boobs bouncing, my clit throbbing to be touched.

Kade's cock slips out as he turns and lifts me into his arms then presses my back to the wall. His head nudges through my soaking slit, and I lace my fingers in his hair.

As he thrusts in, I moan, "Oh God."

There's a sting on my ass cheek, and he grits out, "I'm not putting all this effort in for you to call some other fucker's name." He pummels into me harshly. "Say *my* fucking name."

"Kade," I breathe, barely audible as he sinks deep.

He groans so intensely, so low, I feel it vibrate in my bones.

"Open your mouth," he orders while lifting the gun, the silencer pressing to my lips. "Suck on it while I fuck you."

For a second, I hesitate, but then my lips part as the metal prods between them.

My spine arches as he fucks into me while I suck on his gun, fear and pleasure mixing at the idea he could fire at any point and kill me.

His finger is on the trigger after all.

"Do you know how many people have died from this gun?"

I choke as he pushes it further into my mouth while gripping my ass. I tighten around his dick and moan around the metal as a wave of euphoria hits me.

"Do you know how many times I've pictured fucking you with it? Only to kill you right after?"

My inner walls flutter around him as every nerve ending spark into wildfire all over my body – every cell humming as I see stars. I try to cry his name, the word inaudible.

He pulls the gun from my mouth and tilts my chin up as I try to catch my breath, whimpering as he continues driving into me.

"Such a good girl for me, aren't you?" He swipes the saliva across my lips, my back smacking the wall as he hammers into me with a snarl. "But sometimes you're bad to me, and it makes me really *fucking* angry."

A mumble to the side interrupts us, and Kade's jaw clenches as he slows his thrusts. I flinch and cover my ears as he puts four bullets in No Name before dropping the weapon.

"I'm done having an audience," he says as he pulls out and makes me face the wall, bending me over once more. "Can't fucking stand you. Kissing random guys at the club."

He shoves into me again, and my palms slap the wall to keep myself steady.

"I should shoot you too," he grits out as he grasps one of my breasts, his hips snapping, mercilessly filling me again and again, causing my pussy to throb and pulse around his cock.

"Harder," I moan.

He slaps my ass with enough force to hurt, and my fluttering cunt strangles his thickness. My body nearly crashes into the wall as he slams into me, and my arms struggle to keep me in place.

"You've always responded so well to me. So. Fucking. Well."

Each thrust has me releasing a moan. He tightens his hold on my hair, both of us moving as our moans and curses echo in a perfect symphony.

In my peripheral vision, I see a river of blood trailing towards us.

We're fucking next to a dead body.

I fist my hands against the wall as he pinches my nipple then twists it. "Fuck, *Kade*."

I'm so close again. So damn close. My toes curl, eyes screwed shut as I feel an inferno rushing through my nerve endings.

Kade snatches my chin and turns my head to face him over my shoulder. "Open your fucking eyes. Look at me while you cum."

I do, seeing his lips parting with gasps with each thrust of his cock inside me.

The burning desire wraps around the base of my spine – and I shatter completely.

His hand slips down to my throat, and he nearly cuts off my air as he fucks me through my orgasm. His hold is as tight as my walls around his shaft. Black dots appear from the pressure, but it only amplifies my orgasm.

"That's it. Right fucking there. Shit. I can feel your pussy gripping my cock. I'll cum inside you, Freckles. And I want you to walk around the club with it dripping down your legs, so everyone knows how dirty you are."

My walls tighten around him repeatedly, pulsing with warmth, my heart speeding up to a dangerous rate as my orgasm hits its excruciating pinnacle. My vision shadows, the faint sound of music vanishes, and it's just me and Kade and how he robs me of air.

He stills on a groan as his cock twitches deep inside me, pumping me full of his cum. He's sinking his teeth into my shoulder, but I can't cry out his name; I can't do anything but silently scream as his hold tightens on my throat until he lets go.

Quivering, we both pant, sweat slick on our skins as we try to put ourselves back together. His heart is racing against my back, matching my own.

"You've no idea how long I've wanted it to feel like that."

I exhale deeply as I fill my starved lungs, fully satisfied yet wanting him to stay in place. "Me too."

He lowers his head so we're cheek to cheek, both breathing heavily. "Did I hurt you?"

"No," I manage.

When I glance to the side, his eyes are closed, his nose nudging my cheek delicately. He turns his head more, angling his mouth close to the corner of mine. I fully turn my head too, and he opens his dilated eyes and stares at me, lips parted, gaze dropping to my mouth.

He reaches up to hold the side of my face, caressing his thumb against the glistening skin – the tear from him strangling me. The soft, welcoming, loving touch confuses me.

His hooded gaze drops to my mouth again, and I want so badly to kiss him. To let him kiss me.

But it's too much.

I look away before this gets more complicated. Kissing has always been a big thing to him – to us. He hated casual, unnecessary forms of affection. Us locking lips right now would be an in-the-moment mistake he'll throw in my face down the line.

Besides, I'm nothing but a slut to him.

I wince as he slides out, and I feel the coldness in the night as he backs away and stuffs his cock into his pants. He fixes his hair, his chest rising and falling, then checks No Name is dead before grabbing his gun.

Kade calls someone while I right my dress – my underwear is destroyed – and panic starts to settle in. What I just did was... inhumane. Sick. Wrong. Yet, I felt alive.

He tells someone the location of the body then texts for a minute before he takes a picture of No Name.

My eyes water with rage at how unbothered he is by what he just did, and what he's doing now. I step away, putting distance between us as I smooth my hair. Kade says nothing as he stows his phone, watching me as I back away from the dead body we just fucked in front of.

I feel dirty.

You're dead to me.

"Was it worth it?" I ask him, motioning to the body. "Committing a crime to have half a million in your bank account."

Kade laughs silently and tucks the firearm into his waistband. "I have a lot more than half a million in my bank account."

"It sickens me how proud you are of yourself."

I wipe my eyes again, annoyed at myself for getting emotional.

"You're upset? Why?"

I dodge him trying to touch me.

"Hey. Talk to me, Freckles."

That name triggers so many memories for me.

I could listen to your voice on the phone forever, Freckles.

I miss your annoying face. I'll see you soon, Freckles.

Can I touch you, Freckles?

I'm not asking, Freckles. You're going on a date with me.

Freckles. Freckles. Freckles.

"I wish I could hate you the same way you hate me," I manage, dragging my wet gaze from him, stepping over the trail of blood. "This person you are now, I wish you weren't him." I close my eyes as I take a deep breath and walk to the door, his cum already leaking out of me.

I stop. "You make me feel worthless for something that wasn't my fault. And as fun as it's been messing with you the past few days, you're out of my system."

Throwing the door open, I don't spare him a last look. "Clean your mess up before you get caught. Have a good night, Kade."

27

KADE

FLASHBACK 5

Freckles: Do you still have Jason's car? Is it possible for you to pick me up later? It'll be like two in the morning by the time I get through all my routines. It's okay if you can't. I can get an Uber.

Me: I can get you. 2 a.m.?

Freckles: Yeah. I have no make-up on, so don't look at me.

Me: Do you forget I've seen you without make-up since we were 15? I'll see you at 2.

She goes offline, and I grab a quick shower to try to sober myself after smoking too many joints. I'm really stoned, and I'm thinking the extra roll-up was a bad idea. Dez and Base will be in the pool house until the sun comes up, and I'm debating going back down for an hour. I had to leave after Base started speaking about my sister in Russian and Dez asked me who Freckles was after catching a glimpse at my phone screen.

Safe to say they are more than enthusiastic that I'm no longer frigid.

It's just after one. If I go for a nap and set an alarm for half an hour, then I'll never make it to pick her up. But if I go to see my friends, I'll be too fucked up to drive.

Jason has let me use his car while he has Giana's. I don't think he'll be too pleased to know I've been smoking in it or that I plan on picking up Stacey while baked as fuck.

I lie back on the bed, my hair still damp. I feel like I'm sinking into it, like the duvet is more comfortable than usual, that my pillow is a huge marshmallow.

Without meaning to, I close my eyes. And without meaning to, I fall asleep.

I sit up, my body aching from the angle I slept. I groan, rub my face, getting to my feet, crack my neck left and right and then stretch my arms above my head. I blow out a breath. When my eyes fall on the clock beside my bed, I see it's seven in the morning, and a sudden tearing sensation rips through my chest.

"Shit!" I rush to grab clothes from my dresser, pulling socks on then one of my trainers. I hop along the floor while getting the other shoe on and snatch Jason's keys from my unit. Then I stop, freezing all over. It's seven, meaning I was supposed to get her five hours ago. She's not going to be there. How far away is her house from the studio? What if she had to walk?

Two messages and one missed call.

Freckles: It's too cold. I'm going to wait inside. Let me know when you're here.

Freckles: Sorry. I didn't mean to overstep. We never clarified what we were doing, so I just assumed we were... I don't know? Not dating but not exactly casual, since we've been sneaking around for the last month. I won't ask you again. It was wrong of me.

Me: Fuck, I'm sorry! I fell asleep. Did you get home okay? Don't be sorry – you did nothing wrong. Message me when you wake up.

Tossing my phone on my bed, I think of every single way to slap myself, growing more anxious from her silence.

What if she's still there?

Fuck. You fucking idiot, Kade.

I rush out of my room, nearly knocking Mum on her ass in the hallway.

"I was bringing these to your bathroom. Where are you going?"

"Um... I need to do something."

She grabs my face with one hand. "Your eyes are bloodshot. Are you smoking again?"

"No," I lie. "I just woke up." I get to my feet. "I thought you were working today."

"I was supposed to be. My patient, the little girl, died last night." She gives me a tight smile. She's exhausted. "Don't look at me like that. Get going."

I nod. "Sorry. Make sure you get some sleep. You look like shit."

Mum narrows her eyes. "Leave, before I force you to clean the pool with me."

When I go to turn, she says, "And, Kade? I know Ewan has spoken to you about this before, but if you're sleeping with her, please wear protection."

I pale. "I don't need to hear this from you. And I'm not sleeping with her, alright?"

"Then be patient with her. Stacey will be ready when she's ready."

I stop. "She's the one being patient with me."

Mum stares at me for a second, and then her lips part. "Oh."

Yeah. Oh.

Everyone's assumption that I sleep around is starting to piss me off. As if I'm not getting annoyed at myself for being a skittish prick when around her, I need to deal with my friends, and now my mother, thinking I'm fucking Stacey.

Wait.

"How do you know? Dad told you?"

She starts to walk away. "Your dad tells me everything. Now go. I'll see you when you get home."

Torrential rain pours as I drive away from the manor and out the gates, picking up speed when I reach the motorway. She hasn't replied to my message yet, so I send another while I drive, asking if she's home.

"Hi, you're through to Stacey. Leave a message."

I hang up and drive faster.

I head straight to the studio and get there within half an hour. The doors are locked, and I contemplate kicking them in to see if she's inside.

I call again. No answer.

She might be asleep inside.

I knock on the door – three hard thumps. "Stacey? Are you in there?"

Nothing.

I go back to the car and light a cigarette, debating whether to ask Luciella for Stacey's address so I can make sure she isn't still walking home.

My heart feels weird. It's the reaction I used to get as a kid, thinking one of my parents would catch me out on a lie or give me into trouble when I did something wrong. That uncertainty that something bad is coming.

I know what butterflies feel like, but this is different. I feel sick, as if I could throw open the car door and bring up my guts.

I'm dizzy, and I realise I'm breathing fast and hard.

What's wrong with me?

I get out of the car again, the rain drenching me as I stand staring at the studio building. The coldness helps whatever's ripping me to shreds inside, but I still have the twisting feeling in my stomach.

I walk down the side of the building, checking the other doors and windows, sighing in relief when one opens. I slip in. It closes behind me, and I'm surrounded by darkness. The LEDs are always on, so when I see a pink glow under one of the doors in the corridor, I head for it.

Stacey isn't here. The place is empty and smells of pine – as it always does when she's cleaned up after herself. Poles and hoops crowd me, crash mats piled on the right, a full wall of mirrors to the left.

I find the folder full of everyone's details and scan for Stacey's name.

Five minutes later and nothing. How many students do they have?

I open the file of employee details. Jackpot.

Stacey Rhodes. Teaching qualifications and training in pole fitness, pole dance, erotic dance, aerial hoop, disco dance, kids dance, contemporary dance, silks and fire dance.

Damn. My girl is talented.

I leave the studio as soon as I find her address.

Stacey lives on a fancy estate. Her house is big, with three floors, white bricks and security gates. All the lights are out except for one at the top right. The curtains are closed, but I can see the shadow of someone moving around.

I finish my smoke and flick it out the window, debating what to say. An apology obviously. An explanation. And, hopefully, she forgives me and tells me to come in.

I'll kiss her and go back to sleep in her bed. Then we'll be good.

So why are my hands shaking so badly?

I buzz the gate, wait a few minutes, and when no one grants me access, I climb the wall. I'm not giving a shit if I set off alarms. I need to see her.

Nothing happens though, so her family definitely needs to sack their security team.

I walk around the small fountain at the front steps and knock on the door. Once. Twice. A third time for good measure.

My heart races to an unbearable pace, and I shove my hands in my pockets to stop them from trembling when I hear the door unlocking.

A man with a grey beard pulls it open. "Can I help you?"

Rain drips down my face. "Is Stacey here?"

"Who are you?" he asks, wary. He looks as if I just broke into his house and asked to kidnap his daughter. "How did you get in?"

I shrug. "I climbed the wall. Is Stacey here?"

"You..." He chokes, pushing his glasses up his nose. "Who the hell are you?"

Before I can glare and tell him to watch his fucking tone, a soft voice stops me.

"Dad, it's okay."

A small hand rests on his shoulder, and the door opens wider. My lungs fill when Stacey comes into view in her PJs.

"He's a friend."

I think the fuck not. Instead of showing any hint of how that one word burns me, I keep my hands in my pockets and wait for her dad to fuck off.

Stacey waits until he's out of earshot then turns to me. "Why are—"

"I fell asleep," I cut in, taking a careful step towards her. "I didn't mean to. Are you alright? Did you have to walk? Did you get an Uber?"

"My dad came for me. You didn't need to come all the way over here." Then she frowns. "How did you know where I lived?"

I broke into the studio and violated your privacy, then climbed the wall when the gate wouldn't open.

"I'm resourceful."

"Oh..." She taps the door, chewing her lip. "You need to go."

My insides drop. "Why? I'm sorry. I wanted to come and see you. I really did."

She looks behind her, then her eyes are on me again. "I'll see you later, okay? Thanks for bringing my phone."

I frown. "Eh?"

She gives me a tight smile as she closes the door, and I momentarily freeze.

I knew I'd fuck this up.

I rub my hand through my hair then grab my phone and type another apology out as I leave. The gate opens for me, and I slip into my car.

My heart is beating so hard.

Before I can drive off, the door swings open, and green eyes look at me. "Hi."

I stare at her as she sits. "Hi."

"My phone died – that's why I couldn't text back. You really didn't need to drive away over here. My dad is kind of on edge all the time and isn't a fan of boys near the house." She clips her belt in. "Not that I have boys over. He's just… overbearing sometimes."

"Yeah," I reply. "I thought you might have walked home. I wanted to catch you."

"At eight in the morning?"

I shrug. "Are you… good with me?"

"Of course."

I'm confused. I blink at her.

She sighs. "You scared my dad. He was caught off guard. He's usually really nice."

"So you aren't mad at me?"

"Of course not. I thought I overstepped. Can you drive somewhere?"

I start the engine. "You didn't overstep. You could ask me to drive you to fucking Australia and I'd find a way to do it. Where do you want to go? Luciella is still in Stranraer."

"Anywhere. I can't stay out for long."

I nod, and in comfortable silence, I drive us to Loch Thom and park next to the water.

I don't move my hand away when she takes it, lacing our fingers and resting our hands in her lap. She looks so innocent and sweet and fucking adorable.

I'm going to miss her when I go to America for two weeks.

Stacey doesn't let go of my hand as she unclips her belt and turns her body to face me. I do the same. "As much as I should be giving you shit for breaking into the studio and then into my garden, I find it cute that you went to those lengths."

I tilt my head. "You knew I was in the studio?"

Nodding, she giggles. "I got an alert on my phone. I saw it when I turned it on. You're lucky Tylar didn't get one too. She would've called the police."

"I guess I am lucky."

"Hmm."

"Hmm," I repeat. "You sure you aren't mad at me? I honestly fell asleep."

"I believe you," she says with a spark in her eyes. "You're just my

friend anyway."

I narrow my eyes to slits. "Say that again and I'm going to kick you out of this car and drive away."

"Will you at least kiss me before you do?"

"Maybe," I say, letting go of her hand and curling a strand of hair behind her ear. "Maybe I'll just kick you out and drive away."

She snorts. "You think I believe with the lengths you went to see me, you'd leave me up here?"

"I guess we'll see."

"Okay, friend*."*

I open my door and she lets out a scream, scrambling away from the passenger door. As I try to catch her leg, she dives into the back seat. I climb in with her, and instead of dragging her out, I trap her beneath me, both hands above her head. We breathe heavily. We're both smiling, her giggle making me smile harder.

"Do I Wanna Know?" by Arctic Monkeys is faintly playing on the radio. Her eyes drop to my mouth, fingers intertwining with my own, and as I lower my head slowly, my nose nudges hers.

"I'm not your friend, Freckles. Do you know why?" I kiss her lips. "Because friends don't do this." I kiss her again, her top lip, then the bottom, before dragging my mouth across the sharp line of her jaw. "If I was your friend, I wouldn't think about you every second of the day. I wouldn't want to feel you." Taking flesh between my teeth, I suck, and she gasps. "All of you."

And I mean it. I want her. I want her so bad my cock is fucking sore with how hard it is. I don't want to just fuck her and disappear like Dez and Base do; I want to share every single first with her and stick around.

No matter what, the progression between me and Stacey will be slow. Progress is progress. I truly believe she won't vanish because I need to take things in steps.

I pull my face back to look at her. "Am I your friend?"

"No."

Taking her wrists with one hand, I use the other to move hair from her face, resting it as a collar on her throat. Her pulse is rapid against my palm, her pupils dilating more with each passing second. There's a thrill in watching my fingers flex around her throat, a thrill I never knew existed.

I lean down and kiss her again, sucking on her bottom lip and then

building for years, and stop at the waistband of her underwear.

I feel her with the tip of my middle finger. The material is fucking soaked, and I had no idea Base was telling the truth when he boasted about how wet he could get someone. Stacey is really wet for me as I tease her and kiss her and press against her clit through her underwear.

"Is this good?" I ask, slowly circling my finger.

She moans and rolls her hips up. "Yes."

"You need to tell me what to do," I say, not feeling an ounce of embarrassment. "When you touch yourself, what gets you off?"

Stacey wets her lips and rests one hand on my wrist, the other moving aside the triangle of fabric covering her. "What you were just doing – do it now."

Her head drops back on the seat as I do just that, as I feel the slickness of her folds, the arousal against my fingers, the swollen clit that has her whimpering when I circle it with my thumb. Warm, wet, her eyes wild as I lean down to capture her mouth.

My cock hardens even more. "You're so fucking perfect."

Her mouth breaks away from mine with a gasp as I slowly push one finger inside her. Gently, I wait, feeling her tightness, yet she's soaked enough that I can probably push another in. But I'll wait for her to adjust.

"Does it hurt?"

"No," she replies and pulls my face back to hers. "Keep going."

I slowly ease my middle finger in until I'm knuckle deep, then glide it out and back in. Each time I push, her body shakes. I add a second finger, being careful not to hurt her, and her lips travel to my throat, sucking as she gasps.

I bury my head down, inhaling the scent of her coconut shampoo. I get knuckle deep with both fingers, keeping my thumb on her clit, circling, pumping, feeling her breathing against my neck as I go a little faster, a little harder as I curl my fingers.

"Tell me if I'm doing it wrong," I say, dodging her hand as she tries to touch me. "No. This is about you."

Stacey has a thin layer of sweat on her – her cheeks are red, her hair wild, but her eyes are wilder.

My dick just about explodes as she says, "I think I'm—"

She doesn't get to finish her sentence. Not because I stop her, but because her words are cut off when something erupts inside her, tightening around my fingers.

Shattering like glass, Stacey moans and sinks her nails into my skin. I hiss, capturing her bottom lip between my teeth while I continue fucking her with my fingers. I can feel her pulsing, the wet heat drenching my hand while she rocks her hips through the orgasm ripping through her.

When I slowly withdraw my fingers, soaked in her arousal and cum, she winces slightly. I rest my hand on her thigh. "You okay?"

She nods, and then smiles. "That was unbelievable. We need to do it, like, all the time."

I chuckle, wiping my fingers on my grey sweats. "Fine by me. Do friends go on dates?" I ask her, grinning. "Or would I be crossing the line by taking you on one before I leave for America?"

Stacey snakes her arms around me. "We are friends," she says, and I feel like tossing her in the loch. "But we're also more."

"Hmm..."

She hums back. "You haven't asked me yet."

I narrow my eyes. "I'm not asking, Freckles. You're going on a date with me."

28

STACEY

Dez and Tylar landed yesterday, but I was too tired to go with Luciella, Aria and Base to pick them up. After our night out, I was hit by a migraine and stayed in bed for nearly two days before I peeled myself from the mattress.

I've not reached out to Kade. He's kept his distance too, since I've not seen him. No calls or messages. Although, I only just stopped feeling him inside me – the ache between my legs has been a harsh reminder of the neediness of my body around him.

Tylar pulls me from my daze. "Are you coming to the bar? It has pool tables!"

She's sipping on her cocktail while we sit next to the pool, the sun blazing down on us. Base and Dez are throwing a ball between them while downing beers. Lu is between them, trying to catch it and complaining that they're not playing fairly, and Aria is sunbathing with an open book on her face.

Ewan is working with one of his contractors, a job he's been setting up near Tobias's institution for a while.

And like I said, Kade is MIA.

"Um, are you okay?" Ty asks when I don't reply.

"Oh, sorry." I shake the uneasy feeling off. "Yeah. Sure."

She tilts her head, sunglasses nearly bigger than her face showing my reflection. "Are you sure you're okay?"

I nod once.

To be honest, I'm nervous as hell. I asked Kade's mum if she could put me on the visitation list to see Tobias, and tomorrow morning, I'll be sitting down with him – the psychopath I used to study religiously. Every article, every documentary, even the leaked interview with him from the day he was arrested – I poured over it all, fascinated by his mind and the way it worked; the way his eyes, devoid of anything, darkened whenever Aria Miller was mentioned.

At that point, I had no idea there would be a time I'd fuck his son. *Repeatedly.*

I'm not nervous to see Tobias – I'm terrified.

My phone vibrates as we pack up and head back into the hotel. Dez slaps Tylar's ass as he passes us in the corridor, and she side-eyes me, probably wondering if I noticed.

They aren't very discreet. They haven't taken their eyes off each other since they arrived, and I know the little red mark on her throat was made by his teeth.

He winks at her as he enters his room, Base trailing behind. But I overhear it before I can get into my own room – Dez tells his friend that Kade is leaving his girlfriend's house soon and will meet them later.

Girlfriend. As in, Kade has a girlfriend. He's in a relationship. And we've been messing around.

He was inside me a few nights ago and then he just… vanished.

I can barely control my temper as I slam the hotel-room door, ignoring Tylar's concerned expression as I march into the bathroom and lock myself in. I breathe deeply, staring at my reflection in the mirror.

Kade has a girlfriend. Since fucking when? Why the hell didn't he tell me?

When I was on my knees for him, about to suck his cock, he told me it meant nothing, and I was fine with it remaining as nothing. But this is low. This isn't who I am, someone who sleeps with taken, completely unavailable men.

I feel dirty and used.

He isn't mine, and I lay no claim on the idiot. But I want to slap him hard enough that his *girlfriend* asks who the handprint belongs to.

I practice a fake smile, wash my hands and leave the bathroom to find Tylar texting on the bed while Luciella hunts for an outfit.

I try not to think of that night while I sit down next to Ty. His hands on me. His hips snapping into me, his large cock hammering my tight pussy. The flush I can feel on my cheeks and the way my thighs tense is far too annoying. We fucked. We argued – as usual – and in good old Kade fashion, he vanished. And now he apparently has a girlfriend.

Luciella sighs as her phone dings. "Base keeps asking me on a date."

"Then go on a date with him," I say as Tylar says, "Go for it."

"Absolutely not."

I shrug. "But you like him."

"What? No I don't."

I can see right through her lie, but that's okay. Luciella has always been like this. Her family has a bad name, but she's made it her life's mission to be a good person, to not step out of line or get into any sort of trouble.

Including staying away from Sebastian Prince.

Once we tidy up the room and get dressed, Lu goes to see her mum while Ty paints my nails.

"You're seeing Dez again," I throw out quietly. "I'm happy for you."

She blushes. "Please don't say anything. I'll tell Lu, but I like being in our bubble where it's just us two. She'll get mad and try to make me split up with him, and I'm not ready to even consider that."

"I get it." I watch her stroking the brush on each nail. "Don't break up with him. Promise?"

"I promise." She smiles, painting my thumbnail. "I tried to stay away from Dez, but I felt so lost without him, Stacey." She caps the nail polish, blowing on my nails. "I'll tell Lu soon."

"If you don't want to be caught before then, maybe try to be a little more discreet," I say with a giggle. "He had his hand on your ass at the bar next to the pool and then kissed your cheek."

"Lu was too busy arguing with Base in the pool to notice."

I snort. "That's true. Those two have been bickering this entire trip."

"What about you and Kade?"

I glance up at her. "What?"

She gives me a knowing look before she stands and examines her work. "You suit dark nail polish," she says, changing the subject. "Matches your soul."

"What did you mean about me and—"

"She suits that colour, right, Lu?"

Luciella's back, staring into the mirror and swiping red lipstick on her lips. "As dark as her cold heart."

"Fuck you both."

"Base and Dez are coming out with us tonight and I am *not* happy."

Tylar smirks as she looks away, and I try not to giggle. She has no idea how much Base has got under her skin.

I pull on my jeans and top, looking at my phone as it dings.

> ***Kade**: Are you going out tonight with Luciella and Tylar?*

I peer up at my friends, both now fixing their hair and make-up in the mirror as I type back, my pulse thrashing in my ears.

> ***Me**: Why? Does your girlfriend not want to hang out with you anymore?*

As soon as I hit send, I regret the petty, jealous and downright childish reply. Why can't I just ignore him and get on with my holiday?

"Okay. Let's go!" Lu exclaims, a smile plastered to her face, and when she opens the door, Base and Dez are leaning against the wall, both dressed immaculately. The former looks Lu up and down with a smile that lights up his entire being as she groans and shoulders past him.

She glances at us. "And that leaves tomorrow night to have some girl time before we head back to Scotland. Away from these assholes."

She definitely said that so he'd hear.

"Sounds like love to me," Base mutters, and she elbows him in the side.

While I'm in the Uber, I feel my phone vibrate, but I ignore it. In the bar, it burns in my palm, and I itch to read the messages I'm sure are from Kade, but I refrain.

The place is small, not too busy and doesn't smell. But before I can get a good look around, my gaze lands on a tall, muscled figure at the bar, a tattoo crawling up his neck, dark hair a mess as usual. Kade turns to us, lifting his beer bottle up as his friends head towards him.

I look away and go find the chair furthest from the pool table the boys have chosen, and Tylar orders us drinks. My phone vibrates again, my eyes flickering to Kade as he taps on his screen. Another notification comes through.

Groaning, I give in and check it.

***Kade**: The fuck are you on about?*

***Kade**: I don't have a girlfriend. When would I have time for that? You think I'd fuck you when I was with someone else?*

***Kade**: Although, jealousy looks cute on you.*

I narrow my eyes at the screen. Muttering a *prick* under my breath, I type back quickly before my friends see.

***Me**: Cockiness looks ugly on you. I'm not jealous either. And don't lie. Dez said you were leaving your girlfriend's place to meet them. I really don't care, but don't come near me again.*

Glancing up, I see his thumbs rapidly work his phone, his brows knitted in anger, and I can't help but feel a little relieved, because somehow, I believe him. I watch him chew on his lip, still typing back to me. When the notification comes through, he looks up at me, and we hold each other's stare until I feel treacherous heat creeping up my spine.

***Kade**: I don't have a fucking girlfriend. I had to lie to them. Once I finish this game, go to the bathroom when I walk out. It's easier to talk.*

***Me**: Now you want to talk? No thanks.*

"Who has you scowling at your phone?" Ty asks, and I quickly turn my screen off.

"No one," I reply, and her eyes flicker to the boys.

"Is this my drink?" I point to the red cocktail, and when she nods, I take a huge gulp. "Please tell me we aren't staying here all night."

Ty and Lu both say the opposite at the same time. Luciella grumbles and drops her face into her hands.

We then talk about what our plans are for when we get home, since Lu is desperate to get away from Base and cutting the trip short. The conversation goes on for hours, and Tylar and Dez stand at the bar multiple times, smiling between themselves. Lu has watched them a few times, but after I mouth to her to stop it, she shrugs and downs a drink Base has bought her.

She doesn't drink much, so I reckon she'll be going home soon. Either Aria will pick her up, or I'll take her, or Base will get an Uber back to the hotel with her like he did last time. He even put her into bed and sat with her until she fell asleep.

Another drink, and Ty and Dez are nowhere to be seen. I've given Lu a bottle of water while we sit on a pool table opposite the one Kade and Base are playing at.

I try to ignore him. But I'm struggling, especially when his fingers trail down my spine as I squeeze past him to place my drink on the small table.

Luciella boos her brother's best friend as he pots one of his balls. "You are shhhhhockingly bad, Sebastian."

He chuckles, taking a drink of his beer and leaning his hip against the table. "Will you scream my full name when I pin you to the table with my dick?"

Kade nearly chokes on his drink. "Come on, man."

"I'm going to the bathroom," I announce and jump off the table.

The place is next to empty, so I can hear the footsteps behind me as I make my way down the small corridor, into the narrow passage that has three doors.

"Stacey."

My skin buzzes. I stop, taking a deep breath. "What?"

He pulls my elbow. "I don't have a girlfriend."

"I saw your message – I'm aware."

His blue eyes watch me, and I can tell he wants to say something. Maybe to say it was a mistake.

Because it was.

I cross my arms. "You said you wanted to talk. So talk."

An older man appears behind us, and we move out of his way – then when someone else walks out, he swears and pulls open the door to the maintenance room and tugs me inside.

As the door closes, we hear the squeal coming from Tylar as Dez pulls out of her – both completely naked with the smell of sex in the air.

I cover my eyes and turn around. "Sorry!"

Kade mutters, "Fuck's sake. Put your dick away."

"Why are you guys here?" Ty asks, and I turn around to see them thankfully hidden. She covers her breasts with Dez's top. "Were you looking for us?"

"I wanted to talk to Stacey," Kade says. "Can you fuck off?"

"We were here first, asshole!" Dez zips his jeans up and stands in front of Tylar while she fixes herself. "What are you two doing in here? Screwing around again?"

Tylar doesn't even flinch at the words. And when I stare at her, she gives me a tight smile. Of course she knew. *Perfect.*

She kisses my cheek as they leave, and Dez – very disgustingly – tosses his condom into a box full of rubbish.

The door closes, and it's just us two. The force is igniting, but I refuse to let any heat build or think of how well we fit together so intimately – how addictive it is.

"I didn't mean to vanish right after that happened," he says, taking a step towards me, hands in his pockets. "I know you think I'm disrespectful and whatever else you've thrown my way, but I fully intended to approach you the next day."

"And what would you have said if you did approach me? Thanks for the quick fuck, snake? Sorry for fucking you while killing someone?"

"Do you want me to apologise for that?"

I gulp. "No. I just want you to leave me alone."

"Do you?" Another step. "Because I'm a killer?"

"Because you're my ex who can't stand me."

Kade tilts his head – another step. "What if I have good intentions? What if I said I don't want to sleep with you but be your friend?"

"I could never be friends with you," I say, unable to move as Kade invades my space. His muscular form towers over mine, and I strain my neck to glare up at him. "I'm nothing but a slut to you, remember?"

His eyes are burning into my apparently dark soul. "And I'm nothing but a piece of shit to you. It must be the entire aspect of loathing each other that draws us together."

"I'm not drawn to you," I lie.

I don't move away when his hand comes up to push a lock of my hair behind my ear, his thumb stroking my cheek. "Well, I'm drawn to you, Freckles. And it infuriates me that I am. I could be inside someone else, yet all I can see is you."

My brows furrow. "I don't know if you were trying to be sincere there, but it made you sound like a total prick."

"I'm not a sincere man. Maybe when I was a teenager, when I worshipped the ground you walked on, but now? I want to rip your clothes off and sink my teeth into your skin."

My breath hitches as he comes even closer.

"I want to degrade you while you sit on my cock. Praise you as you swallow every drop of my cum. I want to brand every inch of your skin with my mouth and make sure you're unable to even look at another man."

I suck in a breath, holding it in my lungs as he lowers his forehead to mine.

"I want you, but I can't have you," he says. "You deserve way better than me. If you knew half the shit I've had to do, you wouldn't be in this tight space with me now."

"What have you done?"

Kade sighs, slightly pulling away. "The company I work for has their claws in me – that's all you need to know."

"What do you need to do for them?"

"Mani pārdod seksam un nāvei, lai aizsargātu visus, kurus mīlu."

Kade leans into me more, raising his other hand between us to tuck another strand of hair behind my ear. I tilt my head, utterly confused by whatever language he's speaking.

He licks his lips. *"Tajā skaitā jūs, vasaras raibumi."*

"You're speaking in a different language again..."

"Latvian, from when I was sent there for six months. I know four languages. Not well, but I'm working on them. It comes with the job."

I tilt my head. "What does it mean?"

He half-smiles, backing away from me, his hands leaving me until I have enough room to breathe. He opens the door and pauses. "I hope you never find out."

29

KADE

FLASHBACK 6

How Luciella has talked me into coming to a nightclub in America is beyond me, yet here I am, sitting at the bar while she has a full-blown conversation about biosynthesis.

Here, I'm technically underage but Base got us fake IDs last year and they've somehow worked a treat.

I'm three beers down, and she's still talking to the girl.

"Oh! This is my brother." She shoves me towards her. "Kade, this is Annika."

I tip my beer to her. "Howdy." Then turn to the side and lean on the bar.

Luciella nudges me with her elbow as blondie smiles and goes to walk away. "Talk to her, you idiot!"

I chuckle. "There's no chance I'm letting my sister wingman me."

"You're annoying," she replies before asking the bartender for another glass of Coke. "Base is an hour away. He came over in his jet with his grandfather and two of his guards for some meeting. He said he'd come see us."

"Is that why you wanted to come here and made an effort with your hair?"

"I always make an effort!"

I snort out a laugh. "Your denial is far too obvious. I'm going for a smoke. Come with me."

"No," she replies, turning to Annika. "I'll stay here."

"Don't go anywhere," I warn.

As soon as I get outside, the coldness hits me, and I light up a cigarette. Music blasts, and I get a weird feeling, so I text Luciella and tell her to come outside and stand with me.

Luciella: Stop being overbearing. I'm fine.

Me: If someone kidnaps you, I'm not coming to look for you.

Luciella: It would be a blessing if someone kidnapped me away from you.

My eyes land on a message from Tylar. I don't remember having her number.

Tylar Spence: It's Stacey. Are you free to talk?

I press call before I can even think. We've never spoken on the phone, so this is weird, I think. This could also be a bad call, since I haven't heard from her.

She answers on the first ring. "Hey."

I shut my eyes and drop the back of my head against the wall behind me. "Fuck. It's good to hear your voice."

"It is?"

"Yeah. Why are you using Tylar's phone?"

"She left it in the studio. Mine's broken. I smashed the screen and I'm waiting for it to get fixed."

"I thought you were patching me on purpose."

She giggles. "I was debating patching you."

I raise a brow. "Really?"

"Yep. You were supposed to take me on a date before you left."

"I'll make it up to you," I respond with a grin. "Tell me about your day."

"It's been slow," she starts. "No. I want to know about your night. Luciella said in our group chat that she was talking to a beautiful girl and thought you two had great chemistry. She said she was going to introduce you both."

I smirk. "Is my Freckles jealous?"

"You can obviously do what you want. We didn't talk about exclusivity. Was she nice? Oh God. Don't tell me. Does that mean we're seeing other people? Do you want to see other people? It's okay if you do." She goes silent. "I'm embarrassing myself. Feel free to hang up at any point and put me out of my misery."

I laugh. "It wasn't like that at all. She kept talking to her at the bar and wanted me to flirt with her. I said no obviously. And I'd never hang up on you."

"I would hang up on me," she mutters. "You didn't answer my questions, but don't feel like you need to. I just want to know where I stand."

"Meaning?"

"Are we seeing other people? I don't mean boyfriend and girlfriend. I mean are we casual or not?"

I can tell she's face-palming.

"I'm doing it again. I'm sorry. I know it's only been six weeks. I'll shut up now."

"I'm new to this, so I have no idea how it works. If you want to see other people, then go for it." The words taste like poison. "I can't promise their bodies won't show up in the River Clyde though."

Silence, and then: "That was kind of cute."

I inhale deeply, blowing out smoke. "If it makes you feel any better, I have no interest in anyone else."

"Okay," she replies quietly. "That's, um, good."

"And when I see you, I'm going to touch you again. Just so you know."

"I'd like that. Only if you let me touch you."

My dick responds to her words by twitching.

"Oh, Lu just said in our group chat that she can't find you."

The twitch is gone just as quick.

"Shit," I reply. "We'll talk when you fix your phone."

"Yeah."

I don't want to end our call, but I say, "See you soon, Freckles."

"See you soon."

The call ends, and I'm in a much better mood. So much better that when Base finally appears, I get drunk and dance around the club with him and my sister to some sort of electronic dance music until we give up at six in the morning.

As soon as I see her walking along the hallway on my side of the manor, my sour mood after travelling for hours vanishes. Her eyes find mine as I get to the bottom of my stairs, and like something from a movie, Stacey runs. Her long hair flows behind her, her robe unfastening to reveal her Grinch PJs, and when she leaps into my arms, I catch her by the thigh and lift her into me.

"This is dramatic, but I missed you. I really missed you."

I smile. "I missed you too," I reply, kissing her bare shoulder as her robe hangs from her body. I take a step. "Come to the kitchen with me."

She shakes her head, leans back and runs her fingers through my hair. "Kiss me. Then take me to your room."

Stacey tastes fruity with a hint of mint when my lips press to hers. Her soft mouth moves with my own while her legs tighten around my waist, and my grip on her thigh trails to her ass.

I somehow manage to keep kissing her while I carry her up the stairs and into my room, not breaking it as I lower us to the bed. Our mouths slant, heads tilting as we devour one another – hands in hair, lips between teeth, names dropping from our mouths with how much we missed each other.

"I meant it when I said you could see other people," she whispers against my lips. "But I'd rather you didn't."

I part her legs with my knee and settle between her thighs. "Why?"

She gasps as I press against her.

"I like you," she admits. "Is that too soon? I'm sorry."

"Stop apologising."

"But is it too soon to say that? I don't know about timelines."

I kiss her once, twice, three times. "We make our own timeline. If you feel a certain way, then you feel a certain way. If it helps, I like you too."

She beams, smiling so hard I think I might just hug her to death. "I get butterflies."

"So do I."

Stacey lowers her hand to the hem of my top and tugs it up. I sit back, reach behind my head to pull it off and toss it across the room. She drags her hand down my chest, which is only starting to properly show now that I'm doing work with Ewan. She stops at the waistband of my shorts.

Her green eyes stare into my soul, the soul I would rip apart for her. "I get nervous."

"So do I," I reply, my heart speeding up as her fingers bend into the waistband, playing with the fabric instead of taking them off. "Are you nervous now?"

"Yes. But I want to..." She tugs at my shorts. "I want to touch you."

Fuck.

I've wrapped my own hand around my cock more times than I can count, but the thought of having hers around me is like being on a high. Well, I assume. I've never taken drugs, apart from smoking joints with Base and Dez.

"Lie beside me, on your side."

I shift onto my back, and I can tell she's really nervous. Instead of telling her to take my shorts off, I pull her to me and kiss her mouth, her nose, her forehead, everywhere I can.

"We don't need to be nervous," I say to her but also to myself. "We like each other, and this is what people do when they like each other."

"Can I tell you something?"

Shit. "Of course."

She shakes her head. "I want to tell you how I feel about you, but I can't say it." Then Stacey lowers her head to my chest. "God, I really am an embarrassment."

I lace our hands together. "Tell me. I can assure you the feeling will either be mutual, or my side is on a higher level."

"I listened to a song, and it made me think of you instantly." Her cheeks go red. "You can tell me to stop now."

"What song?"

She covers her face with her free hand. "'Spiracle' by Flower Face. The lyrics. They were so powerful and beautiful and... explained how I feel about you." She tries to get up from the bed. "I'm going to hide from the world now."

"Stop getting so embarrassed," I say, laughing and dragging her back to my side. "I'll listen later."

"I will totally understand if you want to call this off with me."

"Shut up."

She stares at me. "Rude."

"Tell me three things about you."

She tilts her head and doesn't say anything for a full five seconds. "I like to dance."

"Evidently."

"Sandwiches."

"Chicken," I say. "You always eat them."

Stacey grins. "I like dogs."

"What kind?"

She shrugs. "Big ones. I always get scared I'll stand on the smaller ones. Do you like dogs?"

"Yeah. I want two Dobermanns."

"Dobermenn."

I frown. "What?"

"Dobermenn... plural."

"I don't know if you're serious or not."

She sighs with a smile. "Think about it!"

I absolutely will not.

"There are two. So – Kade!" She is silent when I start to unbutton her PJ shirt.

She shivers as my fingers glide against bare skin. I bring my mouth to her neck. "Are you going to stop talking now and show *me how you feel?"*

When she nods dramatically and kisses me, I pull the duvet over us, devouring her until she's tugging at my hair and breathless.

"Take off my shorts," I order against her throat, sucking at the erratic pulse as my hands explore her body. I palm her tits, rolling her nipples between my fingers and finally feeling the restraint of my shorts vanishing.

I sink my teeth into her skin and grow harder, thicker with her soft moans. I drop to my back again, not breaking our contact as I take her hand and place it close to my dick.

I trail kisses up her throat, along her jaw until I reach her mouth. "Show me what it's like, Freckles. Show me how it feels to have you fuck me with your hand."

Slowly, dangerously slowly, Stacey slips her tongue through my parted lips at the same moment her hand moves over my cock.

I hiss into her mouth as she palms me, as she gently trails her fingers up and down the warm skin, the solid length that throbs and twitches with each glide of her fingers. Sensations rush to my head, and I try not to thrust.

My eyes screw shut as she wraps her fingers around me. My heart restarts, a low buzz at the base of my spine while she swipes her thumb up, wiping the bead of precum from my engorged head.

She's studying me as she pulls my mouth to hers. A distraction, maybe, because I can feel her heart pounding as I cup her tit and squeeze.

"Relax," I whisper. "This is okay. This is us."

"I like the sound of that," she replies quietly. "Is this right?" she asks as she starts to move her hand up and down my length. "Or is it too tight?"

She's kind of crushing my cock in her grip. "Loosen it a bit."

Stacey does, and my eyes roll as she twists her wrist when she reaches the tip, slamming her mouth on mine.

My balls tighten as she continues, all the blood in my body rushing to between my legs. I groan as tingles start travelling from my groin up my spine.

"Go faster," I tell her, my teeth clenching when she does. I reach under her to grab her ass, raising my hips to fuck into the grip she has on my cock. My free hand clutches her jaw, tilting her head to the side so I can kiss her throat.

She pumps faster, base to tip, rotating her wrist and moaning as I suck on the skin above her collarbone. My muscles spasm all over, and I'm so fucking close already.

I nip at her throat, breathing heavily, my vision blurring, and when I feel the pull in my balls, I groan from the building pressure and say, "Go slow. Fuck, go slow."

I chase the soaring high just as she sinks her teeth into my bottom lip, and everything smashes into me at once. The back of my head presses into the pillow. Slower, yet still as tight, Stacey keeps stroking but pulls back to watch me through my release. Heart pounding, my eyes close and my muscles bunch at my thighs; I fist both hands, gritting out curses and her name, my breaths completely stalling.

Strings of cum hit my chest in the hardest orgasm I think I've ever had. My heart beats rapidly, my lungs desperate for air as my mind goes blank. Satisfied, and relaxed, I find her free hand and hold it while I float back down to reality.

When I open my eyes properly, she grins at me as she lets go of my dick. "That's something else we should definitely do again."

I chuckle, moving curls from her face and tucking them behind her ear. "Only because I like you."

Stacey grins wider, kissing my cheek. "I like you too. Now where are your towels? I have cum on my hand, and you have it everywhere."

She goes to my bathroom and throws me one. "I need to go back to Lu's room. I'll see you later?"

I tilt my head while I wipe myself. "Did you just use me?"

"Yep. Arrange our date, asshole." Then she puts on her robe and climbs onto the bed to peck my lips before vanishing from the room.

I stare at the closed door for far too long with a goofy smile on my face, then grab my headphones and listen to the song she mentioned.

It seems we are on the same level.

As soon as it's done, the only thing stopping me from hunting her down and dragging her back to my bed is that I'm searching for places to take her where we won't get noticed. Between her not wanting my sister to know, and people constantly following me around with a camera and a fake story, I can't take her out around here.

I find something perfect, and when I tell my dad the next day, he pays for the entire thing. I don't know how the hell he has access to money or a bank account, but he's got a lot of connections. He sends me extra to play with and tells me to have a good weekend.

When she texts me later, telling me her phone's fixed, we meet at the pool house, where we kiss then touch then kiss some more, before slipping back out and trying not to look at each other during dinner.

I basically tackle her into the spare room the following day and feel her coming undone with my fingers again. It's becoming one of my favourite things, watching the orgasm rip through her, seeing her glazed eyes as she floats in euphoria before coming back to me – that and having her hand wrapped around my cock.

The day after, I slap her ass as I walk past her in the kitchen and tell her to cancel any plans she has next weekend. She texts me later to say she's free and demands to know where we're going, but I say it's a surprise.

I'm going to take Freckles on the best first date ever.

30

STACEY

Sitting in the reception, I check the time again, waiting patiently to be called.

I hold the book containing my notes on the way Kade's been acting, the signs of him taking drugs and the words he's said. I have everything ready to pass to his dad, and hopefully, he'll know what to do.

I just want to help.

"Visitor for Tobias Mitchell."

I get to my feet and walk slowly through the corridor, following a woman in clicky heels. My chest hurts from how much I'm holding my breath.

She shows me to a small room. There's a single bed in the corner, a table in the middle with two seats, two cups of water and two apples.

I thought Kade said they meet up with him in an artificial park?

I sit at the table, fidgeting with the notebook for the longest minute of my life.

My nerves nearly shatter when the door opens, and the tall, muscular presence takes over all the energy in the room. Either the oxygen has been sucked out of my lungs, or I'm just not breathing as Tobias Mitchell, in all his savagery, trains his eyes on me.

"You," is all he says.

I gulp. This was a mistake.

But I can't control my body, can't make myself stand and run from the room, not as he takes careful steps towards me and lowers himself onto the seat opposite me.

The vein in his neck is thick, and damn does it look the exact same as Kade's. I knew he was handsome, from pictures and videos, but up close? I feel like I'm wandering into forbidden territory even considering such thoughts about him.

"What the fuck do you want?" he snaps, and the notion of finding him hot vanishes. "Where's Aria?"

"You know who I am?"

"I've seen pictures," he snarls. "Why are you here?"

"I need to talk to you about Kade."

Silently, he watches me as I place the notebook down, my hands shaking.

"You have some nerve coming to see me."

I swallow the large lump threatening to strangle me. "I just want to help him."

"Help? You don't think you've helped enough by ruining him?"

"I didn't ruin him," I snap and instantly regret the way the words come out.

Tobias leans back in his chair. "As much as I tried to make him hear you out, my son hasn't been the same since he told me his perfect little fucking girlfriend cheated on him. He's become destructive. He's like me that way."

"He isn't like you though," I say, meaning it in the most genuine way. "His emotions—"

"His emotions are learned and controlled," Tobias interrupts. "But when he first started going out with you? He was constantly on the phone with me or sitting down with Aria, trying to figure out what was wrong with him. He wanted to know why he felt something that made no sense to him. My son wanted medication to suppress urges and impulsiveness, to make sure he didn't ruin you like I did his mother. But little did he know all he was feeling was love."

I swallow a lump. I knew Kade had struggled at the beginning of our relationship. All his senses and emotions were wild and personal. He asked me if I thought he was abusive, manipulative, coercing me into a relationship. I did my best to reassure him I was in it because I wanted to be.

Kade was an angel back then, but now he's definitely a manifestation of Tobias.

Tobias continues when I stay quiet. "He felt it had become an obsession, the thought of having you to himself. That I could understand. That is what I could help him with. I take it you're aware of our story? Me and Aria?"

The entire world knows their story.

"The articles I've read say a lot of things."

"I destroyed her because I wasn't in control. I don't mean that I gave her a rough time. I gave her *hell,* little one. I stopped taking my medication, I stopped going to therapy because I thought it would be good for her to have a normal boyfriend. Most of it's a blur, but I remember what I felt when she left me, what I felt when I watched her spiral into alcohol abuse and come close to losing her job. Did you know I drugged her with my medication? I thought, at the time, I was helping her."

"I read you swapped her contraceptive pill with your meds to get her pregnant with the twins."

He glares at me. "Not true. I had no intention of getting her pregnant. Why would I want to pass on my genes?"

I shrug once. "And you locked her and her best friend, Gabriella McGhee, in dog cages. Gabriella died because of you. Then you slit the throat of one of her lovers in front of her – his blood went all over her."

"It was a dark time," is his reply, monotone and careful. "I don't remember most of it. I can only be thankful that Aria forgave me after years of trying to be better for her."

"Is it true you stabbed her?"

"No. That wasn't me."

His eye twitches, and I regret mentioning any of it. I need to learn to keep my mouth shut.

"Those were mistakes I can *never* take back. I lost control of parts of me. But like you said, my son is not me; he has every chance in the world to have a normal life."

I'm not too sure.

"Can anyone hear us?"

A smirk pulls at his lips. "No cameras. No microphones. Nothing. Just us, little one. But be careful – I have one type and her name is Aria. Kade did say you prefer them older though."

I roll my eyes. "What chance does he have at a normal life when he's killing people and taking drugs?"

Tobias, frozen in his seat, eyes darkening, watches me carefully. His hands are steepled, his fingertips pressed together. "Elaborate."

"I watched him shoot two people," I say, forcing the words out. "One was for money. The other was because the man touched me." My thumbs twiddle together, and I swallow. I feel like I'm doing Kade dirty, but he can't do this alone. He needs help, and I know Tobias will do what he can. "I'm positive he's taking drugs. Drinking excessively."

"What else?"

I grit my teeth to stop myself from getting emotional. Tears burn at the back of my eyes, and my chest caves. Not because I'm telling his dad that he's in trouble, but because this version of Kade isn't real. I hate that we're even in this position.

The Kade I knew didn't even know how to hold a gun, never mind shoot one.

And now I'm sitting down with his psychotic father, trying not to cry while I tell him about what happened at the warehouse. The nickname he has. Being able to speak different languages. The money. The suitcase full of white powder.

Each time I explain something, Tobias drops his head, and his knuckles turn white.

I should be telling this to his mother, but as much as he loves

Aria, she won't be able to stop him.

I'm not too sure his dad can either. But it's worth a try.

"What about you?" he asks when I finish going through as much as possible. "When did you start caring about him again?"

I frown. "I never stopped caring about Kade."

He shakes his head. "That's a lie. Do you know how horrible it felt to sit there and watch my son fall apart because of what you did to him? How many times he had to call and tell me that the urge to drown himself, to throw himself off a bridge was getting worse, and he was scared. I may not fully understand how true love and trust and loyalty works, how it feels to have one's heart ripped out, but I saw it all through my son as you broke each one of his emotions. How dare you sit here with me and claim to care about him?"

I go to speak, but I shut my mouth when he narrows his eyes at me.

"Aria found him close to overdosing on her boat. If he hadn't managed to send her his location, he'd probably be dead."

What?

"I didn't know," I respond quietly, a vivid image in my head of Kade frantically trying to reach his phone, his body shutting down as he coughs and shudders. I stand. "I... I didn't know."

"You didn't deserve to know."

My gaze shoots towards him as I stop pacing. "I didn't deserve to know? Why? Because I *apparently* cheated?"

"*Yes*! He didn't understand certain emotions until he met you," he yells, getting to his feet so fast his chair falls over. "You certainly showed him how to understand the negative ones. So much so that he was fully prepared to *end his life* because of it."

"I'm sorry your son did that, I really am, but if he ever sat down and let me explain, he'd know that the ten-second video he was sent was heavily edited from three hours of drugging and non-consensual activity."

My heart stops at finally getting the words out. Tears fall down my cheeks, and I wipe them away as my voice falters. "Help me, before he ends up dead, and we both lose him."

I push the notebook towards him as he studies me, silent –

thinking.

"I know you believe Kade can do better than me, and that's fine. But I have *never* stopped loving him. Not once. But this..." I tap the notebook, our gazes still locked. "This is more important. You're the only one I know who can help him. I'll try to find out more for you, but please don't do anything until I figure out who his boss is."

"You expect me to sit here and do nothing?"

My lip trembles. "Please. I'll be in contact."

"Aria and I have a private line you could use; I'll tell her to give you the number."

"Thank you."

And with that, I wipe my face with my sleeve and pull my bag up my shoulder.

Still watching me, Kade's father places his large palm over the notebook. "It broke him. What he thought he saw happening... broke him."

Before I leave, I reply, "We're all broken in some way, Tobias. But we can also be fixed."

My hand lands on the doorknob. A deep voice stops me.

"You didn't fall down the studio stairs, did you?"

For a split second, I feel my heart shatter. My composure slips, and I try not to burst into tears and pull him in for a cuddle, to bury my head in his powerful chest. Lu always said her dad's hugs were the best.

I shake my head. "No."

"Did you abort the baby?"

My eyes close. "No."

"Does my son know the truth?"

I grit my teeth, clenching my jaw painfully as I turn to him. "It would have made things worse. I'll tell him when I'm ready to. This is more important."

"You were attacked."

I nod.

"Who?"

"Please." I shiver. "We need to focus on Kade first. What's done is done."

Tobias gets to his feet, walking to stand in front of me. I don't flinch as he rests his hand on my shoulder.

"She was my granddaughter. No one takes from me and gets away with it. Once I deal with Kade, I'm going to hunt down whoever is responsible. I promise you, little one."

I smile weakly. "You don't need to hunt for him – he lives right under my roof."

31

STACEY

The screen above us flashes up *Check In* for our flight home.

The number Aria gave me for Tobias's secret phone burns in my pocket – where my phone starts to buzz.

I slide my bag down my arm and pull it out to see Kade's name on the screen. I glance up at his sister, who's none the wiser, whistling to herself while a crowd in front of us argue about their baggage weight.

I don't answer, but I do send him a text asking if he meant to call.

Then his name is on my screen again.

On the third call, I eventually tell Tylar I need to answer and wheel my suitcase out of the line. There's no point trying to talk to a drunken Kade while checking in. I'll just join the queue once I'm done talking to him.

As soon as I answer, I frown at his silence, covering my other ear. "Kade?"

"I don't... I don't want to work," he says, and I can tell he's really drunk. "Talk to me, Freckles."

"I'm here," I reply, moving hair behind my ear. "I thought you were out with Dez and Base? Did you leave the club?"

"I don't want to work," he says again, but I can hear his voice going strange, as if he's trying to stay awake. "I don't."

"Where are you?"

He coughs, then I hear the sound of his lighter flicking, him inhaling and exhaling a lungful of smoke. "Did I wake you?"

I sigh. "No. Where are you?"

"An alleyway." He slaps his hands together. "I can't get rid of the blood. My palms are red as fuck."

My eyes widen. "You're bleeding?"

He laughs once – low and deadly. "Not mine. It's dark here – I kinda like it."

"Where's Dez and Base?" I look over at Tylar and Lu, still waiting impatiently. The airport is so loud, I decide to quickly go outside to hear him better. "Kade?"

"Club. I had to go do a stupid job."

I lean my back against the wall next to the entrance, the cold nipping my skin. "Why did you call me?"

"I wanted to," he replies, inhaling more smoke. "Do you remember when we made a deal to quit smoking?"

"Yeah?" I haven't touched a cigarette since.

"I used to sneak one behind your back."

I laugh, my cheeks heating. "I knew. You were never good at hiding your cigarettes."

We talk about those times, and I try not to think about him trying to kill himself after we split up. Fifteen minutes go by, maybe longer, and I'm hoping one of his friends finds him soon, or he gets an Uber to his hotel. He tells me that Barry is coming, but then says Barry might be dead, and I gasp.

"I'm kidding."

"That's not funny, Kade. My gate closes soon, so I'll need to come off the phone."

"I guess I wanted your voice to be the last I heard..."

I straighten. "What? What do you mean?"

"I took something I shouldn't have, and I needed to hear you before..." he slurs. "Wait, I'm not hallucinating, am I? Are you actually talking to me?"

"What did you take? What kind of drug?"

I pull up the handle of my suitcase and rush back into the airport. But I freeze in place when I see the board closed and the desk empty. Where are my friends?

I have a text from Tylar saying they're going to lose their signal and to hurry up.

"Freckles, please talk to me."

"Where are Dez and Base?" I ask for the tenth time. "You need to get to them. Go back to the club."

He doesn't reply.

"Where are you?" I ask. "Tell me where you are."

"I already..." He breathes deeply. "I already said I'm at... the alleyway."

"Send me your location – I'm coming to get you."

Kade groans, but a notification pops up, and I rush to the first Uber I see. An elderly man greets me and places my things into the trunk, and I show him my screen, the call still active. He inputs it into his database and the route shows up.

"I'm tired."

"Stay awake."

I beg the driver to speed, and Kade repeats the same thing over and over – that he wants to hear my voice. He doesn't believe it's actually me and thinks someone is playing a trick on him. The longer the drive takes, the more confused he gets. I place him on hold quickly, but Lu and Ty both go straight to voicemail, as do Base and Dez.

"Are you still there? You sound like my ex. Her name is Stacey."

I press my forehead to my knees. "I *am* Stacey."

"Hmm. You wish."

I close my eyes. "Are you okay? How do you feel?"

"I can't get the blood off my hands, and someone is doing

cartwheels in front of me." He huffs. "Kind of creepy. Hey! Fuck off, will you?"

"Calm down. I'm nearly there."

There's another voice. Barry. "What the fuck are you doing?"

Kade yawns. "Chilling."

Barry takes the phone. "Who is this?"

I hang up as soon as the car reaches the alleyway. The driver sets my bags on the kerb, and I rush down to see Barry standing over Kade, his phone light shining down on him.

I gasp when I notice him slouched on the ground between two large bins, back to the wall, another joint between his fingers. He screws his eyes up against the blinding light, raising a red hand to shield himself from it.

"You two here to kill me?"

Barry sighs.

I kneel between his legs and shine my own phone light on my face so he can see me. "It's me. Come on." I offer my hand and blanch at the red stains all over his clothes. "Put your arm around me."

"That's very forward of you, but okay."

He takes my hand, and I try not to stare at the crimson on his skin – or his eyes, which are going in every direction possible. Barry and I help Kade up, and he staggers, throwing one arm across my shoulders, the other over Barry's.

"The car is over there," Barry says, and we hurry.

Kade studies my face. "You look like my ex."

"I know," I say, looking at Barry. "Do you have a hotel to take him to?"

"No," Kade blurts out as Barry tells me yes, pulling away from me as I sit down beside him. "I don't want to work."

I stop him from trying to open the car door. He's that fucked he can't fight me off.

"I'm not fucking working!"

"You aren't," I reply. "Please calm down, Kade."

When we reach Barry's hotel, I'm still rubbing his back; he's slouched forward on the seat with his head between his legs.

We manage to get him inside. The receptionist doesn't ask why there's a man standing with his head against the lobby wall, talking about flavours of chocolate. She does offer me water and lets me know there's a cleaning service if I need it.

Trying to get Kade into the elevator is difficult. He thinks I'm putting him into a prison. He tells me he isn't an animal that can be caged. So me and Barry carry him up the stairs, which he falls down four times. The last time he manages to grab my arm as he topples.

He laughs as I fall on top of him, telling me that not only do I look like his ex, but I'm also as clumsy as her too.

Kade has already unbuttoned his trousers and is asking me how much I paid as Barry grabs water from his fridge.

"I need to go clean up this mess. I'll be gone for a few days. Stay here. Make sure he drinks plenty of water and rests."

"Where are you going?"

He looks at Kade. "If I don't sort this out, Kade will most likely end up in prison for the rest of his life. He shot a political leader in front of a lot of witnesses."

I look at Kade as Barry leaves – he's swaying around the room, humming "From Now On" from *The Greatest Showman.*

"Drink this." I hand him the water. "And try to make yourself sick."

He grimaces. "Sick? No thanks."

He downs the water and tosses the bottle, then proceeds to talk to me about recycling.

Kade then lies on the bed, staring at the roof. "Can you pretend we had sex?"

I frown. "What?"

"Just… tell her we did. I don't want to work," he says, slurring some more.

Slowly – and messily – he starts to strip off his clothes. His top first, then he attempts to pull his trousers down, which I eventually help him with. Everything is muddy and covered in blood. Even his socks and hair.

"I probably won't get hard."

"Did you kill someone tonight?"

"A few someones, yeah." He pulls a joint from behind his ear and attempts to light it with a lighter that isn't there. "Fuck." Both hands drop, and he groans. "I hate this."

I go into the bathroom and soak a cloth, coming back in to find him sitting up on the edge of the bed, elbows on his knees, only in boxers. I rinse the cloth off after wiping his face and come back for his arms, his chest and the back of his neck.

I'm standing between his legs, scrubbing at his hair, when he captures me in his arms. My body reacts to his possessive touch – I stop wiping when his strong arms tighten and rest my hands on his shoulders.

"Are you okay?" I ask quietly as Kade presses his forehead to my midsection.

"Can I hold you and pretend you're her?"

I tilt my head, narrowing my brows as I look down at him. "Who?"

"My ex-girlfriend."

I toss the cloth aside and brush my fingers through his hair. "Okay," I say softly. "Lie down."

"Will you tell her we had sex? I won't take money from you. I promise."

"Tell Stacey? Pay you for… sex?"

"Fuck no. She'd hate me even more." He furrows his brows in confusion. "Obviously for sex. Why else would you be here?"

"Oh," I respond, feeling ill. "Sorry."

"Don't be. Did you pay her yet?"

"No. Just…" I swallow. "Lie down."

He flattens himself on the bed and looks at me. "You're really pretty though."

I chew the inside of my cheek. "Thanks."

His eyes are closed, and his skin is hot, so I tell him to stay above the covers. I chew my lip, debating if I should stand here and see if he falls asleep without me beside him.

He'll wake up tomorrow and tell me to fuck off.

I think.

I'm not entirely sure anymore. He's made it clear I disgust him yet still approaches me. I've never been so confused in my life.

I'll stay with him and fly home tomorrow. My friends will be worried sick.

I pull off my hoodie, but keep everything else on, and lie down beside him. His powerful arms drag me into him, and I fight a smile. This is wrong. This is so, so wrong. He has no idea that it's me.

I take a deep breath. "Who was I to pay to have sex with you?"

"The she-devil." Kade yawns. "She's horrible, if you haven't met her yet."

"What's her name?"

He shakes his head. "Not allowed to say."

"Are you a male prostitute?"

"You could say that, yeah. An escort with perks..." His voice trails off.

There is silence, and I tackle the uneasiness.

"Tell me about your ex?"

I'm an idiot. A chancing, idiotic idiot.

I can sense the grin as he replies, "She has freckles everywhere. I used to trace them when she was asleep. You even wear the same perfume."

He tightens his hold, and I link our fingers and trap our hands against my chest.

"You feel like her as well. Are you okay with me hugging you? When I get all fucked up, I think about her, and this is helping."

I nod and wipe a tear. "Yeah."

"Thank you."

My heart is racing, but he doesn't make it obvious if he can tell.

"She was my first kiss. First... everything. She's my sister's best friend. Does that make me a bad person?"

I shake my head. "No."

He chuckles low. "She's funny. If she was here and in a good mood, she'd say something along the lines of... *Let's dance. Horizontal. In bed. Preferably naked.*"

His attempt at my voice is terrible, but it makes me laugh.

"She sounds funny," I say. "What else?"

"I want to fuck her on my motorbike."

My eyes ping open.

"I reckon she'd love it."

My insides turn to liquid heat – having him nearly naked against me and saying things like that is making my heart pick up its pace even more. "I might take her out on it when we get home, if she gives me the time of day."

I turn on my back, and Kade lowers his head onto my chest, snaking one arm under the small of my back, the other draped over my waist – cuddling into me.

"I'm going to take her to my apartment in Stirling." Nodding against me, he slowly adds, "Maybe she'll stay the night."

"You have your own place?" I always thought he stayed in student accommodation at university.

Kade laughs, and the sound makes me warm. "I'm a grown man. Of course I have my own place, silly."

I smile – the tone of his voice has turned cute as he grows sleepier. He curls into me more, and I play with the dark strands of his hair that are sticking up.

"How do you feel now?"

He sighs, stuttering a little as he replies, "F-Fine. I wanted to hear her voice. She didn't answer though."

I frown.

"I have a lot of money, but it's dirty," he admits randomly, eyes closed. "She'll never let me spend it on her, will she?"

"Do you want to? If she's your ex..."

Ignoring me, he relaxes completely. "I miss her," he mumbles. "But we have no chance of getting back what we had."

I fight the burn in my eyes. "I know."

"She was pregnant. A girl. We lost her."

My heart shatters. "I'm sorry."

"It sucks."

Kade's temperature has lowered, and a light sweat has broken out on his skin. The room is hot, so I pull off my bottoms.

I miss her, he'd said.

I miss him too.

But Kade is right – we would never work now. Too much has happened. Chris would intervene again and ruin it, and Kade isn't stable enough to hold down a relationship with all the skeletons locked away in his closet. He needs help, and he needs it fast.

The pillow shifts, and I gasp as Kade pulls me to him tighter;

I fit against him like the perfect puzzle piece. I feel at home in his arms and almost burst into tears from the intensity of the moment.

Turning in his hold, I bury my head into his chest, inhaling his scent as he breathes steadily. My eyes finally fall shut when the sunrise splits through the window, and for the first time in a long time, I'm in Kade's arms, feeling safer than ever.

32

KADE

FLASHBACK 7

Stacey has always been the girl out of reach for me. The girl I wanted but could never have. My sister's best friend who hated me with every fibre of her being.

I was the deranged kid. The mentally fucked-up kid. A boy who struggled with basic emotions.

But whenever I'm around her, I want to learn everything there is to feel. I want to be good enough for her. I want to be able to feel this way and not worry about it turning into something dark and sinister, the way it did with my parents.

Hurting Stacey would kill me.

I doodle while I wait for her to get out of the shower. We're in a hotel in London, just after seeing The Greatest Showman *live in theatre. Stacey cried the entire fucking show, and it triggered something protective inside me I never knew existed.*

Without realising, I've drawn a rough design of both our initials interlacing with each other – unrecognisable, unless you know what to look for. I want to add vines and some roses to make it pretty for her, maybe a scripture of something meaningful, but I have no idea what it should say.

I leave it blank and work more on the details.

When the door unlocks, I quickly shove the paper into my pocket and get to my feet.

Holding a towel to her wet body, she stops in the middle of the room. "Hi."

I smirk. "Hi."

"I didn't mean to fall asleep," she says. "When I woke and you were gone, I thought..." She pulls her lip between her teeth.

I approach her, eating up the distance slowly. I'm still hard from devouring her pussy. She fell asleep right after.

"You thought what?"

She shivers as I drag my knuckles down her arm. "I..." She trails off, her head tilting to the side as I come closer and press chaste kisses against her fluttering pulse. My fingers tease across her towel, testing her reaction, and I pause when she hesitates. "I'm very inexperienced, Kade."

"I nearly passed out when you sucked my dick in the studio before we came down here."

The room was spinning, and I'm not ashamed to admit I slid to the floor and had to take a second. She did it again while I drove us down here, and I have no idea how I didn't crash.

She blushes. "I'm still inexperienced in other stuff."

I cup her cheek gently, lowering my voice. "So am I."

"Doesn't it bother you that I don't know what I'm doing?"

I let out a disbelieving laugh. "Stacey, I don't know what the fuck I'm doing either." I caress her cheek with my thumb. "We're the same. When we're ready, we'll learn from each other. No rushing. Okay?"

She stares at me, and I swear I see a shield behind her eyes lowering.

"Do you want to wait?" she asks softly, her eyes dropping to my mouth. Her towel stays on her as she wraps her arms around my neck, rising to her tiptoes. "For more?"

"Only if you need me to."

"I think I need you now," she says as her nose nudges mine. "I want to experience it all." Her voice drops to a whisper against my mouth. "With you. Now."

The kiss comes first, then her body is crushed to mine as I lift her into my arms, the towel dropping to the ground. With a hum of satisfaction, her back hits the mattress, and I'm on her.

She's unbuttoning my shirt as my hands explore her body. I dig my fingers into her hips and press my hardening cock between her legs.

Then I pull away and unbuckle my belt, yanking the leather out and tossing it across the room. She reaches inside my boxers and palms my cock, gliding her nails up the underside.

I kick the rest of my clothes off the bed and settle between her legs again, kissing up the column of her throat.

Her nipples are hard, and they rub against my chest as I slide the head of my cock against her inner thigh, swallowing her whimpers when my fingers push inside her.

She feels so wet, warm and ready.

She feels like mine.

Stacey Rhodes is mine.

While I fuck her with my fingers, I suck a nipple into my mouth, and her body starts shaking. With my free hand, I palm the other breast, rolling her nipple between my finger and thumb.

I groan as my name falls from her lips, kissing along her collarbone, her throat, then coming back to her mouth.

"Is this okay?" I ask her as my fingers speed up, curling to find that sweet spot that has her eyes rolling. "Answer me, Stacey."

"Yes!" She gasps into my mouth, and I taste each moan with my tongue. "Can I" – she reaches between us and takes my dick in a fist – "do this?"

"Yes," I hiss, pushing my hips forward as I slide another finger inside her.

The room grows hot as we kiss and fuck with our hands, whimpering and moaning into each other's mouth. She bites my lip and sucks, and I kiss a trail up her throat while all the blood in my body goes to my cock.

It throbs in her hand; the kisses grow hungrier – and messier.

"I want you," she says against my lips, releasing my cock and hooking

her ankles at my calves to pull me to her. "All of you."

I stare at her, feel her beneath me, feel my heart pounding in my chest as I take in her beauty. Dark hair surrounds her on the pillow, and with her freckles and the flush in her cheeks, her long lashes and pouty lips, I honestly couldn't think of a more perfect person to be experiencing all of this with.

She's the definition of beautiful, and she wants me.

She belongs to me.

I'm whipped, and she isn't even my girlfriend.

But I might hurt her. I will hurt her. I'll do it wrong and make this a nightmare for her.

"What if I hurt you?"

Stacey takes my face in her hands. "I heard it can be uncomfortable the first time. But I'm ready, Kade."

My brows narrow. "But I don't want to hurt you."

"We'll go slow. It doesn't hurt when you use your... If I'm uncomfortable, I'll tell you, okay?"

I nod then feel like stabbing myself in the dick. "I didn't bring condoms."

She smiles. "Front zip of my suitcase."

"I should be ashamed that I forgot, but it's kind of hot that you brought them."

Stacey grins as I go to her suitcase and pull out an unopened packet of condoms.

"You even knew to get large." I chuckle and pull the plastic off. "Good girl."

She crawls to the edge of the bed, and she distracts me. "Stand here." She points in front of her.

I don't hesitate. When I'm in place, she tells me to open the box, but I nearly drop it on her head as she sucks my cock into her mouth.

She pops it out from between her lips. "Open the box and unwrap one."

As her tongue glides up my twitching cock, I gulp, quickly ripping the box to shreds.

"Do you know how to put one on? Or do you want me to try to do it?"

I don't want to admit that I've tried on every condom imaginable while bored in my room, so instead, I shake my head and tell her to do it.

She doesn't take her eyes off me as she rolls it down my cock and finds her place in the middle of the bed, head on the pillow.

As I climb on top of her and line the tip of my dick up to her entrance, I try to focus on her and not the panic rising in my chest. If I do this wrong, I might hurt her. If I'm a failure and unable to perform, then I'm never having sex again.

I'll cut my dick off if I hurt her.

What if I'm no good?

I've heard Dez and Base discuss fucking people plenty of times, even had a full description from the latter of how warm and tight and fucking heavenly it feels to be inside someone.

But that's not what I'm thinking about.

All that's going through my mind is that I'm a fuck-up in most things. This will inevitably suck for her.

She had to talk me through going down on her, for fuck's sake.

"Hey." Her soft voice breaks my inner thoughts, her hands on my face. "Be here with me."

"I am." My voice shakes. "Sorry."

Her hand slips down my chest. "Don't apologise."

I bite my tongue to stop myself. She notices, smiles that beautiful smile that warms my dysfunctional heart, then rises to press her lips to mine.

We don't rush anything as we kiss. The tip of my cock is easing inside her, and my arms are shaking so fucking badly. I feel like she's trying to push me out, like there's a fist around my dick trying to force me away.

I stop pressing my hips forward. Take a breath. Kiss her forehead and ask if she's okay, and when she nods and presses her heels to my ass, I slowly push into her.

Inch by inch, eyes locked, lips parted, we become each other's firsts. And if I can help it, lasts.

"Fuck. You're gripping me so tight." I try to move a little deeper, but she winces, so I stay still. "We don't need to do this if it's hurting you."

I ease back, her inner walls pushing me out with the pressure. With my head still inside, I wait for her to speak.

"No." She hooks her ankles behind my thighs tighter. "It doesn't hurt – it's more of a pressure. Just..." She gently rolls her hips, and I hiss from the sensation. "Keep going."

I lower my body to hers, my elbows resting on each side of her head as I kiss her. Stacey sucks on my tongue as I slowly move out a few inches then slide back home, which earns me a whimper.

Stomach muscles tightening with each carefully controlled thrust, I keep my eyes on Stacey. Looking for any sign of discomfort, showing her that she has my full attention, that this might be sex, but it's her and her soul and fucking heart that have got my emotions running wild.

Her fingers dig into my biceps as I go deeper, a mixture of a moan and a gasp filling the space between us. I keep my forehead to hers. "How does it feel?"

Stacey rocks her hips into mine, nearly taking all of me and moaning, "I want more."

"More?"

She nods. "Yeah. Give me more, Kade."

I give her one hard thrust to test how it feels and grit my teeth. Fuck. Her pupils are fully dilated; she's drunk with pleasure, and when I drive inside her, her body trembles beneath me. I hit that spot that has her seeing stars and then do it again, hooking my arm behind her knee to open her wider.

I fuck into her, not in the slightest fast, but deep. Each glide of my dick, the way I'm strangled by her walls, has me groaning and kissing her. Each stroke of my tongue is a push of my hips, her rolling into me and us letting sounds fall from our lips.

I was fifteen when I met her, and that's when my obsession began. Now, as I feel her body shattering around me and beneath me, orgasm slamming into her with my name on her lips, I know it's an obsession I'll never get over.

Because as the pleasure blooms through me and rockets through each muscle in my body, my balls tighten, and I empty into the condom.

I collapse on her, careful not to crush her as I catch my breath, then pull back to ease out of her. Once I toss the condom in the bin beside the bed, I caress her cheek. "Talk to me, Freckles. How do you feel?"

She grins. "Amazing."

"You're not sore?"

"A little," she admits, and we glance down between us, noticing the spots of blood on the sheets.

I stop her hands from covering her face. "You don't need to be embarrassed about this stuff. Not with me, okay?"

"It doesn't disgust you?"

I shake my head. "As long as you're okay, I don't care about anything else."

"I'm okay."

I kiss the tip of her nose. "Then so am I."

In her post-orgasmic state, Stacey leans up and kisses me. It's a chaste kiss, but it means more than all the others we've had the past hour.

And it's now, as I carry her to the bathroom and clean us both, that I realise I might be feeling an emotion I've only ever heard about. One I had no idea existed for me – never knew I was capable of feeling.

An emotion that makes me want to blind everyone in the world so they can never see how beautiful she is. I'll stick a screwdriver deep in their ear canals, so they'll never hear her laugh. The idea of anyone thinking they can have her after me makes my blood boil.

Dangerous. This is so fucking dangerous.

I think I'm falling in love with Stacey Rhodes.

33

KADE

The dream – or more like the nightmare – ends where it always does, and it takes me a long minute to realign with reality.

Hair is in my face, a head resting on my dead left arm, our fingers linked. My other hand is against a warm chest, a palm holding me in place between two tits.

I never sleep over when I'm working. I fuck and leave, then report back to Bernadette.

When I open my eyes, the familiar smell of coconut shampoo and the feeling of being content makes sense as I see dark hair, freckled, inked skin, and Stacey in my arms.

I blink a few times.

Stacey… In my arms. Long bare legs tangled with mine.

My painful morning wood is pressing into her ass through my

boxers. Because that's all I'm wearing.

If I've fucked Stacey and have no memory of it, I'll be so fucking pissed.

She shifts, and a part – a *huge* part – of me doesn't want her to wake, so we can stay in this position a little longer. My eyes close again, and I pull her a little more into me. Our knees are bent, my form large and dominating hers, but I still feel comfortable and… I don't know.

I don't remember much of last night. As soon as I was held down by five guys and felt a needle pressing into my arm, everything kind of went black.

She's supposed to be home with my sister and Tylar. Why is she here, in a random hotel room, cuddling into me?

Morning grogginess slips into my mind, my eyes falling closed again as I try to move my legs. My pulse spikes as she backs into me.

She shifts once again, grinding her ass against my cock and stopping when I let out a groan. I stay where I am, burying my face into her hair and snaking my arm around her waist.

The deep, low buzz between us is almost too intense to handle.

I know she's awake, probably in her head and wondering what the fuck is happening. Her stomach muscles tense as she lifts her head from the pillow ever so slightly.

Stacey's breathing getting heavier and her heart racing against my chest shouldn't be turning me on, but I'm losing it here, desperate to turn her around, yank down my boxers and shove my cock deep inside her.

Do you know how many times I've wanted to wake up like this over the last two years? With her in my arms? I'd hated myself for wanting it so badly, but I would have broken every single one of my rules to be in this position.

And now I am.

Bernadette would have Stacey killed if she found out. I'm already putting her in danger just being here.

A groan is torn from my lungs as she opens her legs a little, so my cock – straining in the material of my boxers – settles against her pussy. I whisper, "Why are you in bed with me?"

She doesn't speak but does grind against me. We're a perfect fit – two puzzle pieces with tattered edges. Her fingers tighten around mine, her breathing heavier, and I thrust my hips forward to close the infinitesimal distance between us.

I lift my hand from around her waist and splay my fingers against her ribs. "No bra," I say as my thumb strokes her skin.

My palm slowly, lazily travels down. Lower, until skin meets skin on her thigh. "No," she confirms, breathless.

"Will I find you bare for me if I do this?" I ask as my fingers trail to her inner thigh and delicately drag up and close to where liquid heat is pooling against the material, separating the head of my cock from her cunt. "Hmm… Little tease." I hook my middle finger into the string of her thong and glide it against her slick folds, rubbing her clit.

So fucking wet for me.

Just when I think she's going to moan my name, she blurts out, "Kade! No! I need to pee!" And tugs my hand away from between her legs, breaking the connection.

Before I can reply or even open my mouth to let words pass my lips, she's scrambling into the bathroom and slamming the door.

I stare at my middle finger then slide it into my mouth, tasting her as my confusion grows worse.

It takes her five minutes to come back out, and I watch her nervously rub her arm.

"I'm a little confused why we're here," I say, tilting my head and watching her take a few steps towards the bed and stopping. As if she wants to climb back in but doesn't know how I'd react.

I'd be more than happy to drag her back in, but she speaks before I can debate whether to actually do it.

"Drunk Kade decided to take something and then called me. You sounded like you were in a bad way and couldn't get any of your friends, so I left the airport to come and get you from some alleyway. Barry was there and told me to stay here with you."

I don't remember even seeing Barry last night.

But I do remember getting pissed off at a function and shooting someone important.

I hum, trying to calm my erratic pulse, but as my gaze drops down the perfect curves of her body, it only gets more rapid. "That was nice of you. Giving up your trip home to come to my rescue."

Stacey laughs derisively, and it causes my cock to harden even more. "Shut up – I'm still going. This is Barry's room; I'm just making sure you're okay before I leave."

I slide both hands behind the back of my head. "Did we fuck?"

She scoffs. "You didn't even know it was me in bed with you – why would we? Besides, you made it clear you just wanted to cuddle."

The corner of my mouth curls ever so slightly. "I just wanted to cuddle."

"Yes. It seems some things never change."

"So you slept in bed with me, in only your shirt, and held my hand to your tits?"

She clenches her jaw. "If you're going to point out the obvious, I'll get another hotel room."

I quirk a brow. "You want to stay a bit longer?"

"I never said that."

"No," I reply. "I'm asking you."

Say yes.

Say fucking yes.

I don't want her to be here if she doesn't want to, but I also don't want her to leave.

"You said you took something you shouldn't have, and thought I'd paid to have sex with you." Shaking her head, she adds, "I've never seen you like that. The Kade I knew hated drugs and never got himself into that kind of condition."

"The Kade you knew died two years ago," I tell her. "Forget about him."

She chews on her lip. "He isn't dead."

I will be soon.

Or she will be.

I want to speak, but I'm frozen by how sad she looks.

"You scared me last night."

She slips back into the bathroom to brush her teeth and wash her face, and I watch her through the crack in the door. She pauses and lowers her head as she holds the sink, takes a deep breath and comes back out.

"I have a spare toothbrush you can use, and your clothes should be ready soon. I had to put them into the cleaning service because they were covered in blood."

Once I freshen up and take a piss, I notice she washed blood off me again – there's a cloth soaked in blood in the trash.

I slip out the bathroom and try not to care that she's still here.

She cheated on me. And it's annoying me that I'm starting to ignore that fact.

My phone is off, thankfully, so no one can contact me. Barry would have made sure I can't be traced here either.

Technically, I should be safe here.

"I'll call an Uber in a while," Stacey says, sitting on the edge of the bed. "It's a bit early yet."

"An Uber?"

Nodding, she says, "I can't be here with you. I just booked another flight, but it's in two days, so I'll stay somewhere else until then."

I don't want her to leave. I kind of like having my phone out of battery, and being here…

With her.

I'm putting her in so much danger. Even though Bernadette shouldn't be able to find me here, there's still a chance, however small, that it could happen.

Then she'll find Stacey. And keeping my ex off her radar will be fucked.

Bernie can't find out about her, or what she means to me.

Meant.

"I'm too ill for you to leave," I lie, dropping back onto the mattress. "Go later." I take a bold chance by looking up and saying, "Come back to bed."

Stacey stands from the edge of the bed and turns with wide eyes. "What? No. I can take the sofa." She points at the small, definitely uncomfortable couch next to the window. "Go to sleep. I'll call an Uber when you wake up."

"Suit yourself," I reply and close my eyes.

It takes her a few huffs, an attempt to lie on the sofa, a scroll on her phone, before she gives in and pulls the duvet aside to climb in.

I smirk. "Knew you couldn't resist me."

She slaps my chest. "I hate you."

I roll onto my side and yank her back to my chest, so we're in the same position we woke up in. Yet, this time, I'm awake and sober. "I hate you too."

But I love how fucking much our bodies respond to each other.

"You're getting hard," she says, pointing out the obvious. "Stop it."

I laugh – a real, genuine laugh I haven't let out in so long. "I can't help it."

My brain restarts when she giggles. Fuck me, I've missed that sound.

"Turn around," I demand.

She gasps and tenses her shoulders as I skim my teeth across her skin. "Why?"

"So I can look at you."

"You've seen me a billion times," she replies, turning around to face me. "Plus, that's kind of creep—"

"Don't finish that sentence, Freckles," I warn, grabbing her ass and slamming her into my front.

"Or what?" she teases, hiking her knee so it rests on my hip. Her top rides up, my hand on her bare ass. She looks between us, my dick solid against her.

What the fuck did she expect?

"Wow. You're *really* hard."

I smirk, her heat radiating against me. "And you're really wet."

She shakes her head. "Nope."

I narrow my eyes, and she yelps as I roll her onto her back, grabbing her wrists with one hand and forcing them above her head. I shove my hand into her panties, groaning deeply when I feel how soaked she is. My fingers tease her clit, then I spread her folds with my pointer and ring fingers, and sink the middle one deep.

"Little liar."

She whimpers when I pull my hand away, eyes widening as I press my middle finger to her mouth.

"Open."

Her lips part, and I slide my finger against her tongue, letting Stacey taste herself. "You still taste like mine, Freckles."

She rocks against my cock, and I tense.

"Keep doing that and I might fuck you."

"If I let you."

My hand pushes her wrists further into the bed, and I hear the hitch in her breathing. "Will you let me?"

Stacey, being a little cock tease, rubs herself against me again instead of replying. I groan, snatching her throat with my free hand. I know she loves this side of me – dominating, angry yet full of desire and lust. The rage between us mixes with the need to fuck each other's brains out.

The crown of my dick is pressing against her entrance, but our underwear is in the way. I've never hated material so much in my life.

"As well as having a soaked pussy, your nipples are hard, your pupils are dilated and you're breathing heavy. If you don't tell me you'll let me fuck you, I'll use them as indicators and fuck you anyway."

"Do you want to fuck me?"

"Obviously I want to fucking fuck you." I push against her, wanting the barriers between us to rip. Her pulse hammers in her throat, and I run my thumb across her jaw before dragging her bottom lip down. "I'm not hard for nothing."

"If you want me" – she grins as she pushes out two words I'm sure will make her feel powerful – "then *beg*."

"You want me to beg? How would you like me to plead for your pussy? Vocally or on my knees?"

Her eyes spark. "Both."

I loosen my hold on her throat. "Fine."

She shrieks as I yank her to the edge of the bed by the thighs, her legs dangling as I kneel on the floor between them. "I'm going to eat first though, if you don't mind?"

Perched on her elbows, she watches me take her thighs, spreading them wide. I can see her arousal through her thong, and I salivate, desperate for another taste.

I still hate her for what she did, but for some reason, the feeling is lessening the more time I spend with her. Is this me slowly forgiving her?

Am I breaking rule five?

No.

We watch each other as I kiss her left inner thigh then lick and suck my way towards her underwear. Her legs shake when I reach her pale pink thong, right at the area next to her clit. I move over it with hot breaths before kissing my way down her right thigh.

"Fuck you, Kade," she seethes, her chest rising and falling, her hands fisting the bedcovers. "I *really* hate you."

"Really?" She gasps as I speak against her clit, the material grazing my lips. "Even when I do this?" Her body jerks as the tip of my tongue swipes up the side of her pussy. "And this?" The other side, and she's whimpering. "What about here?"

She drops her head on a moan as I tease her entrance with the tip of my tongue, the thin material doing nothing to stop me from tasting her arousal.

"Your cunt has been mine since you first opened your legs for me." I hook my fingers into her thong. "Since you sat beside me at the pool house." I slide the material down her legs, then throw the thong aside as her pussy welcomes me. "Since you walked into that fucking tent and kissed me."

Her thighs tense as I plunge my tongue inside and pull it out just as fast, my eyes closing, teeth gritting as I attempt to control myself. *Fuck*. I might finish before she does.

"I'm going to kill you," she mutters as I go back to kissing her thigh, trying to control my breaths, making sure I dodge her throbbing clit, breathing against it before I kiss the other thigh. "I'm going to find your gun and shoot you – or strangle you."

"I dare you to try," I reply, gripping her thighs in a deadly hold, spreading them as wide as her flexibility will allow. "I'm rather skilled at ending someone's life though. But yes, do try, Freckles. I'd love to fuck you while you attempted to kill me." And then I'm burying my face between her legs, devouring her.

Her entire body jolts as I shove my tongue into her cunt, before sucking and biting at her folds and clit, letting spit drip from my mouth as I lick from ass to clit. Her hands release the sheets and tangle in my hair.

"Please don't stop," she moans, grinding her pussy against my mouth.

She's drenched, soaking for me. She tastes divine, addictive; I'd happily drown in her cunt.

I suck harshly on her clit as I ease two fingers inside, her inner walls immediately clutching them tightly.

I add another finger. Another gasp from her, and I'm painfully fucking solid in my boxers. I want to release her thigh and stroke myself, but I'll leave that to her.

"Oh *shit*, Kade!" She moans loudly as I curl my fingers, hitting that sweet spot that has her perfect fucking cunt pulsing.

Hearing her say my name is better than drugs. My chest tightens like her hand does in my hair, nearly ripping the dark strands out. I want to hear her scream it louder. I want my name to stay on her lips forever.

Stacey's legs try to clamp shut as she unravels against my tongue, crushing my fingers. I pump them in and out, hard and fast, her eyes rolling to the back of her head as I circle my tongue on her throbbing clit.

She's suffocating me with her thighs through each pulse and jolt of her orgasm, but I don't mind. I'll happily pass out right where I am with her juices all over my face.

"You taste so good," I say as I lap up each drop of her arousal. "So fucking good."

She pants, a sweat building on her skin. "Yeah?"

"Fuck yeah." I pull my fingers out of her, and she winces.

I climb up her trembling body, pressing my hardness against her pussy, desperate to be deep inside her. "Open your mouth." To piss her off, I add, "Filthy little slut."

She snarls, nails dragging and splitting the skin of my stomach, causing each muscle to constrict. "Don't call me that."

My cock twitches at the pain, the raging look on her face. She still wants me though – she's hooking her ankles behind my back and pulling me against her more.

I snatch her jaw and pry her mouth open. "Tongue out."

I gather her taste in my mouth then spit into hers.

Her orgasm-dazed eyes stay on me as it slides down her throat.

I hum. "See? You're delicious."

She nods and takes my wrist, bringing my fingers to her mouth to suck her own cum from them. I grow harder at the sight of her gagging as I sink them right in, my knuckles hitting her teeth.

"Good girl."

Her eyes are on fire with my praise, watching my mouth as I sink my teeth into my bottom lip. When I pull my fingers out, she glares at me. "You called me a slut."

I nod. "I did."

She wipes her mouth and sits up, shoving me onto my side. Then she gets to her feet, fisting her hands as she walks towards the bathroom.

"What are you doing?" I ask, standing from my position on the floor. My cock hardens even more when she pulls her top off, giving me her naked back.

I gulp as she glances over her shoulder at me. "I'm going for a shower."

I hold my breath. Does she have any idea how fucking beautiful she is?

She's completely naked. And my cock is painfully hard.

She walks into the bathroom, not bothering to close the door.

Shit.

Don't follow her.

Don't follow her.

Don't follow her.

What's the worst that can happen? I've already screwed her on this trip.

"Fuck it."

34

KADE

As soon as I climb into the shower with her, it takes me everything not to drop to my knees and beg for her forgiveness for who I've become.

Even if I did, and she asked me to stop all that I've been doing, I can't.

I lied when I said I'd had two years to get over her.

Her green eyes drop to my dick, and she wraps her hand around it, using her grip to yank me towards her. "Am I a slut?"

I bite my lip. "You're *my* slut."

She narrows her eyes, watching me as she starts to pump me in her hand. "Better. But I'm not yours."

"And I'm not yours."

She keeps stroking my cock, but I grip her wrist, because I'm far too turned on to hold back if I need to cum. I want to spill inside her. I want to see it drip from her cunt, only so I can use my fingers to stuff it back inside her.

Not once have I ever wanted to cum inside someone, but with Stacey, I crave it. Maybe it's because she was once carrying our child and I witnessed the start of the swelling of her womb. I loved her already, but knowing she was going to be the mother of my child made me worship her in ways I had no idea existed.

I wanted to marry her at the age of nineteen, for fuck's sake.

We were young, but we were fully prepared to take on every single hurdle that would've been thrown at us.

Until that last one.

I shake off my thoughts and stare at the beautiful woman in front of me – her freckled, tanned skin, the curves she hates but I love.

I walk her into the water, turning her then pressing my front to her back and caressing her tits. I roll each nipple between my finger and thumb. My cock twitches against her ass.

"I need more."

I pinch her nipple, and her head drops back to my chest. "More what?" I ask.

"Of you. This. The way it feels."

Same. Fucking same here.

"How does it feel?"

"Good," she replies, grabbing the back of my head with one hand and reaching the other behind her for my dick. "It feels good like this, Kade."

My balls tighten as she carefully works me in her palm.

"That's all?" I ask, sucking drops of water off her heated skin, working my lips up the side of her throat. "I'm going to make you feel more than fucking *good*."

I could thrust forward and be fully sheathed in her depths. One wet movement, and I'd be inside her. One thrust, and she'd be full of my cock.

I move Stacey's grip off my dick, both my hands on her ass now, spreading her cheeks. The swollen crown eases between them, and I stop pushing forward when the head reaches the entrance of her pussy. "You want this?"

"Yes," she breathes, fisting my hair and arching her back so I have a better angle. "Please fuck me, Kade."

"So pretty when you beg," I whisper against her ear as the tip of my dick slowly sinks into her. "So *fucking* pretty."

A hard thrust, and I'm wrapped securely by her cunt.

We both gasp, and I stay still, trying to stop my pounding heart from jumping out of my chest.

"Hands on the tiles."

She lets go of my hair and does as she's told, bending slightly.

I wipe my palm down my face, watching her body, my cock inside her, her pussy firmly capturing it. I run my hand down her spine, stopping at the base and pressing my thumb against her tight hole, making her flinch. "Can I fuck you here?"

"Absolutely not."

I chuckle and move my thumb. "Next time."

She doesn't respond, so I grab her nape and force her to bend further.

I kick her legs apart and grab her hips, pulling out to the tip then sinking inside again. So tight. I pump slowly, rolling my hips against her. Each thrust is carefully controlled and deep.

She moves with me as the water soaks us, as we find a rhythm where my cock is buried deeper into her depths. "Harder," she begs.

I pull out completely, and Stacey nearly screams as I thrust back in with force. Again. Again. Fucking her faster and harder until my lungs are seizing and my balls are slapping her clit. My teeth crash together, and I grab both of her wrists, slamming her body against the tiles as I keep shoving my cock inside her.

She moans repeatedly, reaching back to grip my hair again and tugging with full force while I devour her throat with my mouth and teeth. Pain and pleasure wrack my body, and my cock swells inside her.

She turns her head, her eyes finding mine, and I want to press my mouth to hers. She's looking at me like I used to mean everything to her, and it pisses me off, but not because I don't feel the same.

We're each other's dirty little secret. And it will probably always be that way.

The shower is raining down on us, our bodies slamming

against one another, strangled noises ripping from our throats. She's whimpering, gasping, and I want to kiss her so fucking badly. Our mouths are so close.

I haven't kissed anyone in a long time. Not willingly. If someone pays Bernie extra, she forces me to kiss them. She even paid me a grand to feel my lips on hers.

Stacey will never let me kiss her. I know that. But that doesn't mean I won't fucking try.

I thrust deeper. Her eyes are still trained on mine as they begin to glaze over, pupils fully blown. She's so close to tipping over the edge again.

She's stunning.

I curl my hand between her legs, watching her as I circle her clit. She drops her gaze to my mouth before screwing her eyes shut.

My teeth snatch at her bottom lip, and she's erupting. I don't tip her over the edge when her orgasm hits – I fucking launch her as she detonates around me, cunt clenching my cock, strangling me hard enough I think I might be stuck. I keep going, fucking her tightness harder, rubbing her clit as she unravels.

Stacey yanks her bottom lip from between my teeth, and I taste her blood in my mouth, feel the warmth of it on my lips. I lick it as I watch her fall apart while I keep thrusting into her.

"Fucking love being inside your tight pussy. It was made for me," I say, pressing my forehead to her and holding her to me. "*You* were made for me."

Her eyes roll to the back of her head as her nails sink into my scalp and wrist.

She shakes in my hold. "*Kade.*" Her voice is strangled through a moan. "K—"

I can see the crack of thunder within her body and feel it around my dick when her entire body seizes, her legs like jelly. Her eyes widen on a scream, my name spilling from her mouth as she hits the pinnacle.

She goes limp in my arms, breathless.

It's possible I just gave her the hardest orgasm of her life.

I grin as Stacey looks at me, her chest and cheeks red.

"Shut up," she says with a quiet laugh, catching her breath. She wipes her mouth. "You bit me and cut my lip."

"You pulled away," I say with a shrug. "Self-inflicted."

She winces as I pull out of her and turn her to me, cupping her face in my hands. Her eyes are glazed from her euphoria. "We aren't done yet."

I lift her into my arms, gripping her ass and carrying her to the room. Stacey captures my earlobe between her teeth, and I hiss at the sting of pain, but it only makes me harder.

I drop her on the bed and settle between her legs, sucking along her jaw then lowering to her throat. She shoves her hand into my wet hair, tugging hard and making me groan with fuckable rage.

We're soaking the bed as we explore each other as if we haven't a million times.

I take her tightening nipple into my mouth, and suck and bite and kiss while she whimpers. I watch her as I trail gentle kisses down the scar between her breasts, the raised skin she's hidden until now, and vow I'm going to find out what happened.

If I ask, she'll lie. She always lies.

My mouth travels up her throat, along her jaw, and I chance my luck.

But Stacey dodges my mouth when I try to kiss her, and it fucks me off enough that I lean up and press my hand into the pillow beside her head.

"I want to kiss you," I tell her, taking her throat and cutting off her air. "Let me fucking kiss you."

Her lips part, and I release her enough to speak. "It's too intimate."

A gasp rips from her throat as I force my cock into her pussy, sheathing me in her warmth. "And this isn't?"

She flutters around me, still sensitive from her orgasm.

"You... You fuck all the time. I'm no different from the rest."

That isn't even slightly true.

I fist her hair, tugging her head back, and start slamming into her, hiking her leg to my hip to go deeper. "Is this too intimate?" I grit my teeth as she tries to shake her head, groaning loud as my cock threatens to spill inside her already. "Will I go harder? Faster?"

"F-Faster."

I do. I fuck her with every ounce of speed I have.

I pull out, flip her over, pushing her down so she's flat, and hammer into her again. Her sensitive area grinds into the mattress with each thrust, and every nerve within me sparks, my balls tight.

My body completely covers her. I'm taking what she's giving, and none of this is forced. We want each other. We want this. We want the fucking orgasms causing havoc in our bodies.

"One more, Freckles. Come on." I link our fingers in one hand and take her throat with the other. "Give me one more."

I grit my teeth as she pulses around me one more time, screaming my name and gripping the sheets between our entwined fingers. Her cunt clenches around my cock, her throat working under my grip, and as my vision blurs, heat floods the base of my spine, muscles bunching at my thighs.

I see black before I'm falling over the edge with her, spilling every drop inside her.

I collapse, crushing her as we pant through the euphoria, slowly dragging my length through her depths until I can't handle it anymore and pull out.

But I don't move – I stay on top of her, pressing my lips to her shoulder and trying to fill my lungs.

I shift off her, my hand on her back. "You okay?"

Stacey manages a nod and quietly says, "Yeah. Are you?"

I frown. No one has ever asked me that after sex – am I okay? Fuck yes, I am.

"Yeah."

There are so many words I want to blurt out, but I'll regret them as soon as I do. We can never be together, not with our past and secrets and my life. I can't have a girlfriend then go fuck and be fucked by both men and women while drugs are pumped into my body.

Against my thoughts, I lean forward to kiss her, but she turns her face away from me.

"I need to go get your clothes from dry cleaning," she says, sitting up and hiding her tits from me. "I'll call an Uber when I get back."

I frown as she quickly collects clothes from her suitcase and hurries into the bathroom to clean up and get dressed.

I sink into the mattress and rub my hands down my face. Reality is slowly creeping in, and I want to kick it the fuck back to where it was. As soon as I charge my phone, the bubble we're in pops.

Not a fan of that idea.

Stacey comes out, hoodie and leggings covering her now. "You should get something to eat. I think they do room service."

I glance at her as she sits on the sofa and studies her phone, acting like I didn't just make her explode numerous times, though her legs are still trembling slightly. "Why did you book your flight for two days' time?"

Her eyes find mine over her screen. "It was the next one."

"To Glasgow?" I shake my head. "They're on every day."

"Maybe I wasn't in the mood to fly?"

I grin. "Or maybe you wanted to spend more time with me."

She scoffs. "Don't flatter yourself, Kade. I'm going to another hotel, and you can do what you want."

"Nope. When I get my clothes, you're coming to the mall with me. We'll eat while we're out." I tilt my head. "I'll let you drive whatever car I rent."

I hate renting, but I haven't had a chance to buy a new car after wrecking my Bentley.

Stacey's phone screen gets her attention. "I can't drive."

I inwardly groan and get up from the bed as I pull on my boxers. I walk to her, tipping her chin up so she stops looking at her phone. *Fuck*. She's gorgeous. I've never once thought any differently. "I taught you how to drive, remember?"

She knocks my hand away and tosses her phone aside. "Why? Why do you want to spend time with me?"

I shrug, knowing I've won. "Because you're hiding, and I want to hide with you." I caress her cheek and press my lips to her forehead, catching her off guard. "Let's hide together, Freckles."

35

STACEY

I can't think straight.

My forehead rests against the shower tiles as I mentally bash myself, inner Stacey calling me every shameful word under the sun. Yet I'm fighting between smiling and breaking down.

Oh God. I fucked Kade. Or… he fucked me. Again.

Jesus. What were we thinking?

My mind goes over everything while I watch water swirl down the drain.

Kade is using my phone – I assume in private mode – talking to Dez and Base. I made sure I deleted every single message Chris sent, and I'm praying he doesn't reach out while Kade has it.

He lets out a deep chuckle, and his tone is warm when he tells them he'll meet up with them tomorrow, that they'll go out and party.

The area between my legs is aching as I rinse the conditioner from my hair and scrub the sweat from my body, my skin sizzling with the after-effects of multiple orgasms from my ex.

After agreeing to hang out with him for a little while, he pinned me to the couch and made me unravel *again.* His fingers know exactly how to drive me insane, and I think if I cum once more, I'll pass out.

The tremble in my bones is still present as I lather soap into my skin, jumping as Kade opens the door and casually strolls in wearing a towel around his waist.

"Hey! You can't just walk in here while I'm showering!"

Confused, he raises a brow through the lightly steamed glass. "I was just inside you."

"So?"

Silence, and then he opens the bathroom door again to leave. "Hurry up."

Kade lies on the bed, staring at the ceiling, his fingers gliding over his naked chest repeatedly as I leave the bathroom. Dressed, my wet hair in a ponytail, I grab my phone and check the notifications.

"You're good. No boyfriends tried to contact you."

I scoff and pull on my shoes. "I'll go get your clothes."

Kade says nothing as I leave the room. I make my way down the hallway, pull out the piece of paper his mother gave me and quickly type the number scribbled on it into my phone.

It answers on the first ring. "Aria?"

I clear my throat. "It's Stacey."

"Ah. What can I do for you, little one?"

I skip the elevator and take the stairs to make sure I don't lose my signal. "I'm in a hotel room with Kade."

"You aren't about to tell me you've been fucking my son all night, are you?"

I'm stunned into silence.

"What do you want?" he asks when I fail to respond.

"I was supposed to go home with Luciella, and he called me. He... he'd taken something, a drug, and was in a bad way." My feet carry me down each flight of stairs. "I got to him the same time as his assistant. He was so messed up he didn't know who I was. He thought I paid to… to have sex with him."

Tobias stays quiet, his breathing all I can hear.

I keep going as I descend the steps. "He was covered in blood too. His assistant said he shot someone he shouldn't have."

Voice low, Tobias asks, "He has an assistant?"

I stop walking. "That's your question? He shot someone, Tobias."

"Did he tell you what happened?"

"No. He was hallucinating quite badly and kept asking me how much I paid and if I'd pretend to *her* we had sex."

I can't believe I'm talking about this with him.

"Who's her?" he asks.

"I don't know. He called her the she-devil."

"Anything else?"

"Just that he gets paid to kill and… I guess he's a male prostitute, but I'm not fully sure on that part." I hate myself for telling his dad, but how else can I help him? Tobias is my only shot at getting Kade out of this. "He wants me to stay with him until I fly home, so he can hide with me."

"Hide from who?"

"I don't know," I reply, handing my card to the receptionist with the receipt for Kade's clothes.

Kade's father doesn't respond.

I chew my lip.

"I think the old Kade is still there," I say. "I can try to find out more today."

"Okay. Stay safe, little one."

The call ends as the receptionist hands over the clothes, and I make my way back to the room.

Kade doesn't speak as I toss him the bag and head for the sofa, so I can message my friends and ask how their day has been.

We have a chat between the three of us, and Lu sends screenshots of a conversation between her and Base – him calling her Moodypants and telling her she's missing out by refusing to go on a date with him.

***Lu**: Can you believe this guy?*

***Ty**: Moodypants is funny though.*

***Lu**: Don't you dare tell him that or I'll never hear the end of it.*

***Me**: Why are you two talking to each other if you're together?*

***Ty**: She's been in the bathroom forever.*

***Lu**: Hey! Anyway, what should I do? Block him? Tell Kade? Threaten him with my father?*

***Ty**: You could say yes?*

***Me**: I agree with Tylar.*

***Lu**: I'll pretend neither of you just said that. Do you both forget who we're talking about here? He flirts with my mum* and *Ewan, for God's sake!*

***Ty**: Um, hello? Have you seen Ewan?*

***Me**: You have kissed Base before.*

***Lu**: Stop talking about my stepdad, Tylar. And a dare doesn't count!*

***Ty**: Whatever you say, Moodypants.*

***Lu**: Ahhh!*

I chuckle at the pair bickering. As much as I wish I was with them, I'm still feeling butterflies that Kade is in the bathroom, only ten steps from the couch. I keep battling a grin, remembering his hands and mouth all over me, at the same time as scolding myself for letting it happen.

My friends are kind of pissed at me for vanishing – they think I left my passport behind. But Ty knows the truth – she knows I'm with Kade and told me to enjoy myself while I can. She knows as soon as we're back in Scotland, normality will settle in, and the spell will break.

My phone dings again, and my heart sinks, blood draining from my face as Chris texts from another new contact.

***Unknown**: I'm sorry, okay? I'm so fucking sorry for the way I've been with you. How come Kyle gets all your sisterly love and I get tossed to the side? It's always been that way. My own mother prefers you and my brother. Do you let Kyle touch you? Do you let him sleep beside you and hold him? Have you fucked him? You smile at Kyle a lot. I wish you'd smile at me the same way.*

***Unknown**: I'm in your bed, baby. I'll always be in your bed. Even when you're married to someone else, I'll be the one who puts a kid in you. I'll be the one who has your love. I'll be the one who'll grow old with you. Think about it, okay? Forget that we're step-siblings. Forget everything I've done in the past and just... fucking love me back.*

Bile rises in my throat, the bubble I've been hiding in since flying to America finally bursting. My reality is that when I go home, Chris can control me again. His hold on me has loosened right now, but if I attempt to run, he'll find me.

And if I tell Kade, Chris will hurt him.

Chris is the reason my life is upside down, and I don't want to risk him getting worse.

I somehow managed to tell Tobias a snippet of the truth, but getting the words out to Kade? Impossible.

"Can you call an Uber?" Kade's deep voice travels through the bathroom door.

I can still feel each inch of him inside me, and I'm exhausted from how many times he made me orgasm. I reckon I have bruises between my thighs from how hard he pounded into me too.

I'm so fucking confused with it all.

All I keep thinking is that it might mean something to me, but he hates me. It terrifies me that I'm just going to break my own heart, because I meant it when I said we can't be together.

It would be far too toxic. No relationship should have secrets.

There is no future with Kade Mitchell.

I call an Uber, and I try not to let the fresh, dressed and dangerously handsome Kade affect me as he walks out with damp hair hanging over his forehead, fixing his collar.

He stops dead when he sees me staring. "What's wrong?"

I shake my head, eyes following him as he picks up his expensive watch from the bedside table. He clips it around his wrist, checking the time, then inspecting the small crack on his phone screen.

"Where exactly are we going? There's a place across the street that sells phone chargers."

"I'm not charging my phone," he says, tossing the dead iPhone onto the bedside unit again. "I'll do it later. I'm going to rent a car; I can use it to drop you off at the airport."

"Why?"

Why are you even here? You hate me. Every harsh word you've sent my way proves that. I'm dead to you, remember?

He only shrugs. "I won't try to fuck you again, if that's your issue."

I roll my eyes. "My issue is that a couple of weeks ago I was nothing but dirt to you. Are you still drunk?" I walk to stand in front of him as he sits on the edge of the bed, putting on his shoes. "Is that why you're tolerating me?"

I want to throw the lamp off his head as he laughs and replies, "Probably."

"You know what? I'm not doing this." I gesture between us, holding eye contact as annoyance seeps into my bones. "Me and you are over. You made sure of that when you left me. So what the hell are you doing now, Kade?"

He stands, towering over me. "Why are *you* here? Why did you leave the airport to come get me?"

"You needed help," I reply, crossing my arms in front of me. "Don't answer my question with a question."

Kade steps forward, and I step back. "I want you to answer it. I treat you like shit, so why did you come for me?"

Another step forward from him, and one back from me. I breathe deeply until my back hits the door. He doesn't stop until he's right there, toe to toe, an inch away.

I flinch as he lifts his hand to touch my cheek, but he stops when he sees my eyes screwed shut. It's an instinct I've picked up from Chris attacking me every chance he gets. He's had me in this position several times.

Kade notices my reflex, instead resting his hand on the door next to my head. "Answer me, Stacey."

His eyes are so beautiful, light like his father's. But they're also troubled and tired. My voice is quiet as I say, "I'm allowed to still care for you."

Knocked into silence, Kade's brows knit together.

My phone dings, and I slip away from him. "I'm not the snake you think I am. Despite what you think, I care. Probably more than I should."

I open the door and walk out, and Kade follows.

36

STACEY

We grab a burger, chips and a drink from a fast-food place. We haven't spoken in the two hours since we left the hotel. He grabs my hand while we walk through the mall to one of the stores but quickly drops it when he realises his mistake.

I scowl at him when he asks if I want anything while walking past clothes that would take me years to afford.

When Kyle calls me to tell me Nora is going in for her annual scan on her liver, Kade keeps his eyes on me, smoking a cigarette.

I want to go back to the room, alone, and lie in bed. I want to get away from this imbecile who just did about four one-eighties in his mood.

Him and Lu really are twins. Moody bastards.

"Do we need to go anywhere else?"

Kade nods once.

"Where?"

"You'll see," is his response.

"I've had better conversations with your grandmother," I say, intentionally shouldering him as we walk. "And that's saying something."

We get in another Uber, and Kade's knee bumps mine. I glance at him, but he's staring out the window. "Just pull in here."

My eyes widen when I see where we are. "No."

"Yes." He gets out and pulls my door open. "Come on."

"No."

He laughs and grabs my hand, yanking me out and thanking the driver. "Stop being a shitebag."

I point at the sign. "I'm *not* going on a motorbike!"

Kade ignores me and saunters into the building, fingers wrapped around my wrist lightly. I sit at the reception in a huff, debating whether I should run now or pretend he kidnapped me.

To my horror, *he buys one.*

Buys. A motorbike. Outright.

Ten minutes later, he walks towards me with two helmets. "Let's go."

"Absolutely not."

"I'll throw you over my shoulder.."

Disregarding the building terror in my gut, I get up and walk towards the back, through the doors and into the car park, where a black motorbike sits, waiting to end my life.

"Jesus, Kade. No. I'm not going on that huge thing! It will honestly kill me."

He gives me a look. "Are we still talking about the bike?"

"Shut up."

The worker chuckles, arms folded and leaning against the wall. "Our most recent model. And most expensive."

I scowl at Kade. "Stop throwing money around."

He shakes his head and nods to the death trap. "Get on the bike."

"No," I reply, my heart beginning to race as he approaches me, lifting his hand and tucking a loose strand of hair behind my ear.

"Stop that." I knock his touch away. "I'll get a ride back to the hotel."

"You either climb on or I bend you over it."

He's serious. The heated look in his eyes is enough to make my pussy instantly wet.

"I'm happy with both. You choose."

The man behind us clears his throat and dismisses himself.

"What will it be then, Stacey?"

I force a snort. "Neither are realistic."

"If you think I won't pull off your little black dress and make it realistic, you're wrong."

My inner walls clench on nothing but the image of him doing just that. I swallow hard, the pulse in my neck fluttering, and I try to appear unaffected. I wet my lips with my tongue and note his gaze dropping to my mouth. "There are cameras."

He smirks. "You better get on the bike then."

Idiot.

I know for a fact he means it too. If I tell him to bend me over, he will. Why is there a daring part of me that wants him to? We'd get caught and arrested for indecent exposure and public sexual acts, no doubt.

Not that we haven't fucked in public.

When he sees I've given up the argument, he looks amused with himself and goes over to the bike, checking all the buttons or whatever it is that has his attention.

"Where are we going?"

He shrugs. "A drive. Somewhere to pass time."

"Because you're hiding from the she-devil?"

Kade glances up at me as he turns on the bike, the roar of the engine making me jump. My insides flip, and I'm not sure if I'm turned on or terrified. Maybe both.

"Exactly. Who are *you* hiding from?"

"Why do you do what you do?" I ask instead of replying as Kade hands me my helmet. "Like, the bad stuff and the… escorting."

He rubs the back of his neck before pulling on his helmet, visor up. "The money?"

"Are you asking me or telling me?"

The stupid helmet won't sit right, and when I try for the fourth time, he steps towards me, taking it from my hands. "It's good money. There's nothing wrong with being a sex worker."

"I never said there was. I'm a pole dancer, and we're always sexualised. I'd never shame someone for their profession."

He doesn't respond, loosening the straps. His dark lashes are so long and thick. I stare at them, at his brows and the small bruise on his cheek.

Let me fucking kiss you.

I wanted him to kiss me. But it would be too complicated if I let him. My feelings are still there – he's just passing time.

I gulp. I was his first, and at one point, he told me he couldn't imagine ever fucking anyone else. We were in love. We had a future, and we were going to make Luciella understand what we meant to each other. No one could come between us. Ever.

Then someone did.

"How did you get involved in that line of work?" *Please, just tell me. I need to understand. I* want *to understand.* "Is that why you were trained to use a gun?"

"I was trained to use a lot of weapons." He reaches up behind me and pulls at my ponytail until it's loose, wrapping the band around his wrist. Kade runs his fingers through my hair, messy in my face. His tone is soft. "Stop asking questions."

"When did it start?"

"Why did you fuck him?"

I stare at him, wide-eyed. "I… I…" *Say it, Stacey. Say it!*

Kade shakes his head at my silence. "Exactly. Stop asking me questions and I won't ask you."

I lower my gaze. "I just want to understand."

The helmet fits over my head perfectly now, and he fastens the clip at my chin. His closeness is making butterflies go wild, and I want to hug him. I have the sudden, annoying urge to crush my body into his in an embrace.

I want to cry – to sob in his arms.

Kade steps back, his eyes tracing my body, from my dress to my shoes and then up to the large helmet. "You don't need to understand. It's my life now."

"Do you enjoy it? You can at least tell me if you're happy."

Lips thinning, he pulls his visor down then throws his long leg over the bike and taps the seat behind him. "Get on."

"Will you ever quit?"

He sighs. "Come on, Stacey. It's been two years. There's no reason for you to know any of this."

I cross my arms. "*Can* you quit?"

His head drops in annoyance. "It's very improbable that the opportunity to walk away comes up. Now, get on, unless you want the second option? Fucking you in only a helmet sounds hot."

I stand beside the bike. "But—"

He hits my visor, and it closes over my face, ending the conversation. He can't see through the tint, but I'm narrowing my eyes at him as he holds out his hand to help me climb on behind him.

Kade looks over his shoulder. "The helmets are hooked up to the bike's Bluetooth. Connect your phone."

"Why would I do that?"

I can tell he's raising a brow. "Music."

"While you're driving?" I ask, mortified. "No! You need to concentrate."

"Stop being annoying. I've shot guns while driving and have never even come close to crashing."

I slap his shoulder. "You did *what*? And what if you go too fast and I can't hold on and fall off?"

The bike vibrates under me as he kicks the stand. He raises his voice so I can hear. "Just connect your fucking phone, Stacey."

I lean back and pull my phone out. "You know, Base shouldn't be calling Luciella Moodypants when she has you as a brother." The helmet beeps as my Bluetooth connects and I open my music playlist. "You're by far the moodiest person I've ever met," I say under my breath.

"I heard that," he replies, his voice now echoing in my helmet.

Of course. "Just when I thought I'd get some peace from you."

I don't hear what he replies as "4runner" by Brenn! starts playing.

He reaches behind him and takes my arms, snaking them around him. "Hold tight, Freckles."

I shriek as he takes off, and I decide that this will be my last day on earth. He's going far too fast, and I think I might fly off.

The bike dips to the side as he takes a right, and I'm sure I'm about to lose a kneecap.

"I'm scared," I admit, screwing my eyes shut on a scream as he pushes forward through traffic. "Slow down!"

"Every time you scream, I'll go faster."

"Fuck you!" I yell over the music. "Fucking fuck you, Kade Mitchell!"

I hear the smile as he says, "I will as soon as we stop."

"I'm going to kill you."

He laughs again.

I wrap my arms around him tighter as he sets off to the right, the wind whipping my hair around us. He zips to the side more, so close to hitting the ground, and I find myself gripping his top.

"I'm so cold," I gasp.

Kade quickly slows down and pulls off to the side. "You should've said." The helmet comes off, then he pulls off his hoodie and gives me it. "Here."

"Won't you get cold?"

He shakes his head as he puts the helmet back on.

Kade helps me get my helmet off and pulls the hoodie over me before putting the helmet back on. I sigh at the warmth. I feel him around me. My helmet rests against his back as he starts off, going at a steady pace before he speeds up, and my pulse spikes from the adrenaline.

I keep my eyes open this time, enjoying it, the view around us merging until it becomes a mass of lights and colours, and I find myself smiling.

I'm smiling so hard my face hurts.

He slows as we approach a stop sign and waits for cars to pass at the intersection. "I heard you giggle, Freckles. I think you secretly like it."

"I did not," I say through a grin, my arms still around him, even though we're not moving. "I coughed."

"That's a lie."

My leg tenses as he reaches back, circling his fingers around my thigh and sending flutters everywhere. Waiting. The lights are still red, and a huge part of me wants them to stay red.

"Your cough sounds like you have asthma."

I swallow as his thumb moves against my leg. "Shut up."

He chuckles deeply.

The lights turn green, and his touch vanishes as we set off once more.

We eventually stop near a beach, where the sun is nearly gone behind the sea. Orange, red and yellow hues dance together as people still surf, a group of underage teenagers drink around a fire, music playing on a speaker, and a couple sit in the sand, watching the sky like us.

We keep our helmets on, and when Kade's hand finds my leg again, I keep my arms around him. A few minutes go by before I speak. "I don't want to go home anytime soon."

"You want to go somewhere else?" he asks, and when I nod, we sit for another ten minutes, comfortably, before he drives us to a quiet pier.

The bike moves over the wood until we come to a stop between loads of boats. He kicks the stand out. We're invisible. No one can see us. Was that his plan? Is he going to try to fuck me here?

Is this all about sex?

"Get off," he orders me, and I frown in confusion.

When I don't move, he says, "Sit in front of me."

Deftones is playing through the helmets, a band I've noticed Kade's also been listening to a lot recently. He helps me off, and before I can ask what's going on, he lifts me up and sits me in front of him, so we're face to face. He shifts back, so it's more comfortable, my legs draped over his.

He flips his visor open, then mine, his eyes as breath-taking as ever. "You want to sit here for a while?"

I bite my lip, the bike warm beneath me. "And do what?"

"I can think of a few things."

I tilt my head as he reaches up and unclips my helmet, then pulls it off. It drops on the pier beneath us, the hoodie following. We can still hear the music.

The breeze hits my skin, but that's not the reason for my hard nipples or the shivers running up my spine. His touch is electrifying.

"Are you going to let me kiss you yet?"

I shake my head, and Kade huffs.

My heart pounds in my chest as he traces his finger along my collarbone then hooks it under one of my dress straps and pulls it down my arm. The other follows. He unclips my bra and throws it aside.

The cold air hits my breasts, and Kade grazes his fingers over them both until I'm panting.

He's hard.

Is it even possible to have sex in this position?

"There are so many things I want to do to you right now. I don't think I can wait until we get back to the room."

My breath hitches as one hand cups my breast, caressing it as his thumb rubs over my nipple, his other hand sliding up my bare thigh. "What are you going to do to me?"

Kade looks at me with a dark, hooded gaze. "Everything."

The bike stays steady as Kade moves aside my underwear to feel how soaked I am.

My head drops back as he circles his thumb on my clit, pulling his helmet off so he can capture a nipple in his mouth. It lasts seconds before he tugs it between his teeth and draws back, sliding me fully into his lap.

I grind against his cock, and my lungs stutter from the sensation. He snakes an arm around the small of my back to help me move against him.

Then Kade halts me by grabbing my hip, shifting me as he frees his cock and positions me above him, crowning my entrance.

He pauses. "Are you on birth control?"

My eyes go wide. "*Now* you're asking? You've cum in me like five times in the past ten days."

"Are you though?"

I nod, shivering as he rubs the head of his cock up and down my pussy. "I'm on the pill."

"You got pregnant last time on the pill," he says, pulling me down and sinking deep, making me bite my lip to stop from moaning out in the open. We might not be able to be seen, but someone might hear us. "Who's to say it won't happen again?"

"It won't."

"Fuck," he mutters as I slowly roll into him, taking control while he keeps us upright on the motorbike. "I love how responsive you are to me."

Whimpering, I take more of his length. "It's a hot setting – don't let it get to your head."

He releases a breathy laugh. "Sure, Freckles."

I gasp as he thrusts upwards to meet my movements.

"Fuck me faster," he demands.

I lean forward, my spine tingling, toes curling as I ride him, hitting that sensitive spot that has me seeing stars already. "Kade," I breathe. His mouth bumps against mine, and I pull back a touch.

Our lips are so close, we're breathing the same air. His gaze drops to my mouth, and I dig my teeth into my bottom lip.

"Kiss me," he says. "If you want me to beg, then I'll fucking beg you to kiss me, Stacey. Please." The last word is a whisper.

My fingers brush through his hair as I contemplate pressing my lips to his. Just once. I can kiss him once.

"Am I interrupting?"

We flinch and abruptly pull away from each other, Kade's cock slipping free, and he yanks up my dress to conceal my breasts. He shoves his erection away and stands, but he freezes when he turns around.

"You're a hard man to find, Kade Mitchell. I thought you were smart though. You're supposed to use your *untraceable* bank account when you don't want to be found, remember?" the man says.

He's Scottish, and I know his face from somewhere.

"Do you want to introduce me to your lady friend?"

I clamber off the bike and grab Kade's hoodie, holding it to my body. My heart hammers in my chest, my building high completely gone.

The tall, older man reaches his hand out. "Archie Sawyer. I'm pleased to meet you. What's your name?"

"Don't speak to her," Kade snaps, pulling me behind him. "What the fuck do you want?"

Archie hums. "Right now, I want to know who has your attention more than your work. Who is she?"

Kade is silent.

"She's a beautiful little thing," he says. "Is she a client?"

When he tries to move around Kade, Kade stops him with a hand to his chest – walks him back a few steps then shoves him. "Stay the fuck away from her."

"Interesting."

My body trembles as he looks intently at me then glances at Kade.

"I'll leave you two to it. I highly suggest you turn on your phone, so I don't need to have my men track you down again."

He turns away from us, takes a few steps and stops. But then he lifts his phone. Kade isn't fast enough to stand in the way when he takes a picture of me.

The man stares at his screen then peers up at me and winks, before slowly making his way back to a black SUV parked near the pier.

"We need to go," Kade bursts out as the car drives off. He's panicking as he lifts me onto the bike and straps my helmet into place. "I've put you in so much danger. I'm sorry."

37

KADE

Why the fuck won't this stupid bike go faster?

My blood roars in my ears as Stacey holds on tight, asking me repeatedly through the Bluetooth what's going on. I overtake cars, checking around me to see if we're being followed. I know for a fact we will be. Archie isn't about to walk away and leave me to it. Bernadette's husband is a fucking wanker.

I check the mirrors as we slow at lights. Two of my cars are following close. Barry must've dealt with my fuck-up if he's here already. I'm going to fucking lose it with him if he's been tailing me all day and didn't think to check me and Stacey weren't being followed.

My team is surrounding us, boxing us in to protect us. A beep echoes in my helmet and Barry's voice comes through. "Five cars, boss. I have all of them tracked."

"Armed?"

"Yeah."

I swear to myself and grip the throttle. "Didn't think to tell me he was nearby?" I snap, venom lacing my tone. "He took a damn picture of her."

"Apologies, sir. We only arrived as he left, and your phone is off. I found you because you used your bank card."

The lights turn green, and we move again, the wind whipping Stacey's hair everywhere.

"I suggest you drive faster. They have orders to kill her. We can distract them."

Fuck.

Thankfully, Barry is only connected to my Bluetooth, so Stacey can't hear what he's saying. She does, however, tighten her hold on my midsection, and it annoys me how comforting the feeling is, despite our circumstances.

I take a sharp right. "Get us to the hotel and shut it down. I want everyone we have nearby ready."

Three SUVs are tailing us, following Barry speeding through the busy streets. I can swerve through traffic, so Archie's cars slowly fall into the distance. Each time I zoom through a red light, Stacey screams at me to be careful as cars sound their horns at us.

If she had any idea how much of a risk I'd be taking by letting them catch up to us, she'd tell me to go faster.

They have orders to *kill* her. Not fucking happening.

There are rules for me. I'm not allowed to fuck around without asking for permission. I'm not allowed to have a girlfriend. And I'm definitely not allowed to take pretty girls on motorbikes – on a borderline date.

But when I'm around Stacey, all common sense fucks off out the window – even my five rules are void. It shouldn't be this way. When I woke up with her in my arms, I should have snuck out and got the hell away from her. I shouldn't have called her when I was high, when I was covered in blood and so far from reality that I thought she was paying for my services.

I should have left her alone when I walked away from her two years ago. I should have kept my distance – cut her out of my life completely, but I had to watch her. I *needed* to watch her. The only things that held me together were the moments I'd see her true smile, hear her laugh when I tapped into the manor's security system and she was with Luciella. Watch the way she'd move in the dance studio, unaware of my prying eyes.

When she goes home, my connection cuts off. There's something about that place. I was never able to hack into it – still can't. Even her phone is untouchable, and no matter how much Barry and I try, we can't get into that either.

Barry thinks this obsession with my ex is unhealthy. I disagree. It's the only thing keeping me sane in my world.

Watching her isn't a problem. I'll most likely still watch her when I get her the fuck out of this country. I just need to be more discreet.

I should never have picked her up from that house. Being so close to her, being in a hotel room with her, triggered something animalistic in me, and watching her from afar was no longer enough.

I shouldn't have forced my way back into her life.

She'd be safe.

"Did you hear gunshots?" Stacey asks, her voice full of panic. "Kade, I think they have guns!"

"They do."

"Oh my God," she cries. Her fingers grip my top. "I don't want to die."

"You're not going to die."

Blackmailing me with my father was enough to make me agree to Bernadette's terms, but if she finds out who Stacey is to me – or *was* – then I dread to think about the punishment. Coldness wreaks havoc inside me as I consider how much worse this can get.

Barry drives in front, another car trailing behind, and tells me that the hotel has been evacuated. We'll drive in through the back, and we already have a team waiting for us. He also tells me that Archie already sent Bernadette the photo of Stacey and they're conducting a search for her identity.

I fist the handlebars of the motorbike. "Fuck!"

Fucking Archie. One move and I'd be able to snap his neck

without even blinking. But that would only piss off his wife and I'm not ready to attend the funerals of my loved ones anytime soon.

Fuming, I zip and zoom between vehicles to make sure they don't catch up while two of my cars distract them. My blood boils as I realise Archie would have seen her before making himself known at the pier. He would've seen her body, heard her breathy moans and the way my name sounded on her tongue. The fucking predator probably got off on watching us, waiting for the perfect moment to announce himself.

Fuck. This is what I wanted to avoid. I thought by being in America, I'd have some privacy. I should have known keeping my phone off and accidentally using my main account would've sent signals to them. I was already in the shit for shooting one of Bernadette's friends. A political leader, or whatever the fuck he was.

A bang sounds, and Stacey flinches around me.

I swerve as another gunshot misses us by an inch.

I tighten my thighs around the bike and lean back. "Sit in front of me," I tell Stacey while one of my guys hangs out the window and fires back. I try to keep my voice steady as I say, "Swing your leg around and I'll catch you."

"What?"

"I need to shield you."

When she doesn't shift, and another bullet nears us, I grit my teeth. "Move, Stacey."

I try not to freak the fuck out as a whistle passes my helmet. She shakes, but her nails release my top, and she slowly moves to my side, clinging to me for dear life.

I take her leg first and pull it around me while her arms wrap around my neck. Stacey climbs around me, and I help her as I control the bike.

Her voice trembles as her legs drape over my thighs. "Kade..."

"Don't wrap your arms around me – hold my top at my front." I narrowly miss a truck as I pull the throttle, bullets whizzing past me as I shield Stacey at the same time as dodging traffic.

Her body is so small against me, and it pisses me off that she always feels like home.

Now I have her in front of me, the bullets are aimed at my guards instead.

They won't kill me. I bring in too much profit and am one of the best assassins; plus, Bernie seems to be obsessed with me. She's possessive and controlling, and if it had been her who'd caught us, Stacey would be dead already.

My heart races as I repeatedly reassure Stacey that I'll get her to the hotel, that I'll get her out of the fucking country before they find out who she is.

She cries and holds me tighter, legs dangling over my own and tensing as I push right. I can hear her heavy breaths, the little squeaks she makes when I dodge cars left and right.

Another red light, but there are far too many cars passing in front of us to risk going through it. I finally stop and search my surroundings. Barry and the rest of my men are in a chase.

"Who was he?" she asks, breathless. "He looked familiar."

"Someone I never want you to meet again," I reply, rubbing her thigh over mine, trying to comfort her at the same time as holding her dress down.

I hear her gulp. "Is he dangerous?"

"Dangerous is an understatement." I look at her through the visors. "Once we deal with them and know it's safe, I'll get you to the jet. I want you to go straight home and tell your brother Kyle not to leave your side. I'll make sure they don't find out who you are."

"No. I already have a flight booked."

"Don't argue with me on this. Hold tight."

The lights turn green, and I shoot off, her helmet hitting into mine.

I hear gunshots behind us again, the fight gaining on us. If I had a weapon, I'd help, but not only am I annoyingly unarmed, but I also need to protect Stacey.

"Go left, sir. We'll go right. Go through the back of the hotel. It's clear."

"Be careful. If you get killed, I'll fucking kill you."

Barry snorts, the connection growing weak. "Got it, boss."

38

KADE

We make it to the hotel in under an hour, and as Barry said, the place is clear, bar all of my guards standing outside and inside, patrolling the stairways and the surrounding area.

I slip in the back, Stacey in hand. The place is like a ghost town.

As soon as we get to the room, I can breathe.

Stacey pulls the helmet off and drops it on the sofa, hands on her hips. "Talk. Now."

"No." I point to her suitcase and the clothes surrounding it. "Pack."

One of the guards gave me a charger, so I plug my phone in and wait impatiently for the screen to turn on. I look up when I don't hear movement. She's still standing in the middle of the room, glaring at me.

I groan and pinch the bridge of my nose. "Move. Pack your things. We don't have time for you to fuck around."

As soon as a bunch of notifications pop up from Base, drunk and being his annoying fucking self, I drop to the edge of the bed, elbows to my knees. Stacey cuddles herself in my peripheral, lowering to the couch. "Kade. Please. I need you to tell me what's going on here."

She deserves to know. But I also don't want her to know. Will she look at me differently if I tell her everything? Will she understand why she needs to stay away from me?

I came back home because Bernadette loosened her leash on me after putting me through a hard month of brutality, and the only reason I didn't snap her neck then and there was because she threatened to have my dad killed and make it look like a suicide. All this shit with my ex just... happened.

The connection between us is too strong, and I didn't even want to fight the pull.

I welcomed it. Since the moment I picked her up from that house, I've felt less dead inside. A speck of light in my darkness with her name on it.

Stacey broke my teenage heart, but there are more problems in my life than dwelling on the past. I'm not going to marry her and have children; I don't get to have a happy ending. There was no harm in us having fun. Messing around. I made it clear when she was between my legs on the plane that it meant nothing, but I think I was telling myself more than her.

I'd just hurt her or get her killed.

I've taken so many lives that I'm numb to death. What does that say about me? I don't deserve anything good in my life.

She can do way better.

"Kade."

My name is a caring whisper, breaking me away from my erratic thoughts. She kneels in front of me, gently taking my wrists to halt me from texting a reply to Base.

"Who was he? And why are you trying to rush me out of the country?"

Tingles attack me, and I stare at her fingers on my skin, but she quickly pulls them away like I've burned her.

I close my eyes, wiping my palms down my face before looking at her. "I work for him and his wife."

Correction: I work for Bernadette Sawyer. Archie is just a filthy disease that floats around in her rotten shadow.

She frowns, a deep line forming between her brows. Whether she's mad, confused, happy, aroused or sad, Stacey is the definition of beautiful.

"They're the ones who get your contracts?" she asks.

"Among other things, yes," I reply, nodding once.

Her eyes are mesmerising as she takes me in; as she studies my anxious expression. If I bring her closer to me, I'll see each shade, the little clusters of gold circling her pupils.

I remember when we found out we were going to have a kid, I wanted them to have her eyes. I wanted them to have everything that made Stacey who she was.

Smart.

Brave.

Confident.

Beautiful.

I wipe a tear from my face as I hold my girlfriend in my arms. "We can try again, okay? We were supposed to be parents. We were supposed to have a family. I love you, Freckles. I love you so much."

Stacey weeps into my chest, her body shaking through each sob as she shakes her head. "I can't. I can't go through that again, Kade."

I want to take in everything about her while I can. Because I'm certain this might be the last time I see her.

Having her so close to me is cruel, even for a man like me.

"Why are they coming after me?"

Fuck. How do I even explain this? Oh, Bernadette tricked my heartbroken teenage self into her house, groomed me until she got me into bed and has been blackmailing me ever since?

How about adding they got me addicted to drugs?

Or Archie having his way with me while I was unconscious because I was three hours late on finishing a job?

I wanted to fucking die for weeks after waking up in my own blood and piss. No one, let alone a helpless and scared nineteen-year-old kid, should go through that.

I've been planning his death for a while now. When I get out of these shackles, I'll make it fucking hurt.

A hand presses to my cheek, pulling me back to the now. "Where did you just go?"

Where I always go. The void in my head.

I gulp. Stacey takes my other hand, which has been rubbing the side of my leg repeatedly. "I'm... I'm not supposed to have any relationships outside of work."

Stacey tilts her head, releasing my cheek to take my other fidgeting hand. "Why?"

A rush of humiliation courses through me. "Because I belong to them. If I don't do what they say, people around me pay the price."

"What?" Her eyes go wide. "Go to the police!"

I force myself to laugh. "They own them too."

Technically, they own Scotland and over half of the underworld.

Sighing, I stare at her, take in how concerned she is for me. I pull my hands from hers and cup her cheeks, stroking my thumbs under her watering eyes. "Don't worry about me, Freckles. I told you – this is my life now. I'm not dragging you into it as well."

"You need to tell someone," she says, holding my hands to her face. "Please."

"And watch my family disappear, only for their bodies to show up months later?" I let go of her face. "No."

"I... I told your dad."

My eyes go wide. "What?"

"I went to visit him; I was worried about you and needed help."

I tamp down my anger and close my eyes, fisting my hands. "You shouldn't have done that, Stacey. If they find out, or he tries to do something, it'll make it all worse. Don't talk to him again, okay? Don't talk to anyone about me. You'll make it worse and my job harder."

Her bottom lip shakes. "But..." She trails off. "How do I help you?"

"By leaving."

Stacey goes ramrod straight at my bluntness. "What happens when I leave?"

"You don't need to worry about that. As long as you're safe."

She's quiet for a moment but then catches me off guard by climbing into my lap and burying her head into my shoulder.

For a brief moment, I have no idea what to do. She's bracketing herself around me, hugging me, as my palms press into the mattress to keep me steady. I swallow, but when I feel wetness on my neck from her tears, I wrap one of my arms around the small of her back, fisting her hair.

I'm freefalling into a sea of tranquillity in her arms. My head is silent. My bones don't shake, and I fill my lungs with her scent, wishing I could stay here forever.

I close my eyes, holding her to me. Her body cuddles into mine, one hand twisting into my hair and the other gripping my top at the back. Her hot breath is on my neck as she quietly weeps.

I massage my fingers into her hair, trying to keep my emotions in check. "Please don't cry."

"You weren't supposed to have this life." She's shaking in my arms. "We should have moved away when we planned to. When I found out I was pregnant, we should have left and never turned back."

There's a tug against my heart. "I know." I rub her back in small circles. No one has hugged me like this in so long. She was the only person I ever let get close to me, and I need to savour this while I can.

I lean back, remove my hand from her hair and tip her chin, so she looks at me.

"What we've been doing is risky. We can't..." I blow out a breath, hating my words. "This." *Fuck.* "We can't."

Silent, her eyes are lined with silver as another tear drops down her cheek. She doesn't stop me as I kiss her forehead.

"Please pack your things."

When she climbs off me, I check my phone, and I pale.

***Bernadette:** Five missed calls.*

One voicemail.

> ***Bernadette**: Sebastian Ivanovich Prince. Twenty-three. Dark hair. Brown eyes. Six foot one. Father is a successful Russian CEO. Mother is a Scottish accountant. Bisexual. Drives a red Aston Martin. Has a scar on the back of his head from being hit with a glass bottle when he was seventeen. Shall I continue or do you understand?*

Fucking shit. That means one thing.

Base officially has a target on him.

Keeping this side of my life a secret from my best friends has been hard going. So many times I've lied to get them off my back, but I think I need to tell them if Bernadette is going to start targeting them too. Base has a powerful family in Russia who could protect him. If Bernadette kills him, she'll have a fucking war heading her way.

Relief fills me as Barry walks in – alive, watching me pace while Stacey zips her suitcase. "We need to leave now."

I look at Stacey, at how shaken and emotional she is. It's all my fault.

"Get her a vest," I order, checking my gun is loaded, then shoving it into my waistband and gathering more weapons.

Stacey stares at the armoured vest in her hands, her brows knitting together.

I sigh. "Come here."

She stands frozen as I take it from her hands and unfasten the straps to pull it over her head. Unblinking, she stares at my chest as I tighten it around her body.

"Breathe," I say, and she blinks, looking up at me.

"I'm scared."

I stare at her: the freckles dusting her skin – which is turning paler by the second – the still windswept hair, the forest-green eyes I've pictured an unhealthy number of times. "You'll be fine."

She doesn't shy away when I grab a rifle from Barry and leave the hotel room.

Slowly, we walk down the corridor, Stacey in the middle. We're joined by more of my men, and we circle her, shielding her, taking each step carefully in case Archie decides to ambush us.

When we reach the bottom of the stairway, one of the guards opens the back entrance, and we slip out.

The blast of a gun vibrates in my ears as one of my guys takes a bullet to the head. Stacey screams as I cradle myself around her and rush us towards the car while bullets fly from each side. I shove her inside the car, slam the door shut then open fire with rapid bursts until my rifle runs out of bullets.

I throw it down, grabbing my pistol from my waistband and shielding myself with the passenger-side door so I can start shooting again.

"You need to leave, sir," one of my guards says. "We can hold them back."

I swear to myself, because I never leave my guys behind, but I need to get Stacey out.

Barry rushes into the front, and we slide down the windows and shoot as he reverses out of the lot, swinging us into the road and accelerating.

Stacey stares at me, wide-eyed, breathless. "This is your life?"

I shrug.

She wipes a tear. "What happens now?"

I stop her from taking the vest off. "You go home. I'll have you watched for a bit to make sure they don't track you. You go on and live your life the way you have been."

Maybe I'm being stupid, but I have to believe it's possible, that she'll make it out of this shit okay.

Stacey doesn't say anything; eventually, she yawns and rests her head on my lap, and it stills me as she gets comfortable while Barry drives us to the hangar that's over two hours away.

When she falls asleep, I lace our fingers, my other hand playing with her hair. "You should have stayed out of my life," I whisper. "But you've always been there. Always."

"Do you know what you're doing?"

I glance up, my eyes clashing with my assistant's. "What?"

"The more time you spend with her, the more danger she'll be in."

"I know that, Barry. Why the fuck do you think I'm rushing her out the country?"

"Sorry, sir, but she's innocent and you're..."

"I know," I reply. "I fucking know."

The drive takes forever and no time at all. I spend every moment of it staring down at her.

When we arrive at the hangar, Barry scans his badge to open the gates. The jet comes into view as we veer around the corner of an abandoned building.

"Wake up, Freckles," I say softly, stroking her hair. She stirs, then blinks her eyes open. The corner of my mouth tugs absently, and I flatten my lips. "We're here."

The car stops as she rubs her eyes, trying to wake herself up. She looks out the window at the jet, my team waiting to both help her escape and fight the fight that will inevitably come here.

"Wait. What happens when I leave? Where do you go?"

The pilot appears as the stairs lower, his messy grey hair a sure sign we've dragged him out of bed.

I stare at Stacey. "I told you not to worry about me."

"Well I'm going to!"

Someone's radio beeps, announcing that four SUVs are trying to enter the area.

I briefly close my eyes; I hate that my team is dying. "You need to leave. Now."

Barry takes her things, standing beside her. "Miss, if you'd board the jet please."

Another radio goes off. A casualty. Two. Three.

Bernadette's army is coming.

When Stacey takes a step back, ready to leave, I snatch her wrist and pull her to me, crashing my mouth down on hers with my hands on each side of her face. It's not deep or passionate but enough that I won't regret watching her walk away without kissing her.

And fuck me, feeling her lips on mine is a dream, especially when she kisses me back and the world ceases to exist.

I'm no longer standing in the airfield. I'm playing dares in a tent with the girl I've fancied since I was fifteen. Her lips are on mine, and I'm no longer in darkness, swallowed by the shadows of my wrongdoings.

The butterflies are still there. The nerves and the shake of my hands.

She told me not to kiss her, but she isn't pushing me away either.

I taste her tears as she whimpers against my lips. "Come with me."

I release her and step back, putting distance between us, and shake my head. "I can't."

Another gunshot, and I turn to Barry. "Get everyone on. You included."

He frowns. "Why?"

"Because they'll kill you all, and I'm not letting that happen. Get on the fucking jet – that's an order."

He nods, but I see his hesitation over leaving me.

"Miss Rhodes," he says to Stacey, trying to usher her on.

She shakes her head. "Please, Kade."

"Go," I tell Stacey. "Don't reach out to me. They'll have my phone."

She looks broken as she nods in agreement, taking a few steps towards the stairs, then stopping and running back to me.

Time stands still as our mouths collide in a deep, desperate kiss as she throws herself into my arms. I pull her to me as her lips move, part, and we open to each other, letting our tongues finally taste. I lift her off her feet and walk towards the steps. Her legs wrap around me, and I revel in the softness of her mouth.

It's like I'm visiting heaven while living in hell. But I want to steal her and bring her to my chaos, set fucking fire to her world and keep her in mine.

Not even the devil could take this moment from me.

This is what I wanted to do earlier. I wanted to taste her moans and suck on her tongue, to swallow her gasps as I pushed into her.

Instead, I'm tasting her tears, swallowing her inconsolable sobs as she begs me to come on the plane with her.

"I'll tell you everything," she says. "I promise I'll tell you everything."

I've no idea what she's talking about. *Everything?*

"We can make it work," she adds. "We can help each other."

"Sir, we need to leave right now."

My nose nudges hers. "It's over. It's been over for two years. If we keep doing this, you'll be killed."

She sobs and shakes her head. "No."

I press my mouth to hers again as I lower her to her feet. "I can't be selfish."

Stacey takes a step back, covering her mouth with the back of her hand, tears falling down her face, and I don't want to let go of her other hand. A lump is in my throat, my chest is tight, and I want to keep kissing her. I want to go with her.

But then our fingers separate, and she turns away.

It's over as soon as it starts – I let go of her forever, and she's vanishing into the jet, not daring to give me one last look. Everything else is done. We're done. And that's how it needs to be. I'll stay away from her. I'll do anything to make sure Bernadette never finds her.

Barry stands at the top of the metal stairs, looking behind me, and I know I'm screwed. "Keep her safe," I say. "Don't worry about me."

The door of the jet closes, and I blow out a breath and shove my hand into my hair. I can hear all the cars now. Speeding. I guess the team I had on the gates is dead. Everyone who was on shift and didn't make it to the jet is dead. So many innocent lives lost, all because they were loyal to me.

At least Stacey is safe.

I light a joint and watch the jet back into the runway, and relief fills me as it takes to the sky, carrying Stacey away from trouble. I blow out toxic smoke as a gun is pressed to the back of my head.

Everything goes dark as pain smacks into my skull.

39

KADE

My body jerks as frigid water splashes over me. "Wake the fuck up."

I gasp and try to catch my breath. I'm strapped to a chair in front of a table. Archie is sitting opposite me with a folder, ankle to his knee, dressed in his usual navy suit.

A guy with an empty bucket is standing beside me, bulletproof vest and all, and I make sure to remember his face, so I can fucking mutilate him.

"You're a sneaky son of a bitch," Archie says, getting to his feet and leaning his hands on the steel table.

"My dad would have your tongue for speaking about my mother that way," I reply with a smug grin. "But you're too much of a pussy to say that to his face, aren't you?"

Archie argued until his face was blue that it was stupid to be involved with the son of Tobias Mitchell and they should stop messing with me before my father retaliated, but Bernadette, being the horrible bitch she is, convinced him to keep going.

He started watching me with her, with others. Then he took his turn.

It was sickening. I'd broken up with Stacey weeks prior, and the sting from her betrayal was still there. I just wanted to get drunk all the time, but they introduced me to ecstasy, cocaine, acid and whatever the fuck else they pumped into me.

Then the violence started. They made me strangle someone to death. My first kill. Then they sent me to other countries to be trained. Russia. Poland. France. Latvia. Spain. Italy. Austria. Brazil. Beijing.

When I attended private parties with Bernadette on my arm, other women began inquiring about me. My bank account started filling up, surpassing one million, then two, three. Kill contracts amped it up to eight figures.

As rich as I was becoming, I was an empty vessel. I still am, but in the past week or so, I became that teenager again, who had no idea how to use a gun or the deep horrors of the underworld. Just the nervous kid who fancied his sister's best friend.

Archie punches me out of my trance.

"Your father is nothing but a mindless drone. Can he even speak with all the medication he's on? Does he even remember who the fuck you are when he spaces out?" He scoffs. "Fucking Tobias Mitchell. You're just like him. Useless, pathetic, pieces of shit."

I smirk. "Sure. And that's why you need to beat me while I'm tied to a chair, right? I'm a piece of shit like my dad, yet you can't take me one-on-one. You're an embarrassment, Archie. Your wife got so bored of your dick that she had to fuck a teenager for excitement."

I tip back as he boots my chair, and the air rushes out of my lungs as I hit the ground.

I laugh through my coughing.

He drops to my level on the ground and grips my hair, whispering harshly into my ear. "I'm going to sneak into your little mansion, slit your stepfather's throat and shove my cock in your mother's mouth until she can't breathe. I'll fuck her corpse and send you the video. Then, after that, I'll take your sister."

My blood boils, my smile dropping.

I keep myself controlled, my expression blank. "When I get the chance, I'm going to make you suffer," I snap. My forehead smashes into his nose, and I hear it crack. He yelps and quickly stands. "You go anywhere near my family, and I'll fucking kill you."

He holds his bleeding face. "You little—"

"Oh shut up the both of you." Bernadette's voice echoes in the room – it's coming from the speaker on Archie's phone. "Kade. What the hell are you playing at?"

One of the bodyguards rights my position as Archie's blood drips on the floor.

I hope it hurts, the motherfucker.

"I don't know what you're talking about," I reply to Bernie.

"Who is working for you? Who was firing back at us?"

I hold my breath, refusing to speak.

"You created your own little team, didn't you? Sneaky, sneaky boy. It's a shame they'll all be dead soon."

"Doubtful," I snap. She'll never find them.

"Who was she? Who was so important to you that you went to such extremes to protect her?"

"No one."

"You know the goddamn rules, boy," Archie spits, his stupid bloodstained moustache twitching with his anger. He rips open the folder, spreading pictures over the table. Different angles of me and Stacey at the club. Standing at the bar, me touching her. Her dancing with my target then us out back.

Me fucking next to my target and killing him while deep inside Stacey.

Then the one he took of her. She looks so innocent and frightened, and my insides twist that I put her in that position.

"Who is she?" Archie asks.

His fist connects with my face before I can spit on him.

Another from the left – one of his men wearing knuckledusters on both hands. My mouth fills with blood as my teeth cut into my gums.

Good. I want pain. I want to feel every single fucking blow they throw my way.

They question me on who the mystery woman is, and to be a prick, I ignore them, just so they can throw more punches and pour ice-cold water over me. It soothes the raging heat inside.

Bernadette eventually tells them to stand down and to get out of the room, leaving just me and a phone sitting on the desk, surrounded by images of my ex.

"If you tell me who she is, I'll call off the hit on Prince," she says, and my face drops. "All I want to know is her name."

"She was just a fuck to pass time," I lie. "I met her at the club, then we met up again tonight."

"How many times did you sleep together?"

I grit my teeth, spitting crimson on the floor. "Twice. It won't happen again. Call off the hit."

She hums. "Then why did you hide her?"

I lick my burst lip, tasting metal on my tongue. "She was innocent and didn't deserve whatever shit you were about to throw at her. You going after her was petty fucking jealousy."

She chuckles. "Fine. I want you on the next flight home. Come to me and apologise in person." She's smiling. "Earn your forgiveness."

I gulp down the sick rising in my throat.

"I don't like hearing about you sleeping with other people I'm not aware of. No more sneaking off with cheap whores on motorbikes. Do you understand?"

My knuckles turn white. Did she just call Stacey…

I close my eyes to tamp down my building fury.

Hearing Bernie speak about her like that is fucking irritating. She doesn't come close to how stunning Stacey is. But if I bite, I'll give it away that she was more than just a fuck.

"Do you understand, Kade?"

I glare at the phone, forcing the words out of my mouth. "Fine. But you stay the fuck away from my friends."

"Beg me not to kill him, and all will be forgiven."

I click my neck to the side, shaking my head. "Please," I grit out through my teeth, a headache coming on. "Please don't kill him."

"Done. Hold your fire, James. Go back home."

They must've had a sniper aiming into the hotel room.

Then she speaks to me. "You have a lot of making up to do. I look forward to seeing you."

My body tenses. "Right."

She laughs. "Don't make any plans for the rest of the month. I'll need some extra company while I'm in Italy."

The call cuts off as one of her men enters the room, and as my hands are cut from the zip ties, five more pile in. Two have bats, three have knuckledusters and the other a metal pole. Typical – these fuckers need to use weapons against me.

I prepare myself for a fight as I swing for the closest, breaking his jaw on contact. The pain searing through my knuckles drives me to hit the next one. I hear the snap of someone's neck as I blindly lose my fucking shit.

This I can handle. This I'll take to keep everyone safe. This is the price I'll pay to make sure they never find out who Stacey Rhodes is to me.

At least I got to kiss her.

CONTINUE THEIR
STORY IN
VORACIOUS
NOW

SPECIAL MENTION

For my fur baby who went to doggy heaven while I was in the middle of publishing this book. We got ten amazing years with him, and I wish we had ten more. My comforter when I was down, my little spoon, my sidekick while writing, my four-legged best friend who kept me company throughout my twenties.

A dog's love is unconditional, and that's exactly what we got from him when we rescued him all those years ago. He made our family complete, and now there is a hole in my heart.

Sleep tight, Charlie.

AUTHOR BIO

Leigh Rivers is a Scottish Biomedical Scientist who has ventured into the world of writing dark, morally grey characters with rollercoaster storylines to drive her readers wild.

When she isn't reading, writing on her laptop, or gaming until ridiculous hours, she dances at the pole studio, goes to the gym, and walks her dogs with her sons and husband.

Email: authorleighrivers@outlook.com